Dance with a Dragon

Book IV of The Dragon Archives

Linda K. Hopkins

LOVED BY A DRAGON

CHAPTER ONE

"Mistress Anna!"

Anna turned to watch Peggy as she rushed along the stone passage.

"I've lost the twins again," Peggy said. She clutched her skirts as she tittered nervously. "They are always escaping me."

Anna sighed. It was true that Zachary and Lydia were quick on their feet, but this was the third time *today*. "Have you searched the gardens?"

"Yes. They aren't anywhere!" The last word ended on a wail, and Peggy quickly covered her mouth with her hand, her gaze searching the walls and ceiling as if expecting to find a monster lurking between the stones. Or maybe she was just looking for a pair of four-year-olds. Her voice dropped to a whisper. "Do you think they are ...?" She nodded at the ceiling, indicating the floor above, where the master's chambers were situated.

Anna shrugged. "Probably. Why don't you go and check?"

Peggy's face paled slightly. "I couldn't possibly," she whispered. "What if *it* is there?" *It* was the dragon of

1

Storbrook Castle, a huge, winged beast that came and went as it pleased. It was well-known amongst the servants of Storbrook that Master Aaron Drake had no fear of the dragon, and allowed it free access into all the upper chambers, including those of his wife, the lady Keira. He even allowed his children to play with the monster, quite unconcerned about the danger it posed.

Anna knew it was pointless to try and convince Peggy that the dragon was harmless. "I'll go find them," she said. "Wait for us in the nursery."

"Oh, thank you," Peggy said. "It's just that their supper is growing cold and …" She trailed into silence as Anna turned away and headed towards the staircase.

Anna's shoes rang against the hard stone as she mounted the wide staircase that led to the upper floors. A low growl reached her as she walked along the dingy passage, followed by childish shrieks. The sounds came from the direction of the master's chambers, and the growl was definitely not human. Pushing open the heavy wooden door, Anna stepped across the threshold, taking in the scene before her.

The room she'd stepped into was huge, stretching thirty feet from one side to the other. The ceilings soared high above her, while overlooking the range of mountains was a series of large, arched windows that reached almost as high as the ceiling. The center of the room was bare of all furnishings, and lying in the middle of the stone floor was an enormous, golden dragon. Anna paused, staring at the magnificent creature. She never failed to feel a sense of awe at the beast who was now a member of her family. He had a long neck, which, when raised, stretched taller than her, while golden horns curved from the top of his skull. Sharp rows of teeth lined his long snout, from which blazing flames sometimes spewed. His cat-like eyes gleamed yellow, but when aroused by emotion, they were windows into the flaming furnace that burned within him, revealing leaping flames. Huge wings lay folded over his scaly back, and a long tail armed with sharp spikes curved around his body. Keira, Anna's sister, was leaning against his side, her feet drawn up beneath her, a book resting against her knees. She looked up as Anna entered the room.

"We've been reading a story," she said.

"I can see you have a rapt audience," Anna replied in amusement. The children Anna had come to retrieve were clambering over the huge back of the dragon, clutching the folded wings in tight fists.

"They're still listening!" Keira said, frowning when Anna laughed.

"I'm sure they are," Anna said.

The dragon, who was watching the children on his back, looked up at Anna with a grin. "They've heard the story so many times, they know it by heart," he said.

Anna laughed, then nodded at the children. "Peggy is looking for them," she said. "Again!"

"Oh dear," Keira said with a sigh. "They do seem to frequently escape her attention."

"And she is far too scared to come here to look for them," Anna added.

"So she should be," said the dragon. He turned to look at Keira. "Perhaps it is time to hire a tutor for them."

"They are only four," Keira protested.

"Ah, yes, but they are dragons, so they will learn very quickly."

Keira laughed. "Of course! How dull of me to forget that the children of the Dragon Master will be superior in every possible way to any other children." She rose to her feet and turned to face the creature. "But maybe they inherited their intelligence from their mother."

Aaron brought his face close to hers. "Then they are doubly blessed, my sweet," he said. She smiled and ran her hand down his snout, before turning to look at her offspring.

"Zachary! Lydia! Nurse Peggy has been looking for you."

Neither of the children paid their mother the slightest

attention, but were instead intent on the task of walking bravely along the length of their father's back towards his tail. Opening his wings, he gave a gentle shake and they fell onto the outstretched appendages, sliding onto the stone with a thump when he lowered them. Anna winced, but the children rose to their feet unhurt. Lydia looked at her mother, then dropped her gaze to the ground, but Zachary placed his hands on his waist and gave his father a defiant stare.

"I don't want to play with Nurse Peggy. I want to play with you."

"I want to play with you, too, son," said the dragon, "but you should never have run away from Nurse." Zachary glared for another moment, but at his father's upraised eyebrows, his expression crumpled.

"But I want to be with you," he said. "Make Nursey go away."

"No. You need to learn to listen to her and be more obedient. But if you go with Aunty Anna now, then I will come see you in the nursery after supper." Zach smiled.

"Like this?" he said.

"No, silly," Lydia said with a giggle. "Nursey's scared of Papa when he's a dragon." Zach's expression went from incredulity to outright disbelief.

"Papa's *not* scary," he said, with a stomp of a foot.

"Off you go with your Aunty," Keira said. "You have kept Nurse waiting long enough, and your father has said he will come find you later."

"Will you take us for a ride?" Zach asked the dragon as Anna took him by the hand.

"We'll see, son. Perhaps if you behave yourselves." The dragon pushed himself to his full height, and looked down at them with his bony eyebrows raised.

"Yes, Father," said the boy with a sigh, allowing Anna to finally take him by the hand and lead him and his sister from the room.

Anna marched the children down the stairs and delivered

them to their relieved nurse, waiting in the nursery. She watched for a while as they dutifully sat down at the table and waited for Peggy to serve them their food. Peggy had been hired at Storbrook when the children were toddlers. Only a few years older than Keira, she had spent the years of her youth caring for an elderly parent. Shy and slightly awkward, she was never completely comfortable around other adults, but she loved being with the children. Her biggest fear, however, was for the dragon who was a regular feature of the Storbrook landscape. Although the creature never came near her, she trembled when it circled the skies, or when its roar rang through the stone mountain-top castle, certain that the beast was about to eat them all. Zach watched Peggy as she bustled around the room, giving her a penetrating stare.

"What is it, Zach?" she finally asked.

"Are you scared of Papa?" he asked.

Peggy looked at him in surprise. "Scared of your Papa? Why would you think that?"

"Well, because he's —"

At his words, Lydia, with an insight that went beyond her years, smacked her brother on the arm.

"Shh," she said loudly, her finger over her lips as she glared at Zach. She turned to Peggy. "Papa can be scary looking sometimes."

Peggy stared at Lydia for a moment as the color rose in her cheeks, before turning and brushing nonexistent crumbs from the table.

"I'm not scared of your father," Peggy whispered, "although he can be quite, er, stern at times. I do wish he wouldn't let the dragon near the castle, though."

"But the dragon is ..." Zach began, and Anna quickly intervened.

"Zach," she said, "I have a surprise for you." The boy looked at his aunt eagerly.

"What su'p'ise?" he said.

"If you are very good, I will ask Cook to bake you a

honeyed apple."

"Me too?" Lydia asked.

"Yes, you too," Anna said with a smile. She knelt down between the two chairs, watching for a moment until Peggy's back was turned before speaking again, her voice low.

"Do you remember what your Papa said about keeping secrets?" she said. Zach and Lydia both nodded. "Nurse must never know that your Papa is a dragon. All right?" Lydia stared at her in silence as Zach nodded. "You can only have a baked apple if you keep the secret." Again both children nodded. "Good," Anna said with a smile. She rose to her feet, and watched as Peggy poured warm milk into wooden cups and placed them on the table, before turning and leaving the room, confident that the importance of keeping the family secret had been impressed on Zach, at least for now.

Descending the stairs, Anna crossed the low hall, where the servants slept, and exited the castle into the warmth of a late spring day. She skirted the courtyard and headed into the gardens, pausing at a large spreading oak. They had celebrated the twins' fourth birthday beneath the shade of the tree just a few days before. A quilt had been spread over the new grass, and Cook had made honeyed cakes and sticky buns, served with warm milk, straight from the cowshed. The twins had polished off the treats, complaining later that their stomachs ached.

Anna smiled at the memory. It was hard to believe four years had passed since the twins were born – and more than five since she and Keira had been abducted by Jack, a rogue dragon seeking vengeance against Aaron, the Dragon Master. Jack had been killed in the resulting fray, and Keira had been grievously injured, saved only because Aaron had insisted she drink his blood a few days before. And then there had been Max. Anna closed her eyes, and pushed the memory away. She had not seen Max since the day he left the dragon domain, and although he often crept into her thoughts, bringing with him a tangle of yearning, regret and shame, she was determined to put him from her mind and get on with her life.

Anna leaned back against the tree and lifted her face to the sunlight, the new leaves painting a pattern of shadows against her skin. The sounds of the castle rose in a hum behind her, while closer at hand, birds twittered in the trees. It was calm and serene, but her soul was anything but serene. She took a deep breath, then pushed herself away from the knobbly trunk, annoyed at the disquiet she felt. She loved living at Storbrook, being with her sister, and helping with her young niece and nephew, but there were times when she felt like Storbrook was a cord wrapped around her neck, slowly choking her. It wasn't Aaron and Keira's fault, of course, but there were times when all she wanted was a life of her own. She sighed and turned back towards the castle, waving at Garrick, the castle groundsman, as he led a horse across the courtyard. He waved back with a smile, his eyes lifting to watch her as she walked. The smile turned to a grimace when he stepped into a pile of muck that had not been cleaned away, and Anna snorted back a laugh as she continued towards the doorway. She had friends and family – surely that should be enough?

CHAPTER TWO

Anna adjusted herself in her saddle, leaning back as the horse picked its way down the steep path that led through the mountains to the village where she had grown up. Garrick rode a few feet ahead of her, and she watched his back as he rolled easily with the movement of his mount. A year younger than her, he had filled out from the gangly youth she first met almost six years ago when she moved to Storbrook. His sandy-colored hair had darkened to brown, and his blue eyes creased at the corners when he smiled.

He was a man of few words, and did not seem to notice the glances that were frequently thrown his way by the young maids at Storbrook or in the village. When Anna had returned with Keira and Aaron after the troubles with Jack, it was Garrick who teased her out of her doldrums, dragging her through the forest while he trapped rabbits and hunted deer. He was an excellent marksman, and often it was his skill that placed meat on the tables at Storbrook. He had taught her about birds, pointing out the secret places where the hidden nests of robins and sparrows could be found, then dragging her away so the birds would not be anxious. He made her lie still for hours on end as they watched a spider spin her web, until finally Anna's fidgeting grew too much for even him to ignore. They swam in the river, and lay on the rocks in the sun afterwards, and once, he had kissed her on the forehead, then turned away in embarrassment. There had been a few moments of awkward silence, before he jumped into the deep pool formed by the river, drenching her from head to toe, and she had yelled at him while he laughed. Later, when she thought about it, she decided that it had been a brotherly kiss, and meant nothing more. She was relieved at this conclusion, although she did not think to wonder why. As the years went by, she sought him out while he mucked in the stables or chopped wood behind the shed. He would stop and smile at her, and occasionally tease her into helping him. She smiled now at the memories. Garrick was a good friend – probably better than she deserved.

It was over thirty miles to the village from Storbrook, but they made it in good time, reaching the outskirts of the village before noon. Garrick turned to face Anna. "I'll fetch you from your parents, shall I?" he asked.

She shook her head. "No, I'll meet you at the churchyard. I don't plan to visit for long, since I have a list of purchases I want to make in the village." Garrick nodded, then turned away, taking the path to the village smith, while Anna took the path that led to her old home. She made this trip every few weeks, sometimes with Garrick, other times with Thomas, Aaron's steward. Keira would often accompany her as well, bringing the children along, and then Aaron would carry them all on his back. But Aaron had urgent matters to attend to this day, and it was too far for the children to travel the distance on horseback in one day, so they had remained behind. Anna did not mind. She knew she was quite safe with Garrick, and his silence gave her time alone with her thoughts as they rode down the mountain.

Richard and Jenny Carver lived in a small house at the edge of the village. Richard was a Master Craftsman, and his wooden wares were sold in many of the surrounding towns and villages, gracing the tables of poor and wealthy alike. He was also the village reeve, employed in the service of Lord Warren to represent the people of the village as well as serve the lord's interests. The previous reeve, Matthew Hobbes, had been intent on killing the Storbrook dragon, a foolish mistake which had almost cost him his life, and left him with a serious injury. Richard had also been injured – not by the dragon, but by another villager who had accidentally impaled him with a pitchfork. It was the dragon's blood, spilt over his wounds, that saved Richard's life, an action that had won Richard's undying gratitude. He looked up through the doorway of his workshop as Anna approached, and with a wide smile hurried out to greet her.

"Are you here alone?" he asked, glancing behind her, and Anna could hear the slight regret in his tone. He loved his daughters, but it was Aaron that he revered.

"Yes, just me," she replied lightly. She hooked her arm around Richard's and led him towards the house. "Aaron and Keira send their regards, of course," she said as they crossed over the threshold. Jenny was sitting near the fire when Anna entered the small parlor at the front of the house. The passing years had not been kind to Jenny, and she looked far older than her forty-eight years. She smiled at Anna, but her eyes were dull, lined with black rings, while the skin sagged around her cheekbones.

"Anna, you have come to visit. How lovely."

"Yes, Mother," Anna said, dragging a stool towards her parent and taking her frail hands. "How are you doing today?"

"Not well, Anna, not well. I believe I'm not long for this world." Anna glanced at Richard, and he smiled sadly.

"Dame Lamb came to see your mother this morning," he explained. "She says there is nothing more to be done."

Anna turned back to Jenny, who was already patting her hand. "We are all marked for death, daughter," she said. "I have many regrets in life, but at least I know one daughter has a secure future, even if he is not the man I would have chosen. Now if I can just see *you* married, I could be at peace, ready to meet my Maker."

"Well, Mother," she replied, "it may be that God has seen fit to leave me a spinster. There are few men as worthy as Father, or Aaron, so I am quite content to remain in the unmarried state." She saw the dismay in Jenny's face, but was saved from reproach by the announcement that dinner was served.

"Come Mother," Anna said, helping Jenny to her feet. "Let me help you to the table."

Anna did not stay long after the meal was finished. She led Jenny to her room and helped her lie down on the bed. The fire had died down a little, and she stoked it back into flames before shutting the light from the windows and closing the door behind her. Richard had already returned to his workshop, but he lifted his head to give a distracted wave goodbye as she walked past.

Nothing in the village was a great distance apart, and it took Anna only a few minutes to reach the high street, with its collection of shops and services. It ran perpendicular to the churchyard, and Anna paused to tie her horse next to Garrick's before continuing on her way. Someone called her name, and she turned, her heart sinking when she saw Sarah Draper hurrying towards her.

"Anna! How lovely to see you! You have become quite the stranger!" She hooked her arm around Anna's, dragging her along the street. "I must confess, I am surprised to see that you are still alive and well."

Anna pulled her arm free. "Why?"

Sarah laughed shrilly. "Well, you do live in the mountains with a dragon."

"The dragon would never harm me."

"It would if Aaron Drake allowed it to," Sarah responded knowingly. "But I'm not really interested in hideous monsters. It is Garrick Flynn I want to hear about. Did I see him at the smith?" Anna shrugged. "He is so handsome," Sarah continued. "I'm sure he would kiss a girl very prettily."

"I wouldn't know," Anna said.

"He wouldn't be able to resist *me*," Sarah said, slyly. "I'm going to tell him you are delayed, and that you sent me to tell him."

"No." Anna was aghast. "Do what you will, but do not drag me into your affairs."

"Oh, la," Sarah said with a wave of her hand, before running lightly down the road, and disappearing around the corner. Anna watched her for a moment, then with a slight shrug of her shoulders, turned in the direction of the shops.

Anna took her time completing her purchases. She ordered new boots from the shoemaker, selecting the softest and most supple leather; she stopped by the parchmenter to pick up a roll of parchment; and she spent twenty minutes selecting a fine woolen worsted at the milliner to make a new gown. It had been dyed a soft blue, and Anna was sure the color would become her. She reached the end of the high street, where the cobbled paving petered into a muddy lane, before she turned around and headed back in the direction she had come. She had forgotten Sarah Draper and her plans to trap Garrick, but as she neared the end of the street, she was startled to see Sarah stomping towards her, scowling furiously. She glared at Anna as she walked past, but said nothing. Anna glanced towards the trees where the horses had been tied, and saw Garrick staring angrily after Sarah, arms crossed and eyes narrowed.

"That woman is entirely lacking in propriety," he growled as Anna drew near, "and refuses to even consider that her advances may not be welcome. She would have thrown me to the ground if given half a chance. Even so, I had to endure her touching and stroking me until I was forced to give the harshest putdown."

"Am I correct in understanding," Anna said with a grin, "that Sarah Draper is not the kind of woman you admire?"

Garrick's angry gaze swung to Anna, until a reluctant grin tugged at his mouth. "No, Sarah Draper is not the kind of woman I admire."

"Tell me, then," Anna said playfully, "what kind of woman *do* you admire?"

The smile dropped from Garrick's face, and he turned away to check the straps on Anna's horse. "A woman who can engage in a good conversation without being coy. A woman with spirit and fortitude. A woman who knows how to endure trials and still be cheerful."

Anna was silent, taken aback at the directness of his response, and she wished she hadn't posed the question. Garrick moved to the horse's head and checked the bit, before turning towards Anna, cupping his hands to boost her into the saddle. He did not meet her gaze, but when he placed his hand on her back to steady her, it lingered a moment longer than necessary. She saw a frown crease his brow before he turned away and mounted his own horse. He turned onto the path that wound behind the church and towards the forest at the foothills of the mountains. He did not speak as they crossed the open fields, but when they gained the shade of the trees, he drew his horse to a halt, forcing Anna, who was a step behind, to stop as well.

"Anna." He paused.

"Do you think we will reach Storbrook before nightfall?" she said.

Garrick shook his head. "Probably not." He was staring at her, and she looked away, suddenly uncomfortable.

"Well, I hope it won't get too cold. My cloak is not very warm," she said. "Perhaps if we –"

"Anna." Garrick's voice was firm. "There is something I would say."

She glanced back at him, and shook her head. "No."

"I cannot keep silent any longer. It is destroying me to see you every day, and not speak of how I feel. I have waited for some sign from you – anything that I could take as an encouragement, but my patience is wearing thin."

"Please, Garrick —"

"Tell me, Anna, do you feel anything for me?" he said.

Anna turned away and stared into the trees. "Garrick," she finally said, "I like you very much. You are a good man, and I consider you a great friend."

"A good man. A great friend." Garrick laughed dryly. "Words of the damned. You're still hankering after that dragon, aren't you?"

Anna turned to him with a look of surprise as her heart skittered within her chest. "What are you talking about?"

"Don't take me for a fool, Anna. I have lived at Storbrook most of my life, and like everyone else who lives there, I know exactly what Master Drake is. Don't worry," he added as she pulled in a startled breath, "we all know that there are some secrets that must be kept. But that does not change what Master Drake is, or the friends that arrive at the dead of night, through entrances other than the gate. Friends like Max Brant." The air was suddenly too heavy to breath. "You still have feelings for him," Garrick continued. "Even after all these years. But where is he now, Anna? He left you, didn't he? Probably without a backward glance."

Anna looked away as a pounding grew in her ears. "No," she whispered. "It wasn't like that."

"No? Then where is he now? He's not here, Anna." Garrick paused, then added gently, "But I am." Anna glanced down at the ground. A small, brown beetle was clinging to the edge of a leaf, dry and speckled with spots, and she watched as it fell on its back, its little legs waving furiously in the air, before it righted itself. Garrick leaned closer. "Anna," he said, "I love you. I know your feelings for me are not the same, but I love you enough for both of us. I want you to become my wife." She glanced up at him in dismay. "We could be happy," he continued quickly. "We already have friendship, which is more than many couples start with, and in time you will learn to love me." She opened her mouth to respond, but he covered her lips with his fingers. "Think about it, please," he said. "At least give me that much." She stared at him for a moment, then dropping her eyes, nodded slowly. "Thank you," he said, pulling his fingers away. He stared at her for another long moment, then turning away, nudged his horse down the path, as Anna did the same.

The rest of the journey was traversed in silence. Anna's first thoughts had been of bewilderment, dismay, and wild refusal, but as the initial shock wore off, she was able to consider Garrick's words with more composure. She didn't love him, it was true, but she had been honest when she said he was a good man, and she knew he would treat her well. And she could learn to love him. It wouldn't be wild or passionate, but steady and enduring. She would have a husband who loved her, and a home of her own, filled with children. She would have a life that did not depend on Keira or Aaron. A life that was hers alone. That was what she wanted, wasn't it?

CHAPTER THREE

Anna lay in bed that night, tossing and turning under the heavy quilts. She pushed them off, but when a breeze blew through the crack in the shutters, she pulled them back up with a shiver. Her chemise, although fresh and clean, felt scratchy and uncomfortable. A dull pain hovered behind her eyes, and her shoulders ached. Garrick's words would not be forgotten, but she could find no peace in them. She knew he was a man who was not only kind and generous, but also determined and strong. He would be a good husband, of that she had no doubt. But then why was she not happy? Why could she not bring herself to accept his offer with pleasure? Not only would she have her own home, but being married offered far greater freedom than she currently enjoyed. A reasonable man like Garrick would allow her to run her household as she chose, and with the protection of his name, she could travel and conduct business in a manner she could not do as a single woman. But even as she acknowledged these advantages, she was not content. She had seen the look of love in Keira's eye when she gazed on her husband, and recognized Aaron's happiness when he looked back. It was clear to Anna that Aaron and Keira were tied together by something far stronger than a mere contract. And there was the rub. She wanted what Keira had, even as she acknowledged that it was a strange and rare thing.

She lay restless through the long night, until the light of dawn started to penetrate the darkness. She stared blearily at the windows, but after the passing of another restless hour, finally pushed herself from the bed. A few glowing embers were all that remained of the fire from the previous night, and Anna stoked up the flames, watching as they licked the logs she placed over them. She crossed the floor to the window and threw open the shutters. A dark shadow was circling in the distance, and for an instant she thought it was a dragon, until it turned and she saw it was an eagle, gliding on a current of air.

Her gaze drifted downwards to the gardens of Storbrook. She could hear the cheerful twittering of birds as they fluttered between the trees, searching for grubs and insects. Early morning mist still clung to the mountain, and Anna could see a layer of dew covering the lawns, like a finely spun spider web. The sun had risen above the horizon, but the sky was still streaked with pinks and grays. A slight breeze stirred between the plants, and Anna caught the scent of roses drifting up past her window. All was peaceful and still, so unlike her own turbulent thoughts, and she reached for a gown, quickly fastening the laces as she slipped on a pair of slippers and headed out of the room.

Anna could feel the damp rising through her slippers as she walked across the grass, the back of her gown leaving a trail through the dew. She paused for a moment to watch two birds fighting over a worm, until a vicious peck convinced the smaller of the two to surrender, chattering angrily as it hopped away. The path twisted slightly as it meandered through the gardens, and she followed it around a corner, pausing when she saw a figure crouching on the ground a few feet away. Garrick had his back to her, but when she started to retreat, he held up his hand with a soft 'hush' and she paused, watching him cautiously. He wore a crumpled shirt, hanging over a pair of leather breeches and rolled up to his elbows. His hands were close to the ground, but his back hid what he was doing. It was only when he turned, his expression intent, and motioned her forward with his chin, that she could see a small bird in the palm of his hands.

"It's been hurt," Garrick said, his voice low. "I think it may have broken a wing. I found it lying on the ground."

"What are you going to do with it?" she asked.

"I'll find a box and nurse it back to health until it can fly on its own," he said. He was looking at the bird again, and as he spoke, Anna watched his face. His expression was gentle as he carefully stroked the trembling creature in his hands.

"Why?" Anna asked. Another man would choose a quick death for the injured bird, rather than taking time to care for it. "Why would you do that?"

Garrick turned to her with a smile as he rose to his feet. "Even the smallest creatures are of value to God," he said, "and no life should be taken needlessly." His smile stretched into a grin. "Even dragons know that."

"Well, some dragons, maybe," Anna said, suppressing a shudder as the memory of a black dragon rose in her mind – black in heart and black in appearance. And black Jack Drake had had no qualms about killing innocent people – whether they be human or dragon – in his efforts to try and wrest the Mastership from Aaron and pay him back for perceived wrongs. She glanced back at Garrick, who was watching her carefully; but when he met her gaze, he held his hands out towards her.

"Would you like to hold it?" he asked.

"All right," Anna said, cupping her hands together as she stepped closer. She could feel the roughness of his skin as he placed his hands over hers, carefully opening them and allowing the bird to slip into her palms. The tiny creature was trembling, its little heart racing with terror, and Anna felt a stab of pity for it. How easily its life could be snuffed out, its death completely unnoticed. She gently stroked her hands over its feathers, before smiling at Garrick.

"It's so tiny," she said.

He smiled back, but said nothing as he cupped his hands together once more, placing them beneath her own. She could feel the calluses on his hands as his skin pressed against hers, and she darted a quick glance at him, but his gaze was intent on the bird. He was so gentle as he handled the small creature, and she wondered what made him care for something so insignificant. But that was what set Garrick apart from many other people. She knew he loved nature, and whatever he loved he cared for and nurtured. Perhaps, Anna thought, that was what love was about. Not the searing blaze of flame that burned a path across your heart, but rather smoldering embers that warmed and comforted, gently spreading heat through your soul. She had yearned for the searing flame, but perhaps she should welcome the glowing embers.

"Garrick," she said. He lifted his gaze from the bird and looked at her upturned face, his eyes softening as he gazed at her. He took a step closer, and her name left his lips in a whisper.

She drew in a deep breath. "Garrick. I —"

The sound of her name being called made her turn around. Keira was coming along the path.

"There you are," she said. "You're up early! I went to find you in your chambers, but you were already gone. Aaron and I have something we need to discuss with you. He's waiting …" She had been looking at Anna, but paused when she glanced at Garrick. "There's no rush, however. Just come to the study when you're ready."

"I'll come with you now," Anna said. She glanced at Garrick, then hurriedly looked away. She had felt an unsettling sense of relief at the interruption.

"We can talk later," he said, and she nodded before quickly hurrying away. Anna could feel the weight of Keira's gaze as they walked, although she kept her eyes steadily on the path before her. "I interrupted something, didn't I?" Keira finally said. Anna glanced at her quickly, then looked away again.

"It was nothing."

Keira nodded, and silence fell for another few moments.

"Garrick's a good man," Keira said.

"Yes," Anna said with a sigh, "he's a very good man." She smiled wryly as she met Keira's gaze. "But maybe just too good for me."

CHAPTER FOUR

"Anna, come in," Aaron said. He was leaning against his desk, his long legs stretched out in front of him as Anna followed Keira through the door. A roll of parchment lay on the desk beside him, and he took it in his hand. "This arrived last night," he said. "The king is dead, and Prince Alfred is to succeed him to the throne. He has requested my presence at the funeral and subsequent coronation."

"Why?"

Aaron laughed dryly. "He knows what I am, and wants to ensure he has my support and cooperation. Keira and I wondered whether you would like to accompany us to the city. We will take the children and travel by coach. We leave in the morning."

"So soon?"

Aaron nodded. "Traveling by horseback would be faster, and flying even more so, but the children still tire too quickly to travel so far on my back."

"What about Peggy?"

"She will remain here." Anna nodded. "I have already sent Richard a message, informing him that we will be away for a while. But the choice is yours," Aaron continued. "If you would prefer to stay here, you will be quite safe under the protection of, uh, the servants here." Anna looked at Aaron sharply, catching his amused gaze. "I believe Garrick will consider it a privilege to keep you safe." He paused a moment. "He's a good man, Anna."

"I know," she groaned, "why does everyone keep telling me that." Her eyes narrowed suspiciously. "How do you know?"

"That Garrick is a good man? Everyone knows that," Aaron replied with a laugh. He grinned at her for a moment before relenting. "You forget that I can smell someone's emotions. And Garrick's feelings for you are very strong."

Once more Anna groaned, covering her face with her hands. "You're not helping me at all," she said.

Keira laughed. "Maybe a trip to the city is just what you need, Anna, to get your thoughts in order. Do you want to come?"

Anna lifted her head to look at her sister. There really was only one answer, after all. "Of course I'll come," she said.

Anna left the study a short time later, hurrying straight to her chambers. There was packing to be done if she wanted to be ready to leave in the morning, and she did not want to waste a single moment. She did not see Garrick again until much later, but she felt his eyes on her when Aaron made his announcement at supper about the king, followed by the news that they would be leaving Storbrook to travel to the city the following morning. Anna gave Garrick a weak smile, then looked away as the heat rose in her cheeks.

Despite the lack of sleep the previous night, Anna rose early the next morning, and was outside by the time the sun gained the horizon. Aaron had arranged to hire a carriage, and he and Keira had already left to fetch it and bring it to the crossroads at the foot of the mountains, where they would meet Thomas, Aaron's steward, and Anna, traveling with the children.

Thomas was in the courtyard when Anna arrived, and a

few moments later the children stumbled through the door of the low hall, rubbing their eyes sleepily while Peggy fussed behind them. Garrick had strapped the trunks to the packhorses, and these would be transferred to the roof of the carriage when they met Aaron and Keira. Satisfied that all was in readiness, Thomas helped Anna into her saddle. He had been Aaron's steward for years, and was one of the few humans who knew Aaron as a dragon. Of course, as Anna now knew, the other staff had also guessed Aaron's secret, but Thomas served Aaron both as a human and as a dragon, at Storbrook and beyond. It was Thomas who traveled with Anna and Max when they had made the trip to the city before, all those years ago when Aaron went to face Jack. He shared a smile with Anna as he lifted Lydia onto the saddle, settling her in front of her aunt, and in another moment he had mounted his own horse. Garrick lifted Zach into his arms, and he settled the boy in front of him as Anna had done with Lydia, while Peggy watched from a few feet away. The packhorses were tethered to the mounts, and Garrick took a few moments to test that the ropes were secure. He had not spoken to Anna, but as she sat on her horse, he stepped up beside her. She had dreaded the recriminations she was sure she would see in his eyes, but he looked at her calmly, with a slightly rueful smile.

"I'm sorry, Garrick," she said softly. "I need to do this."

"I know," he said. "Perhaps you will find what you are looking for while you are in the city, but when you have finished your adventures and are ready to return home, I will be waiting here for you." He laid a hand over hers. "My feelings for you will not change, Anna. No matter how long it takes, I will still be here, waiting in hope."

She bit her lip and nodded. She wished she could say something reassuring, but no words came, and she looked away as Garrick's hand slipped from hers. He took a step back, slapping the horse on the rump to get it moving as Thomas led the way. They were already passing under the portcullis when she risked a quick glance back. Garrick was standing with his arms crossed over his chest, his eyes staring at the departing party. She lifted her hand in a wave, but he did not acknowledge it, and she turned back to look at the path once more.

Lydia lay heavy against her chest as they made their way down the mountain. Ahead of her Zach chattered away to Thomas, and Anna smiled to hear Thomas answering his childish questions with all manner of seriousness. As the sun rose higher, Lydia became more attentive of her surroundings. Traveling on horseback gave her a new perspective on the forest, and she bubbled with questions.

"Antana," she asked, "why does the spider make his web across the path? Doesn't he know it will get knocked down?" Anna patiently explained that the spider did not know about paths, but Lydia already had another question. "Antana, why don't the birds sit together and talk, instead of shouting across the trees?" Before Anna even had a chance to respond, Lydia was speaking again. "Eew. Master Thomas's horse just pooped in our path!"

Anna laughed. "Where are his manners?" she said.

"Antana," Lydia asked a little while later, "What is the city like?"

"It's very big," Anna explained. "With lots of people. There are jousters and jugglers and troupes of actors performing wherever they can."

"Will I see them?" Lydia asked.

"I will take you myself," Anna said.

Aaron and Keira were waiting for them when they reached the crossroads, with a single horse standing in harness at the front of the coach. Working quickly, Aaron and Thomas soon had the carriage re-hitched with two pairs, while the remaining packhorse was tied to the back. The luggage was transferred to the roof of the carriage, and they were ready to go. It was roomy inside the vehicle, with two benches covered in cushions running across its width; but

Anna did not doubt that even with the cushions, the benches would soon feel hard and uncomfortable. Perhaps Thomas would allow her to sit next to him on the driver's seat sometimes.

The children climbed inside, eager to be off, and within a few minutes, Thomas was urging the horses to a trot with his whip, the beat of their hooves measuring the miles as the trees and villages rushed past. It did not take long for the children to tire of the new adventure, their freedom restricted by the ever-shrinking space in the carriage.

"How long till we get there?" Zach said.

"We have many days of travel ahead of us," Aaron answered. He leaned forward. "Perhaps you would like to ride with me for a while?"

"What about me, Papa?" Lydia's hand crept out to rest on Aaron's leg, and he looked down at her with an affectionate smile.

"You'll have a turn, too," he said. He looked at Keira, his eyebrows raised questioningly as he waited for her approval of the plan.

"Of course, as long as I also have a turn," she said with a laugh. He bent his head down and wrapped his hand around her neck as he whispered something into her ear that made her blush, before bringing his lips to hers. The moment was intimate, and Anna looked away, but the children had no such delicacy.

"That's de-yus-ting," Zach said. A moment later Aaron pulled away from Keira, his hand still on her neck, and raised his eyebrows in Zach's direction. The boy flushed and looked down as Aaron grinned.

"Come along, son," he said, tugging his tunic over his head and dumping it onto the bench behind him. "Let's leave these women to their business, shall we?"

Aaron grabbed the boy in his arms, and opening the door while the carriage still moved, shot himself into the air. Anna got a glimpse of golden wings unfurling behind him as Keira quickly pulled the swinging door shut, before a bright flash lit up the sky, extending in every direction then pulling back into nothingness. A loud whoop sounded in the air above the carriage, and they were gone, driving up into the sky and disappearing behind the clouds.

CHAPTER FIVE

It was a long and tedious journey, and it did not take long for Anna to be heartily sick of the carriage. The last time she made this journey it had been on horseback, and although she was unable to sit comfortably for days afterwards, at least it kept her mind occupied. The tedium of traveling in a coach, she decided, would eventually drive someone straight into their grave.

Attacks by highwaymen were not of the slightest concern to Aaron, and they traveled late into the night, stopping at roadside inns for just a few hours of sleep and a brief rest for the horses before continuing their journey. The inns were usually modest, offering nothing more than a warm bowl of stew, a roof over one's head, and animated conversation. At every stop Anna overheard people discussing the death of the old king, and speculating about the new.

"Prince Alfred may have been acting as regent, but he was still guided by his father's wisdom. But with the old king gone, he will allow his brother drag us into war," Anna heard someone remark at one of the inns. "I won't mind if he attacks to the north," another man retorted. "Terran's taxes against our goods are making it impossible to trade in the towns there." Terran was king of the neighboring kingdom, and he had imposed stiff tariffs on wool and linen brought in from beyond his borders. But despite the lack of love for Terran, the general consensus amongst the people seemed to be that Alfred lacked wisdom, while his brother, Rupert, hungered for a war Alfred could ill afford to wage.

The funeral of one king and coronation of another meant that there were many travelers on the road, and there were nights when it was impossible to secure more than one room for the party. On such nights, the men would sleep on the floor of the common room, along with the other male guests of the establishment, while the women and children shared a chamber. Often the inns were so full, some guests had to share their chambers with strangers, but Aaron always seemed to manage at least one room for the comfort of his family.

During the day, Aaron took his children out for short rides, and his wife for longer ones. Anna noticed in quiet amusement that Keira often returned from these excursions with cheeks that glowed and eyes that sparkled, but she kept silent about her observations. For herself, when she grew tired of the confines of the carriage, she climbed onto the driver's box and sat with Thomas. Sometimes he allowed Anna to take the reins while he leaned back with his cap over his eyes, and she would loosen her hold, enjoying the feel of the breeze through her hair.

They arrived at Drake Manor, the home of Aaron's cousin Favian, late in the afternoon of the sixth day. The home was shared with Owain and Margaret, Aaron's uncle and aunt, who occupied one wing, while Favian and Cathryn lived in the other, along with their two children, Will and Bronwyn.

It was five years since Anna had last been at Drake Manor. As the carriage barreled up the long drive that led to the house, she could see Favian and Cathryn waiting at the end of the drive, while a girl who was no longer the child she remembered stood at her parents' side. Aaron leaped out before the carriage even came to a stop, and Favian strode forward, his right hand clenched into a fist which he pounded over his heart.

"Master," he said, bowing his head for a brief instant, before looking up and meeting his cousin's gaze with a nod. Aaron smiled and nodded back, before turning to look at his aunt and uncle, who had come out as the carriage drew to a halt. Like Favian, Owain placed his fist over his heart and beat his chest.

"Master," he said.

"Power and might to you, Owain Drake, and strength be over your home."

"Thank you, Master," Owain said. He lifted his head. "It's good to have you back, Aaron."

"Keira! Anna! Welcome!" Anna turned with a smile to see Cathryn hurrying towards them, while Margaret walked at a more sedate pace a few steps back. Behind her hung Bronwyn, but as Anna glanced at her, she looked up and met Anna's gaze with a shy smile.

"Anna," Margaret said, taking her by the shoulders and studying her face intently, "you no longer carry the look of a girl, but have matured into a woman. It is good to see you again."

"Thank you," Anna replied with a faint flush. Cathryn, who had been greeting Keira, turned to her, and pulled her into an embrace.

"I am so glad you made the trip this time. We see Keira and Aaron so often, but never have the chance to see you!"

"Well, if Aaron would deign to carry me like he does Keira, then I would see you more frequently," Anna retorted. Cathryn grinned, and flashed a quick look at Aaron. If he had heard the comment, he was choosing to ignore it. A shout rang through the air, and the women turned to look at Zach and Lydia, running in wild circles around the carriage.

"They must be heartily sick of traveling," Margaret said.

She turned to the young woman at her side. "Bronwyn, why don't you take them to the kitchen and find them some milk?"

Bronwyn nodded. "Yes, grandmother," she said. She smiled hesitantly at Anna. "I'm very glad you came as well," she said shyly.

Anna stepped forward and took the girl by the hands. "Me too," she said. "It has been so long since I last spent time with you." She glanced around. "Is your brother here?"

The words were just out of her mouth when a long rumble filled the sky.

"That will be Will," Bronwyn said with a sigh. Anna looked up, following the glances of the others, to see a red dragon trailing through the air above them.

"That's Will?" Anna said in disbelief.

"When did that happen?" Aaron asked Favian in amusement.

"Oh, a few months ago," he said. "Your arrival could not be more timely, Aaron. Hopefully this newly transformed dragon will listen more closely to his Master than he does to his father or grandfather when he is advised to exercise more caution around humans."

"Oh? Should I be concerned?"

"Not yet," Favian said wryly, "but a stern lesson from you would not go amiss."

Aaron laughed. "Do I have to remind you what we were like at that age?"

Favian grinned. "That is exactly why I am concerned."

"Come," Cathryn said, linking her arms with Keira's and Anna's. "Let's leave the men and go and find some refreshment. I'm sure you must be quite weary of traveling." She nodded at Bronwyn, who gathered up Zach and Lydia, taking each of them by the hand, and led them around the back of the house.

That night Anna slept better than she had since leaving

Storbrook. She was given different chambers than before, for which she was grateful – there were far too many ghosts waiting to haunt her in the other room. She slept late the next morning, enjoying the luxury of lying in bed instead of climbing back into the carriage. They were leaving again that day, traveling the short distance into the city, but they would leave the carriage behind and traverse the rest of the distance on horseback. Or rather, she and Thomas would, taking Zach and Lydia with them, but Aaron and Keira would fly, landing near the city and traveling the remaining distance on foot. Favian, Cathryn and Bronwyn were also joining the party, but Will had chosen to remain behind with his grandparents.

"I would much rather stay here," he had resolutely declared. "What do I care about human kings and their coronations?"

It was early afternoon by the time the party left Drake Manor, but with the long days of late spring the city gates remained open until late, giving them plenty of time to enter. Anna could feel Lydia sagging against her as they drew closer, and she had to shake her gently as they neared the city gates.

"Look, Lydia," she said softly. The girl opened her tired eyes, then sat up when she saw the metropolis spreading along the valley below them.

"Is that the city?" she asked, her tone one of awe.

Anna nodded, remembering her own amazement the first time she had seen the capital, seething and pulsing with life, surrounded by walls almost ten feet wide that wound around the city in a drunken circle. Tall spires and rounded domes glittered in the late afternoon light, despite the pall of smoke that hung over the buildings, and occasional shouts rang through the air, carried along by the breeze. "Yes," she said to Lydia. "It was built by the Romans. They called it Civitas, which simply means 'city'. That's what the people who live here call it, too."

The path they were on joined a road that led to a bridge

over the river, right up to the tall wooden gates of Civitas, and Anna followed Thomas as he led the way. The dragons had landed behind a small knoll a mile outside the city, and they and their passengers had joined Thomas and Keira, traveling the last mile on foot.

As Anna crossed the bridge, she was once again struck by the teeming mass of humanity that pushed and shoved within Civitas's walls, but she also noticed a heaviness that hung over the city like a smothering blanket. The people within the city still went about their daily business – housewives did their shopping, hawkers sold their wares, craftsmen and merchants conducted business. But the atmosphere was subdued. And then there were the clothes – blacks, grays and dark browns. As they moved along the street, Anna saw that black drapes hung in the windows, and when they passed a church, she saw that not only the windows were covered, but the walls and doors as well.

But even the bleakness of mourning could not fully suppress the vibrancy of the city, and it pulsed with a beat that strained to be free. Anna wondered what Garrick would think of this place, but she knew he would not like it. Too many people, too little space. But Anna felt as though her heart was beating faster, desperate to match the rhythm of the great city.

"Why's everyone wearing black?" Lydia whispered.

"Because the king has died," Anna explained.

"But why?"

"The people want to show their respect for the king, so they are dressed in mourning."

"What's mourning?"

"When someone dies the people left behind dress in black to show how sad they are that they won't see the person again."

"Oh. Why did he die?" Lydia asked after a moment's pause.

"He was sick for a long time, and then he died. But we

will have a new king soon."

"Will the new king also die?"

"Eventually. But hopefully not for many years."

Lydia seemed to be pondering that as Thomas pulled his horse to a halt outside a large house, black timbers stark against whitewashed walls. As he dismounted, the wooden door was cautiously opened from within by an aging man with skinny legs and a large, hooked nose.

"Harry," Favian said, stepping forward.

The man bowed stiffly. "Master," he said. Squinting his eyes, he peered at the people gathered around Favian. "You brought visitors, Master," he said, his tone suggesting that this inconvenience was a personal affront. He glanced down at the two children who were staring at him, and his brows gathered together in a frown.

"I did. But perhaps you will allow me entry into my own house?"

"Of course, Master," said the man, pulling himself stiffly from the door with a bow. Taking Lydia by the hand, Anna followed the others into a hall that, even though it stretched the length of the house, was only half the size of the hall at Storbrook.

Favian turned to face the others. "Welcome to Drake House," he said with a wave of his hand. "Not as grand as Storbrook, to be sure, but comfortable enough for a few nights."

"You are right," Aaron said, his face straight as he glanced around. "This place is very pokey." He turned to Keira. "Should we find more comfortable accommodations elsewhere, my sweet?" Keira glared at him in mock consternation, but her attempt at sternness was lost when she laughingly turned to Favian.

"Please forgive his rudeness – he can be quite uncivilized at times. In fact, there are times when I think he's no better behaved than a wild beast. But *I* am very grateful for your kind hospitality, so thank you."

Beside her Cathryn laughed. "No need to apologize, Keira. We are all familiar with Aaron's, er, manners." She turned her attention to Harry. "Please send some refreshments to the parlor, and let Hannah know that we have arrived." The man bowed again, and left the room as Cathryn turned once more to her guests. "Follow me, and I will show you your chambers," she said, leading the way out of the hall and up a narrow flight of stairs.

CHAPTER SIX

The following day dawned cool and damp, despite being late spring, as though nature itself was joining the residents of the city in mourning the loss of their king. Anna's room overlooked a narrow lane, and the rain made the view even more miserable. Puddles filled the ruts, creating cesspools of mud and manure, while a large, gray rat scurried along the side of the wall. Anna slammed the shutter closed with a shiver and made her way downstairs where she joined the others.

"Alfred most humbly requested the pleasure of my presence when I arrived in the city," Aaron was saying to Favian as Anna entered the room. "Keira and I will go there today to pay our respects. And a reminder of our presence in his kingdom wouldn't do any harm." Aaron glanced at Keira, seated by his side. "You know I would prefer you not come, but your presence will make mine less of a threat."

"You worry too much, Aaron," Keira said. "I promise to take no notice of the beautiful ladies at court, nor be plagued by unpleasant memories." She turned to Anna and asked, "Would you like to come?" but Anna shook her head.

"The city looks too dismal. I would rather just stay here

and keep dry."

The day passed drearily, the rain dampening the mood of adults and children alike. When Zach and Lydia grew bored of playing in their chambers, Bronwyn cheered them up by playing hide-and-go-seek. And when they tired of that, she told them tales of a king who had become the loyal subject to a powerful dragon.

Aaron and Keira were gone until mid-afternoon. When they walked into the hall, Aaron's skin was steaming from the rain, but Keira was shivering beneath her damp clothes. Anna handed her a cup of wine as she went to stand before the fire. "Why anyone would choose to be out today is beyond me," Keira said, "but the rain did not keep people away from the palace to view the body of the king."

"Did you see it?" Anna asked.

Keira shook her head. "No. People were lined up out the building, across the courtyard and through the gardens. Besides, Aaron complained that he could not bear the smell. He moved so quickly past the hall, I had to run to keep up!"

Anna laughed. "A dragon who does not like the smell of dead flesh!"

Aaron walked over to where the women stood by the fire. "Dragons do not eat carrion!" he said with mock consternation. "It needs to be warm and fresh!"

Anna shuddered. "That sounds ... delicious!" Aaron grinned.

"So you saw the new king?" Favian asked, entering the room.

"I did," Aaron said. "I gave him a little reminder of who I am, to make sure he remembered his promise to keep our secret for the safety of his kingdom. And I also assured him of my loyalty to him as sovereign king of the human realm."

Favian nodded. "Do you think he has kept his silence?"

"I think so, for now at any rate. But he has a long reign ahead of him, and the burden of our secret may become too heavy for him to bear alone. But there is no more we can do now. We will just have to wait and see what happens."

The funeral service was the following day, and although the rain had stopped, the clouds were low and ominous, and the air was damp. The service was to be conducted in the large cathedral that soared high above the city skyline, but despite being the largest edifice in the kingdom, no more than a few hundred people could be squeezed into the nave, and the guest list had been strategically pared down to include only the most important guests. The nobility, of course, were invited – a new king had to ensure he offended no-one who could pose a threat to his rule; foreign dignitaries also made the list; the church elite – the kingdom's scribes and bearers of blessings – had also been invited; and the Dragon Master. These people would bear report to the rest of the kingdom of the ceremony given to the old monarch. Of course, anyone who chose to could watch the coffin proceed from the palace to the king's final resting place within the cathedral.

Except for Aaron and Keira, the entire Drake household, including the staff, set out early in the morning to find a good spot near the cathedral to watch the procession, the children jumping excitedly at the thought of seeing the knights in their armor. Despite the early hour, crowds of people were already lining the streets as they huddled together, laying claim to their spaces along the funeral route. The street was a sea of black which grew thicker and deeper with each passing hour. An air of grief hung over the city, and Anna saw more than a few elderly women pressing handkerchiefs to their eyes. Lydia tugged at her hand.

"Why is that lady crying?" she asked.

"Because the king is dead," Anna said.

"Does she miss him?"

"Yes," Anna said, "I think she misses him very much."

The hours passed slowly as they stood waiting in the chilly air. Hannah had brought a basket filled with cold meats, bread and wine, which she passed out among the group, but still Anna shivered, and the children complained of the cold. The only one unaffected was Favian, and slowly the family edged closer to him, seeking out his warmth. It was already well past noon when Anna heard the muffled stamp of hooves in the distance.

"I can't see anything," Lydia complained, pulling on her hand. Anna was standing next to Cathryn and Bronwyn, with the children in front of her, but with so many people milling about, it was difficult to get a clear line of sight. Behind them stood Favian, who towered over everyone else in the crowd.

"Pass her to me," he said, and a moment later Lydia was seated on Favian's shoulders, while Zach scrambled onto Thomas's. Lydia wrapped her hands around Favian's head with a laugh, and Anna turned to shush her as people looked on disapprovingly.

"I can see everything," Lydia said in a loud whisper.

"I wish I was still small enough to sit on Papa's shoulders," Bronwyn said with a sigh, pushing herself up on her toes to try and get a better view of the road. Cathryn turned to her daughter with raised eyebrows, her expression more eloquent than words as she looked at the daughter who already topped her by an inch. Bronwyn grinned, but said nothing.

Still the minutes dragged by, and the silence on the street was eerie as the people waited for the funeral procession to appear. The bells hung silent, and even the birds did not sing on this dreary day. The horses' hooves had been wrapped in cloth to muffle the sound of their tread, which added to the surreal mood. Finally, a small gasp rippling through the crowd announced that the procession had turned the corner and was approaching the gathered onlookers. Anna craned her neck to see the twenty-four liveried knights, bearing the colors of the royal house, mounted on battle steeds and riding in pairs. The open hearse followed, drawn by six black horses, their manes and tails braided with black ribbons. The royal coffin was draped with a cloth bearing the royal coats of arms. Behind the hearse walked the new monarch, King Alfred, and his younger brother, Prince Rupert. Dressed in black from head to toe, they both had their heads bowed, and they marched with even footsteps as they followed the vehicle carrying their father to his final resting place. Behind the royal sons came the Lord Chamberlain, a black mantle over his shoulders; the Lord Mayor, his chain of office hanging around his neck; and the city Aldermen, representing the Merchant Guilds. They were followed by the Knights of the Garter, the blue strip of fabric that was tied around each calf the only contrast in the sea of black. Lastly came a glittering carriage, gilded in gold, which carried the new queen, the royal children, and the ladies-in-waiting to Her Royal Highness.

The silence thickened as the hearse drew closer, even the children recognizing the solemnity of the occasion. An elderly woman standing near Anna sobbed quietly, her shoulders heaving as she pressed a sodden handkerchief to her face.

As the procession slowly moved past, the crowds fell in behind the carriage, walking quietly behind. It was not far to the cathedral from this point, and Anna watched as the hearse pulled to a stop alongside the wide stairs that led up to the large arched doors. The crowd watched in silence as the coffin was pushed from the hearse and into the waiting hands of the new king, his brother the prince, and the deceased king's two younger brothers, the Dukes of Sufford and Eastwich. The wagon moved away and the four men slowly marched up the steps towards the door. They were almost at the top of the stairs when Alfred stumbled, his foot missing the next rise. The coffin swayed precariously for a moment and a collective intake of breath was heard through the crowd before he finally found his footing.

"A bad omen, mark my words," a woman mumbled behind Anna. The pall-bearers reached the top of the stairs without further incident, and entered the church, where the archbishop stood waiting for them. The rest of the procession followed in dignified silence, and the archbishop pushed the door closed behind them.

All around Anna the crowds pushed and surged. Lydia and Zach were still seated on Favian and Thomas's shoulders, but Anna grabbed Bronwyn's arm as someone pushed between them. They turned in the direction of Drake House, forcing a path through the heaving crowds. It was slow going, and they were still some way off when they heard the tolling of bells, jangled and confused as they sadly delivered the news that the old king had been placed in his final resting place within the cathedral. Anna shivered slightly, before hastening her footsteps to keep up with the others as they neared the warmth of Drake House.

CHAPTER SEVEN

A new wind blew through the city in the week following the funeral. Gone were the clouds and rain, and instead the sun shone in a sky of blue. The black drapes disappeared from the windows and mourning clothes were set aside. The city resumed its frenetic pace, and the street sounds returned to their usual volume, all air of reverence and respect gone.

There were many dragons who lived in the city, and Aaron's days were full as he dealt with clan matters and met with his clansmen, sometimes going beyond the city walls where his dragon form would not be seen by humans. Favian often joined him, and the two were gone from morning till late each night. Cathryn, too, took the opportunity of being in the city to deal with matters of business. As a wool merchant, there were guild meetings to attend and brokers to entertain. Which left Keira and Anna plenty of time to explore the city, Bronwyn and the twins in tow.

The city was abuzz as it prepared for the coronation of the new king – tapestries were hung from windows, banners were strung across the streets, and the inns concocted special brews in honor of the new monarch. Foreigners filled the city, speaking languages unfamiliar to common city folk, and wearing clothes that made people stare in astonishment. To Anna, it was exciting. Every day there was something new to see, and some new treat to taste. She heard words she had never heard before, and gaped at the latest fashions, brought from foreign courts. She felt as though she could wander the streets forever and never tire of the pace and rhythm.

A few days before the coronation, Anna was surprised to come downstairs and find Aaron waiting in the hall with Keira, while the twins ran in circles around them.

"I'm taking a break from clan business," Aaron told Anna as she entered the room, "and will be joining you on your excursions today."

Bronwyn soon joined them, and they pushed their way into the crowded streets. Turning in the direction of the river, Aaron led them to some quieter roads, away from the shoving crowds. Even here, jugglers, jesters and mummers arrayed themselves along the street, and Zach and Lydia watched wide-eyed when knife jugglers and sword throwers impressed the crowds with their skills. Keira teased Aaron when a man who breathed fire set a long branch alight, but Zach was fascinated.

"Is that man a dragon, Papa?" he asked in wonder.

"No, son," Aaron answered with a laugh. "He's not actually *breathing* fire."

"Oh," Zach said, but his tone was doubtful.

Aaron and Keira walked ahead of the small group, the children at their sides, while Bronwyn fell in step with Anna. Her long dark hair was tossed carelessly over her back, but the sun caught tints of red within the brown tresses that shone as her hair swayed on her shoulders. Her eyes were blue like her father's, and like him, her smile came easily.

"You are so fortunate to live so close to the city," Anna said.

"Really?" Bronwyn said. "We don't come very often. Father prefers being in the country, away from prying eyes." She glanced up at Aaron, her eyes narrowed in consideration.

"I can't blame him. I'm sure I will want to stay in the country too, when I change."

Anna looked at Bronwyn, confused for a moment, before understanding dawned. Of course, she too was a dragon, and although her body had not yet started changing, her turn would soon come.

"How do you feel about being a dragon?" Anna asked, curious.

Bronwyn shrugged. "I don't really think about it. It is what I am, and nothing will change it. It will be wonderful to take to the sky with my own wings, but I wish I didn't have to eat … certain things."

Anna shuddered. "No, I can understand that."

"But Father says if you don't think about it, it's not so terrible."

"Well, I suppose he would know," Anna said, a little doubtfully. She looked at Lydia, who was riding on her father's shoulders. She hadn't given much thought to her little niece being a dragon before, but she too would one day sprout wings and breathe fire. As Anna considered this, Aaron turned to look at her, his amused expression convincing her that he had guessed the direction of her thoughts.

A group of actors a little way ahead caught Anna's attention and she watched as they played out a coronation scene. As would be expected from a troupe of actors, the coronation went horribly wrong – the prince tripped on his way to the throne, the archbishop dropped the crown, the princess whacked the prince with the scepter, and the orb rolled down the aisle as the noblemen hopped over it, until one of them picked up the rolling sphere and raising it above his head, declared himself to be the new king. Anna joined the crowd in laughing, amused at the spectacle.

Later that evening, Anna sat with Keira and Cathryn in the small parlor behind the hall. Anna was telling Cathryn about the play they had seen, laughing as she related the farcical coronation. Aaron and Favian had gone out a few hours earlier, and Bronwyn, Zach and Lydia had all gone to bed.

"It sounds like you enjoy the city," Cathryn said.

"Oh, yes! It is the most wonderful place," Anna replied. "It's so alive! There is something happening on every street corner – a play, or jugglers, or some other entertainment."

Cathryn smiled in amusement. "It does begin to tire after a while."

"Oh, no, I cannot believe that! I don't think I would ever grow tired of Civitas!"

"I enjoy coming here for a short while," Keira said, "but the place is too chaotic for me to spend too long. I will be glad to return home."

"Will we leave immediately after the coronation?" Anna asked, a tone of wistfulness creeping into her voice. Keira smiled, then glanced at Cathryn, who gave a small nod.

"Aaron is eager to start the journey back to Storbrook as soon as possible following the coronation," Keira said. Anna nodded her understanding. It was as she expected. "We will stop overnight at Drake Manor," Keira continued, "and if you would like to, you can remain there with Cathryn and Favian."

"At Drake Manor?" Anna said in surprise, looking first at Keira, then turning to Cathryn.

Cathryn nodded. "Yes. I know you would like to be in Civitas, but we are not so far away, and can come in anytime."

"But ... are you sure?" Anna could not help smiling.

"Yes. We would all welcome your company. Bronwyn is very fond of you, you know."

"Oh, yes, that would be wonderful!" Anna said. She turned to Keira, and her smile dimmed slightly. "But what about Zach and Lydia?"

"We will all miss you, Anna, but you can come home to Storbrook anytime." Keira took Anna's hand in hers. "I know you have not been happy lately," she said. "It is time for you to discover your own destiny." She paused for a moment. "Is there anything else that would hold you back at Storbrook?" Anna glanced down at the hand that lay in her sister's, then lifted her head to meet Keira's gaze.

"No," she said. She smiled. "I would love to remain with Cathryn and Favian."

"Well, you don't have to decide right away," Keira said, but Anna was already shaking her head.

"I won't change my mind," she said. She turned to look at Cathryn again. "Thank you so much for the offer, and I would love to stay with you at Drake Manor."

Cathryn smiled. "Excellent," she said.

CHAPTER EIGHT

The good weather held, and coronation day dawned fair and bright. The excitement in the city was palpable, and along every street and alley people were in a joyous mood. Children danced and sang in the streets, women smiled and laughed as they chatted with their neighbors, and the men nodded to one another in friendly greeting. By order of King Alfred, mourning clothes had been set aside, and the citizens of Civitas wore their brightest hues. The procession route had been laid with branches and petals, while hanging overhead were brightly colored banners. Pageants and pantomimes, extolling the virtues of the new monarch, had been written by the greatest playwrights and musicians in the city, and had been performed in the streets and on the stage throughout the week.

Once again, Favian had ferreted out a good spot for the family to watch the passing procession, and they stood waiting amongst the crowds on the street. As they waited, bells began to toll in the distance. "The king and queen are leaving the palace," Cathryn told the children.

Lydia nodded wisely. "We'll see them here," she said, pointing to the road in front of where they were standing.

"That's right," Cathryn said.

The royal couple were to travel along the river by barge from the palace to the city steps, where they would be met by the Lord Chamberlain, the Mayor, and the city Aldermen. The bells continued to toll in the distance as they waited, and after a while they were joined by others, their notes ringing out much nearer.

"Listen," Cathryn said. "The king and queen are drawing closer. As they pass each church, the bells will begin to ring."

"We see them soon?" Lydia asked.

"Soon," Cathryn promised.

But the sun was high in the sky and little trickles of sweat were running down Anna's neck by the time the royal couple finally came into view. The king rode a magnificent white stallion, while behind him came the queen, traveling in an open litter mounted between two white horses. The bells in the surrounding steeples pealed furiously as the royal couple waved to their loyal subjects. The queen wore an exquisite gown of cream silk overlaid with gold lace, and the jewels in her hair glittered in the sun. The king was just as splendidly arrayed, with breeches made of gold cloth and a purple doublet embroidered with gold thread. The queen smiled and waved at the adoring subjects as the procession moved on. A chatter rose amid the crowd, but the people remained standing where they were, aware that the newly crowned king and queen would pass this way again at the end of the ceremony.

If it was possible for the bells to peal more joyously, they did so an hour later when the ceremony was complete, and the doors swung open to the cathedral. The news quickly spread along the streets that the king and queen were returning to the palace, and indeed, not very much time had passed before Anna saw the procession coming down the street once more. Circlets of gold rested on the heads of both the king and queen, and a mantle of ermine hung from the king's shoulders. In his hands he carried the orb and scepter of the kingdom, which he held up for the crowds to see. They moved quickly along the route towards the waiting barge, and the crowds broke up as they disappeared from sight.

Anna was hot and sticky by the time they arrived at Drake House, and the children were complaining that their legs were sore, their heads hurt and they were hungry. Even Bronwyn seemed to be miserable. The problem with the city, Anna thought to herself, was that there was no escape from the heat and smog – no shady woods to walk in and no cool lakes to dive into.

Aaron and Keira returned to Drake House soon after, and Keira eagerly shared the details of the ceremony. "It was very solemn," she said. "The king swore an oath that he would serve and protect the kingdom according to the law of the land, before the archbishop recited a very long prayer and anointed him with oil. Then the royal mantle was placed on his shoulders and the crown placed on his head, and he was given the orb and scepter. The queen didn't swear an oath, but she was also anointed with oil before being crowned. They kneeled throughout the ceremony, their eyes downcast, even when Prince Frederick started crying."

Anna smiled in amusement. "What happened?"

"He was hot and bothered, I suppose. Prince Rupert was sitting behind the children, and he gave his nephew his dagger to play with."

Anna looked at Keira in shock. "You're jesting!"

Keira laughed. "I'm not! It was a ceremonial dagger, but still very sharp. However, it did the trick. Frederick spent the rest of the ceremony scratching the wooden pew."

Anna laughed. "I'm sure the archbishop appreciated that! How old is the prince?"

"Frederick or Rupert?" Keira smiled. "Frederick is four, and his uncle Rupert is about twenty-five. You will see him at the banquet tonight. Speaking of which, we should probably start getting ready."

All the city noblemen and merchants had been invited to

attend a banquet on the palace grounds to celebrate the coronation, and Anna had been included in the invitation as well. New gowns had been ordered and delivered earlier in the week, and Anna had purchased a new pair of slippers for the event.

The rest of the afternoon passed in a flurry of activity as the women hurried to prepare themselves for the royal banquet. Maids hurried between the rooms, hauling water and bringing linens. Hannah, Cathryn's personal maid, rushed between them, helping pull on gowns, don jewels and dress hair. Anna's gown was a pale yellow silk, which hung in gentle folds from her hips, accentuating her narrow waist. The long sleeves were tight over her upper arms, and then flared wide, ending at her wrists over the front of her hand, but hanging down low at the back. Her new slippers peeked out from beneath the hem of the gown, and around her neck hung a simple string of pearls, a gift from Aaron and Keira on her twenty-first birthday. Seed pearls, tucked into the long braid that hung down her back, sparkled in the afternoon sun.

Aaron and Keira were waiting for her when she walked into the hall a short time later.

"Ready?" Aaron asked.

"Yes," she replied.

"Then let's be off," he said. "Favian and Cathryn will meet us there." He picked up a shawl from the bench, and with a flourish, draped it around Keira's shoulders, before heading towards the door.

CHAPTER NINE

It was late afternoon by the time they arrived at the palace, but the sun was still high in the sky. The river was a highway of boats, with ferrymen poling their way around each other as they strove for the palace landing, often pushing other ferries aside. Anna stared in astonishment as the boatmen yelled insults and curses at their rivals, while passengers joined in the fray, shouting their encouragement at their own ferrymen, promising silver to urge them on. It was a wonder that more people did not land in the river, Anna thought, but she saw only one boat knocked so hard its passenger fell into the water, unnoticed by the two ferrymen hurling insults at one another. The passenger was rescued from the tangle of weeds by another boat, and he gratefully tipped the rescuing boatman with a large silver coin, before shaking his fist at the other ferryman.

The stairway leading to the palace lawns was crowded with people, and as Anna stepped off the boat Aaron grabbed both her and Keira by the arm, pulling them through the crush. It was just as well, for no sooner had they reached the safety of the lawn than a woman, alighting from a ferry, slipped on the mossy stairs, dragging her escort with her into the muddy river with a shriek.

The crowds thinned the further they drew from the river, and Anna looked around in interest. Dozens of trestle tables had been placed on the lawns near the palace walls, covered with snow white linen. Gleaming silverware glittered in the sunlight, while liveried footmen rushed about, finishing the place settings with crystal glass and white napkins. A raised dais was placed to one side, with a table and gilded chairs on the raised platform. Huge swags of white fabric created a canopy above, and flowers and vines twisted around the trellises that held the fabric. To the left played an orchestra, partially hidden behind an embroidered screen, while between the tables and the river mingled hundreds of guests, the doyens of society keeping up a flowing commentary behind open fans as they watched the new arrivals with raised eyebrows and upturned noses.

Beyond the palace to the right lay the formal gardens, and Anna stared at them for a moment. It was there that she and Keira had been snatched by Jack and flown away to a rocky fortress where they were held prisoner. Jack was long since dead, and Anna knew that no dangers lurked in the garden tonight, but she could not suppress an involuntary shiver. A hand laid on her arm had her turning towards Keira.

"We're quite safe," Keira said.

"I know. It's just the memories."

Keira nodded. "I know." She glanced at Aaron. "But we mustn't allow them to ruin our evening."

"No," Anna said. A bump on her shoulder made her stumble forward slightly, and she turned around to see a young woman stepping backwards, her hand to her mouth as she stuttered out an apology.

"I'm so sorry," the girl said, her expression dismayed. "Someone jostled me and I lost my balance."

"No harm done," Anna said with a smile. "There are so many people here, I'm surprised I haven't been jostled and knocked a hundred times! I'm Anna Carver."

The girl smiled gratefully. "Kathleen Hobart." Kathleen took Anna's outstretched hand and gave it a limp shake, meeting Anna's gaze very briefly before dropping hers to the ground. "I'm not very good with crowds," she whispered. "Father insisted I come today, but I would have preferred to stay at home. I've been reading the most wonderful story, and would have liked to finish it." She looked up for a moment, then dropped her gaze once more. "I don't know very many people." Kathleen stood a few inches shorter than Anna, and was demurely dressed in a gown that rose high up her neck, making her look more like a married matron than a girl of seventeen or eighteen, which is what Anna guessed her age to be.

"Well, nor do I," Anna said. "But I can introduce you to *someone*. This is my ..." Anna turned to see that Keira and Aaron had moved away. Anna turned back with a smile. "I was going to introduce you to my sister, but I'm sure there will be another opportunity later. Would you care to walk around the grounds with me? We can watch the matrons who are so intent on watching us. 'Look, there goes Mistress Kathleen,' they will say, 'with ... who is that girl again? Ah, yes, I remember now – she has a sister – I've forgotten her name – who's married to Aaron Drake, the most handsome man to have ever graced this kingdom.'"

"Aaron Drake?" Kathleen breathed. "Your sister is married to Aaron Drake?"

Anna looked at Kathleen in surprise. It had been years since Aaron lived at court. "Yes," she said, "do you know him?"

"I don't *know* him," Kathleen said, "but everyone knows *of* him. He slayed that terrible monster a few years ago. And my grandmother says he is the most beautiful man she has ever seen."

Anna laughed. "I wouldn't go *that* far," she said.

"Well, please don't introduce me to him. I would be too nervous to even say good evening."

"Nonsense," Anna said. "There is nothing scary about Aaron at all. At least," she amended, "nothing that could scare you if you saw him tonight." Kathleen looked startled, and Anna hurried on. "Do you live in the city?" she asked.

"Oh no. Except … what I mean to say is … yes, I do. Father brought me to the city a week ago so I could be introduced at court. He intends for me to live here with him, but the city…" There was a slight catch in her voice, and she took a deep breath before continuing. "Civitas is not my home."

"You lived in the country?"

Kathleen nodded. "Before my mother died, we lived on an estate in the west. After she passed, Father came to the city, but I went to live with my grandmother, the Duchess of Southbury. She retired from court life about five years ago, and I have lived with her ever since." She lifted her eyes to meet Anna's. "Father has said I must be happy here, and I am determined to be so."

Anna smiled. "I've only just arrived in the city, too, but will be leaving tomorrow."

"Where do you live?"

"I live with my sister and Aaron at their home in the north, but I am not returning with them to Storbrook. I will be staying at Drake House, just a few hours from the city."

"Will you visit sometimes?"

"Whenever I am able."

"Good! Then you can visit me whenever you are in town, and we can be friends." A clarion sounded, and Anna turned around to see people crowding towards the palace entrance.

"Come," Anna said, "the king and queen are making their grand entrance." Looping her arm through Kathleen's, she tugged her along as she followed the mass of people towards the palace courtyard. Slipping through the crowds, she pulled Kathleen to the far side, where they had a good view of the doorway. A moment later movement could be seen from within, and the new king and his queen stepped through the entrance. A cheer went up from the crowd, and Anna added her voice to the throng as the king and queen waved at their guests. Standing side by side, the queen stood a few inches shorter than her husband, although her long, golden hair, braided and coiled around the top of her head, made her seem taller. The thick mass shone in the sunlight, encircled by the crown of gold that had been placed on her head earlier that day. Alfred, too, wore a gold circlet upon his light brown locks. The royal children stood behind their parents, but a quick word from Matilda had them stepping around to stand in front. Alfred dropped a hand onto the shoulder of the oldest, Prince John, while the two little ones looked at the crowd in bewilderment. The youngest, the princess Mary, turned her face into her mother's legs, but little Prince Frederick stared stoically at the ground. Anna could see someone else standing just behind the king, and she shifted slightly before seeing that it was the king's brother, Prince Rupert.

Prince Rupert was a direct contrast to his brother. In appearance, Alfred was lean and fair, while Rupert was swarthy and well-built. Alfred was charming, Rupert was brooding. When Alfred smiled, Rupert glowered. Alfred loved pleasant society, talking, dancing and feasting, whereas Rupert wanted nothing more than to leave the palace and go hunting. He had a hunting lodge a day's ride from the palace, and he would retreat there with only one or two servants for company. Alfred's caution and restraint were well-known, but Rupert's resolute decision-making was praised. Alfred had been overheard more than once complaining that Rupert cared nothing about the loyal subjects of the land, whereas it was known that Rupert considered his brother dull and witless, his love of clothes and dancing an indication of his simplemindedness. The only thing the brothers seemed to have in common was a love for women. Both men had mistresses and lovers scattered around the countryside, but whereas the whole court gossiped about Alfred's affairs, the names of Rupert's lovers were only mentioned in quiet whispers. But that did not stop the women loving him, and Anna could hear his name being whispered as the women in the crowd strained to catch a glimpse of the darkly handsome prince.

He was standing in the shadows behind the king, but the look of boredom in his countenance was clearly evident. He wore his hair short, unusual for men at court, and his clothes, while fine, did not display the bright hues so many other noblemen paraded. His glance fell on Alfred's back, and his eyes narrowed slightly, but when his gaze moved to his nephew, John, his features softened, and a slight smile tugged at his lips.

Anna's gaze returned to the royal couple as King Alfred and Queen Matilda stepped out from the doorway while the crowd parted to make way. The women sunk into low curtseys while the men bowed. Rupert stepped out behind them, his arms crossed over his chest, followed by an entourage of royal courtiers. His eyes swept over the crowd, lingering for a slight moment on Anna before moving on.

"Isn't he handsome?" Kathleen whispered next to her.

"He's all right, I suppose," Anna said with a shrug. There was only one man Anna considered truly handsome, but he was gone forever. From where Anna stood, she could see Aaron and Keira, and she watched as the king drew close to the Dragon Master. Aaron nodded briefly, his eyes meeting Alfred's, and Alfred nodded in return before moving on. She could hear people whispering around her, surprised at Aaron's lack of homage.

"Who is that man?" Kathleen whispered, nodding in Aaron's direction.

"Aaron Drake," Anna replied.

"He didn't bow to the king."

"No. He's a ..." Anna paused. "He's a good friend of the king's."

As the royal couple made their way across the courtyard

to the lawns, the musicians, who had stopped playing at the royal appearance, started once more. A group of women trailed after the queen, and from time to time she turned to say something to them.

"Who do you think those women are?" Anna said to Kathleen.

"Probably her ladies-in-waiting," Kathleen replied. "My grandmother served the last queen."

As Anna and Kathleen walked behind the crowds, Anna saw Aaron just a short way up ahead, towering over the rest of the crowd. "Aaron," she said softly, knowing he could easily hear her above the hubbub. He turned with a smile and a quick word to Keira.

Anna led Kathleen towards them. "I was wondering what had happened to you," Keira said.

"I found a friend," Anna said. "This is Mistress Kathleen Hobart."

"Mistress Hobart," Keira said with a smile. Kathleen smiled back, but the smile fled a moment later when she looked at Aaron.

"Mistress Hobart? Daughter of Richard Hobart? Earl of Riverton?" Aaron said. Kathleen looked down at the ground and nodded slightly. "I know your grandmother, my lady," Aaron continued, his tone softer. "She's a good woman." Kathleen glanced up with a shy smile.

"Thank you, sire," she said, before quickly looking away again. Aaron met Anna's amused expression with a wry smile, before turning back to Keira, who was looking at him with slightly upraised eyebrows. He lifted her hand, and brushed his lips over her fingers as he gazed down at her. Keira stared back at him as his hand moved to her neck, and she gave a tentative smile.

"I believe dinner is served, my sweet," Aaron said. "Shall we?"

"Are you coming?" Keira said, turning to Anna.

"I will be right behind you," she assured her sister. She

watched as they moved away before turning back to Kathleen.

"I cannot believe Aaron Drake spoke to me," Kathleen said.

"Why? You are the daughter of an earl, and Aaron Drake is just an ordinary man."

"There is nothing ordinary about Aaron Drake," Kathleen said. "There aren't many men who have conquered a dragon. Grandmother says he is as great as the king, and deserves the same amount of honor." Kathleen leaned closer to Anna as she whispered, "I think she knew him quite well."

"Oh." Anna glanced up at the retreating forms of Aaron and Keira. Aaron's hand was resting on Keira's back, and she was leaning towards him slightly. Anna smiled. "Let's go find our places," she said.

Anna had been placed next to Aaron and Keira, while Kathleen was seated with her father near the dais. "I'll look for you later," Anna said as they parted company. Kathleen smiled, and hurried away to join a short, balding man, tapping his leg impatiently.

CHAPTER TEN

Anna sat with Aaron to her one side, while on the other was seated a young man a few years older than herself, who spent the entire meal pointing out various objects and enlightening Anna on their geometrical qualities. Anna nodded a few times, until she realized that the man needed no encouragement to continue with his conversation, and an occasional glance in his direction would suffice to keep him assured of her rapt attention.

Cathryn and Favian sat on the opposite side of the table, but the hubbub made it difficult for Keira and Anna to maintain a conversation with Cathryn. The distance, however, did not prevent Aaron and Favian from conversing; it took Anna a few minutes, though, to understand why Aaron kept moving his lips while looking across the table. She could not hear his words, but when Favian's lips moved in response, she understood. She glanced at Keira, smiling when she saw the amused glances she was sharing with Cathryn.

Dish after dish was served – fifteen courses in all – the highlight being the stuffed swan served to the queen, its feathers artfully replaced after roasting. It was served on a bed of lily pads and water lilies, and Matilda laughed and clapped her hands, delighted at the wonderful spectacle. Wine flowed endlessly as laughter rang between the tables, and at one point the king rose to his feet to sing a song to his queen, kneeling down on one knee before her. Matilda looked away with a slight blush and said something to one of the women seated beside her, who laughed as Alfred finished his song.

It was dark by the time the meal was finally done, and lanterns and torches around the gardens blazed in brilliance against the darkening sky. Shadows danced along the branches of the trees, and for a moment the memory of her last time in these gardens made Anna shudder. She glanced at Keira who gave her a weak smile. Aaron squeezed Keira's hand while he looked at Anna.

"There is no danger here tonight," he said.

It wasn't until after the king and queen rose from the table that the rest of the guests rose to their feet, their chairs leaving gouges in the green lawns. The musicians struck up a lively carol, and the king led the queen to the middle of the lawn, where they were quickly joined by other dancers. Prince Rupert stood in the shadows, his eyes narrowed as he watched the dancing. A woman stood next to him, and he whispered something in her ear before turning and walking away.

"That's Lady Blanche," Keira said, nodding her head in the woman's direction. "And on either side of the queen are Lady Joan and Lady Elizabeth. I've heard that Lady Joan is getting married, so she will be retiring to the country soon."

"What will the queen do when Lady Joan leaves?" Anna asked.

"She will find someone to take her place. There is no shortage of young women clamoring for the chance to serve the queen and extend their family fortunes."

"I think it would be great fun to live at the palace and be part of the royal court."

Keira shuddered. "I cannot think of anything worse. I don't think I would enjoy all the palace intrigues swirling around court. I prefer the simple life."

Anna laughed. "Your life has been anything but simple since you met Aaron."

"True." Keira glanced at Aaron. "But living with a dragon is far less dangerous than living at court."

A waving hand on the other side of the lawn caught Anna's eye. It was Kathleen, weaving her way through the crowds to reach Anna's side.

"Thank goodness I found you again," Kathleen said as she neared Anna. "There are *hundreds* of people here!"

"Let's dance," Anna said, grabbing Kathleen's arm and pulling her into a line of dancers that was forming across the lawn. Her feet faulted slightly when she recognized the Basse Danse, the court dance she had danced with Jack so many years before, but she pulled herself together in an instant, and following the other dancers, easily executed the steps.

One dance led to another, sometimes carols, which were danced in circles or long lines between the trees, other times the line dances, where couples danced in pairs. Anna danced with Aaron and Favian, admiring the lightness of foot exhibited by the dragons, and allowed the mathematician who sat next to her at supper to escort her into one of the formations. He was quite a nice young man, Anna thought, as long as he didn't speak. When no men offered themselves, Anna danced with Kathleen, who remained in the shadows except when Anna pulled her onto the lawn.

It was close to midnight when Anna went in search of refreshment. She had not seen Kathleen for a while, but as she headed towards the table with jugs of wine and ale, she heard her name being called, and turned to see Kathleen hurrying towards her.

"My father says it is time for us to go, but I wouldn't leave until I had a chance to bid you goodbye."

"Goodbye, Kathleen," Anna said with a smile. "It was

most fortuitous that you bumped into me this evening."

"Oh, yes! I would have been quite miserable, otherwise." Kathleen paused, dropping her gaze to the ground. "Will you call on me when you come into the city?"

"Of course I will," Anna said. Kathleen looked up with a smile of relief.

"Goodnight."

Turning back to the table, Anna poured herself a cup of wine. The crowds had become loud and rowdy, and more than once Anna'd had to fend off the attentions of an overeager dance partner. Beyond the crowds she could see the river, shimmering in the lamp light. As she watched, a slight breeze stirred the water, making the light dance over the uneven surface. It looked peaceful, a far cry from the unruly crowds. Replacing her cup on the table, she headed towards the banks, away from the jostling masses. She was eager to put a little distance between herself and the crowds, but she stopped before she went too far, unwilling to move beyond calling distance. It had grown a little quieter, and the occasional plop marked the entry of a frog into the water, while crickets chirped, their quick, shrill sounds repeating each time they leaped. A weeping willow hung over the water and she headed towards it, watching the faint ripples made by the branches dangling over the water. An owl flew low over the river, then swerved towards some unseen target. She watched for a moment before turning around, startled to see someone watching her from beneath the tree. She took a step back, suddenly nervous, but when the figure moved from the shadows into the soft moonlight, she saw who it was and paused.

"My apologies, Your Highness. I didn't realize anyone else was here. I didn't mean to intrude."

Prince Rupert waved his hand, dismissing her apology. "I hate these events. Low, common people fawning over me, paying compliments they don't mean in order to win my favor." He took a step closer. "I suppose you're just the same."

"That," Anna said with an indignant tilt of her chin, "is quite unjust. You know nothing about me to pass such a judgment." She stopped, suddenly remembering to whom she spoke. "Your Highness," she added, dropping her gaze to the ground. Why could she not hold her tongue? He barked out a short, dry laugh.

"Clearly I have misjudged you. You certainly are not like any of the other guests here this evening." He walked around her, and she could feel the weight of his gaze as he looked her over, before stopping before her. "You have the benefit of knowing who I am, while I don't know who you are."

"Anna Carver, Your Highness."

"Anna Carver? I don't know that name. Do I know your family?"

"My sister is married to Aaron Drake."

"Aaron Drake. Our slayer of dragons." Anna nodded. In the distance she could hear the musicians start another tune, the music for a popular line dance.

"I should be getting back, Your Highness," she said. "My sister will be wondering where I am."

"No. You should dance with me," he said. Anna gave him a startled look, then glanced over her shoulder to where the guests were forming the lines. She had walked further away from the crowds than she realized.

"I think I should ..." she started.

"I insist," he said, his lips thinning slightly while his voice took on a harder undertone. Anna nodded and placed her hand on the one he held outstretched. "How long do you remain in the city?" the prince asked as they danced.

"We leave tomorrow."

"Tomorrow? That's unfortunate. I think I would enjoy getting to know you more."

Anna remained silent. Rupert was taller than Anna by a few inches, and despite his aversion to society, danced very well. His hand touched hers lightly and when Anna took a misstep, he easily covered the mistake. He did not smile, although he watched her closely as they danced, until she could bear the scrutiny no longer.

"Do I have a spot on my nose, Your Highness?" she said.

"No," he said. "Why?"

"You keep staring at me." His eyebrows rose slightly.

"I'm just curious about the kind of woman you are."

"And staring at me will reveal who I am?"

He gave a short snort. "Perhaps." In the distance the strains of music started fading away, and he released her hand and took a step back.

"I trust our paths will cross again, Mistress," he said.

Anna smiled politely. She had no doubt he would have long forgotten her by the time the evening drew to a close. "Goodnight," she said, then turning away, hurried back to the crowds in relief, glad to be away from his presence. She wondered why he had insisted she dance with him, when he disliked the pastime so much. Was it because she had spoken so impertinently? She saw Aaron and Keira standing with Cathryn and Favian and hastened towards them.

"Ready to leave?" Keira asked.

Anna nodded. "Yes."

CHAPTER ELEVEN

Anna was awoken the next morning by a loud knocking, followed by the door being pushed open. "Come along, sleepy head," Keira said, walking into the room and flinging open the shutters. "Aaron wishes to leave within an hour."

"Go away," Anna mumbled, but instead Keira pulled the covers off the bed.

"Come on, up you get," she said. "Everyone else is already up and dressed." Anna groaned and pushed herself into a sitting position. "Aaron wants a few hours to spend with Owain this afternoon," Keira continued, "and then our plan is to start our return to Storbrook tomorrow."

"So soon?"

Keira nodded. "I want to get the children home. We will travel through the night, since the days are already so hot. Not that it matters to Aaron," she added, "but the horses suffer with the heat."

Anna took the gown Keira held out and pulled it over her head, before turning to the mirror to consider her reflection. Her eyes looked back blearily, and she dipped a linen in the basin of water placed on the table.

"I'll send a maid to do your packing," Keira said. "Meet

us in the hall." Anna nodded as Keira left the room.

It was early afternoon by the time they arrived back at Drake Manor. Owain and Margaret were waiting outside, but there was no sign of Will.

"I called him as soon as we saw you coming, but the young whelp needs a lesson in obedience," Owain said as Aaron and Favian landed on the ground beside him.

Aaron raised his bony eyebrows but said nothing as Favian let out a frustrated growl. "Perhaps you would like to take him back to Storbrook with you?" he said to Aaron.

Aaron laughed. "I'll have a word with him before I leave." He lifted his head and sniffed the air. "He's not far away. I'll go talk to him now," and spreading his massive wings, he launched himself back into the air.

The rest of the party entered the house, joining Owain and Margaret in the parlor, where they talked about the funeral and coronation. When Aaron returned sometime later, it was with a quiet Will, who trailed behind his Master, his eyes on the ground.

Lydia clung to Anna before she went to bed that night, her arms wrapped around Anna's neck. "See you again soon?" she said.

Anna blinked away the tears before replying. "Soon, baby girl," she whispered.

"Lydia sad," sniffed the girl.

"I'm sad, too," Anna said, "and I'll miss you terribly. "But I'll be thinking of you every day."

Lydia nodded. "Me too," she said.

That evening, after the others had retired, Keira sat with Anna in her chambers. "Are you sure you want to stay?" Keira asked.

Anna nodded. "Yes. If I don't, I will always wonder what might have happened." She paused. "Tell Garrick I'm sorry," she added softly.

"I will," Keira said.

Anna was quickly absorbed into the routine of Drake Manor. Each day she helped Cathryn with the children's lessons. Will complained that at the age of fifteen, he had no further use for learning, but a stern lecture from his father made him reconsider. A dragon he might be, but with a life expectancy of three to four hundred years, it would behoove him well to gain whatever knowledge he could. Will was quick to point out that he had plenty of time to gain all the learning he could ever need, but when his grandfather joined the conversation, the argument died on his lips. Of course, there was dragon training, too, and every afternoon Favian or Owain took Will out for a few hours.

Lessons with Bronwyn were far easier. Already, at the age of thirteen, she knew about the four humors of the human body, and understood that as a dragon, she tended more towards yellow bile and blood. Of course, a dragon's make-up was somewhat different from a human's, since a dragon is almost exclusively fire, fueled by flesh; and once she started changing into her dragon form, her inner workings would bear little resemblance to those of a human.

Bronwyn spent the afternoon hours with her grandmother, learning needlecraft and music, unless Margaret was called away to tend to one the tenants. Margaret was well-known in the area as a healer, and would be sent for whenever someone was injured or ill. It had been under her ministrations that Keira was nursed back to health after she was injured by a dragon. Sometimes Cathryn would accompany her as a helper, and it was on one such afternoon that Anna suggested to Bronwyn that they saddle up the horses and ride through the estate. Anna had been at Drake Manor for nearly four weeks, and had spent many hours exploring the grounds around the house, but the hills that lay in the distance, beyond the river, were new territory that she was eager to discover. The stables lay beyond the courtyard, and it did not take long for the horses to be saddled and Anna and Bronwyn to be on their way.

It was a fine day in late summer. The air was heavy with summer heat, and bees flew around lethargically between the flowers, while butterflies flittered gently about. The scent of lemon from the formal gardens hung in the air, and Anna could taste it on her tongue. They turned their horses towards the woods, which lay a fair distance from the house, beyond the wilderness where wild flowers and grasses grew without check. In the distance Favian and Will circled around the hills, moving lazily through the hot air. It was a relief to reach the shade of the trees, and Anna pulled the neck of her gown away from her skin in an effort to cool herself down.

The path through the woods was narrow, and the women rode single-file. The moist, earthy smell of mulch and decaying matter had replaced the dry scents of the gardens, and Anna breathed in the cool fragrance deeply. Under the canopy of trees, the birds chirped as they flitted from one branch to another. Squirrels jumped above their heads, and between the trees, light caught the delicate threads of a spider's web. In the distance Anna could hear the burbling sound of water rushing over rocks. It grew louder as they continued on the path, and then the river was before them, cool and inviting. Without a moment's hesitation, Anna slid off her horse, and slipping off her boots, walked into the water, Bronwyn a step behind.

"Ah," Bronwyn said, "that feels so good." Stepping back onto the bank, she shrugged out of her kirtle, and with just her chemise covering her body, stepped back into the water, sinking down to her knees. At its deepest point, the water reached her chest, and she dropped her body lower, letting the coolness wash around her.

"I thought you didn't feel the heat," Anna said with a laugh.

"I don't really," Bronwyn said, dropping her head back in the water. "It's just that my skin is so itchy."

"Do you have a rash? You should ask your grandmother for a balm."

"There isn't much Grandmother can do for me." She moved closer to Anna and held out her hand. "Look."

Just beneath the surface of Bronwyn's skin Anna could see faint circles swooping around her hand and up her arm. Reaching out a finger, she touched Bronwyn's skin, drawing back in surprise when she felt how hot it was. She glanced up at the girl, startled.

"What's it caused by?" Anna said.

"Scales."

"Scales?"

Bronwyn's eyes were closed as she held her head back. "Mmm hmm."

"Then ... you're already ... you've already started changing." Bronwyn opened her eyes and turned to look at Anna. Faint specks of yellow showed against the blue. How had Anna not noticed that before?

"Yes," Bronwyn said. "It won't be long before I will be flying like Will." She pulled herself out of the water, the thin fabric of her chemise steaming. "But I will be a much better dragon than him."

"Oh, uh, I'm sure you will," Anna said. Although only thirteen, Bronwyn was moving into a world in which Anna had no part – she would be nothing but an outsider looking in, and she felt a moment of sadness. "Are you ready to carry on riding?" Anna asked.

"Yes," Bronwyn said, pulling on her kirtle.

They mounted their horses and nudged them into the river. The splashing water wet the hem of Anna's gown but she scarcely noticed. She rode ahead of Bronwyn, leading her horse towards the shallow rocks on the other bank and onto the deep path that cut through a steep cliff rising above the river on the other side.

Anna felt her horse's hooves slip slightly in the loose sand, and then they were moving, quickly climbing the ridge.

She gained the height and paused, turning to watch as Bronwyn nudged her horse forward. Water from Anna's horse had made the path slicker, and Bronwyn's horse struggled for a moment to find a firm footing.

Bronwyn was a few feet from the top when it happened: a hawk, tracking a small animal in the grass, suddenly dived down towards the cliff, missing Bronwyn and her horse by a mere few inches. Bronwyn ducked and clutched the reins close to her chest, and the horse reared.

It lost its footing and plunged backwards down the cliff, landing on its back. Bronwyn screamed as the horse rolled onto its side, trapping her legs.

The horse slipped further down the hill as it struggled to regain its footing, keeping Bronwyn pinned against the stony ground.

In horror Anna jumped from her horse and stumbled to the edge of the cliff, shouting Bronwyn's name. Bronwyn's eyes were wide with fright and pain as she struggled to pull herself free. Anna started down the cliff, half-slipping, half-scrambling, grabbing whatever there was at the side of the path to prevent her own fall – rocks, tufts of grass and small bushes.

Anna reached the horse, grabbed the reins and pulled as hard as she could. The horse lifted its head and Anna shouted to Bronwyn to move – but the effort was too much for the horse, and it dropped its weight down again. There was a loud crunching and Bronwyn screamed.

Again Anna tugged on the reins, placing her feet against a rock as leverage. The horse lifted its head and this time heaved itself higher into the air. Anna closed her eyes as she mustered every ounce of energy she possessed, and pulled harder. She could feel the horse rising another few inches.

"Move!" she yelled. She opened her eyes, but could not see Bronwyn.

She glanced around, wondering if she had made her escape, when the air was suddenly filled with flames. They seared across her skin, and she dropped the reins once more, but instead of falling back, the horse lurched to its feet.

More flames rolled through the air, and the horse screamed as it leaped into the river below and took off at a frantic pace. It was not the horse that Anna took note of, however, but the raging dragon that had risen into the air above her. The dragon's head swung from side to side, and flames spewed with every breath, setting alight the grass and scrub on the cliff. Huge wings were open on her back, holding her aloft in the air above Anna.

"Bronwyn," Anna screamed, and the blazing eyes swung in her direction. The dragon roared, then plunging forward, threw a searing blaze in Anna's direction. Terror gripped her as she dropped to her knees, then scrambling on her hands and feet, climbed her way back up the path. Fear gave her renewed energy, and she quickly gained the ridge, then rolled away when she felt the heat of searing flames inches above her. She rose to her feet, and waved her hands in the air.

"Bronwyn," she screamed again. The dragon was racing through the air towards her, talons outstretched, and Anna gave up any further attempts to try and reason with the beast. She turned and ran, ducking when she heard the dragon roar once more. "Favian," she screamed. "Help!" It was only a matter of seconds before the flaming dragon reached her. "Favian!" she screamed once more. She felt something swoop low over her, and she dropped down to the ground, covering her head with her hands, but then a loud clash rang through the air. She glanced over her shoulder. A huge red dragon was on top of the smaller one, pushing it down to the ground. With a sob Anna rolled over, and drawing her knees up against her chest, watched the two dragons as the tears streamed down her face, unheeded.

Now that she was no longer running, Anna could see that Bronwyn's hide was a rose-bronze color. Like the other dragons, she had horns that rose from the top of her head, but they were smaller and not quite as lethal-looking. Her wings, outstretched a moment ago, were now folded over her back. Favian had landed on top of her, and she lay on the ground, quivering. Her eyes were no longer blazing, but were yellow. She closed them and lay still beneath the weight of her father, her neck stretched out on the ground. Slowly, Favian pulled his weight off her. He stood for a moment watching her, then glanced towards Anna, who was still curled up on the ground.

"Are you hurt?" he asked. She shook her head no. "Close your eyes," he instructed. She did and a bright light flared through the air, then died away. When Anna opened her eyes again, Favian was in his human form, crouching next to the head of the dragon.

"It's all right, baby," he crooned. "You're fine." He ran his hand down the length of the dragon's neck, and then up to her skull. She shuddered slightly, then opened her eyes, staring at her father.

"Anna?" she whispered.

"Anna's right here," Favian replied. "She's fine. Just a little surprised." He glanced back at Anna with a slight smile, then turned back to his daughter. "Do you think you can change again?"

"I'm … I'm not sure." He ran his hand back down the length of her neck.

"Whenever you're ready. Just close your eyes, and imagine yourself in your human form. Don't force it; just feel it." Bronwyn stared at him for a moment, then closed her eyes. "That's right," he said. "Take a deep breath, and imagine you are going for a swim in the lake. Stretch out your arms – do you see them? And dip your toes in the water."

As Anna watched, she saw the air around Bronwyn start to shimmer, then glow, and she closed her eyes in the instant before a white light brightened the sky. She waited a moment for the light to fade, then opened them. Favian had pulled his little girl into his arms and was stroking her hair.

"Papa," she said. "I don't know what happened." Her eyes fell on Anna, and they widened slightly, before she buried her face in Favian's shoulder. "I'm so sorry," she said.

"It's all right," Favian repeated.

Anna watched in silence, uncomfortable and uncertain. Bronwyn's clothes had been shredded when she changed, leaving her naked. Favian had managed to grab a length of fabric and wrap it around his waist, but Bronwyn's body was exposed. With a shrug, Anna pulled off her kirtle, leaving only her linen chemise. She stepped over to the girl, gently pulling her from Favian's grasp and dragging the kirtle over her shoulders. Bronwyn looked up, startled, and then gave a tentative smile. Her face was streaked with tears, and Anna pulled her into an embrace. She still could not believe what she had seen, nor Bronwyn's actions when she'd changed, but she knew that despite what had happened, Bronwyn was still a young girl, just as shocked by the turn of events as herself.

"It's all right," she said. "Everything will be all right."

"I'm so sorry," Bronwyn whispered. "I didn't know what I was doing."

"I know," Anna said. She swallowed hard. "I know you didn't mean to hurt me. Next time you will be more in control." She glanced at Favian as she said this, and he nodded his head in confirmation. "And," Anna said, dropping her voice to a whisper, "you are a beautiful dragon."

Bronwyn pulled away slightly. "Really?" she said.

"Absolutely!" Out of the corner of her eye, Anna saw Favian smile. "Where is Will?" she asked.

"I told him to wait for me. But what were you doing here?"

"We were going for a ride. Bronwyn's horse fell down the slope and landed on her. That's when …"

Favian nodded. "That makes sense. Fear will often trigger the first change." He glanced at Bronwyn. "You were scared when the horse fell?"

Bronwyn nodded. "It fell on top of me – the pain was agonizing. Then all I could see was orange. I didn't even know what I was doing." Her voice trailed to a whisper and she dropped her head.

"You didn't do anything a dragon changing for the first time wouldn't do," Favian said, pulling her close and dropping a kiss on her forehead. Bronwyn looked up with a tentative smile, and Anna squeezed her hand before looking around. She could see her horse in the distance, but of Bronwyn's there was no sign.

"Your horse must have bolted," she said to Bronwyn. Favian lifted his head and sniffed the air, meeting Anna's amused glance with a shrug.

"It hasn't gone far. I'll find it for you, and bring it back while you round up the other horse."

Anna nodded, and with one last squeeze of Bronwyn's hand, headed towards her horse, which was quietly grazing on some nearby grass. It looked up when Anna approached, then dropped its head again as it continued to graze, allowing Anna to grab its reins and lead it back to where Bronwyn stood. Below the ridge on the other side of the river she saw Favian leading the second horse. His hand was holding up the strip of fabric he had tied around his waist, and he looked up at Anna with a sheepish grin.

"I would offer to walk back with you, but I think it would be better if I accompanied you in my natural form." Anna nodded, and turning her head away, waited for the flash of light. The dragon changed, and when she looked back, he was already in the sky. In the distance another dragon could be seen hovering, and with a movement of his head, Favian called him over.

"It looks like your sister will soon be racing you," Favian said as Will drew near, and Anna turned away in amusement when she saw the dragon scowl. "Don't say anything to your mother about this until Bronwyn and I have had a chance to talk to her," he warned, and Will nodded. He looked down at Bronwyn, who met his gaze with eyebrows lifted, and he turned away, slowly spiraling in the sky in the direction of the house.

Favian flew just above Anna and Bronwyn as they journeyed back to the house. Anna rode behind, and she looked at Bronwyn wonderingly. There was nothing about her now to suggest that she had turned into a dragon just minutes before. Instead, all someone would see was a disheveled thirteen-year-old girl – certainly not a terrifying or threatening monster. As they approached the house, Favian swooped lower. "I will find your mother and meet you in your chambers," he said. Bronwyn nodded, and then Favian flew off, heading towards the flat roof of the house. It was there that the dragons were completely hidden when they changed form, although Anna supposed that the humans at Drake Manor had by now figured out the dragons' secret, but a combination of loyalty and fear kept them silent.

A stablehand came out to meet the two returning women, and they slid off their saddles, handing over the reins. The boy's eyes widened as he took in their unusual attire, but he said nothing. Bronwyn gave Anna a shy smile before turning on her heel and running into the house, disappearing into the shadows.

A few hours had passed when Favian sought Anna out. "I just wanted to thank you for being so kind to Bronwyn earlier," he said. "I can only imagine how scared you felt when she turned on you."

Anna shrugged. "I could see she didn't know me. I'm just glad you arrived when you did." Favian gave her a wry smile. "Why is Bronwyn already changing? I remember Max telling me..." she paused for a brief moment, pulling in a short, quick breath, "...telling me he was fifteen when he first changed. And Will is fifteen, too."

"Girls usually change earlier than boys," Favian said, "and sometimes when a pubescent dragon is scared or startled, it can trigger the change even earlier."

"And that's what happened to Bronwyn?"

"Yes. But as you said, the next time she will have more

control. She won't lose herself again. You have nothing to fear."

Anna smiled. Favian's reassurance calmed the fear she hadn't wanted to admit – that she was scared of a young girl.

CHAPTER TWELVE

A week had passed when Cathryn found Anna seated in the parlor early one morning.

"I'm going into the city. Would you like to join me?"

Anna jumped to her feet. "Yes, when do we leave, and how long are we going for?"

Cathryn laughed. "We will leave in an hour, and we will stay one night."

"Perhaps I can call on Kathleen while I'm there."

"Kathleen?"

"The girl I met at the coronation ball. I gave her my word I would call on her when I'm in the city. I'll send her a note when I arrive. How are we traveling?"

"Favian will take us."

"Favian? Is he staying?"

"No. He doesn't want to leave Bronwyn for too long." Cathryn sighed. "At the moment, I'm not much use to my daughter. It's her father who is helping her through this."

Anna walked over to Cathryn and grabbed her hands. "I have no experience with either teenage girls or teenage dragons, but one thing I always wished for, and Keira too, was the knowledge that our mother would always give us her love and support. We didn't have that, but Bronwyn does. So you are helping her, even if you cannot show her how to hunt a stag."

"Thank you, Anna," Cathryn said softly.

Anna was ready to leave before the hour was up, and she went outside to wait in the sun. She heard someone come out the door, and turned to see Bronwyn.

"How is our young dragon, this morning?" she said with a smile.

Bronwyn smiled for a brief moment, then turned away. "I wish you hadn't been there to see me like that," she said.

"Me too," Anna said. She met the girl's startled gaze. "I know it makes you feel bad," she said, "and I don't want you to be upset about what happened. You are a dragon, a beautiful dragon, and if I'm honest, I'm a little jealous."

"Jealous? Why?"

"I will always just be me," Anna said. "Plain old Anna. I will never have wings to fly me wherever I want to go. And in another fifty years or so, I'll be dead from old age, but you will still be young and beautiful."

"Oh." Bronwyn dropped her eyes to the ground, watching as an ant scurried over the stones. "I like being a dragon," she said, "but sometimes I wish I was just plain old Bronwyn, like other girls my age."

"Well," Anna said slowly, "I suppose you will just have to be the best dragon you can be, and I will be the best human I can be." Bronwyn nodded, but remained silent as Cathryn came out of the house. The sound of heavy wings beating the air made Anna look up, then cover her eyes from the dust that swirled as Favian landed gracefully beside them.

"I'll see you tomorrow," Anna said to Bronwyn. The girl nodded, then turned away and disappeared into the house.

It was mid-morning when Favian, Cathryn and Anna walked into Civitas, and already the streets were teeming with people. The cries of hawkers mingled with the sounds of horses and carriages, and joined together with the hubbub of the streets to create a rhythmic vibe to the city. Their path took them along the river and past the cathedral, before they turned onto the wide avenue where Drake House stood.

Anna did not waste any time sending a letter to Kathleen, and an hour after she sent it, she received a reply. 'I anxiously await your arrival,' it read.

"How do I get to Hobart House?" she asked Cathryn and Favian after she had shown them the note.

"Hobart House, hmm? I'll take you," Favian said. "I'm leaving now and it is on my way." He paused a moment to give Cathryn a lingering kiss, before motioning Anna towards the door. They may have been married for seventeen years, but their affection for each other was clearly evident.

Hobart House was situated next to the river in the same direction as the palace, and half an hour later, Favian was walking Anna up the stairs to the entrance, pounding on the door with his fist. The door was opened by a uniformed butler, who stared at the visitors on the steps with a frown.

"Lady Kathleen," Anna said, and after a long pause, the man step aside and ushered them into the hall, where he left them. Huge tapestries, worked in bright hues, ran down the length of the room, and Favian looked at them appreciatively, before lifting his head to examine the carved beams that spanned the ceiling. At the sound of footsteps Anna swung around, smiling at Kathleen as she approached, eyeing Favian nervously.

"How lovely to see you," Anna said, before gesturing to Favian. "Kathleen, this is Favian Drake, a kinsman of my sister's. Favian, may I present Lady Kathleen Hobart." Favian swept a deep bow in Kathleen's direction.

"Lady Kathleen, it is my honor to make your acquaintance." Kathleen blushed, and looked at the floor.

"Master Drake," she whispered.

Favian smiled, then turned to Anna. "Will you find your way back to Drake House?" he asked. Anna nodded. "Good.

Then I'll see you on the morrow. Enjoy your visit." With a nod in Kathleen's direction, he left the room. Anna smiled at her friend.

"I am sorry for the short notice," she said. "I only learned of our visit to the city this morning, so I'm glad you were not otherwise occupied."

"I would have foregone almost anything to see you," Kathleen said with a shy smile, "unless it meant disobeying a royal command. Come with me." Turning down a passage, she led Anna past the hall and into a small study. A large desk took up half the space, while shelves lined with ledgers were secured to the walls. Two chairs stood in a corner, a small table between them, and Kathleen led Anna over to them.

"How are you enjoying the city?" Anna asked.

"I miss being in the country," Kathleen said, "but Father says I must be happy. There are just so many people, and although they treat me nicely, they are not my friends. They only do it to please Father."

"I can be your friend, if you want," Anna said.

"Oh, yes, please!" Kathleen glanced at Anna then looked away. "Only, I've already been telling everyone that you are my friend," she said.

"And so I am," Anna said with a laugh.

"Father has invited some people to our house tonight," Kathleen said. "He says I'm not in society enough to be noticed, and he has invited a few people here so I can become better acquainted. I asked him if I could invite you, and he said yes. Please say you'll come."

"Of course I'll come," Anna said, then paused. "I'm here with Mistress Cathryn, and I really shouldn't leave her for the evening."

"You can bring her too," Kathleen said.

"But I don't have anything to wear!"

"You can borrow something of mine," Kathleen said.

Anna looked at Kathleen consideringly. She was taller than Kathleen by a few inches, but otherwise they were of similar size. A strip of ribbon along the hem would give the required length.

"Very well," Anna nodded. "But I still need to check with Cathryn first. I can send her a note, if you like. I believe she can be found at her father's warehouse – can you send a page boy to deliver it?"

. "Oh, yes," Kathleen said. There was paper and ink on the desk, and Anna settled down to write while Kathleen rushed out to find someone to deliver the note. A few minutes later a young boy of around ten set out with the missive clutched in his fist, along with a promise of a shiny coin if he returned with a reply.

Anna and Kathleen passed the time talking about happenings in the city. The king had passed a curfew, ensuring that the lower classes were off the street by ten in the evening, while Prince Rupert had been embroiled in a rather unsavory affair involving a young woman. It had been hushed up, however, and Kathleen was unsure of the details. An hour passed and the young boy returned, the response from Cathryn grubby and wrinkled, but still readable. 'I will be delighted to accompany you this evening,' she had replied.

"Good, it is all settled," Kathleen said. "It will be so nice to see a friendly face."

Anna left soon after, followed by the page boy, who carried a lime-green gown wrapped in linen. Kathleen had also found a length of wide white ribbon that Anna would use to add to the hem. It was already mid-afternoon, and Anna walked at a quick pace, smiling when she heard the boy running to keep up behind her.

CHAPTER THIRTEEN

Anna lifted her borrowed gown a few inches from the ground as she stepped into the carriage after Cathryn. The ribbon had added enough to make the gown an acceptable length, and Hannah had added a few little nips and tucks to ensure it fitted her curves. All in all, it was not too bad. Cathryn had not had the same problem. She had a few evening gowns that remained permanently at Drake House, for times such as these.

Hobart House was awash with light as they stepped into a hall filled with people a short while later. Anna looked around in surprise. She had expected twenty or thirty people in attendance, but there must have been at least a hundred.

"I was expecting a more intimate evening," she whispered to Cathryn. "Do you know any of these people?"

"A few." Cathryn glanced around the room. "Even the prince is in attendance," she said.

Anna looked up to see Prince Rupert standing amongst a small group of people, his expression bored as they laughed at some joke. She wondered if the king had ordered him to attend tonight – from what she knew of him, only coercion would bring him to an affair such as this. He wore a doublet of lavender and breeches of dark purple, the colors incongruous with what she had heard and seen of the well-built, short-haired man. In fact, Anna decided, his garments made him look quite ridiculous.

Turning away, Anna followed Cathryn into the sea of people, her eyes searching the room for Kathleen. They hadn't gone more than a few feet when a short, older man waddled up to them.

"Cathryn, my dear! What are you doing here?"

Cathryn turned and smiled at the gentleman.

"Master Grant! This is Mistress Anna, a kinswoman of my husband's. Lady Kathleen is a friend of hers." The man turned a pleasant smile on Anna.

"Indeed? Mistress Anna, my pleasure." He gave her hand a limp shake, then turned back to Cathryn. "Tell me, my dear, what news of your father?"

Anna turned away as Cathryn fell into conversation with the man, her eyes searching the crowds for Kathleen, until she finally spied her at the other end of the long hall. An elderly gentleman was leaning over her, his hand firmly wrapped around Kathleen's arm while Kathleen stared at the floor. She reminded Anna of a small, quivering mouse, trapped by a cat teasing its prey before pouncing. Anna was wondering whether she should go and rescue her friend when Kathleen glanced in her direction. A smile of relief flooded her features as she saw Anna, and tugging her arm free, she made her escape.

"I'm so glad to see you," she whispered as she drew near. "I was so anxious that something would keep you away at the last moment. Can you believe all these people?" She glanced back at the elderly man who was watching her beadily.

"Who is that man?" Anna asked.

"Lord Baxter," Kathleen whispered. "Father says he has influence at court, so I need to make myself amenable."

"You poor thing," Anna said. "What about all these other people? Do you know them?"

"No," Kathleen said, dropping her voice. "Only Mistress Bianca, who visits Father every day. But you are my only friend."

"Well," Anna said, hooking her arm through Kathleen's, "let's find a quiet spot where we can be more comfortable." Benches and chairs lined the hall, and Anna led Kathleen towards a shadowed corner, but before they reached it, a voice called out Kathleen's name. Anna turned to see Kathleen's father beckoning her from across the room. Kathleen gave Anna a look that spoke volumes before turning and crossing the floor to where her father stood. At the sound of Lord Hobart's voice, the prince, who was standing close by, glanced over his shoulder. He turned when his gaze fell on Anna, and in a moment he was making his way towards her.

"Mistress Anna," he said.

"Your Highness," she said, dropping a shallow curtsey, surprised he remembered her name.

"I thought you had left the city."

"I did. And I leave again tomorrow."

"Tomorrow?" He walked towards a spot near the wall where fewer people stood, glancing back with raised eyebrows when she did not follow. She sighed before joining him. "Where do you live?" he asked.

"I'm staying with friends in the country."

"In the country? Where, exactly?"

"About thirty miles away."

"Mistress Anna," he said, a hint of irritation coloring his tone, "what is the *name* of the place where you are staying?"

"Drake Manor."

"That's better. Drake Manor, hmm? And do you come into Civitas often?"

"No, not often."

"More's the pity," he said. He stared at her narrowly. "And are you enjoying living at Drake Manor, with your sister's kinsmen?"

Anna's eyebrows rose slightly. "I am, Your Highness. The Drakes are kind people, and we are not too far away. And we receive news from the city when people pass by. In fact, I've even heard ..." She stopped, chagrined, and the prince pounced.

"Yes," he said, "you've heard ...?"

"Um," Anna glanced at the floor, looking for inspiration, but found none. She looked back up at him. "I've heard you've been busy," she said. At her words, Rupert's eyebrows lifted, and Anna held her breath, waiting for an explosion of anger, but after a moment he gave a dry laugh.

"That's one way to describe it," he said. He tilted his head. "Tell me, Mistress, do you always speak your mind so freely?"

"My apologies, Your Highness," Anna said. "I often speak before I think. I should not have been so bold."

"Actually," he said, "it is refreshing to hear someone speak plainly."

"In that case," Anna said, "perhaps I should tell you that purple does not become you." This time the prince's eyebrows rose even higher, but then he laughed. It was a sound of genuine amusement, and for the first time she saw his features soften slightly from the hard planes that usually lined his face.

"I will tell my Lord Hindley."

"Lord Hindley?"

"One of the lords of my chamber. He has been nagging me to wear something more becoming to my station, and I confess I gave in to get him off my back. The man has known me since I was in the cradle, and refuses to take no for an answer. I will tell him that the ladies concur with my position and I will make sure these damned clothes are burned."

"Only one lady," Anna said, glancing around the room. She was startled to see quite a few pairs of eyes trained on them. "The other ladies seem to appreciate what they see."

The prince glanced around and his expression hardened.

"They're looking at you."

"Only because you are talking to me," she said. He nodded.

"True." He gave her a slight nod. "Excuse me, Mistress."

"Of course," she said, but he was already striding away from her. The people who had been watching her averted their eyes and returned to their conversations. Cathryn glanced her way with a smile, motioning her over.

"This is Mistress Bradshaw," she said, introducing the older woman she was talking to. "She is a friend of Margaret's." Anna smiled and nodded, listening as Mistress Bradshaw and Cathryn conversed a little longer. When the lady moved away, Cathryn turned to Anna with an expression of concern.

"You need to be careful," Cathryn said softly. "The prince's good favor is not always to be desired."

"I know! But what must I do when he approaches me?"

"Just be on your guard," Cathryn said. "That's all I'm saying."

Anna nodded. "I will," she said.

She looked up to see Kathleen coming towards her. "I think I have been introduced to everyone in this crowd," Kathleen said, "so perhaps we can have a few minutes of conversation." She glanced over to where Rupert was standing. "I saw the prince talking to you," she said. She leaned a little closer. "He hardly ever talks to people he doesn't know. What were you saying?"

Anna caught Cathryn's gaze before replying. "I told him that purple doesn't become him," she said.

Kathleen's eyes widened. "No," she whispered. "You wouldn't have dared."

"I did," Anna said, amused. "And he vowed to burn his garments and return to his usual style." She glanced at Cathryn again, and saw a slight tug at the corners of her mouth. Their eyes met, and Cathryn grinned, shaking her head.

"How could you speak to the prince like that?" Kathleen's tone was awed.

Anna shrugged. "He may be a prince, but I suspect a dragon would find him as tasty a morsel as any other mortal." Beside her, Cathryn coughed, but Anna could not hide a shameless grin. "Now let us forget the prince. Tell me, did you finish the story you were reading the night of the banquet?"

CHAPTER FOURTEEN

With Cathryn's business in Civitas completed, Favian was back the next day to fly them home again. The days quickly passed from late summer into early fall. Anna received a letter from Keira, letting them know that they had arrived safely back at Storbrook.

'Everything is just the same,' she wrote. 'Garrick received the news that you were remaining at Drake Manor stoically, but he went out hunting the next day, and we didn't see him for a week. The children are well. Missing you terribly, of course, and running Peggy off her toes. Aaron has started looking for a tutor for them – a dragon, not a human. Write soon. We long for news of you.'

Bronwyn and Will continued with their morning lessons, but instead of doing needlework with her grandmother, Bronwyn now spent the afternoons with her father, working on controlling her transformations and strengthening her wings. Anna spent most afternoons with Cathryn or Margaret, but when Cathryn pulled out her needlework, Anna excused herself. She had never had the patience to master the small, intricate stitches. Instead, she wandered around the gardens, collecting herbs and blossoms that

Margaret used in her different brews and elixirs. She was out one afternoon, collecting green sage and thyme, when Bronwyn caught up with her.

"How are the lessons going?" Anna asked. Bronwyn smiled shyly.

"Fine," she said. She met Anna's gaze. "I can control my transformations now. Do you want to see?"

"Well…" Anna said, but Bronwyn was already tugging the laces of her kirtle free. "Should I turn around?" Anna asked.

"If you want," Bronwyn said, with a mischievous smile. "I've had to transform so many times with Father and Grandfather that it doesn't matter if you see me too. But you must cover your eyes when I change, because of the light." She was shrugging her shoulders to loosen the chemise, and Anna quickly turned around. A bright flash filled the air, and Anna turned back, lifting her gaze to look at the dragon towering over her. She sparkled in the sunshine, her coppery-rose color catching the light. Anna stumbled backwards, then stopped when she saw the dragon looking at her intently.

"I won't hurt you," Bronwyn said, her voice surprisingly small for a creature so large. Anna drew in a deep breath.

"I know," Anna said. She closed her eyes for a moment, then took a step towards her. "You are so beautiful," she said. The dragon smiled, and lifted huge wings into the air. She was not as large as either Favian or Will, and lacked the broad frame typical of the other dragons Anna had seen. Instead, her lines were longer, more graceful and feminine. Her shorter horns curved more over her head, and her tail, though still armed with sharp spikes, was not as thick and heavy.

"Come for a ride with me," Bronwyn said.

Anna looked at her with surprise and took a step backwards. "No, no, I couldn't do that."

"Why not?"

"Because …" Anna searched for a suitable answer.

"Because I don't like flying. And besides, your father might not like it."

"Oh," she said, "he already knows I'm asking you."

"But you're just a girl!"

The dragon laughed, a few sparks escaping her mouth until she lowered her head to Anna's eye level. "I'm not a girl, Aunty Anna. I'm a dragon. Look at me. Do I look like other girls my age?"

"No, but –"

"Please, Anna," she said, widening her huge yellow eyes beseechingly, in a very human-like manner.

"Well…" Anna started, and Bronwyn, sensing her wavering will, smiled.

"I'm not as good as lifting someone onto my back as Father, but keep very still and I'll try."

Anna closed her eyes and held her breath as Bronwyn's tail snaked around her, closing around her waist. "Not so tight," she gasped, and the tail fell away.

"I'm sorry," Bronwyn said.

"It's all right. Try again."

Once more, Bronwyn wrapped her tail around Anna, inch by inch, until it was coiled securely around her middle. "Are you all right?" Bronwyn asked. Anna nodded. Carefully she lifted her tail into the air and Anna felt her feet leave the ground. Bronwyn wasn't as steady as her father, and the ground rocked and swayed below Anna, but then she was being dropped down onto Bronwyn's broad back, where she landed with a thump. "Sorry," Bronwyn said again, and Anna gave her a weak wave.

"I'm fine," she said.

"Next time will be better," Bronwyn assured her. She stretched out rose-bronze wings, and launched herself into the air. The ground grew distant as the dragon pushed her way higher, turning in a huge circle. Anna wrapped her arms around the long neck, and looked down at the ground flashing below them. Although Anna lived with dragons, there were only a few times she had actually ridden a dragon. She had done so once with Max, when he had taken her to a snow-covered peak near Storbrook. It was the first time she became aware of Max as someone – or something – other than the man who annoyed and irritated her, and it had left her confused. The other time had been in the dark, when Favian fetched her from the rocky island where Jack was keeping Keira and her prisoner. All she remembered of that ride was shame and regret.

Bronwyn did not fly evenly as Favian did, but swooped and swerved with childish enthusiasm. She turned when she saw the river snaking through the woods below, following the silver ribbon as it rushed its way between the mountains and the forest. Anna gasped when Bronwyn's belly skimmed the tops of the trees, snapping huge branches like kindling, but Bronwyn just laughed. "It tickles," she said.

Anna saw the spot on the ridge where Bronwyn had changed, but Bronwyn cruised right past it, pushing onwards towards the mountains where the river started its journey. The land below changed to rolling hills then grew steeper as Bronwyn pushed higher and higher. Tall peaks rose directly ahead of them, and the river tumbled from its mountain height and down a rocky face. As Bronwyn drew closer, the cold spray from the waterfall covered Anna in a fine mist. She gasped when Bronwyn directed her body at a sharp angle, and when Anna felt her body slipping backwards she wrapped her arms even tighter around Bronwyn's neck.

The dragon flew up the length of the waterfall, her wings laboring through the air as she lifted her huge body. A moment later she leveled out once more as she gained the height and swept over the small stream that flowed to the precipitous fall. Bronwyn made a huge circle above the stream then plunged down the cliff, angling her body downward. A thin scream escaped Anna's mouth.

She closed her eyes, grasping Bronwyn's neck in a death grip, and didn't open them until she felt Bronwyn level herself out again. They were downstream from the waterfall and following the river's course once more.

When Bronwyn finally landed on the ground outside the manor house, Anna's legs were shaking. She had to keep her hand on Bronwyn's back to prevent herself from falling.

"That," she said, "was terrifying."

"I wouldn't have let you fall," Bronwyn assured her.

"You wouldn't have been able to do much if you had crashed into the ground," Anna retorted, but she smiled when she saw Bronwyn's stricken look. "I know you wouldn't have crashed," she said, "but I'm just human, after all. You cannot expect me to be fearless like a dragon."

"I'm sorry," Bronwyn said, turning away. "I thought you would enjoy it."

"I did," Anna said, "just warn me next time you plunge your nose straight to the earth."

Bronwyn turned back with a slight smile. "Next time?" she said.

Anna groaned. "Well, we'll see."

When Anna walked through the door, her legs still a little shaky, she heard Cathryn calling her from the parlor.

"Anna, is that you?" She looked up as Anna walked into the room. "A letter arrived for you today."

"From Keira?" Anna asked as she smoothed down her hair, disheveled after her ride.

"It came from the city," Cathryn said. She held out the missive to Anna. "Were you flying with Bronwyn?"

"I was," Anna said, taking the letter.

"And ...?"

"I was terrified," Anna said with a wry laugh.

"Oh dear," Cathryn said, but Anna waved the concern away.

"She's young, and giddy with her new abilities. But she'll soon learn."

Cathryn nodded. "She's been nagging me to go with her,

but she's my daughter. How can I let my daughter fly me around?"

Anna smiled her understanding. "I know, but this is not a temporary thing. Eventually you will have to go with her."

"I know," Cathryn said with a groan. She glanced at the letter. "Who is it from?"

Anna slid her finger beneath the seal, lifting it, and opened the sheet of paper. "It's from Kathleen," she said, running her eyes to the bottom of the sheet. Returning to the top, she started reading, first to herself, then a second time out loud for Cathryn's benefit.

'To Mistress Anna Carver of Drake Manor,' she read. 'Warmest greetings. I trust you are in the best of health. I'm afraid I have some terrible tidings to impart. Please do not fear – I am quite well, and am trying my best for Father's sake to put on a very brave face, but my dear Anna, you will understand the dread I feel when I tell you that Father has arranged a position for me at court, where I will serve Her Majesty the queen as one of her ladies. Lady Joan is leaving in a month when she marries Lord Lamont, but I must present myself two days hence! I cannot bear the thought of going without seeing you again, but since Father says that is quite impossible, I am sending you this notice in my stead. I can only hope you will still be able to visit me while I am at court, although, I must confess, I don't see how that will be possible. I must go, for I hear Father calling, but I remain forever your friend, Lady Kathleen Hobart.'

"Poor Kathleen," Anna said, sitting down on a chair. "How can her father do that to her?"

"We have to trust that Lord Hobart is doing what he believes is the best thing for his daughter," Cathryn said gently. "Perhaps he thinks this will help her become more confident and advance her in society."

"Or advance himself in society," Anna said bitterly.

"Perhaps. But we cannot judge a man we do not know. And I think Kathleen will be fine."

"I hope you are right," Anna said.

CHAPTER FIFTEEN

"I need to go into Civitas again," Cathryn said to Anna one morning a few days later as they sat at the dinner table. Anna looked up at her with a smile.

"You don't need to make a trip for my sake."

"Well ..." Cathryn started. "I don't want you to be worrying about Kathleen. We will just go for the day and return in the evening. I will use the time to visit my father, and Favian has agreed to escort you to the palace."

Anna glanced at him. "Thank you, Favian. That is very kind of you."

"I am happy to be of service, Anna. Like Cathryn, I don't want you to be worrying about your friend." He looked at Cathryn. "We will leave at first light tomorrow."

The next morning Anna left the house to find Cathryn and three dragons on the grass outside.

"I insisted the children come visit their grandfather," Cathryn said by way of explanation. "So you have your choice of mounts."

"Hey," Will protested. "I'm not a 'mount', like a stupid horse."

"Of course not, dear."

"I'll carry you," Bronwyn said. "I promise to try and fly more steadily." Suppressing a slight shudder, Anna nodded, and allowed Bronwyn to curl her tail around her waist while Favian lifted Cathryn onto his back.

"You've been practicing," Anna said with a smile as she was gently lowered onto the dragon's back.

"I used a log," Bronwyn said, looking down at the ground as she spoke. She glanced back at Anna with an appealing look, and Anna patted her neck.

"That was excellent," she said. "I hardly felt you lifting me at all." Bronwyn's smile broadened, and she spread out her rosy bronze wings.

"Thank you."

They landed in an open field near the city gates, and were soon walking across the bridge and into the capital. As always, Anna paused to take in the tantalizing sights and smells that were peculiar to Civitas. She smiled to herself, and quickened her pace to catch up to the others who had not slowed down.

At the river, Favian waved over a ferry to take him and Anna to the palace, while the others continued on their way to the home of Master Forrester, Cathryn's father, a few blocks away. It didn't take long for a ferry to reach them, and taking a seat on one of the benches, Anna lifted her face to the sun shining in the clear sky.

"I love days like this," she said to Favian. "Clear blue skies where you can see for miles. Difficult for a falcon or hawk to come unawares on his prey when the sky is this clear," she added with a mischievous grin.

"Hmm," Favian said, glancing at her. "But sometimes a predator can find unwary prey sitting right in front him."

Anna laughed. "When the wolf is dressed in sheep's clothing, you mean."

"Exactly!" Favian grinned, and turned to look at the palace. "There's no guarantee we will be able to see Kathleen. She may be running errands for the queen or otherwise occupied."

"I know," Anna said. "But I'm hopeful I can snatch a few minutes."

Favian nodded. "We will see what we can do."

They arrived at the palace steps a short while later, and made their way across the courtyard. They were nearing the doors when a voice called out her name. Anna turned to see Prince Rupert coming towards her. She dropped a shallow curtsey as he approached. "Your Highness. I did not expect to see you here."

"Nor I you," he said.

Next to her, Favian turned towards the prince. "Your Highness," he said.

Rupert glanced at him. "Favian Drake. What brings you here?"

"I'm serving as escort to Mistress Anna."

"Indeed?"

"Yes," Anna said. "I came in the hopes of seeing my friend, the Lady Kathleen."

"Lady Kathleen?" The prince looked perplexed for a moment. "You mean that mousy little thing Matilda has taken on?"

A spark of annoyance made Anna lift her chin slightly. "Lady Kathleen is a very dear friend of mind," she said. She could feel Favian's look of amusement as he glanced down at her, while the prince's eyebrows rose slightly.

"Well, there is no accounting for some friendships," he said. Anna glanced down at the ground to hide her mounting irritation.

"If you'll excuse us," Favian said, taking Anna by the arm and turning her away.

"Stop." Favian paused, then slowly turned to face the prince once more. "The queen and her ladies are in the garden." The prince's eyes narrowed as his gaze met Favian's. "You wait here. I will escort Mistress Anna."

"Your Highness is very kind," Favian said, "but I cannot

do that." He was taller than the prince by half a foot, and although the prince was broad and stocky, compared to Favian he appeared quite slight. "Anna is under my protection, as both my guest and a member of my family, and it is my duty to ensure her safety."

"Do you question my honor?" Rupert's voice was low and hard.

Favian shrugged. "Take it how you will. I will not leave her alone with you."

"Very well. You can find your own way." He nodded towards Anna, then turning towards the palace, marched away. Anna turned a questioning look on Favian, but a slight shrug was his only reply.

Anna could hear the sounds of voices as they approached the gardens, and as they rounded a corner, she saw the queen walking along a path, a parasol in her hand providing some shade against the sun, while around her walked her ladies-in-waiting. Kathleen was next to the queen, speaking earnestly as she played with a flower in her hand, while behind them trailed two other ladies, laughing and whispering. It was impossible for anyone to overlook Favian, with his huge build and flaming red hair, and within a moment, the queen and Kathleen had paused in their tracks.

"Anna!" Kathleen exclaimed. A look of consternation crossed her features and she dropped her head. "My apologies, my lady," she said.

"You know this woman, Kathleen?" Matilda demanded.

"Oh, yes, Your Majesty. She is a very dear friend." The queen gave Anna a scrutinizing look.

"Mistress Anna." Anna gave a low curtsey while the queen's eyes moved back to Favian. "And Favian Drake. How come you to be here?" she said.

"I came with Mistress Anna. She is a guest in my household."

"I see." The queen looked back at Anna. "Kathleen, leave us alone. I would like to walk with this friend of yours for a while."

"Yes, Your Majesty." With a quick smile at Anna, Kathleen turned and walked a short distance away.

"Come," Queen Matilda said to Anna. "Walk with me. You," she said, pointing at Favian, "may remain here." Favian nodded, and crossing his arms against his chest, leaned against a low wall.

"So," the queen said, "you are here to see your friend, I suppose." Her blue eyes watched Anna carefully, their sharp intensity contrasting with the soft, plump lines of her face and figure.

"Yes, Your Majesty."

"You are worried that she is unhappy?"

"Well ... yes, Your Majesty."

"As you should be. Court can be unkind to a girl of Kathleen's timidity. But I believe she just needs some encouragement."

"Yes, Your Majesty."

The queen pulled a flower from a bush, and brushed the bloom against her cheek. "Rupert told me about a woman he met at Hobart's house. One who offered comment on the color of his wardrobe. Tell me, Mistress, would that woman be you?"

Anna looked at the queen in surprise. "Yes, Your Majesty."

"Enough 'Yes, Your Majesty!' You offer your opinion quite freely with Rupert, and I desire you to do the same with me." She paused in her walking to look at Anna.

"That's only because the prince says so many disagreeable things," Anna said.

Queen Matilda laughed. "Yes, you are quite correct." She continued her walking. "Do you enjoy the city, Anna?"

"I do, indeed. I love the vibrancy and smells. On every street corner people are hawking their wares, while plays and music fill every street."

"That is not a side of the city I get to see. Tell me, what

kind of plays do you see on the streets?"

"Well …" Anna tried to think of one. "During the week leading up to the coronation there were many plays. There was one very funny one …"

"Yes?"

"I'm sorry, Your Majesty, I should not have mentioned it."

"You have piqued my curiosity. Tell me."

Anna looked at the ground uncomfortably. "It was a play about the coronation."

"Yes?"

Anna took a deep breath and looked up at the queen. May as well be hanged for a sheep as a lamb. "It pantomimed Your Majesty hitting His Royal Majesty the king with the scepter, while a nobleman picked up the orb, which was rolling down the aisle, and declared himself king."

The queen laughed. "There are times when I would very much like to hit the king with a scepter, but I must confess I would be hard pressed to do it in the cathedral. Perhaps one day I shall dress like a commoner and see some of these plays myself." She glanced at Anna. "If I asked you to, would you come with me?"

Anna looked up, startled. "If Your Majesty asked me to, then of course I would obey my queen."

"Of course. But would you do it willingly?"

Anna smiled. "Yes. I would love to show you the city from a commoner's view."

"Good." She turned. "Let's return to the others." They walked back to where Favian still stood, completely ignoring the looks thrown his way by the other women.

"You may have a few minutes with your friend before we retire indoors," the queen said to Anna.

"Thank you, Your Majesty," she said.

She passed the next half hour with Kathleen, getting hopelessly lost in the maze as they wandered between the high hedges and around tight corners.

"The queen is very kind to me, and so is Lady Elizabeth," Kathleen said. "And Lady Blanche ... well, she leaves me alone. It is not what I would have chosen, but I am not unhappy."

"I'm glad," Anna said. "I have been so worried for you. But knowing you are happy sets my mind at rest."

They reached the center of the maze, where they paused to admire the statue of Athena, before turning slowly to look at the four exits, one on each side of the four lengths of hedge that surrounded them.

"Which one did we enter through?" Kathleen asked.

"That one," Anna said, pointing to the archway in the hedge behind the statue, but they had no sooner gone down the path than they saw it was a dead end. They retraced their steps back to the center of the maze, and tried another exit, but it was soon clear that this too would lead them nowhere. A few more failed attempts had them back in the center, and Anna indicated a bench.

"We'll just wait until Favian comes to find us," she said.

"Master Drake? But how will he know we are lost? And what if he gets lost too?"

"He'll know," Anna said. "And he never gets lost." And sure enough, before a few minutes had passed, he rounded a corner and entered the center square.

"Ready to go, ladies?" he said.

Anna rose to her feet. "I knew you would come," she said.

"Of course," he replied. "Follow me."

It only took a few minutes to get through the maze as Favian unerringly led the way, deftly avoiding the dead ends and detours. The queen and the other ladies were waiting near the entrance to the maze as they came out, trailing Favian.

"There you are," she said. "I was wondering whether we would have to send in the guards."

"My apologies, Your Majesty," Kathleen said, dropping to a curtsey before the queen. "I didn't mean to cause you alarm."

"No harm done," the queen said indulgently. She looked over at Anna. "I expect I will see you at court again. You are welcome to come any time," she said.

"Thank you, Your Majesty," Anna replied. The queen nodded and Anna turned to Favian, taking his outstretched arm and allowing him to lead her away from the queen, the gardens and the palace.

CHAPTER SIXTEEN

The days at Drake Manor were passing quickly as the leaves started to change color and the nights became cooler. Anna had been there for close on three months, traveling with Cathryn into the city whenever she had cause to go, or spending time around the manor, helping the children with their lessons or Margaret with her healing potions. Evenings were often spent in the parlor where she joined the others in singing, playing games, or listening to Favian or Owain read a tale from one of the many books in Owain's library. Once, Anna had found a play tucked between two books, and she and the children had acted it out for the enjoyment of the others.

It was just past noon when Cathryn found Anna sitting in the parlor before a blazing fire, reading a letter from Keira. She had been out earlier that day with Bronwyn, and even earlier had struggled with Will over Latin conjugations.

"Aaron and Keira are coming to visit," Anna said, looking up from her letter as Cathryn walked through the door and took a seat across from her.

"I know. Favian has also received a letter. Aaron has some business with the dragon council, so they will convene while Aaron is here." Cathryn paused for a moment. "Are you going to return to Storbrook with them?"

Anna had returned to perusing her letter, but at Cathryn's query, she looked up sharply. "Do you want me to return with them?"

"Not at all," Cathryn said with a smile. "We enjoy having you here, and Bronwyn thinks of you as her big sister."

Anna relaxed slightly as she smiled in return. "It's nice to be a big sister for a change!"

"But perhaps you are feeling homesick?" Cathryn continued.

"I do miss Lydia and Zach," she said. "Keira says they are learning to write their names already! But I'm not quite ready to return to Storbrook yet."

"Well, you are welcome to stay here as long as you wish," Cathryn assured her.

Aaron arrived a week later, landing on the gravel drive outside the house with Keira on his back. Anna flung herself into her sister's arms, hugging her tightly.

"It is so wonderful to see you!" she said.

"It is wonderful to see you, too, Anna," Keira said with a laugh.

Anna led Keira into the house while Favian greeted his cousin. "Cathryn has prepared the same room for you as before," she said. Keira would stay alone at Drake Manor while Aaron met with the Dragon Council. The Council was made up of the eight elders and the Dragon Master. They would not stay at the manor, but would spend three days deep in the mountains, taking their natural forms. Owain was an elder, and although Favian was not, he would join the council in their conferences as Aaron's advisor.

"How is Mother?" Anna asked Keira, after Keira had had a chance to refresh herself and bid farewell to Aaron.

"Not well," Keira replied. "Most days she cannot get out of bed. Mary has taken over the running of the household, and Father has hired another two maids to help. Mother says she will remain in this world just long enough to see you wed!"

Anna sighed. "Then she may have to wait for many more years."

"Do you return with us to Storbrook?" Keira asked.

Anna shook her head. "Not yet," she said.

"Mother is not the only one who hopes to see you again soon," Keira said.

"You mean the children."

"The children, too."

Anna groaned. "Garrick." She dropped her gaze to her hands. "If I go back now ... I'm just not ready!"

"I understand. But if you wait too long ..." Keira let the uncompleted thought dangle. Anna nodded.

"I know."

A clatter of hooves on the gravel outside the house had both women turning to look out the window. A horseman was leaning down towards a serving maid, a missive in his hand which he held out to her. They exchanged a few words, and then the man was swinging away again, kicking his horse into motion as he cantered down the drive. A few moments later the maid entered the room.

"Excuse me, Mistress Carver," she said, "but this has just come for you." Anna took the thick folded paper, nodding in thanks, and inspected it in surprise. It bore the official royal seal stamped into wax.

"What do you suppose this is?" Anna said, turning it over to see her name written in fine script on the front. Slipping her finger beneath the seal, she slid it open and unfolded the paper. "It comes from the queen," she said, her surprise deepening. She spread the letter and read the contents aloud.

'Anna Carver from Her Royal Majesty, Queen Matilda, Queen of this Realm by the Grace of God, we send you greetings.

'It is with Great Pleasure that we send you this Communication announcing your Appointment to our Royal

Household, where you will wait upon our Royal Majesty. As a Lady-in-Waiting, you will have the Privilege of showing your True Loyalty and Friendship to our Royal Person and to this Realm, serving us in the Royal Bedchamber. We expect the Pleasure of your Company at Court Monday next.'

Anna leaned back in her seat and lifted wide eyes to Keira. "Well!"

The contents of the missive were soon a topic for general conversation around the meal table. Cathryn thought it was an opportunity not to be missed, while Margaret advised Anna to consider how long she was prepared to remain away from her family. Keira wanted nothing to do with the royal court, but if Anna wished to go, she would not stand in her way. Bronwyn wanted Anna to remain at Drake Manor, while Will did not see what all the fuss was about.

When Aaron returned to Drake Manor with the other dragons three days later, Anna still had not decided what her course of action should be. When Aaron was brought up to date on the letter from the queen, he offered to support Anna in whatever course she chose. "But," he said, "court life is not for the weak-willed. Be sure you are prepared for life there before you decide to accept. But you need to decide soon. The queen expects you in a few days."

"I know," Anna said. She gave Aaron and Keira a bleak smile before leaving the room and walking outside. In the distance the forest was a sea of reds and yellows against an azure sky, while behind them the hills were still swathed in the verdant green of pines. She headed towards the stables, and was soon picking her way along the path that led to the river. She reached the bank, and glanced up at the ridge. She had not been here since the fateful day when Bronwyn had gained her true form. She hesitated for a moment, then kicked her horse back into motion, leading the mare into the water and up the cliff on the other side. She looked up, and felt her heart speed up when she saw something circling high overhead. It wasn't until the dragon drew closer that Anna could see it was Bronwyn. She landed on the ground near Anna with a slight thump.

"What are you doing here?" Bronwyn asked, settling herself down on the ground.

"Thinking about the queen's directive."

"What does a lady-in-waiting do?"

"She attends the queen."

"Does that mean you cannot leave once you are there?"

"Oh, no! Nothing like that! A lady helps the queen with small things, such as getting dressed, or accompanying her in her duties, but she is more a companion, and will read with her, or paint, or walk. Sometimes the queen chooses just to have one lady attend her at a time, or wishes to be alone, and then the ladies are free to do as they wish."

"So you can come and visit?"

"Yes. I'm sure the queen will grant me permission to visit my family. And you can come visit me, too."

"And how long do you have to stay with the queen?"

"Well, most ladies remain until they get married, or choose to retire from court. The queen cannot force me to stay against my will."

Bronwyn nodded, considering this. "So what are you going to do?"

Anna shrugged. "I don't know."

"Well," Bronwyn said, "I want you to stay here, and Aunty Keira wants you to go to Storbrook, and the queen wants you at court. What do you want?"

"That's the problem! I want to be near everyone!"

"Well, maybe it's the queen's turn to have you for a while."

Anna turned to look at Bronwyn in surprise. "Maybe," she said. She smiled. "Maybe so."

CHAPTER SEVENTEEN

Anna tapped the quill on the desk as she sought the words to write. She had informed Aaron and Keira of her decision to go to court and join the queen's entourage, but the most difficult communication lay before her now.

'To Garrick Flynn of Storbrook Castle, from Anna Carver,' she wrote.

'By the time you receive this communication I will have already taken up residence at the royal court at the behest of Her Majesty, Queen Matilda. I have been appointed to the position of lady-in-waiting to Her Majesty, and do not ...'

Anna stared down at the letter, before scratching her pen through the words and flipping the page over.

'To Garrick Flynn of Storbrook Castle, from Anna Carver,' she began again.

'You have probably received the news that I am now serving the queen at the royal court, and will not be returning to Storbrook in the foreseeable future ...'

With a groan, she crumpled up the paper and drew out a fresh piece.

'To Garrick Flynn, from Anna Carver.

'The queen has appointed me as one of her ladies, and I

have accepted the position. I am so sorry for the hurt I may have caused. You deserve someone far better than me. I wish you all the best. With fondest regards, Anna.'

She folded the letter and sealed it with a wax wafer, before leaning back in her chair and closing her eyes. Once the letter was delivered there was no going back. She rose to her feet – she would give the letter to Aaron right away, before she could second guess herself. Everything else was already in readiness. Her garments had been packed in a trunk and sent ahead to be delivered to the palace, and she had taken leave of the Drakes of Drake Manor the previous day. She had stayed the night with Keira and Aaron at Drake House, and this morning Aaron would accompany her to the palace. She walked down the passage slowly. She was casting herself adrift in the wide ocean of the world. At the palace there would be no family close by to turn to, and no dragons watching over her. And the human world she was stepping into was far more dangerous than the dragon world she was leaving.

Keira was waiting in the small parlor behind the hall at Drake House. Aaron was not in the room, but Anna guessed he wasn't far away. Keira smiled as Anna walked into the room.

"Ready?" she said.

"I am," Anna said.

Keira took a step forward, taking Anna's hands in her own. "You are more than ready," she said. "You are strong and courageous, and I know that you can rise above whatever challenges or intrigues come your way." She smiled, and lifting her hand, stroked the hair from Anna's face. "I will miss you," she said.

"I will miss you, too," Anna said, a sob catching in her throat and making her voice squeak, and then she was in Keira's arms. "I don't deserve such a wonderful sister."

"Nonsense," Keira sniffed.

"Give my regards to Mother and Father," she said. "And

hug the children for me. Tell Lydia she will daily be in my thoughts."

"I will," Keira said, pulling away gently as Aaron came into the room. She kissed Anna on the forehead and turned away.

"Ready?" Aaron asked quietly, and Anna nodded.

"I'll see you later, my sweet," Aaron said to Keira, brushing his hands down her arms. She nodded, and he drew away, turning towards the door and striding out of the room.

"Goodbye," Anna said softly, and quickly turned and followed Aaron, not waiting for a reply. Aaron was already out the door, waiting on the street. He looked down at Anna as she joined him.

"You don't have to do this," he said.

"I know," she said. "But I want to."

Aaron nodded. "Then let's be on our way."

Aaron led Anna to a wooden door on the second floor of the palace, where he gave their names to the guard. The man nodded and disappeared through the door, closing it behind him. There was a small bench on the opposite wall, and Anna sat down while Aaron stood, hands clasped behind his back, a few feet away.

"If you need anything, let me know," Aaron said. He had already provided her with a handsome allowance. "And if you are unhappy and want to return home, I will speak to the king."

"Thank you," Anna said.

Aaron nodded and started pacing along the corridor. "Do not expect the men at court to be honorable," he said. "And never, ever, allow yourself to be alone with any man. The higher the rank, the more dangerous he will be."

"I'll be fine, Aaron," Anna said, a note of exasperation creeping into her tone. Aaron stopped his pacing and turned to look at her.

"I know you will," he said. "But humor an old man, will

you?"

Anna grinned. Aaron did not look more than thirty, although he was well over the century mark. "Please continue, O ancient one," she said.

The door opened and the guard reappeared. "Her Majesty will see you now," he said. "Follow me." Anna rose to her feet and followed the guard through the door, Aaron behind her. The guard led them down a passage to a door at the end, which he opened. Within the room sat the queen on an embroidered chair, surrounded by a small group of people. Anna saw Kathleen sitting in a chair a short distance away, a piece of embroidery in her hands, while closer to the queen were the women Anna had seen in the gardens.

"Your Majesty," Anna said, sinking into a low curtsey.

"Mistress Anna," the queen said. "And Aaron Drake. How wonderful!" One of the women from the gardens tittered behind her hand.

"Your Majesty," Aaron said, greeting the queen with a shallow bow, before his gaze wandered to the woman who had laughed. He frowned slightly. "Blanche." She smiled, her lips thinning tightly in a smile that did nothing to soften her features or remove the glint from her eye. So this was Blanche, Anna thought. The woman who had been so sneering towards Keira when she first met her six years ago. No wonder Aaron didn't like her. Blanche nodded slightly.

"Aaron," she said. Aaron stared at her for a brief moment, then turned to the others.

"Lady Elizabeth," he said. "Lady Kathleen."

"Master Drake," Kathleen said, her voice so soft Anna had to strain to hear it. She was staring at the floor as she twisted her hands in her lap. But she peeked up with a smile at Anna when Aaron returned his attention to the queen.

"How nice of you to accompany your sister-in-law," Matilda said.

"Of course," replied Aaron. "She is part of my family and falls under my protection."

"Why, is she an orphan?" Blanche said with a little laugh.

"Blanche. Enough." The queen frowned, and the tight smile grew tighter.

"No," Aaron replied, "but Master Carver lives many miles distant. However, even if he lived within the shadow of the palace, my name and protection would still extend to Mistress Anna, and I would consider it a personal insult should anyone injure her person or name in any way."

Anna sighed. She knew what Aaron was doing, and as much as she appreciated it, she felt like a bone between two fighting dogs. One side, royal court, other side, Dragon Master. Aaron glanced at her, giving her a wry half-smile and the slightest of shrugs.

"Of course it would, Aaron," said the queen. "I'm sure Blanche did not intend to insult Anna."

"Of course not," Blanche said. "I cannot imagine why anyone would think I meant to insult our dear friend. It was just an innocent question."

Aaron took a step forward. "I have known you for a long time, Blanche," he said softly. "I will not tolerate any slurs against Anna's name. Do not think that because I live away from the city I am unaware of what happens within this court. I am very well informed, my dear Blanche, and will take whatever action I deem reasonable should any member of my family be in any way maligned."

Anna saw Blanche swallow hard and her face grow a shade lighter, but she kept her eyes locked with Aaron's.

"You have made yourself very clear, Aaron," she said. He continued to look at her for another moment, before stepping away and turning to Anna.

"Remember what I told you," he said. "We will remain in Civitas until the end of the week should you need to contact me." Anna nodded. "Farewell, sister," he said, leaning down and kissing her forehead as Keira had done.

"Goodbye, Aaron," she said. "And thank you."

He nodded, and glanced once more at Queen Matilda.

"Your Majesty," he said, then turning on his heel, left the room.

CHAPTER EIGHTEEN

Anna quickly settled into the routine of a lady-in-waiting. She and the other ladies slept in a room adjoining the queen's bedchamber – a long chamber, with four beds hung with drapes that could be pulled closed to allow for some privacy. Two desks stood in the room, and beneath the long window were chairs and benches, covered in embroidered cushions. There were separate alcoves where each lady's garments were stored, as well as other personal items. Each lady had a lady's maid, who woke them every morning with a cup of mulled wine, and assisted them with dressing. Betsy, Anna's maid, was a quiet, young woman, with a shy smile and deft hands.

Once the ladies were ready for the day, they would ensure that the maids of the queen's chamber had everything in readiness for the queen – a hot bath drawn and placed by the fire, mulled wine and warm, buttered bread ready on a tray, her garments laid out for the day, ornaments set on the table, and slippers warming by the fire. The maids would leave the room, and the drapes around the bed would be pulled open by Lady Elizabeth, who would wake the queen, brushing her hands down her arm, as Anna stood by with the tray. It took a few days before Queen Matilda was satisfied with Anna's handling of the tray – it must not rest on the bed, nor be too high in the air; it must not be too close, nor too far; the bread must be placed just so on the tray, with the wine two inches away.

While the queen had her meal, Kathleen, whom the queen declared had the gentlest hands, brushed her hair, seating herself on the bed beside Matilda. Her golden hair reached all the way down her back, falling in gentle waves that glimmered in the candlelight. Oils and spices would be rubbed into it, and Kathleen would wrap it in a strip of linen, in preparation for the queen's bath. Her meal finished, Matilda would rise from the quilts and step into the hot water, perfumed with rose and lavender, and Blanche would wash her body with a linen cloth. Once the queen had completed her bath, Elizabeth would rub oils into the queen's skin, covering her entire body while Her Majesty stood naked in the middle of the room, sighing and groaning in pleasure. Anna never felt entirely comfortable, and would glance away when the task was performed. When the queen was well oiled, Kathleen would bring the royal chemise and gown, and she and Anna would lower the garments over Her Majesty's head. While Blanche coiffed her hair, one of the other ladies would take turns reading aloud for the general amusement of the others.

There was a small chapel in the queen's apartments, and the first duty of each day was to attend mass with the queen. With hands clasped together, she would gaze at the crucifix hanging on the wall, while her lips moved in silent prayer. Half an hour would then be spent each morning with her children in the nursery, sometimes watching them as they had their lessons, other times listening with them as a nurse told them a short tale. After that, however, the routine varied. Every Tuesday and Thursday she held court with the king, listening to the petitions of commoners. The king would occasionally defer judgment to her, and Anna was always surprised at her just and insightful rulings.

On Wednesdays, the queen would order a litter to take her to St. Catherine's hospital, of which she was patron. The hospital was a place of shelter for the weary traveler, a place of refuge for the blind and crippled and a place of care for the sick and dying. Matilda would meet with the Mother Superior to discuss the hospital finances and other matters, while her ladies would dispense words of encouragement to the elderly and infirm housed within.

The queen took an avid interest in the arts, and she would invite playwrights and musicians to perform for her. If she enjoyed their performances, she would sponsor them, allowing them to perform at court or at the new theater recently built in the city. On fair days, Matilda could often be found in the gardens, where she loved to walk. She would stop and chat with the gardeners, and Anna noticed with amusement that although they listened deferentially to her advice, they never seemed to implement the changes she suggested. If the queen noticed, however, she chose to overlook this small defiance.

The queen's chambers consisted of the chapel; a parlor, where visitors would be entertained; a ladies' bower, where the queen and her ladies could enjoy a view of the gardens while they read or embroidered; a dining room; the queen's bedchamber; and the ladies' bedchamber. Every Thursday evening the king joined the queen for supper. He would retire with her to her bedchamber afterwards, leaving an hour or two later.

There were two guards assigned to the queen. Frank and Tobias stood outside the apartments when the queen was within, and traveled with her when she went abroad. The men would nod at the women as they came and went, but Tobias was the friendlier of the two, often exchanging a few words with Anna or the other ladies.

Anna soon learned that the queen thrived on knowledge. She read voraciously, books both spiritual and secular. She invited scholars to visit her, and she questioned them at length on their specialty. She demanded that Anna tell her about her home, the village, and the surrounding countryside. She asked about the city and the markets. She was also an unrepentant gossip, and she would quiz the ladies on the latest rumors and intrigues circulating around the palace. She was always well-informed, and knew who was having affairs with whom, and who had been tossed on the street. She knew that Lord Bartley owed Master Somerton money, or that Nellie was not talking to Fanny. She knew the name of the king's latest mistress, and how often he saw her. She also kept herself abreast of political developments in the land, and although she was never invited to meetings of council, she always knew what had happened in the closed-door conferences within a few hours.

But there were times when the queen tired of having people surrounding her, and she would send her ladies away to follow their own pursuits for a few hours. Anna loved to escape the palace, and exiting through the courtyard, would quickly leave the buildings behind her. Sometime Kathleen would accompany her, and they would meander along the river or through the gardens. Despite Anna's worst expectations, Kathleen was thriving at the royal court. The queen treated her kindly, and Anna noticed that Kathleen would sit close to Matilda, quietly answering her demands on what she thought about this book, or that play. And on the odd occasion, she would even offer an opinion to the other ladies. Blanche took no notice of her, but Elizabeth would smile, and nod encouragingly.

But when Anna was alone, she would head towards the wilderness that lay beyond the formal palace gardens. Since not many people wandered this far from the palace, it was a place of peace and quiet, an escape from the hustle and bustle of court. There was one cold afternoon when she wended her way in that direction. The trees were bare of leaves and stood stark against a gray sky. It had rained earlier in the day, and the hem of her gown was damp and muddy from trailing along the grass.

She had received a letter from Keira earlier in the day, and she pulled it from her pocket to reread it.

Aaron had secured a tutor for Zach and Lydia – a dragon a few decades older than Aaron. 'Corbin is the most unlikely dragon,' Keira had written. 'He is only a little taller than Father, and always lost in thought. He bumps into things – a dragon! – and can never keep track of time. Aaron says he loved a girl once, but before he had a chance to declare his devotion, she married someone else, and he never recovered from the blow. He is a man of science, and already has the children learning the Latin names of plants and animals around Storbrook. He has also been teaching them their letters and numbers, and I am including a page of their writings.'

Anna glanced down at the scribbled page with a smile. The children had carefully spelled out their names in big, block letters. She returned to her letter. Keira did not mention Garrick, although she did write about Mother:

'She rallied for a while, and we thought she might recover some of her strength, but the improvement was of short duration, and now she seems even worse than before.'

Anna was so lost in her thoughts, she did not hear the tramping of feet through the wilderness, until someone shouted out her name. She spun around, startled, and saw Prince Rupert marching towards her, a boy at his side. She recognized the boy as Prince John, Rupert's oldest nephew, and first in line to the throne.

"What are you doing here?" Rupert demanded as he drew near. He wore a simple brown tunic, and on his left arm he wore a thick leather gauntlet. A few yards back were two more men – one carrying a large cage, the other a canvas sack, slung over his shoulder.

Anna crossed her arms over her chest. "I am taking a walk." She glanced at the men. "What are you doing here?"

"Teaching young John the basics of falconry. You should

return to the palace."

"When I am ready," she said. Rupert had already started striding away, but he paused at her words, then looked back at her with a slow smile.

"Perhaps you would like to see my falcon?"

Anna nodded. "Yes," she said. "I would."

He gestured with his head, and she followed him towards the men, who were standing close by. John looked at her curiously, but remained silent. The man holding the cage lowered it to the ground, and Rupert crouched before the cage, flipping open a latch, and dropping one side. He stretched his gauntleted hand into the enclosure, then withdrew it a moment later and rose to his feet. On his hand, its talons gripping the leather of the gauntlet, was the most beautiful bird Anna had ever seen. It was about eighteen inches tall, with black plumage on its back and a pale, spotted chest. Its round, black eyes, ringed in yellow, looked at her steadily, and she found herself staring back.

"Beautiful, isn't she?" Rupert said. Anna pulled her eyes away.

"Yes, she is." The bird moved, and Anna heard a soft tinkling sound. Small bells were tied to the bird's claws, and a thin length of leather was looped around its leg, the other end firmly clasped between Rupert's thumb and forefinger. As Anna watched, he slipped the thong off the leg, and quickly lifted his hand into the air. A clear, ringing sound could be heard as the bird launched itself upwards and rose into the gray, overcast sky, quickly become a mere speck against the clouds.

"How do you know it will hunt something?" Anna asked.

Rupert had been watching the bird, but he glanced at her. "She hasn't been fed today. After she has made enough kills, we will give her a good hearty meal of raw meat."

"But why doesn't she just eat what she kills?"

"She knows I feed her. From the time she was young, the only food she has eaten is what I've given her. I'm not sure she even knows she could eat what she hunts."

Anna looked back at the clouds. Rupert was watching intently, but she couldn't see anything. She was about to look away, when a flash through the sky caught her eye. It was the bird, diving down at a dizzying speed towards the ground. It disappeared behind the trees, then swooped back up, a large creature hanging from its claws.

"Look." Anna had been watching the falcon, but she followed Rupert's pointed finger to see a flock of ducks rising into the air. "She's caught a mallard," he said. He lifted his fingers to his mouth and gave a sharp whistle. The falcon changed direction, and a moment later landed on the ground, the lifeless duck hanging from its claws. With a deft movement, Rupert quickly covered the falcon's eyes with a leather hood, then slipped the leather loop around the bird's leg. A small feather plume rose from the top of the hood, and the feathers shook as the bird moved its head. Rupert held his hand lightly against the bird's talons, and the falcon hopped on, while the man with the sack scooped up the prize.

"Will you feed her now?" Anna asked.

"Just a morsel to keep her going. If I give her too much now, she won't want to hunt again." He turned to John. "Would you like to give her a snack?"

His eyes brightened as he nodded enthusiastically. "Yes, Uncle," he said. Rupert nodded to one of the men, who passed over a piece of raw, red meat. John took it gingerly in his fingers.

"Like this, lad," Rupert said, pushing the boy towards the bird. He glanced over his shoulder at Anna. "Ladies often keep birds, you know. I could find you a merlin and teach you the necessary skills if you wish."

The idea made Anna pause. Did she want to tame a wild beast? "Thank you, Your Highness," she said, "but I'm afraid I'm not very patient." A drop of rain fell on her sleeve, and she looked up to see the clouds had become very dark.

"Thank you for showing me your falcon," she said. The prince nodded.

"Good day, Mistress," he said.

CHAPTER NINETEEN

"There is a newcomer at court," Kathleen told Anna excitedly one day. "He has just arrived after being absent for years. I've only seen him from afar, but they say he is more handsome than any other man in the city."

"Who says that?" Anna asked, amused.

"Well, Blanche, for one. And Mary Pritchard. Even Lady Elizabeth says she could fill her hours just watching him."

"If that is the case, this newcomer is probably a vain, strutting peacock, and equally shallow and simple-minded," Anna said.

"That's an unfair assessment of a man you haven't even met," Kathleen protested.

"I don't need to meet him. His character is already quite decided in my mind."

"And you have decided not to like him?"

"Absolutely! Any man who has scores of women hovering around him, gazing on his beauty, is not worth the slightest ounce of regard or consideration."

"I feel quite sorry for him, already," Kathleen said with a laugh.

"Save your pity for someone more worthy," Anna

retorted.

· They were walking through the gardens as they talked. The queen was in conference with her favorite playwright, Lord Denton, and had dismissed her ladies from her presence. Anna did not think Denton's work was particularly good, being neither witty nor erudite, but the queen had taken him under her wing, offering tips and revisions that he eagerly adopted before presenting his work at court and in the city. There were far better playwrights, Anna thought to herself, although none as pretty, perhaps, as Lord Denton.

It had rained the previous night and the ground was damp, but the stones along the path had dried from the few weak rays of sun that broke through the heavy clouds. To one side of the path lay flower beds, the dormant soil carefully raked over, while on the other side rose a hedge, trimmed to perfection by an army of gardeners. It ran like a dashed line, interspersed with bushes that had been carefully cut and trained into perfect spheres. The hedge blocked the view of the adjoining path, except for the brief breaks to display the globes. It was as they were passing one such gap that Kathleen grabbed Anna by the arm.

"It's him," she whispered excitedly.

"Who?" Anna asked in confusion.

"The man I was telling you about – the new arrival at court."

"You mean the peacock?" She glanced at the hedge, but the line of sight had been blocked once more.

"He's coming our way," Kathleen whispered. "What should we do?"

"Don't be such a goose," Anna said with a laugh. "We will nod politely and continue on our walk."

"Yes, of course," Kathleen said, but she clung to Anna's arm as they walked. "Look, he's coming around the corner," Kathleen said. "He's with a woman." Anna had been watching her friend, but she turned now to look at the couple strolling towards them. The first thing she noticed were the bronze highlights in the man's loosely curling hair, caused by the sun glancing off his head as he bent down in conversation with the woman at his side. The other thing she noticed was how tall he was, and the leanness of his frame. She could not see his face, but her heart started to hammer wildly as she struggled to pull air into her lungs. A humming grew in her ears, and she saw nothing but the man walking towards her. She knew the set of his muscular shoulders, and recognized the cat-like grace with which he moved. It had been over five years since she had seen him last, but every aspect of him was imprinted on her mind. He was still bent towards the woman at his side, but as Anna stared at him, he slowly lifted his head and turned to meet her gaze, his gray eyes holding hers over the distance of the path.

Kathleen was saying something, but the words sounded like they were traveling from a great distance. Anna's mind felt sluggish and dull, and it was only with greatest effort that she tore her gaze away from the eyes that held her riveted. Her legs were trembling, and she wrapped her hand around Kathleen's in an effort to control the shaking.

"You have to admit he is very handsome," Kathleen said.

"No," Anna said, shaking her head. She tugged Kathleen's arm as she took a step backwards. "No, I have to go." Kathleen looked at her in surprise.

"What's the matter? Look, they are coming our way."

Anna nodded. There was no escape. He was only a few feet away, and once more she felt her throat tighten as the air around her thickened.

"Mistress Carver," Max said. Anna barely noticed Kathleen's surprised glance. Max stared at her for a long moment, his eyes holding hers, then turned to the woman at his side. "Allow me to introduce Mistress Jane."

Anna nodded, and heard her own voice as though it belonged to someone else, greeting Max's companion. She introduced Kathleen, then waved at the man standing so close. "Kathleen, this is Master Brant."

Kathleen murmured her greetings while Anna looked at the woman at Max's side. There was something about her that was familiar, but Anna could not place it. She was not exactly beautiful, but had a quality about her that made her attractive. Perhaps it was her bright, lively eyes, or her wide, friendly smile, but whatever it was, Anna was sure it drew the attention of any man passing by. She returned Anna's appraising stare thoughtfully. "Mistress Anna," she said, "I am pleased to make your acquaintance. I have heard a lot about you." She turned to Kathleen with a nod. "Lady Kathleen." Kathleen nodded, darting a quick look at Anna before dropping her eyes to the ground.

Anna looked back at Max. Now that the initial shock had worn off, she felt more composed, although her heart was still pounding furiously. He looked quite unchanged, which was to be expected, of course. She turned to Kathleen.

"Master Brant and I have long been acquainted," she said, "although," she continued, "it has been a while since we last saw each other." She turned to Max. "Tell me, Master Brant, how many years has it been?"

"Oh, I don't know, two or three. The time went by so quickly I barely noticed its passing." A sliver of pain ran through Anna, but when she looked into his face she saw in his expression a challenge that she instantly recognized.

"Really?" she said, arching her eyebrows, "as long as that?" A smile tugged at his mouth, and she looked at Kathleen to hide her own. "He's everything I said before," she said. "Arrogant, rude and proud."

She glanced back at Max, and saw the slight narrowing of his eyes as they caught hers. He took a small step closer, and she felt a wave of heat roll over her. "Proud, Anna? Is that a failing peculiar to me? Or is it perhaps one we share?"

She stared back at him, determined to give a sharp retort, but there were no words. She could see a yellow spark deep in the gray depths, pulling her in, and she forgot they were not alone.

"Nothing to say?" he said softly, and she shivered. "No insults? No further maligning of my character?"

"No," she whispered.

He glanced away, and it took Anna a moment to realize that Jane had lain a hand on his arm, and was saying his name.

"Max? Max! Shall we continue our walk?" The moment was broken, and Anna looked away, relieved and disappointed. The intensity she had seen a moment before in Max's eyes had disappeared, replaced with a friendly smile.

"My apologies, Jane," Max said. "Mistress Carver and I are, er, old antagonists." He glanced at Anna with a look of provocation that immediately evoked a slew of unflattering names, but she compressed her lips, refusing to take the bait. He noticed her struggle, of course. "You were about to say something?" he said, his eyebrows raised questioningly.

"I was just going to wish you a good day and a pleasant walk," she said. He grinned, and she could not help giving a gleeful smile in return.

"Good day, Mistress," he said. He nodded in Kathleen's direction, and with Jane at his side, walked past them.

There was a bench a few yards ahead, and pulling her arm from Kathleen's, Anna headed towards it. Her legs felt weak and her hands were trembling as she pressed them into her lap.

"You still say he is a peacock?" Kathleen asked, following her.

"No, not a peacock," Anna said. "More like a wild, uncontrollable beast." She glanced at the retreating figures as she said the words, and when she saw Max's head cock slightly, she knew he had heard her. He glanced over his shoulder, and catching her eye, gave her a grin. She bent down and picked up a small twig lying on the ground beneath the bench. Despite the rain of the previous night, it was dry, and she snapped it in two with a satisfying crack. How easily it would catch alight, she thought, with the slightest breath of flame. All it needed was a single spark. For a moment, it seemed to her that it grew warmer in her hand. She looked up to see Max and Jane round the corner and disappear from view, and with a sigh, she dropped the broken twig and rose to her feet.

It wasn't until much later that it occurred to Anna to wonder why Max had come to court. Of course, he had been a regular in the years before she met him, but what was surprising was his lack of surprise at seeing *her* there. Had he already known she was attending the queen when he arrived? Or had he scented her presence in the moments before their paths crossed? But she could find no answer.

CHAPTER TWENTY

When Anna and Kathleen returned, they found the queen sitting in her parlor, looking out the window. She turned as they approached.

"Come sit with me," she said. "Denton has just left. What a marvelous writer." She sighed. "And his plays are not too bad, either. His latest work is very tragic." She raised her hand to her heart and lifted her face. "It moved me to tears," she said with a deep sigh. There was a moment's pause as Anna and Kathleen gazed at her desperate expression, before she turned to Anna. "It will be acted on the stage near the river. Are you familiar with it?"

"I am," Anna replied.

"I want to see it performed."

"I'm sure that can be arranged, my lady."

"Yes, I'm sure it can be. However, I want to see it without him knowing I am there. I wish to see the people enjoying his fine work. Perhaps, Anna, it is time to put our plan into action!"

"Our plan, my lady?"

"Yes, of course! Have you forgotten? Our plan to disguise ourselves as peasants and walk through the streets of the city unnoticed."

"As ... er ... peasants, my lady?"

"Yes! Anna, why are you being so dull? We had this conversation before you joined my household."

"Of course, Your Majesty," Anna said quickly. "I just didn't realize you wished to travel as a peasant. Perhaps a gentlewoman would be a better disguise?"

"Peasant. Gentlewoman." The queen waved a hand through the air. "It matters not to me."

"Yes, my lady. When is my Lord Denton performing his play?"

"Three days hence," she said.

"We could go to the market," Kathleen exclaimed, still standing next to Anna. She had listened first in surprise and then with growing excitement.

"Yes! Yes! Splendid idea, Kathleen," Matilda said. "We will travel to market like other good housewives, buy pies and roasted chestnuts, and then go to the play." She turned back to Anna. "We want to keep this a secret – just the ladies. And perhaps Rupert too, so he can serve as an escort. But you must order the litter on my behalf."

"The litter, Your Majesty?" Anna said. "Only noblewomen travel by litter, my lady."

"Of course. We will walk."

"Yes, my lady. And, uh, what will you wear?"

"I'm sure I must have something suitable!"

Anna glanced at Kathleen with a despairing look. "Common women wear, um, plainer gowns than you are accustomed to, my lady."

"I'll make something, Your Majesty," Kathleen said.

Matilda smiled. "Excellent. Nothing too fancy. The plainer, the better."

When Blanche returned to the chambers a short while later, she was dismayed to learn the queen's plans. "But I cannot dress like a commoner," she protested.

"If your queen can, so can you," Matilda said, and that

was the end of the subject. Elizabeth, on the other hand, entered into the plans with enthusiasm.

"What fun," she exclaimed when Blanche gave her the news later that evening. "I don't have any suitable gowns, of course, but I'm sure Kathleen can help me make something too." She turned to Anna. "You will have some ideas of what we can wear, I'm sure," she said.

Next to her, Blanche sniggered. "After all," she said, "you are the most common amongst us."

Anna drew in a breath through gritted teeth before forcing a smile. "I am happy to help in whatever way I can."

The following morning, Anna and Blanche accompanied the queen to St. Catherine's hospital, while Kathleen and Elizabeth remained to work on the new gowns. The queen traveled, as she always did, in the privacy of the litter, its windows draped to keep out the odors of the city, as well as curious stares. Anna and Blanche rode behind on horseback. As they were leaving the palace, Anna caught a glimpse of Max standing in the courtyard. He gave no indication that he had seen her, despite facing in her direction, and she turned her attention back to Blanche's complaints.

"I cannot believe I have to dress up like a peasant woman," Blanche was saying. "It is all very well and good for you, given your upbringing, but I am a noblewoman, unused to things common and low."

"Not a peasant, Blanche," Anna said. "A gentlewoman. There is a difference."

"Really? If I cannot wear my fine gowns and jewels, then I may as well be a peasant," she said. Anna had no response, and they fell into silence as they traveled across the bridge spanning the river and through the city streets.

The hospital was a solid building, built with funds donated by the queen Mother. Crabapples stood on either side of the entrance, their branches now bare, and the whitewashed walls were dull in the winter drear. Inside, however, warm rugs covered the floors, and brightly colored tapestries hung on the wall of the Mother Superior's office. A silver tray of wine and cakes sat on a table, and when the queen entered the room, she seated herself in the tall wooden chair next to the desk. Ledgers were neatly placed in a pile and taking the first one, she opened the book and started perusing the contents. Anna and Blanche stood at the entrance for a moment, but Matilda waved them away and they headed down the passage to the large dormitory where beds lined the long, wattled walls.

"I hate this task," Blanche muttered under her breath.

"It is our Christian duty to impart words of kindness and encouragement," Anna said piously, but although she would never admit concurrence with Blanche, she could not help echoing her silent agreement. Sickness and old age filled her with revulsion rather than pity, and try as she might, she could not muster the patience and kindness that came to Keira so easily. Suppressing a slight shudder, she moved to the first bed, and taking the frail hand of an elderly woman, sat down on the edge of the thin straw mattress. The woman's skin was mottled with brown spots, and her few remaining strands of hair were white. Her withered and shrunken body was frail, and Anna could not help wondering whether she would fall apart like an old, dry leaf when handled. Her eyes were bright and clear, an odd contradiction to the rest of her form.

"I'm thirsty," she whispered. A table at the end of the room held a jug of watered-down wine, and leaving the old woman, Anna went to fetch her a cup. The woman watched as she moved across the room. "You've been here before," the woman said as Anna walked back, "but you don't come as often as the others. You don't enjoy coming to the hospital, do you?"

Anna glanced down at her hands as a blush rose in her cheeks. "I'm afraid I don't have as much patience as the others," she said.

The woman nodded. "Yes. I can see that. But you are

young. You will learn." The woman peered at her closely.
"You're trying to determine your path in life, aren't you? But
you're not sure what you want." She nodded to herself as
Anna looked at her in confusion. "I can see it in your eyes.
You will find it, with a little patience."

"How do you know?" Anna said.

"Because I am old and have lived many years. And with
age comes wisdom. Learn some patience, child, and you will
find your happiness." The woman lay back on the bed and
closed her eyes. "Now go. I wish to sleep." Anna rose to her
feet and moved to the next bed, where a young man lay with
open, weeping sores on his legs. She suppressed a shiver and
kept her eyes on his face as she spoke to him, but when she
moved to the next bed, she glanced back at the old woman.
Her eyes were still closed, and although Anna looked at her
many times during the visit, she did not open them again.

At last the queen was done and they were ready to leave,
and Anna heaved a sigh of relief. "Thank goodness that is
done," Blanche muttered as she followed the queen into the
sunlight.

At the litter Matilda paused. "You ride in the litter," she
said to Blanche. "Today I travel on horseback."

"My lady?"

"I want to see the city." She waved her hand impatiently.
"Go."

"Yes, my lady," Blanche replied.

Although Anna had never seen Matilda ride before, she
mounted the mare with ease, and they were on the move a
few moments later. As they proceeded back to the palace,
Anna noticed the queen intently watching the people on the
bustling, noisy streets. The people paid little attention to the
passing party, except to quickly step away from the horses'
hooves, pulling their children with them. It was well known
that a nobleman would sooner run someone down than
pause in his journey to ensure a person's safety, and anyone
who interfered with the queen's royal litter would have to

deal with the two guards that accompanied the group.

Matilda leaned towards Anna as they rode. "Are the streets always this busy?" she asked.

Anna glanced around. "Yes, my lady, except on holy days."

"But where are they all going?"

"I expect they are just going about their daily business, my lady. Many people are going to market to buy their meat and eggs, or maybe cloth or pottery. Some might be going to watch a joust, or a play. Some are farmers, selling their produce, and others are tradesmen, setting up shop."

Matilda nodded. "I didn't realize there were so many of them."

They reached the gates of the city and crossed over the river, doubling back along the bank. Across the water they could see the bustling metropolis. Hawkers and tradesmen could still be found along the road on this side of the river, but they had left behind the frenetic pace of Civitas, and Anna could hear the occasional call of a bird as they continued along. The palace came into view, its rising walls reflected in the rippled water of the river, breaking apart and reforming as the river ran its course, unconcerned about the affairs of kings and common men.

They clattered into the courtyard where more guards hurried forward to help Matilda from her saddle. From the shadowy interior of the litter, Blanche emerged, smiling contentedly.

"I do not ever intend to travel by horse or foot again!"

"Really?" Matilda said.

"Except, of course, when Your Majesty commands it," Blanche added, dropping her eyes to the ground as she executed a curtsey.

"Of course," said the queen, sweeping past the women and into the palace.

CHAPTER TWENTY-ONE

Kathleen had spent the hours industriously, and as Matilda walked into the royal chambers, she proudly held up a gown.

"Your gown, my lady," she said. It was dark red, and although the weave was fine, the cut was simple, and the gown was single-toned.

"Let me see," Matilda said, taking the gown from her and holding it against her chest. "It's so plain," she said. "Could we not add some jewels? Or another color?" Kathleen's eager look fell away, and she glanced down at the floor.

"It is the style of a gentlewoman," Anna said.

Blanche gave a little laugh. "Anna would know," she said. "This is probably more elegant than she is used to!"

"At least my life has equipped me for all manner of situations," Anna retorted, "whereas you, Lady Blanche, know nothing at all!"

"Ladies, enough!" Anna dropped her gaze, embarrassed, as the queen glared at the two women. "I will not have you insulting Anna," she said to Blanche, before turning her gaze on Anna. "And you, Anna, have to learn to control your tongue!"

"Yes, my lady," she said.

The queen nodded. "Help me change into my new gown. Let's see how these simpler garments become me."

The morning of the play dawned fair, with a pale sun breaking through the clouds. Betsy helped Anna into her plainest gown, and deftly twisted her hair into a braid, before Anna joined the other ladies about to enter the queen's bedchamber. She was already awake, a frown creasing her brow.

"Make haste," she said, waving away a second cup of wine that Anna offered. In less time than usual she was dressed in Kathleen's red gown. It was then that another problem presented itself. There was no way the queen could escape from her chamber unnoticed by the guards at the door to the apartments, and Matilda insisted that their escapade needed to be kept a secret. The only other person who knew of the adventure was Rupert, who had reluctantly agreed to play the role of escort. Anna wondered what enticement the queen had used to convince him to come, because she was sure that accompanying a group of women into the city would be a terrible trial to a man like Rupert. Or perhaps it was just an opportunity for him to tweak his brother's nose.

"We need a ruse," Anna said, stating the obvious, but it was Kathleen who came up with a plan.

"Your Majesty and I are of similar size," she told the queen, her eyes on the ground as a blush rose in her cheeks. "I can wear one of your gowns and will go by myself into the gardens." Kathleen glanced up to meet Matilda's gaze. "The guards will follow me instead," Kathleen continued. "You can slip out the side door. Once the guards realize it is me, they will leave me alone, and I will meet you on the other bank."

"But your hair is much duller than mine," Matilda said.

Kathleen dropped her gaze. "I will cover my head with a cloak," she whispered. "The guards will think I – you – are seeking some privacy and will keep their distance."

"And when they realize their mistake, they will come looking for me," the queen said. "What will you tell them?"

There was a moment of silence. "I have an idea," Blanche said, "but you will not like it, Your Majesty."

"Continue," she said.

"Kathleen can admit it was a ruse to keep people away from your chambers so you could, er, indulge in a little, er, rendezvous. The guards will stay away from your chambers, and Kathleen will be free to leave."

"Ah! And if the king hears of this little deception?"

"Then my lady will tell him the truth – that it was a ruse to go into the city. By then our adventure will be over."

"I see." The queen turned around, her fingers on her chin as she considered. "Very well. It seems that is the way to proceed. Kathleen, let us find you a gown."

All was in readiness twenty minutes later. Kathleen wore a gown of crimson and blue, embroidered in gold with the royal arms. An indigo cloak covered her head, and she pulled the hood close around her face. Blanche went out first to engage the guards' attention as Kathleen slipped out of the chambers. It only took a moment before the guards saw the figure flitting down the passage, and turned to follow at a discreet distance. The queen, dressed in her new, simple gown, her head covered with a cloak, quickly hurried from the room, Blanche and Elizabeth close behind, and turning in the opposite direction, headed to a side door that opened away from the bustling courtyard. Anna, who had chosen to stay and wait for Kathleen, saw them leave, then sat down to wait for Kathleen's return.

Half an hour had passed before she heard footsteps outside the chambers, and the door opened to reveal Kathleen, with Frank, one of the guards, close on her heel. Anna jumped to her feet.

"Out," she hissed to the guard. She glanced back at the queen's chambers. "If the queen hears you here ..." She left the sentence hanging as she looked pointedly at the man. He glanced in the direction of the chamber, then back at Anna.

"My orders come from the king," he said.

Anna sighed. She dug her hand into the purse at her side, and withdrew a silver coin. "Would it really do any harm to allow the queen some privacy for a few hours?" she asked. Frank looked at the coin, then back at Anna with a shrug. With a silent growl, she pulled out another coin as he watched.

"I suppose not," he said with a smirk, which widened when Anna scowled. "Two coins, two hours," he said.

"Fine," Anna ground out, pulling out one more coin and tossing them at the guard. "Three." He caught them easily and with a mocking bow, turned and left the room. She watched him go, then turned back to Kathleen.

"What happened?"

"Tobias believed me, but Frank followed me back. I don't know why."

Anna sighed. "He must have smelled a rat. There's nothing more we can do. Change your gown and let's begone."

They opened the door a few minutes later and walked into the passage. Both guards were back in place outside the chamber. Anna smiled and nodded at Tobias as Frank watched. He gave her a mocking salute as she walked past, three fingers raised in the air. She ground her teeth in annoyance, but kept her silence. They finally reached the courtyard and headed towards the river where the ferrymen plied the waters. A ferry was approaching the small landing as they arrived, and they stepped onboard, sitting down on the cushions that covered the seats with sighs of relief.

Anna had arranged to meet the queen, Elizabeth, and Blanche at a small tavern on the opposite bank of the river. Its main custom was the ferry passengers, unlike the tavern just a dozen yards away where all manner of unsavory persons could be seen entering and leaving. She found the ladies easily. Rupert stood at the queen's side, thoroughly bored, and although the atmosphere was clean and comfortable, Anna could see that Matilda was ill at ease.

"Let's be on our way," she said.

Rupert led the way out of the tavern and along the hard-packed street. It was not far from there to the main city marketplace, and he led them deftly along the winding streets that led to the large square. There were many markets in the city, but this was the largest, where all manner of goods were sold from places both near and far. Before they had even reached the market, Anna's senses were assailed by evocative sights and smells – the aroma of exotic spices from far-away lands, fruits from the sun-drenched south, cloth and furs, and mixed in between, hawkers selling pies and roasted chestnuts. Memories flooded Anna's mind – Max buying chestnuts for her, holding the burning seeds in his bare hand; Max walking beside her, pausing while she delightedly examined goods she had only ever heard about; Max whispering in her ear to stay close as they pushed through the crowds.

"Your Highness, whatever are you doing here?" The voice behind Anna made her spin around to look at Max bowing before the queen, stepping from her mind and into the street. A few people had paused and were looking at Max and Matilda in surprise.

"Shh," the queen hissed. "You can call me, uh, Mistress, uh, Ann."

Max glanced around, then turned back to the queen with a flourishing bow. "Darling Ann, you will always be queen of my heart, so I call you 'Your Highness'."

There were a few laughs as people turned back to what they were doing. Matilda glanced around anxiously, then seeing that people were no longer paying them any mind, looked at Max suspiciously.

"What are you doing here?"

"Why, the same as you," he replied. "I'm browsing the market."

"You didn't follow me on the king's command?"

"Follow you? No, Your, uh, Mistress Ann." He held out an arm. "But why the disguise?"

"I wish to see a play," she replied, wrapping her arm around his.

"Ah! And you do not wish people to know you are in the audience?"

"Correct!" The queen smiled at him. "You are a smart one."

"I do my best," he said. "May I escort you to this play?" Max glanced around, frowning slightly when he saw the prince leaning against a vendor's table. His eyes rested on Anna for a moment before he turned back to the queen. "But I see you already have an escort."

"Yes, but I am happy to have another man in our company," she said. "Rupert can be so dull." The little party moved forward again, weaving through the narrow gaps between the market stalls. Rupert fell in beside Anna.

"I heard you know our pretty new arrival," he said. "What can you tell me about him?"

Max was walking ahead of Anna, and she watched his back as he walked. She knew that there were ridges that ran along the length of his spine, where strong muscles would stretch and grow taut when his massive wings were spread wide; she knew he could breathe fire when he wished to, enough to burn an entire forest; she knew he was stronger than any human he had ever encountered, but did not use his strength unless provoked. She knew he was not actually human at all, but rather a large, monstrous beast.

"It is wiser to have Max Brant as a friend than an enemy," she said, dragging her attention back to Rupert.

"Really?" Rupert laughed dryly. "Are you referring to his physical prowess? Because there is no-one at court who can best me with a sword, or in a hand-to-hand fight."

"Do not let Master Brant's handsome looks and easy manner fool you," she said. "He is more dangerous than you can imagine."

The prince stared at Max, his head cocked slightly as though sizing him up, then turned a speculative glance back at Anna. "How do you know this? Surely you haven't actually seen him fight?"

"No," Anna replied. "But Master Brant is my sister's kinsman. I have heard stories."

"I see." Rupert looked at Max again. He was bending his head towards the queen with a laugh. Anna glanced around, and a table of gilded cages caught her eye. Within each cage were small, yellow birds, twittering furiously. She moved towards them with a smile.

"They are so pretty!" she said. "Where do you suppose they come from?"

Rupert shrugged. "I have no clue. I have no interest in birds, unless they can hunt. They might make a tasty morsel, though."

"You don't eat them!" Anna said. "You keep them. Like a dog."

"Whatever for? A bird such as this has no use whatsoever."

Max had moved to stand behind Anna while she admired the birds. "It will sing prettily for a lady," he said. She shivered slightly as he moved closer, standing next to her. "Those are canaries, and they come from islands off the coast of Africa."

Anna turned to Max with wide eyes. "Africa?" He nodded. She turned back to the birds and chirruped softly, smiling when the birds twittered back.

"Anna!" Anna turned at the sound of her name to see Kathleen standing at a table of intricate lace. "Come look."

"I'm coming," Anna said. She gave the canaries a last, lingering look, then moved away to look at the work that had caught her friend's fancy.

"Which one should I buy?" Kathleen said.

"This one," Anna said, pointing to a broad length with

scalloped edges. She glanced back to where Max had been standing, but he had returned to the queen's side. Anna turned back to watch Kathleen complete her purchase.

CHAPTER TWENTY-TWO

Max stayed with the small group for the rest of the day. After an hour spent browsing the market, he led them to the cathedral steps, where mummers and performers displayed their talents for a few pennies. The queen laughed and clapped her hands when a tumbler rolled and twirled through the air, and gasped in fear when a man juggled knives, the sharp blades cutting dangerously through the air. Max stood next to Matilda, and he turned to look down at the queen with a smile when she gasped. Rupert stood next to Anna.

"I don't see what the fuss is about," he said, his eyes on the juggler. "With a little practice I could do that."

Anna turned to look at him. "And if he was eating fire, would you say that too?"

"Of course." Anna raised her eyebrows dubiously as Rupert continued. "If a man like that can swallow flames, it would be an easy matter for one such as myself."

"Of course," Anna said, turning her attention back to the performer. He had added a sixth knife to his act, and she glanced away when it looked as though a blade would slice right through his hand, not turning back until a sigh of relief ran through the crowd.

It was not far from the cathedral to the open theater that had been erected near the banks of the river. It was close to the fish market, and as they walked along the river, Anna saw boats of all sizes pulled onto the marshy banks and secured with thick ropes wrapped around poles in the mud. The smell of rotting fish wafted over them, and Blanche was not the only who delicately covered her nose with the edge of her cloak.

Rows of benches had been placed before the stage, already filled with people who were crammed together to squeeze as many in as possible. There were some empty gaps on the bench closest to the back, but Matilda shook her head in distaste when Max pointed them out.

"I can only endure so much," she said. "Find a seat for me and place it at the back, away from the crowds. And make sure you place it where I can see," she added as Max strode off with a slight frown. He came back a few moments later rolling a barrel with his foot. From the smell, Anna guessed it had been used to store salted fish. As Max pulled the barrel upright, Matilda eyed it dubiously, then glanced around. It stood higher than the benches, and it was clear that if she wanted to remain unknown, her options were limited. Gingerly she took a seat on the weathered wooden lid, moving cautiously until she was well placed, then turned her attention to the stage. The actors were busy setting up their props, and all around them people were crowding in to see what was happening. A few moments later, Denton clapped his hands together, shouting over the noise to gain the crowd's attention.

"The show is about to begin," he shouted. "It is entitled *The Soldier and His Lady*." He paused and glanced at the audience, waiting as the noise quieted down. "Imagine, if you will, a soldier saying a fond farewell to his love within the walled gardens of her home. She is heartbroken, of course, at the thought of her lover leaving her side. But he must do his duty for his royal sovereign, and will head to distant lands to fight the barbarians who would threaten us." Denton turned away from the audience, and shrugging a coat over his tunic, turned to the woman who had just walked onto the stage weeping copiously.

The soldier, played by Denton, said his fond farewells, but his lover was distraught at the thought of his departure. Refusing to be left behind, she trailed after him, following the army as it marched from one battle to another. As the final battle neared, the soldier knew that the end was close. A passionate kiss was shared between the pair before he pulled away in an agony of emotion. "Farewell, my love," he shouted, before plunging into a bloody and brutal battle against the wicked foe. Swords and spears plunged into him, but he remained on his feet, shouting his lover's name. "Tilly! Tilly!" Anna glanced at the queen, amused to see her watching Denton fixedly. A final spear thrust went through the soldier's heart, and he fell to the ground, the name still on his lips as he breathed his last. His heartbroken lover, watching from the sidelines of the battle, ran to his side, and grabbing the sword from his dead hands, wrapped her own around the hilt. Anna compressed her lips in an effort to contain a grin as the woman lifted the sword high above her head and plunged it into her heart. She fell down, still for a moment, as the crowd watched in silence, then lifting her head, declared to the audience, "I am dead," before once more dropping her head to the ground, never to move again.

A small snort escaped Anna, and she lifted a hand to her mouth with shamed amusement as the queen turned to glare at her. Another giggle escaped her, and she looked at the ground, biting her lip. She felt a movement beside her, and she glanced up to see Rupert looking at her, his eyebrows furrowed in disapproval.

Anna shrugged helplessly. "It's funny," she said as another giggle found its way out. She clamped her lips together, but it was no use. The harder she tried, the more she laughed, until finally, hands over her mouth, she turned and pushed her way to the back of the crowd. She saw Max standing near the queen, his gaze fixed on the stage, but a grin was tugging at his lips, and she laughed even more. Finally, she reached a place beyond the crowds, and leaning against a wall, gave vent to her mirth. People walking by grinned at her infectious laughter, which only made her laugh more, until finally she turned her face to the wall, and biting her lip, brought herself under control.

By the time she made her way back to the others, most of the crowds had dispersed. The queen was standing next to the stage, while Denton knelt before her. She was stroking his head as though he were an adoring puppy, while the others waited a few feet away. Max was looking on with an expression of distaste, but Rupert seemed to have lost all patience.

"Stop making such a fool of yourself, Matilda," he said. "You'll have the city talking about your display if you continue like this."

"Nonsense!" she said, but she drew her hand away nonetheless. Denton reached up to grab it, but she took a step backwards. "I must be gone," she said, "but we will meet again."

"Even a minute will be too long, my sweet Tilly," he said with a sigh. His eyes were fixed on her, but a dry laugh from Rupert had him glancing at the company watching them. He rose to his feet with a flush. "Of course, my lady," he said, before quickly stepping away and disappearing into the shadows.

By the time the small entourage arrived back at the palace, more than three hours had disappeared. Max had accompanied the queen to the river, securing a ferry for her and her ladies before finally stepping away. He had watched as the small craft was pushed down the river, and Anna's last sight of him was standing on the river bank, his arms folded over his chest as he stood against the lowering light of the day. Rupert had also taken leave of the little party, and it was just the women who stepped off the ferry as the ferryman pulled the boat towards the small landing below the palace lawns.

As they walked towards the palace courtyard, a woman came hurrying out towards them, pausing in obvious surprise when she saw the queen amongst the party, decked out in simple clothes.

"Your Majesty," she said. "I came looking for you, but you were not in your chambers, nor were your ladies," she said. "And," she added, laying emphasis on the word, "your secretary did not know of any appointments that would take you from the palace today."

"Oh, hush, Mary," said the queen. "We have just had the most marvelous adventure. You saw through my disguise, but only because you know me. The people on the streets had no idea they were traversing the roads with their sovereign queen."

"You went into the city, my lady? Dressed like that?"

"Yes, Mary," the queen said, impatience creeping into her tone.

"But why?"

"So I could travel incognito, of course."

"Oh." Mary's gaze lingered on the gown for a moment, her mouth tightening in distaste, before she looked up at the queen. "His Majesty, the king, has been looking for you."

"Then go and give the word I will be with him directly," she said. "Oh, and Mary," she added as the woman turned away, "not a word about my escapades. Understood?"

"Yes, Your Majesty."

"The entire court will know by nightfall," Blanche said as she watched Mary walking away.

"I know," Matilda said. "I just hope I can explain to the king before he catches word in the wind."

Frank and Tobias were standing outside the door when Matilda and her ladies arrived at her apartments. They bowed as she entered the rooms, although Anna could see Frank eyeing the group suspiciously, his gaze pausing on her. He frowned for a moment, then turned away. The gown that Kathleen had discarded earlier had been spread out on the bed, and within a few minutes the queen had donned it and was sitting down for Blanche to do her hair. She was still brushing when a sound at the door had all the ladies turning around to see the king enter the room. Anna dropped into a curtsey as the king strode forward.

"Matty, my dear, we have been searching the palace grounds for you," he said. He was smiling, but beneath the friendliness, Anna could hear the note of irritation. "I was growing concerned that some disaster had befallen you."

"As you can see, my lord, I am quite safe and sound. My ladies and I went into the city."

Alfred frowned. "Why?"

"I wanted to see a play."

"You can see plays anytime you wish to," he said, turning away and pacing the room. "You do not need to sneak away to do so."

"I did not wish to be known," she said.

Alfred stopped his pacing and turned to face her. "You went to see Denton, didn't you?"

"I did."

"Good lord, Matty, could you be any more obvious?"

"I traveled in disguise."

"In disguise? And you did not reveal yourself to Denton?" Matilda was silent. "Who saw you speak to him?" he asked.

"Anyone watching the play." She lifted her chin as she met his gaze. "But no one knew who I was. I could have been a fisherwoman for all they know."

"You are clearly no fisherwoman," he retorted. "Whatever clothes you wore to disguise yourself, anyone with an iota of sense would have seen that you were a noblewoman, and they would have wondered why a noblewoman was traversing the city dressed in rags." He paused. "Who traveled with you?"

"Rupert. And when we encountered Master Brant in the city, he joined us, too."

"Rupert! I'm surprised he would go along with a plan such as this. It is unlike him to be so wanting in sense." Alfred turned to look at the ladies, his gaze falling on Anna. "Along with your other duties, you are expected to provide wisdom and counsel to your queen. You should have talked her out of this foolishness."

"Do not blame my ladies," Matilda said, rising to her feet. "The blame is mine alone. And despite what you say, I do not believe anyone who saw me recognized me for who I am. I will not regret the actions of today."

Alfred nodded. "Well, clearly there is no point in saying more. But my dear, if the slightest whiff of scandal reaches my nose, you will regret it." And with that he turned on his heel and walked out the door, slamming it behind him.

CHAPTER TWENTY-THREE

The next days passed by quickly. Whatever private regrets the queen may have had, she kept them to herself. The king said no more about the affair, and since no other action was taken, his annoyance was soon forgotten. Matilda had enjoyed her adventure thoroughly, and talked often about how delighted she was with the city.

"I will keep my red gown so we can go again," the queen said, a pronouncement that made Anna's heart sink. The king's tolerance could only be pushed so far.

Anna was sitting with Kathleen in the queen's private parlor one afternoon a few days later when a soft knock was heard on the door, followed a moment later by Betsy coming into the room. In her hand she held a cage with rounded sides and a domed top. It stood about eighteen inches high, and perched inside were a pair of bright yellow canaries.

"Excuse me, Mistress, but this was delivered for you," Betsy said, looking at Anna.

Anna rose to her feet. "For me? Who's it from?"

"There's a note, Mistress." Anna took the cage from Betsy's hands and placed it on a nearby table. It was similar to the cages she had seen in the market a few days before, but more intricately wrought, with trailing vines and flowers covering the dome. The note was secured to the cage with a narrow ribbon, and Anna carefully untied it and removed the missive. 'I hope you enjoy many hours of cheerful birdsong,' it read.

"Who's it from?" Kathleen asked eagerly.

"I don't know," Anna said, turning the note over and studying the back. "It doesn't say." She nodded at Betsy, who quickly exited the room.

"It must be from the prince," Kathleen said.

"The prince? It doesn't seem like the kind of thing he would do. And why would he send me a gift?"

"Well, who else? I saw him talking to you when we were in the city. In fact, he barely left your side. And wasn't he with you when you were admiring the birds at the market?"

"He only walked with me because the queen was giving her attention to Master Brant. And Master Brant saw me admiring the birds, too."

"Yes, but why would *he* give you a gift? Everyone knows he's pursuing Mistress Jane."

Anna turned in surprise. "He is?"

"Of course. Why, Blanche was telling me just the other day how Jane has resisted all his advances thus far, but he still keeps dangling after her. She also says ..." Kathleen's voice trailed away, and she dropped her gaze to the hands in her lap.

"Yes?" Anna said. "What else does Blanche say?"

"Nothing," Kathleen said. "I shouldn't have said anything."

"Kathleen?"

Kathleen looked up. "Blanche says it won't be long before you are in the prince's bed, if you are not already," she whispered.

"What?"

"Pray, forgive me, Anna. I know it's not true. At least ... I think ... it's not true, is it?"

"Of course not! I have no interest in the prince whatsoever."

"Oh. It's just …"

"Just what?"

"He does seem to give you more attention than other ladies."

"Only because he finds it amusing when I speak my mind!"

Kathleen dropped her gaze, and Anna reached for her hand. "I'm sorry," she said, "I don't mean to sound so cross."

Kathleen nodded and the subject was dropped, but Anna could not get Kathleen's words out of her mind. Later that day, she pulled Blanche aside.

"What rumors have you been spreading about me?" she said.

"What do you mean?" Blanche's eyes widened in surprise as she gazed at Anna.

"About me and the prince."

"I don't know what you are talking about."

"Did you not tell Kathleen that I would soon be sleeping with him?"

"Certainly not!" Blanche took Anna's hands in her own. "We may have our differences, but I would never say such things. Kathleen must have misheard."

Anna pulled her hands free. "How could she have misheard?"

"I told her that the prince seemed to like you. Maybe she leapt to conclusions."

Anna stared at Blanche. "Very well," she finally said. "But do not talk about me with others."

Blanche nodded. "I won't. I swear." As Anna turned away, Blanche caught her by the arm. "I did hear that the prince sent you a pair of canaries."

"The note wasn't signed, so I cannot say who sent it."

"Well, who else could it be?" Blanche said, echoing Kathleen's words. "He was with you when you were admiring the birds at the market."

"I suppose so," Anna said. "It just doesn't seem like something he would do."

"Well I have no doubts at all," Blanche said. "I am quite convinced that our handsome prince sent it to you, and is intent on pursuing you."

As Anna fell asleep that night, she wondered about it again. Her mind refused to accept Rupert as the giver – it was just too out of character – but who else? Not Max, certainly. The queen? But why would she favor Anna with such a gift? It did not make sense. She was still puzzling over it when she drifted off to sleep, with the sound of rain tapping against the shutters.

She awoke early, startled by the call of an owl as it flew past the window. No-one else had been disturbed, however, and the only other sound was the gentle lull of soft snores and heavy breathing. She lay back on the mattress, but the fright had chased away her sleep. It was still dark outside, but Anna could see the faint stain of light on the horizon through the window. The warm cocoon of blankets kept her curled up for a little longer, until finally she pushed them aside, and pulling on a pair of boots, quietly crept from the room. The rain had turned to snow during the night, and the landscape was blanketed in white. The air was cold, and Anna pulled her cloak tighter around her shoulders as she stepped outside. There was a large fire burning in the center of the courtyard, with a few people huddled around for warmth. They glanced at her as she walked past, but she did not pause. Skirting the gardens, she took the path that led to the wilderness. On the horizon the light was no more than a smudge behind the gray, looming clouds, but it was enough for her to pick her way through the dead blades of grass, which were damp from snow and rain. They brushed against her cloak as she walked, leaving trails and muddying her hem, but she took no notice. She breathed in the bracing air, and watched as her breath formed little clouds of mist that hung in the air for a moment before dispersing.

High above she could hear the discordant cries of geese as they flew overhead, chased away by the cold weather that had arrived overnight. She watched as they passed in their 'V' formation, one side longer than the other. From the end of the shorter arm, a goose pulled out of the line, and flying heavily, pushed ahead of the rest until it reached the front of the formation, taking the place of the leader. The replaced goose fell back, slowing down as the other birds pulled ahead, then headed towards the back of the line. It never made it, however. As Anna watched, the goose suddenly quivered and started falling towards the earth, slowly at first, then gathering speed as it dropped lower. It had been brought down by an arrow – she could see the shaft sticking through its neck – and picking up her skirts, she started to run in the direction of the falling bird. She could not have explained what impulse propelled her forward – perhaps it was seeing a winged creature being felled from the sky, or maybe it was just that the early morning peace seemed shattered by the act of violence. She was not unused to seeing animals die – it was a part of life, after all. But something had touched her, and she started to run.

She heard a dog barking, and then the sound of voices. In the low light she could make out the forms of three men, and recognized Rupert amongst the group. She was panting as she reached them, and Rupert turned to look at her in surprise. In one hand he held a bow, and in the other, the lifeless form of the goose Anna had seen falling, the arrow still pierced through its neck. The ground at Rupert's feet was stained red with blood, while a dog sniffed and whined, jumping from time to time at the dead bird which dangled above its nose.

"Anna," Rupert said dryly. "I suppose I shouldn't be surprised."

"Why did you shoot that goose?" she said. Rupert's expression narrowed.

"Do you think I have to explain my actions to you?" he said.

"Well ..." She glanced at the two men standing behind him. She recognized them from the time he had been hunting with the falcon. One of the men was clutching a brown hessian sack, and he stared at her in disbelief, while the other man smiled slyly. Rupert dropped the bird on the ground and stalked towards her.

"I do not need to explain myself to anyone, least of all you," he said.

Anna stared back at him for a long moment, then glanced at the other men. She took a step backwards. "Of course, Your Highness," she said.

"Now go," he said. He turned his back to her and picked up the goose as she slowly walked backwards away from the men. She did not go far, but stopped next to a tree to watch. With a quick motion, Rupert pulled the arrow out of the dead bird, then dropped it in the sack that the man held open. A quiver of arrows was slung over Rupert's back, and reaching over his shoulder, he pulled another one out, glancing up at the sky as he did so. The geese were gone, of course, but something else had caught his eye. Following the direction of his gaze, Anna looked up and saw a creature circling in the sky high overhead, a mere blot against the clouds.

"What's that?" Rupert asked.

One of the men shrugged. "It is too far to tell, Your Highness," he said. "Perhaps a crane."

"Let's find out," Rupert said. He lifted his bow to his shoulder, and notched the arrow. Looking up again, Anna saw that the creature was circling lower and lower. The light was still too dim to make out what it was, but as she watched, she saw a glint of light reflecting from its back.

"No," she whispered. "Get away from here." Had the creature heard her? It continued to circle around. "No," she said, "he's going to shoot." Rupert pulled the bow taut against his shoulder, and she drew in a breath as he released it, sending it straight towards the creature. "No!" she screamed. She saw Rupert turn towards her with a start, but a moment later he was turning back to the creature in the sky. Anna could no longer see the arrow, but surely it must have hit its mark by now. "Max," she whispered. She saw Rupert pointing at the creature, which circled around one more time, then turned in the direction of the river and disappeared from view. Anna watched the place where he had disappeared, willing him to come back, hoping he would stay away. Her heart was racing in her chest, and her mouth felt as dry as sand. Inside her boots her feet were numb, but she barely noticed.

She stayed there for a long time, staring at the sky, but Max did not reappear. What had he been thinking, flying above the prince while he hunted? Surely he had seen the danger! When it became clear that his target had escaped, Rupert and his men moved away without another glance in her direction, heading towards the forest, but she gave them no heed. Had Max been injured? She had no way of knowing, but the thought of him dying, or dead, made her stomach twist into knots. The sun had risen behind the clouds, a dull, milky light, by the time Anna finally made her way back to the palace, dragging her feet slowly through the snow. Her boots were coated in a thick layer of mud, and she could no longer feel her fingers.

She was nearly at the courtyard when a young boy ran up to her. A thick mop of dirty blond hair fell over his forehead, and his cheeks were red from the cold. In his hand he held a long package, which he shoved towards her.

"I was told to give you this, Mistress," he said. She looked down at the package in his small hands, and slowly took it from him. It was long, narrow, and very light. The boy spun on his heel and started running back across the courtyard.

"Wait," she called after him. "Who gave it to you?"

"A man," he replied, shouting over his shoulder. "He gave me a ha'penny to give it to you."

Anna looked at the package again. Wrapped in thick oilcloth and bound with twine, there was nothing to indicate what it was or who it was from. Walking over to a low wall that ran along the edge of the courtyard, Anna sat down and examined the package a little closer. The twine had been knotted, but although the knot was not tight, Anna's fingers were cold, and she fumbled for a few moments in frustration until she used her teeth to loosen the binding. She eased the string off the package, and pulling it open, stared down at the arrow that lay within. Its shaft was slightly bent, and one of the striped feathers had been broken. It had an iron arrowhead, about three inches long, but when Anna ran her finger over it, she saw that the tip of the metal had been bent, folded over like a piece of paper. She lifted the arrow and turned it over in her hand; it was then that she saw the small piece of paper rolled tightly around the shaft. Pulling it loose, she placed the arrow on the wall and opened the note. 'A mere arrow is useless against a beast,' it read. It took another two readings before the meaning sunk into her frozen mind, and then she smiled. Of course, she should have known that!

She remained sitting on the wall until the cold seeped through her clothes. Tucking the note into her bodice with fingers that were turning blue, she wrapped the arrow in the cloth once more, and carefully hid it in the folds of her gown. She had just risen to her feet when she heard a voice calling her name, and turned to see Frank heading her way.

"I have been sent to look for you," he said. "The other ladies are concerned you were abducted during the night. I told them I doubted that, since you are too wily to allow someone to make off with you, but they insisted I search the grounds for your dead and lifeless body."

"Well, here I am, quite safe and sound," she said. She turned towards the palace entrance and he fell in step next to her.

"I know the way. No need to accompany me."

"Oh, I know you know the way," he said. "I'm just

wondering what you are up to. Perhaps you are a spy."

"A spy?" Anna laughed. "What a ludicrous idea. I went for a walk."

Frank grunted. "Ladies do not go for walks when it is this cold," he said.

"Don't you know," Anna replied, sweeping past him, "I am not a lady!"

CHAPTER TWENTY-FOUR

The colder temperatures remained, along with a mixture of rain, sleet, and snow, which made the surrounding countryside bleak and drear. The damp found its way into every corner of the palace, settling into the quilts, worming through garments, and shrouding the rugs placed on the cold, stone floors. Fires were lit in every room, their blazing heat creating a small circle of warmth that drew people around in a huddle.

But the cold did not dampen the spirits of those who lived and worked within the walls of the palace, for Christmastide was fast approaching, bringing with it plans for feasting and music, dances and plays. The courtyard was a hive of activity as entertainers came and went – mummers and musicians, actors, jugglers, and jesters. Children ran through the corridors, their squealing laughter and noisy games adding to the cacophony. The royal children joined in the games, until they were dragged away by a disapproving nurse, back to their lessons. At every meal the great hall was packed with people seeking shelter from the cold and warm food in their bellies, conversation and laughter rising above them all and drifting to the rafters. The king and queen presided over the meals from their table on the dais, and laughed as uproariously as the common folk on the floor. Different entertainments were offered every evening after dinner – a yarn from a traveling storyteller; a conjuror who made items appear out of the air; a haunting tale sung in verse. And when no entertainment had been planned, the tables were pushed away for an impromptu dance.

There was only one thing that disturbed Anna's peace in these happy and busy days. Max was a frequent visitor at the palace, and a favorite amongst the woman at court. Despite Kathleen's assertion that he was pursuing Mistress Jane, there was nothing in his manner to suggest that he held her in any special regard. In fact, it seemed that all that was needed to engage his attention was a swish of a skirt. He smiled at every woman who passed his way, and offered his hand for every dance. When his eye caught Anna's, he would smile in a friendly manner, and nod his head, but then turn to the next woman with a smile equally as warm. Of course, Anna knew that she had lost any chance of engaging Max's heart – the fact that he had stayed away for so long confirmed that – but she had hoped he would give her a little more regard than the other women at court. They were related by marriage, were they not? But he did not speak to her beyond a few words of greeting, and did not seek out her company. In fact, apart from those few polite words, he ignored her completely. And so she ignored him too – as much as she was able. She maintained her distance when the tables were pushed aside for a dance, and took her place on benches far away from where he sat. And when she was near him, she steeled her heart against the man whose memory lay deep in the recesses of her soul.

It had been another gray day, but tonight there was to be a special treat. A monk had arrived at court that morning, and he had in his possession a copy of *Sir Gawain and the Green Knight*. The story of the strange knight who challenged one of King Arthur's men to deliver a felling blow to his neck was not unfamiliar amongst well-learned people, but few had heard the original tale. And tonight, after supper, Friar James would read his precious manuscript in the great hall. The monk had been given a place of honor at the raised table, and ale had flowed freely into his cup all evening. Beside him sat Rupert, who listened resignedly as the man attempted to engage him in animated conversation, crumbs flying from his mouth as he punctuated his sentences with a fat fist clutched around a shank of lamb, the other clutching a hunk of bread.

Anna watched in delighted amusement as Rupert leaned a few inches away from the spray of food and ale, a look of distaste souring his expression. His eyes roved the hall, then stopped when they reached her. She looked away, turning to hear what Kathleen was saying, but something drew her eyes back to the prince. He was watching her thoughtfully, his eyes narrowed, and when his gaze caught hers, he stared at her for a long moment before turning away. Anna glanced down at her hands. There had been something disconcerting in his look, as though he were a hunter, and she, the prey.

The remains of the dinner were cleared away, and there was a scraping of chairs and benches as people settled down to enjoy their evening's entertainment. A high stool had been placed at one end of the dais, where Friar James would sit and tell his tale, while the king and queen remained at the table. The two younger children were in the nursery, but Prince John had been given permission to join the adults in the hall and listen to the story. He sat beside his father, glowing with excitement as the monk prepared to tell his tale. Anna sat near the dais, and when Rupert rose to his feet she glanced up, her eye drawn to the movement. He stepped from the platform and bent over Blanche, whispering something in her ear. Her eyes flew to Anna for the briefest moment as he spoke, and she nodded. Anna watched curiously. There was something strange about Blanche's expression. She wondered what it could mean, then pushed the matter from her mind as the monk began his tale.

"King Arthur lay royally at Camelot at Christmastide with many fine lords, the best of men, all the rich brethren of the Round Table, with right rich revel and careless mirth. Suddenly there burst in at the hall door an awesome being, in height one of the tallest men in the world. All green was this man and his clothing, and the horse that he rode was of the same color too."

The story told of how Sir Gawain rose to the challenge of exchanging blows with the green knight. The unknown knight would accept the first blow, and then, one year later, Sir Gawain would have to present himself to accept his blow. With one swift swing of his axe, Sir Gawain cut off the head of the green knight, who stood motionless before Sir Gawain. But the challenge was not finished, as Gawain quickly realized when the headless body picked up its head and placed it back on his neck.

The crowd gasped in surprise, and Anna shivered. A headless body was enough to give anyone nightmares. She glanced at the dais, and smiled when she saw Prince John's pale face.

A sigh of relief was heard through the room when Sir Gawain's life was spared one year later, and Anna could not help grinning. There had been no dragons, but it was still a marvelous tale.

"Did you enjoy the story?" she asked Kathleen, who was sitting across from her. Kathleen shivered.

"I'm not sure I'll be able to sleep tonight," she whispered, glancing around the hall as though she expected a green knight to appear from the shadows.

"You're not the only one," Anna said with a laugh, looking pointedly at the main table. Rupert had returned to his seat near his brother, and during the course of the story, young Prince John had maneuvered his way to his uncle's side. When Rupert whispered something in his nephew's ear, she saw him turn a wide-eyed gaze on his uncle, who returned the look with upraised eyebrows. A woman came forward – one of the nursery staff – and held her hand out to John, but it was the queen who, turning around to see her son, led the young prince away. Rupert watched for a moment, then he too rose and followed the exiting pair. A hubbub was growing as people rose to their feet and chatted excitedly. The monk had been a wonderful reader, and approval of the evening seemed to be the consensus of the crowd.

"I think I'll return to our chambers," Anna said to Kathleen. Blanche had disappeared a few minutes earlier, and Elizabeth had joined a small crowd towards the back of the hall. "Are you coming?"

"Yes! I don't want to walk back alone!"

Anna laughed. "I think you are quite safe from green knights lurking in the palace corners," she said.

The corridors through the palace were dimly lit with just a few lamps along the long passages, and they walked quickly up the stairs to the wing where the queen's apartments were located. Anna's hand was already reaching for the latch when she heard a voice calling her name. She turned around to see Blanche hurrying towards her. "The queen wants to see you right away," she said.

Anna pulled back in surprise. "Why? Where is she?"

"She was taking the little prince to the nursery when he fell and hurt himself. She asked me to fetch you."

"But why me? Surely it is a nurse you are wanting?"

"I don't know why she asked for you," Blanche said. "Should I go back and ask her?" She crossed her arms as she stared at Anna.

"Very well. I'm coming," she said.

"Follow me," Blanche said, but when Kathleen started to follow, Blanche stopped. "Just Anna," she said.

"Don't be silly," Anna said. "Of course Kathleen can come."

"The queen was very clear. Bring Anna and no-one else."

Anna paused. Some kind of game was afoot. But if the queen had sent for Anna and she didn't come ... She nodded her head, and followed Blanche back down the passage.

"Why are we going this way?" Anna said as Blanche led her up a narrow staircase. "This isn't the way to the nursery."

"We aren't going to the nursery," Blanche said, glancing over her shoulder. "He was in Rupert's chambers when the accident happened."

"What?" Anna stopped. "Where is the queen?"

"She's with her son, of course. What's wrong with you?" She turned, her eyes meeting Anna's in the dull light. "You don't want to keep the queen waiting."

Anna stared back at Blanche. It was entirely possible that the queen had taken John to see his uncle, though not likely. But to disobey the queen would invite censure. She thought a moment, then nodded, picking up her skirts to follow Blanche again. They wound their way through several more passages, down some stairs and up others, until Blanche finally stopped in front of a large wooden door. Anna had never been in this part of the palace before, and she wondered how Blanche knew the way. Blanche paused a moment to push the door open, and then gestured for Anna to enter.

The room Anna stepped into clearly belonged to a man. Dark, heavy fabrics hung over the windows, and the walls were paneled with dark wood, upon which were tapestries and paintings depicting various hunting and battle scenes. A low fire blazed in the hearth, the only source of light in the room.

Anna turned around and saw a figure standing in the shadows, arms crossed over his chest. Rupert stepped forward into the dim light.

"Where is he?" she said. She saw his eyebrows rise slightly. "John," she clarified. "Is he lying down?"

"Ah, John. No, you will not find him here." Rupert glanced at Blanche, gesturing with his head toward the door.

"Go," he said. Anna looked at Blanche.

"You tricked me," she said, but Blanche was already slipping out the door. It closed with a soft click. Anna turned back to look at Rupert.

"I knew it was the only way to get you here," he said.

She took a step backwards. "Why?"

He shrugged. "I find you interesting. You are frank and honest. I am curious to know what you would be like in bed."

"In bed?"

"It will be mutually beneficial, of course. You can learn how to pleasure a man, and I will ensure you keep your position with Matilda."

She shook her head. "No." She swallowed. "I will not sleep with you."

"Come, now Anna. You are an intelligent woman. Surely you aren't prudish?"

She stared at him. "Do you really think I would risk my reputation so easily? For a man I do not love?"

"Love has nothing to do with it. And your reputation as my mistress will secure your future." He took a step towards her. "I see that this comes as a surprise, and I am not a brute who will force a woman against her will. But know this, Anna. I always have my way. I expect you to present yourself, happy and willing, tomorrow evening at this time."

"And if I don't?"

He took another step closer. "Then you will discover what happens when you cross a prince. It was me who brought you to Matilda's attention. As you have been raised up, so I can bring you down."

He was almost on her now, and reaching out his hand, he ran his fingers over her lips. "I can promise you this, however. You will enjoy it when you surrender to me."

She turned her head away. "Never," she hissed.

"Very well," he said, and she could hear cynical amusement in his voice. "You can be soft and yielding, or you can fight me like a cornered cat. But you will be here tomorrow night. Now go." She looked at him in dismay as he took a step back. A cornered cat, indeed! She walked to the door, and without a backward glance, left the room.

CHAPTER TWENTY-FIVE

It was only as Anna walked down the corridor that the trembling started. She could feel it in her legs, and she reached out her hand to steady herself against the wall. Her hands were shaking too, and she felt a tightness in her chest that hadn't been there before. She pressed her hands flat against the cool stone surface, and taking deep breaths, tried to slow her racing heart. She heard voices coming down the corridor and she moved to a corner, pulling herself into the shadows. A group walked by, their laughter ringing against the stone, and she cringed. She needed to get outside, where the cold air would fill her lungs and she could find silence for her turbulent thoughts.

She waited until it was quiet once more, then hugging the wall, hurried along the passage. There was a small spiral staircase in the corner, away from the main corridors, and she headed towards it. Blanche had brought her this way, only minutes before.

At the bottom of the staircase was a narrow arched doorway. Anna grabbed the latch and pushed the door open with a creak. It resisted at first, then swung open into the cold night air. She stepped outside and shivered. Behind her the door swung shut, closing out the meager light and warmth, and she rubbed her arms and stepped away. The door had opened out into a small, frozen patch of muddy ice, bordered by large bushes that looked as though they were seldom tended. A well-worn path led from the door, but the bushes had overgrown it. Ducking her head, she pushed her away past the bare branches, grimacing when she heard the tearing of fabric. Sharp twigs scratched her skin, and shards of ice on the ground cut into her slippers. When she finally broke free of the tangle with a grunt, she gave a small smile of triumph.

She glanced around, trying to decide where she was. The sky was dark, the stars and moon hidden behind a curtain of cloud. She listened for a moment – from the right she could hear the distant sound of music and laughter, but up ahead she could hear a faint ripple of water. Tentatively she felt her way forward, and after a few minutes she caught the merest glimpse of light reflecting on the river. She continued to walk, and finally could make out the gray slash of water cutting through the landscape. A thin layer of ice clung to its edges, but in the middle the river was moving sluggishly.

She walked toward the bank, stopping at the water's edge. A weeping willow dipped its branches in the water – the same one where Rupert had first taken notice of her. She shivered, and moved away. If only she had never wandered to the river on the night of the ball! She drew in a deep breath, and felt the cold stinging her lungs. A drop of rain landed on her arm, and she looked down at it. If she stayed in the rain long enough, would she eventually melt away? More drops landed, on her cheek, in her hair, on her hand. Reluctantly, she moved back to the shelter of the willow.

There was a movement of air, and she glanced around, startled. Someone was coming towards her. Her heart started to race. Was it Rupert? It was too dark to tell. But then she heard her name, and she felt herself relax.

"Max," she breathed. "It's you."

"Yes," he said. She could see his features now in the dim light. "You're trembling." He touched her arm. "And freezing. Here." With a quick motion, he stripped off his tunic and pulled it over her head. It was warm. "What are you doing out here?"

"Just thinking." She looked back at the river. Max stood next to her, looking at her for a long moment, then slowly, gently, placed his hands on her shoulders and turned her to face him.

"What happened?"

She shook her head. "Nothing. It's … nothing." She looked up at him, and he caught her gaze. She could see the flames at the back of his eyes, just a flickering deep within stormy gray. She held her breath.

"Tell me," he said. And so she did. She told him how she had first met Rupert, and how he had mentioned her to the queen. She told him about the falcon, and the canaries. How Blanche had tricked her. And Rupert's demand. And then she fell silent.

"Did he hurt you?" he asked.

"No."

"What will you do?"

"I won't go." She was surprised to see him relax slightly. She hadn't realized how tense he was.

"You could leave here and return to Drake Manor. Or Storbrook," he said.

Anna stared at the river for a long moment. "No," she finally said. "I won't give in to his demands, but I won't run away, either."

For the first time Max smiled. "That's my girl," he said. He took her by the hand. "There's a log further downstream – let's sit." She nodded. The log was a little beyond the willow, and Max sat down beside Anna. He was not touching her, but his heat pulsed though the air, surrounding her like a cocoon. He glanced at her with a frown.

"Rupert won't stop until he has what he wants," Max said.

Anna nodded. "I know. But if I tell the queen —"

"She won't stop him," Max said. Anna looked at him in surprise. "But I don't think she will easily get rid of you, either. Rupert may underestimate the affection she has for you." He shrugged. "Or overestimate the influence he exerts over her. Either way, I think your position as lady-in-waiting is safe for now. Your reputation, however, may not be."

"What do you mean?"

"Do you think Rupert will take your refusal lightly? He will do whatever he can to get his way, including destroying your name, if he thinks it will break you."

"Surely not!"

"He is very determined. Don't forget, I have known him since he was a child."

Anna smiled. "I had forgotten how old you are!"

"Old? No, I'm a youngster compared to your brother-in-law."

"Well, he's ancient." Max laughed, and Anna shivered. They fell silent for a moment. "He gave you a pair of canaries?" Max said.

Anna glanced at him. "It seems quite unlike him, doesn't it? But I cannot think who else might have sent them."

"You admired the canaries at the market. Who else saw you?"

"The queen, of course, but that doesn't make sense. And Kathleen, but why would she hide it?"

"Who else?"

"Well, you." She looked up at him, surprised to see him watching her intently. "You," she whispered. "You sent them to me."

"I could see you liked them." He turned away, and was silent for a moment. "Aaron asked me to look out for you while you were here," he finally said.

"So the canaries are from Aaron?" He didn't reply. "Why did you send them?"

"Aaron and Keira want you to be happy."

"Oh." Anna turned away to look at the river. "Thank you." He nodded. She felt Max's eyes on her, but she kept her gaze on the rippling water.

"Are you ready to return to the palace?" he said. Anna took a deep breath.

"Yes." He rose to his feet and held out his hand. She looked at it for a moment, then placed hers within it. His hand was so much larger, with long fingers that curled around hers. They were warm, and when he rubbed his thumb over the back of her hand, she felt the heat spread up her arm. She rose to her feet, but kept her eyes to the ground. It may have been years since they had spent time together, but he knew her. And if she looked at him now, he would see right into her soul.

They walked along the river, hand in hand. His chest was naked since he had given her his tunic, and she saw now that his feet were bare as well.

"If anyone sees me now, my reputation will be thoroughly ruined," she said. "At least I can argue that the prince commanded me to be with him, but I have no such argument for being with you."

Max smiled. "I can command you, if you like."

"I'm afraid your command does not carry the same amount of weight."

"No?" Max glanced down at her. "You would defy a dragon?" Anna was silent.

The sounds of the palace grew louder as they approached the courtyard.

"Aaron told me to be careful around the men at court," she said. "He said nothing about trusting other women, however."

"There was no reason for you to suspect Blanche," he said. "And being too mistrustful only brings unhappiness." She glanced at him, but he was looking away. She stopped and tugged off his tunic.

"Here, you must take this," she said, handing him the

garment, shivering as the cold air touched her neck.

"You need it more than I do," he said, pushing it back at her.

"I cannot walk into the palace wearing your tunic," she said. He smiled reluctantly.

"No, I suppose not."

"Besides, it wouldn't be proper if you saw Mistress Jane without a tunic," she added.

"Mistress Jane? Why in the world would I see Mistress Jane?" He tilted his head and gave her a scrutinizing look as she raised her eyebrows. He leaned closer. "You know, you really shouldn't listen to rumors," he said.

She smiled. "I know."

Blanche was sitting in the parlor when Anna entered the room.

"Did you enjoy your evening?" she asked.

Anna stopped. "Enjoy my evening?" she said. "If you are referring to Rupert, I left just a few minutes after you." She moved a few steps towards Blanche. "How could you do that to me?"

"Do what, Anna? Set you up for an evening with a prince?"

"You knew perfectly well I was not interested in an evening with the prince," Anna said. "You lied to me! You betrayed my trust!"

"Please Anna, don't be so dramatic. I was just giving you the chance to further your acquaintance with Rupert."

"He wants me to be his mistress!"

"You should be flattered!" Blanche rose to her feet. "Welcome to the real world, Anna," she said. "A world where men have the power and control." Anna was silent as Blanche continued. "I first learnt about men when I was twelve," she said, "when I was raped by my uncle. When I told my father what had happened, he congratulated me on becoming a woman!" Blanche's eyes narrowed. "I also told my mother, and you know what she said? That I was fortunate it happened when I was already twelve. She had been ten when her cousin raped her." Anna pulled in a deep breath as Blanche continued. "My father married me off at the age of fifteen to a man eighteen years my senior. He contracted a fever ten months later and was carried off, thank God. He would come to my room every night, pull down his stockings, drag me to the end of the bed and force himself on me. He didn't even lie down, but did it standing. The first night I thought I would please him by touching him, but he beat me for that. The second night I told him I was feeling unwell, and he beat me for that. I quickly learned that the best thing was to keep quiet and let him do what he wanted. That way it was over in minutes, and I was left in peace."

"Oh, Blanche, I'm sorry," Anna said. Blanche stepped back as Anna drew closer.

"I don't want your pity," she said. "I'm just telling you how things work in the real world."

"And is what you are doing any better?"

"Don't be so naïve, Anna. I am just aligning myself with the winning side. Rupert will get what he wants, and by helping him, I secure my own position."

"How can you be so cruel?"

"Cruel? The world is a cruel place. I look out for myself and no one else."

Anna took a step away. "I'm sorry for all the terrible things you have endured, Blanche, but you are wrong about the world. Not all people are cruel. But you will never know that if you do not allow kindness into your life." She walked over to the door that led to the bed chambers, but paused before opening it and turned to look at Blanche. "I do pity you," she said, "but not because of the things you have endured. I pity you because you will not allow the light to shine into your dark, miserable world."

CHAPTER TWENTY-SIX

The queen was in a state of agitated excitement the following morning. She had received word from her brother that he was coming to the palace. She had not seen him since she was sent away to marry Prince Alfred, twelve years earlier. She had been a princess in her own right, coming from the land beyond the mountains, the youngest of six royal children. The previous king had died three years before, in the prime of his life, from a festering wound caused in a hunting accident, and his death had plunged the country into turmoil. He had expected to live for many more years and had not bothered to name a successor. His son, Prince Roderick, the only son to survive to adulthood, was not popular amongst the nobles of the land, who instead threw their support behind another contender. Prince Roderick's cousin Terran was far more to the liking of the nobles – tall, swarthy and robust. He was clever, but not too clever. Ambitious, but with a sense of justice and an ear for the people. And so Terran's supporters had taken advantage of Roderick's grief to imprison him in his hunting lodge, until Roderick finally escaped through a window at night. He had found a ship to carry him along the coast, away from his kingdom, and ever since had been drumming up support and funds for his cause. And now he had arrived at Matilda's court, having sent a note to his sister to meet him in the hall at eleven o'clock.

Matilda bustled around excitedly, urging her ladies to make haste with her toilette. Finally she was ready, and she set off at a brisk pace in the direction of the hall, her ladies trailing behind along the passages. She paused for a moment as they reached the hall, peeking in through the door as she smoothed her gown and patted down her hair, before entering with stately grace. Facing the entrance was a company of around fifty men, and when one of them stepped forward, his hands outstretched, Anna looked at him curiously. Prince Roderick was a small, slight man, pale and wan. His legs were thin and slightly bowed. His outstretched hands were long, with the slender fingers of an artist or musician. Anna knew he was only a few years older than Matilda, but his face was care-worn, with deep lines around his eyes and mouth. He smiled as he moved forward, his hands grasping his sister's arms as he looked into her face.

"Matty," he said with a smile. "It is good to see you again, my dear one."

"Roddy." They smiled at each other for a long moment, until Matilda turned and indicated some cushioned chairs, placed facing each other near the huge fireplace. "Let's sit," she said.

They sat together for a long while. Roderick told of their father and his last days. He spoke of his escape from the hunting lodge, and the storms he had endured as he traveled by sea along the coast. He talked about the foreign courts he had visited, and the route he had traversed to finally reach his sister. He spoke of his plans to regain his throne and overthrow their cousin, the usurper to the throne. He had amassed a small army, a number of whom had joined him in his journey to Alfred and Matilda's court and now stood arrayed around the hall, listening in silence. He had been promised funds and given gold and jewels to enable his fight. And he had asked for the blessing of God and the church on his mission.

As they talked, Alfred entered the room. He had met Roderick once before, when Roderick served as an emissary to Alfred's court, and he gave him a friendly greeting now. Matilda rose to her feet, and with a smile at her brother, gestured for her ladies to follow her from the room.

Anna trailed behind them in silence. She had slept very little the previous night and was tired. She was already a few paces back when she rounded a corner and saw Rupert coming her way. His gaze fell on her, and his eyes narrowed. She dropped her head and turned away, but he grabbed her arm as she walked past. "What game do you think you are playing?" he said, his voice low and angry. His hand was tight on her arm, and he glared down at her as he spoke.

"I'm not the one playing a game," she said. She tugged at her arm, and his grip tightened, making her wince.

"I elevated you, then singled you out for preferment. But what do you do? Scorn what I offer and throw it in my face. Any other woman in this palace would be honored to be so noticed. But you? A commoner? You seek to destroy me."

"What?"

"You went running to Max Brant, and he spoke to my brother this morning. The king has threatened to exile me if I come near you again." She drew in a breath as he bent his mouth close to her ear. "Mark my words, Anna. I will not be mocked. You will reap the rewards of this treachery." He pulled back and glared at her for a moment, before thrusting her away and marching off. There were marks on Anna's arm where he had grabbed her, and she rubbed them distractedly as she considered Rupert's words. Max had spoken to the king! Why had he done that?

The other women had already disappeared from view, and Anna hurried to catch up. The queen's apartments lay in a different wing of the palace, past the exit to the courtyard and up the grand staircase. She was nearing the stairs when a voice made her glance around. Max was in the midst of a small group of women, Jane among them, laughing at some joke. Changing direction, she headed his way.

"Master Brant, I would have a word with you," she said, stopping behind Max's back. She saw one of the women raise her eyebrows, while another whispered something to Jane. Max stared at Jane for a long moment, before turning slowly from the group and looking Anna up and down. He turned back to the women.

"Ladies," he said, "will you please excuse me. It would appear that I am wanted." He grinned at Anna, who scowled back. He followed her as she walked away from the group, pausing when she stopped and turned to face him.

"Did you speak to the king?" she demanded.

Max's smile vanished as he glanced at the group of women watching them curiously. Taking Anna by the arm, he led her to the far wall.

"I did," he said.

"Why?"

"Why? Because the prince wants you in his bed, and will coerce you into accepting. How did you think he would react when you didn't show up in his apartments this evening? Do you really think Rupert is the kind of man to take no for an answer? He would have forced you to do his will one way or another."

"I would not have allowed him to! I would have made sure I was never alone with him."

"Anna," Max said, a note of impatience creeping into his voice, "You live under the same roof as him. Would you have avoided the hall? And the passages? You enjoy roaming the gardens and the wilderness. Would you have been content to remain indoors? And even if you did manage to avoid seeing him, there are plenty of people at the palace prepared to do his bidding. Your lack of willingness to do as he wished would only have added to the thrill of the chase."

"Well, now he intends to make me pay. The king threatened him with exile, and he is not happy."

"Exile, hmm? The king must have a lot of respect – or fear – for Aaron if he is willing to go that far." Anna lifted her eyebrows in unspoken question. "I reminded him that you are under Aaron's protection, and it might be in his best interests to keep his brother's behavior in check."

"You should have left it alone," she said. "Your interference has made things worse." Max leaned closer, and she could smell the fire emanating from him.

"My interference," he said through clenched teeth, "has saved you the anguish of being forced against your will."

"You are so arrogant," she hissed. "I never asked for your protection. You should have left well alone."

"I'm being arrogant? You haven't changed at all, Anna! Still the same foolish little girl you always were. I have saved you more times than I can remember, and you continue to look at me with disdain." He glared down at her, and she could see the flames growing at the back of his eyes. With a low growl, he pushed himself away from the wall, and turning his back to her, he strode away, flinging open the door to the courtyard with a hand clenched into a fist.

CHAPTER TWENTY-SEVEN

War! The word spread through the palace like wildfire. Alfred was going to the kingdom beyond the mountains to wage war against Terran, usurper to the crown and enemy to King Alfred, and reclaim the throne for the true heir to the throne, King Roderick. The fact that Terran bore no love for King Alfred and had imposed tariffs on goods coming from his kingdom only gave further weight to the case for war. Even so, Alfred, known for his caution, had not agreed easily – it had taken Roderick all of the Christmas season to convince him to join his cause. In the meantime he enjoyed Alfred's hospitality, feasting in his hall and enjoying his entertainments. When Alfred finally agreed to lend his support to Roderick's cause, Matilda had been thrilled. Roderick left the following morning, traveling to other realms to raise further support.

Word of the war quickly spread to the distant corners of the kingdom. Through the cold and dismal weeks of January, knights of the realm, trained soldiers with decades of fighting experience, had started gathering in the city; and in the sodden countryside beyond the palace walls, peasant soldiers and commoners were congregating, eager to share in the spoils of war.

Rupert had been dispatched to organize the inspection of the volunteers and the signing up of new recruits. Men poured into Civitas each day, and were put through their paces before being accepted into the king's forces. Men too old to handle a sword were sent home, while boys as young as twelve were given the tasks of cleaning armor, digging latrines and running messages. Most of the new recruits had little experience with war, being farmers or craftsmen, and were assigned to the infantry – the division that led the charge into battle. They were also the division that would suffer the most losses – the pawns of the battlefield. A few brightly colored tents were erected for those fortunate enough to merit such distinction, but most of the new soldiers made makeshift shelters on the ground with branches, or whatever other materials were at hand. Meat, grains and vegetables were distributed amongst the men each day, which they prepared over fires that sent trails of smoke into the sky day and night, extending the pall that hung over the city. When darkness fell the men huddled in groups around their small fires, trying to find a little warmth in the winter chill.

Smiths set up forges within the camp, sharpening swords and axes for a small price, and making armor for those able to afford such extravagancies. The most popular items were helmets, with a red feather plume so soldiers could identify their compatriots, and something to protect the chest. Chain mail was the more sought-after option, being light and more flexible than the solid and heavy plate armor, but was also more expensive. And so each man supplied for himself what he was able. When he could not afford metal armor, leather armor would have to do; made with a thick padding beneath a layer of boiled leather, it could protect a man from an otherwise fatal blow. When a man was not practicing with his weapons, he spent his time making new ones – long pikes for the infantry; swords for the cavalry; and arrows, with metal tips and feathered ends for the archers.

A war council was convened, led by the king. Prince Rupert was appointed Army Commander, second only to the king, while a team of advisors were selected to serve on the council. Roderick had a seat on the council too, of course, along with Lord Wetherton and Lord Eastwich. Wetherton, the king's cousin, was known as a fearless man who had served well in many battles. He had been injured in his last foray against the enemy, and was unable to fight any longer, but his military knowledge was indisputable. Eastwich, brother to the old king and uncle to the new, was a cantankerous, impatient and indecisive man; a man that Rupert regarded with barely concealed loathing. Council discussions were held in secret, for fear of a spy leaking information from the palace to the enemy, but closed doors did not stop the rumors: Eastwich had given Rupert a dressing down before the rest of the council; Rupert had called his uncle a miserable, old fool; Alfred was reluctant to push the untrained troops too soon; Wetherton was urging him to march on Terran as soon as possible. The palace was rife with speculation, but concrete plans were not forthcoming. Despite this, an air of victory pervaded the palace. For how else could it be than that Alfred's army would defeat the foe, and return home victorious?

With each passing day, new word reached the palace of the despicable and cowardly actions of Terran. How could they not take action, people asked themselves, when Terran taxed his poor people to death? And only the hardest-hearted could fail to be moved when news of his debauchery and orgies reached the delicate ears of the civilized people at court. And when the story spread through the palace that he had given his own daughter to a dragon to feed on, no one doubted the righteous mission they were set upon. They would be failing in their Christian duty if they did not act against such an evil man.

Anna wondered what the dragons thought of the

business. She had not seen Max at court since their angry exchange, but his words still smarted. He had called her a little girl, and she couldn't blame him. She had sent him away – again – and what for? Because she was too proud to admit she needed help? Or because she was angry at the helplessness of her situation? She didn't even know. What she did know was that, once again, she had made Max leave.

"I've asked the king if we may dine with him this evening," Matilda said one afternoon. "I expect you all to accompany me."

"Of course, my lady," Elizabeth said.

Anna looked at the queen speculatively. She never sought out Alfred's company unless she wanted something. Did she need a larger allowance? Anna didn't think so. But it must be of some import for her to insist her ladies attend as well.

The king's apartments were larger than Matilda's, but just as lavish. A dining room led from the formal parlor, with a table that could easily seat twenty people. When the queen arrived with her ladies, they were ushered straight to the table, where footmen stood ready with jugs of wine. The queen took a seat at one end, while the ladies took places on either side. By the time the king made his appearance, followed by the chamberlain, Anna had already finished her second glass of wine. The queen looked at her husband as he entered the room, but made no comment on his tardiness.

"My lady," he said, nodding in her direction. "This is a rare pleasure indeed."

"Thank you, my lord," she replied graciously, bowing her head.

"What is this about, Matty?"

"Perhaps I wished to spend an evening with My Lord Husband," she said with a smile.

"With your ladies in attendance?" he said. The doors opened as two footmen brought in a tray of soup.

"How go the plans for the war?" she asked when the first course was removed.

The king nodded. "Well enough."

"Will you be ready to march when the spring thaws come?"

"Yes. We already have four thousand assembled in the city, with more arriving each day. And I have been promised another two thousand by our fine noblemen. And with Roderick adding the men he has gathered, we will be a formidable force."

"Then our chances of victory are good?"

"My dear Lady," he said, "victory will be ours. The astrologers say our timing is fortuitous, and the bishop has offered prayers for our success. I am quite assured that Roderick will be back on the throne before the spring is out."

The next course was brought in, and the conversation lulled as the diners tucked into the succulent meats and tasty tarts.

"I want to accompany the army when you march," Matilda said as she delicately wiped her mouth with a napkin. Alfred glanced at her in disbelief.

"Have you lost your mind?" he said.

Matilda looked at him steadily. "I have as much interest in reclaiming the crown for Roderick as you do," she said, "and we both know I will be a much stronger rallying point for the people. They will fight for the sake of their princess, but perhaps not as much for a disposed or a foreign king."

"You are crazy if you think I will allow you to come, no matter how persuasive your arguments might be," he said.

Matilda smiled. "I think you will see the sense of what I am saying." She glanced at the chamberlain. "What say you, My Lord Chamberlain?" she said.

He glanced between Alfred and the queen. "A lady does not belong on the battlefield," he said.

Matilda laughed. "Oh, I don't mean to *fight*! Good heavens! I just wish to observe."

"I will lock you in the tower," Alfred said. Matilda's smile vanished as she leaned forward across the table.

"It would behoove you to remember whose cause you are fighting for, my lord," she said. "What will Roderick say if he hears you have locked his sister away?"

"Do you think I care?"

"Will you care when he has regained his throne and is writing his foreign policies? You may be marching into battle with him, but you are not the only king to give him your support."

Anna could see the angry flush mounting in Alfred's cheeks as he glared at his wife. "Very well," he finally ground out. "But let it be known that your blood will not be on my hands."

Matilda nodded, then leaned back with a smile. "Come, my lord, that was not so difficult, was it?"

Alfred pushed himself to his feet with an angry scowl, and throwing his napkin on the table, stormed from the room. The chamberlain watched his retreating back, then rose to his feet, bowed at the queen and followed his angry monarch. Anna glanced at Matilda. One day, she thought, she will push too far, and she will have to suffer the consequences. For now, however, she looked as satisfied as a cat that had gotten the cream. She looked around at her ladies.

"I will not think less of you if you choose to remain behind when I go to war," she said, "but if you will accompany me, I will be glad of the company."

"Will you give us time to think on it?" Elizabeth asked.

"Of course," Matilda said.

"I'll come," Anna said. Matilda looked at Anna with a smile.

"I knew you would," she said.

CHAPTER TWENTY-EIGHT

Anna stood behind one corner of the queen's chair as she listened to a petition from the bishop to help fund new screens in the cathedral. Blanche stood at the other corner. "You should not have scorned Rupert as you did," Blanche whispered. "Becoming his mistress would have given you both wealth and prestige."

Anna turned to glare at Blanche. "I will not whore myself for money or position," she said.

Blanche shrugged. "And how much are you willing to lose for your principles?" she said. "Because you may lose everything."

"At least I will still have my self-worth," she said.

Blanche sniggered. "Self-worth! Will that keep you warm and feed your belly when you are tossed on the street?" The queen turned and gave Blanche an annoyed frown, and she fell silent. Anna focused her attention on the bishop. His petition must have been successful, given his triumphant smile. The queen nodded at him, and he bowed his way out of the room.

"The two of you are like squabbling cats," the queen said once he was gone. "If you cannot find a way to live in peace, then one of you may have to go." Blanche turned an exultant look on Anna. "And don't assume, Blanche," the queen continued, "that it will be Anna that goes. I'm beginning to tire of your spiteful comments."

A knock sounded on the door, and it opened to admit one of the guards. "There is someone in the courtyard asking to see you, Mistress," Frank said to Anna. She looked at him in surprise.

"Who is it?"

"A man. I cannot tell you more than that."

"He didn't give a name?"

"He did not." Anna glanced at the queen.

"Go," she said with a wave of her hand.

Anna turned back to Frank. "I will come down in a moment."

As Anna opened the door to the courtyard, she glanced around. It was drizzling slightly, but that did not deter the palace staff as they went about their duties. Visitors strode purposefully towards the palace doors, heads down against the gray day. One of the footmen had his arm around a young maid, who was giggling and blushing as she pulled herself away. Children chased dogs around the fire that blazed in the center of the courtyard, and one or two chickens wandered between legs, pecking unconcernedly at the slushy ground until a booted foot sent them flapping through the air, squawking angrily. Anna pulled her cloak closer around her shoulders as she searched through the crowd, looking for a familiar face, but it was only when she took a second look at the men standing against the low wall surrounding the courtyard that she saw him.

Garrick was leaning against the wall in the rain, his arms crossed over his chest, watching her scan the yard. His legs were crossed casually, one ankle over the other, but as she looked at him, he slowly pushed himself up to his full height and strode towards her. He wore a long, hooded woolen cloak that covered his brown tunic and leather breeches, with boots that reached his calves. A sack was slung over his shoulder, and his hair was pulled behind his neck, held in place by a leather thong.

He reached her in a few long strides. "Hello, Anna." He dropped the sack to his feet.

She stared at him, surprise stealing her words. "What are you doing here?" she finally said. He glanced away for a moment.

"Are you not happy to see me?" he said softly. She swallowed hard. Pushing the cloak aside, he reached into his pocket, pulling out a letter which he held out to her.

"I brought you this," he said.

"Is something wrong?" she asked, taking the missive from his hand.

"No," he said. "Your sister asked me to give it to you since I was coming here."

"Oh." She turned the letter over, and recognized Keira's neat writing. "Why did you come here?"

"I'm joining the troops going to war for the king."

"What?" She stared at him in horror. "No. You mustn't."

"Why not?"

"Because ..." she paused. "Because you could be killed."

"I could. Would you care if I was?"

"Of course I would!" she said. "You know that!"

Garrick glanced away. "I know."

"When did you arrive?" she asked.

"This morning," he said. "This is the first place I came."

She glanced at the ground. "Where are you staying?"

"I will make my way to the Camp Commander as soon as I leave here. Master Drake gave me a letter of reference, as well as money to purchase armor and weapons."

"That was ... generous."

"Yes," Garrick said wryly. "He was spared the burden of having me join his family, so I think it was the least he could do."

"Garrick —"

He lifted his hand to stop her. "I'm sorry, Anna. That was uncalled for. Master Drake has been very generous. I suppose I came here hoping ... but you have made your choices, and I have made mine. It was not my intent to make you feel guilty. I just wanted to see you, and deliver your sister's letter."

Anna felt a wave of shame roll over her. "Oh, Garrick," she said, but before she could continue, his hands were taking hers, pulling her closer.

"Shh," he whispered. "I'm sorry. I do understand. I didn't expect you to have changed your mind." She looked up at him. "Perhaps ..." He looked away. "Have you made a final decision?"

"I –"

"Well, well, the stablehand." Max's voice cut through Anna's words, and she pulled from Garrick's grasp to see him striding towards them. He met Anna's gaze for a brief moment before turning his attention to Garrick.

"Dragon," Garrick ground out. He glanced down at Anna, and his expression tightened.

"His name is Garrick," Anna said to Max.

"Garrick? I had quite forgotten." He drew closer and sniffed the air. "But I never forget a smell," he said, "and you smell of, well, you smell of the stables."

"Max!" Anna glared at him, her expression horrified.

"Am I interrupting something? A happy reunion perhaps?"

"Yes," Anna ground out in annoyance. "Garrick is my betro–" She froze, her eyes wide, and slowly closed her mouth. *No, no, no*, she screamed to herself. Why could she not hold her tongue? She laughed nervously and turned to Garrick, determined to take back the foolish, unconsidered words, but the look on his face made her stop, groaning inwardly. He was staring at her with an expression of disbelief – and hope. She smiled weakly, then turned back to Max. "We were keeping it a secret."

Max smiled in sardonic amusement. "I see," he said, and Anna had a horrible feeling that he saw all too well. "Then let me be the first to congratulate you." She nodded, and glanced back at Garrick. He was still staring at her.

"Is it true?" he said softly. "Do you mean it? I thought all hope was gone, but here you are calling me your betrothed. Am I really so fortunate?" Anna glanced down at the ground. She could not take back the words now, while Max stood watching. "I love you," he whispered.

"Oh, Garrick," she said. In one foolish moment she had rewritten her own future as well as Garrick's. She heard Max snort, and looked up to see him walking away. She glanced back at Garrick. He had already dismissed Max from his mind.

"I'm sorry I doubted you," he said. He was grinning. "I thought when I saw the dragon ... but I was wrong. We will be happy together, you will see! And right now, I don't think I could be any happier!" Anna forced a smile. It was not within her to destroy his moment of joy. Tomorrow, maybe, but not now.

CHAPTER TWENTY-NINE

Anna sat in her chambers, staring unseeing out the window that faced the formal palace gardens. Icy tendrils of frost swirled over the cold glass panes, the delicate feathering glimmering in the low winter light. In the background the canaries given to her by Max – no, Aaron – were chirping brightly, competing with the crackling of sparks that leaped from the fire. She had parted from Garrick a short time ago, his joy unabated as he set off to find the Camp Commander and join the king's fighting forces. She closed her eyes, remembering how he had looked at her, his vivid blue eyes sparkling with happiness as he lifted her hand and kissed it gently before he said farewell.

She had created a tangled web and ensnared herself completely. She could not untangle the threads without causing pain. She dropped her head into her hands. She may not love Garrick, at least not love in the way of lovers, but she still could not bear to hurt him.

She leaned her head against the cold surface of the window, her breath creating patches of steam against the glass. It was slightly uneven, and she could feel the ripples beneath her forehead. Was it so terrible to be betrothed to

Garrick? How many men truly loved the woman they married the way Garrick loved her? And she cared deeply for him. He had been her friend at Storbrook when she would have sunk into despair. He always treated her with dignity and respect – something that seemed to be lacking between so many couples. He was easy to talk to, and she enjoyed his company.

No, she decided, it was not a terrible thing to marry him. They could build a happy life together. He would not leave her when things became difficult, or turn away from her when she used careless words. He would stand together with her, and they would face whatever the world had to offer, together.

The sound of voices through the walls broke her reverie. The queen had been meeting with her secretary earlier in the day, consulting her calendar, and had now returned. Rising to her feet, Anna went to the next room.

"I am planning a ball," Matilda said as Anna entered the room. "We will delay the winter ball until spring, and make a celebration of our victory in battle. We will invite the officers!"

"But the battle will not have been fought yet, my lady," Anna said, cautiously.

"Oh, pish," she said. "Victory is already assured. Alfred says that our forces are far superior to Terran's, and Rupert has assured him that our men are quite ready to face the enemy."

"Well, I think it is a splendid idea, my lady," Elizabeth said. She had followed the queen into the parlor. "We will have a military theme."

"Yes! Yes!" said the queen. "All the ladies must wear red on their gowns to show their support of King Roderick – and Alfred too, of course – in this important mission. I will have a gown specially made for the occasion."

When Anna saw Garrick again, he could not stop waxing lyrical about the superior forces he had joined. "The men train every day," he told her. "I have been given command of a company of archers, and we spend six, seven hours a day in training."

"Hitting targets with a bow and arrow for seven hours a day? That sounds exactly how you would like to spend your days!"

"I would like to spend seven hours a day with you," he said, smiling down at her. They had left the courtyard and were heading towards the gardens, brown and dormant in the dull, winter light. The ground was damp from the rain that had fallen overnight, and the heavy bank of cloud left everything gray and colorless. "But I'm not shooting for seven hours. I am setting my men to marching, moving stones and digging trenches. They need to be strong and ready for a battle."

"Oh. Well that might not be quite as much fun as playing at war."

Garrick laughed. "I don't mind. My muscles ache at the end of each day, but I am used to hard work." He had pulled her hand through his arm as they walked, and he stroked the backs of her fingers where they rested in the crook of his elbow. "I wish there was somewhere we could go and be alone together," he said softly.

Anna glanced back at the palace. "I know," she said. "But I cannot be away for too long at a time."

He nodded. "Have you written to your sister yet?"

Anna drew in a breath. "No, not yet." She looked into his face. "I think we should wait until this war is over before announcing our news."

"Wait? But why?"

"The queen may not let me stay if she knows that I am betrothed."

"I see." Garrick paused. "Very well. On one condition."

Anna looked up at him, and saw a hint of a smile. "What condition?"

"You must give me a kiss."

Anna glanced around in dismay. "What? Here?"

He grinned. "I'm sure there are some nooks and crannies that can give us a moment of privacy. Come!" He led her into the gardens, laughing as he dragged her along the paths. There was a small alcove overhung with vines that in the summer provided a leafy hiding place, but was now just a tangled roof of bare branches. There was no-one else about, however, and he led her beneath it. "Perfect," he said with a smile. Placing a finger beneath her chin, he lifted her face. The dull day made his eyes seem darker, more brooding, and she stared up at him as he moved closer. He brought his hand to her cheek, then ran it along her neck to the base of her skull. He leaned a little closer, and she could smell campfires and damp earth. He brushed his lips against hers, a gentle touch like the wings of a butterfly. Her back was to the wall, and when he pressed closer, she could feel the cold surface behind her. He pulled back slightly to look into her eyes, and then his mouth was on hers, gentle at first, then becoming more demanding. She could feel his lips move against hers, and the brush of his tongue. It was startling, and she closed her eyes. He drew away, and she opened them to see his staring down at her. "I love you," he whispered.

He placed his forehead against hers, and took her hands in his. He stood still for a long moment, then took a step back. "Shall we continue our walk?" he said. He pulled her hand into his arm once more and they continued along the path. They passed the place where Anna had first seen Max at court. The hedges, bare of leaves, no longer blocked the view of the intersecting pathway, but the spot still brought back memories. She seldom saw Max these days, and when she did, he never seemed to notice her. Which was just as well, she thought. It made her decision to marry Garrick so much easier.

"Do you remember the bird I found?" Garrick was saying. She nodded. "Its wing healed beautifully, and I released it a few weeks later. It returned later to nest in the same tree it fell from."

"How do you know it was the same bird?" she said.

He smiled. "I could see it in her eyes. She looked at me without fear."

Anna laughed. "That doesn't mean anything. There is no creature that fears you." But she knew, deep in her heart, that that was not true. Because she feared Garrick, and the love he had for her.

Kathleen and Elizabeth were sitting on a bench in the parlor when Anna returned, quilts covering their legs as their needles flew through the canvases they were embroidering. They were deep in conversation, but at Anna's entrance, Kathleen looked up, an expression of dismay crossing her features when she saw who it was.

"What's wrong?" Anna said. Kathleen glanced at Elizabeth, but remained silent.

"We heard a rumor," Elizabeth said. "About the prince."

"What about the prince?"

"It seems the king has threatened to send Rupert from court over an affair with a woman."

Anna sat down heavily in the seat across from the two women. "What woman?" she whispered. Kathleen looked down at her needlework.

"We don't know," Elizabeth said.

"I'm sorry," Kathleen whispered. "I know the prince was showing you his interest, and then to go off with someone else ..." Her voice trailed off as Anna stared at her friend.

"Did you think I would be upset?" Anna finally said. She laughed dryly. "You can be sure I have no interest in Rupert whatsoever." She glanced back at Elizabeth. "How do you know this?"

Elizabeth lifted a shoulder. "I heard it from Mary, who heard it from Hindley. The whole palace is seething with the news."

"The prince won't be happy about that."

"No! Mary said he's in a towering rage over the whole

matter. Whoever this lady is, she had better make sure she stays far away from the prince." Anna clasped her hands together. She was shaking slightly.

"I'm quite sure," Anna said, "that is exactly what she is doing!"

CHAPTER THIRTY

Anna had spent the morning in the chambers with the queen, checking the guest list for the royal ball. The secretary had drawn up the list, but Matilda was not convinced it was accurate, and so she and Anna had gone through each and every name. Anna was finally dismissed from the queen's presence when Denton presented himself. He had stayed away for a few weeks after the last play, but was once more a regular visitor to the queen's chambers. The previous play had not been as successful as he had hoped, but this one, he knew with complete certainty, was going to enshrine his name as one of the greatest playwrights of his time.

"I was thinking the lady could use poison this time," he was saying to the queen as Anna closed the door behind them. Her head was pounding from the lists of names and the stale air she had endured all morning. She slipped out a side door, avoiding the courtyard, and headed in the direction of the wilderness. She had heard that Rupert was inspecting the troops today, or she would not go outside alone and risk a chance encounter with him.

It had once again rained the previous night, but the sky had opened up to reveal a few weak rays of sun through a small patch of pale blue. Anna left the muddy path, instead picking her way over fallen logs and sodden leaves. In the distance she could see the low hills that lay beyond the wilderness, hiding at points behind curtains of mist. She rucked up her skirts and tucked them into her belt, revealing her booted feet. The forest lay before the hills, and then there was the brook. She had never crossed the stream before, but she knew that once she reached that point, the ground was flat until it reached the gently undulating hills. Arms swinging, she hastened her step, determined to reach her goal and return to the palace before it grew dark.

The forest smelt of damp leaves and mulch, a rich, earthy smell. A bird chatted in a tree above her and then fell silent. She could hear the fall of her feet against the soft forest floor, and the rustle of dead leaves when the air stirred slightly. A large bush of holly grew at the base of a tree, its crimson berries a splash of color against the gray forest. Anna remembered a time when she had collected holly with Keira to decorate the halls of Storbrook. Garrick was there, and they had a snowball fight. And when they returned to Storbrook, she had met Max for the first time. She glanced up at the sky, wondering if a dragon was circling overhead as he had been that time, but all she could see were gray clouds against the small patches of blue.

The trees started thinning and she could see the clear outline of the hills again. The stream was hidden from view, but she knew it cut across the flat ground a little beyond the forest. An eagle screamed above her, and she looked up to see it diving to the ground, then lift itself back into the air with a small animal in its talons, its strong wings carrying it towards the hills. She reached the stream, which was far wider than she remembered, swollen from the winter rains, and she paused at its banks, wondering whether she could ford the small river. A large rock lay in the water a little further upstream, and she walked towards it, looking at it with consideration. The distance to the rock from where she stood on the bank was about two feet, but from the rock to the other side was further. Stretching out her leg, she sprang from the bank onto the rock, tipping slightly as her foot touched the slick surface. She leaned forward, thrusting her arms out to regain her balance and twisting about as she found her footing. She took a deep breath and considered the opposite bank. It was a lot further than she realized. Lifting her skirts above her knees, she rolled the extra fabric into her belt. The rock was too small to take a step backwards, but she inched back as far as she could and pushed herself forward, stretching her leg as far as she could. Her toes touched the other bank, and she pushed her weight forward, falling onto the damp and muddy ground. Her back foot splashed into the water, and grabbing the weeds at the edge of the stream, she hurled herself forward. The water had not seeped into her boot, but beneath her knees her gown was muddy and wet. She pushed herself to her feet and shook out the grubby fabric, before turning to face the hills. They were still a short distance away, beyond a meadow of long, damp grass, and she set off once more, determined to reach them. The sun had disappeared behind the clouds while she was in the forest, but a few rays broke through, bathing the meadow in soft light.

By the time she reached the hills the sun was already halfway to the western horizon. She would not be able to stay long. But the low peaks were drawing her, insisting that she at least reach the first height. They were not very high, but even so her forehead and underarms were damp as she gained the elevation, and she was glad of the cool air. She had to scramble the last few feet, and she used her hands to haul herself up. She rose to her feet, turned and looked over the valley, rubbing her muddy palms against the soiled gown. The palace looked squat from this height, with thin trails of smoke rising from its many chimney stacks. The army camp lay a mile beyond the palace, a smudge on the horizon. Weaving its way into the distance was the river, separating the palace from the city, while closer she could see the shadowed forest and the narrow stream she had almost fallen into. There was a wide, low rock near where she stood, and she sat down, glad for a few moments of rest before she started her descent. She lifted her face to the weak rays of sun and closed her eyes, listening to her heart as it settled back to its usual pace after the exertion of gaining the summit.

A slight breeze blew over her as she sat on the rock, her eyes closed. There was a rustling sound, and she wondered what little creature was scurrying around. She was too lazy to make the effort to look, however. The sound came again, followed by the swish of something sweeping over the ground. She opened her eyes, suddenly concerned about the possibility of snakes, but what met her eyes was something quite different. A huge, bronze dragon was settling on the ground behind her. His tail wrapped around the front of the rock and rested against her feet, while his long neck stretched around the other side, his eyes locking with hers. She could feel the heat wrapping around her as she stared back at him.

"Lean back," Max said softly. His huge body was pressed against the rock, his side a heavy wall behind her. She stared at him for a moment, then shifted herself and leaned her back against his side.

"I have to get back," she said. "It will be dark soon."

"I'll carry you," he said. His head was at her eye level, and reaching out a hand, she touched his neck. It was covered in scales that gleamed in the light. Her fingers glided over the warm surfaces, smooth as polished stone and just as hard. His yellow cat-like eyes held hers, while his hot breath washed over her. She dropped her hand and turned back to the view.

"Do you know I was with Bronwyn when she first changed?" she said. He turned and followed her gaze.

"Bronwyn? Favian's daughter?"

"Yes. We were out riding when her horse fell, crushing

her beneath its weight." Max lifted his head as a thin stream of flame blew from his mouth.

"Did she hurt you?"

"She would have, but Favian reached her before she could do anything." Max brought his head closer again.

"That must have been terrifying."

"It was. But I feel worse for Bronwyn."

Max lifted his eyebrows in surprise. "She could have killed you, but you feel bad for her?"

Anna nodded. "She has to live with that knowledge for the rest of her long life."

He turned back to the view in silence. She could feel his chest moving as she leaned against him, the sound of his heart like a wave rolling against the shore and crashing against the rocks, over and over. She had only seen the ocean once, when she had been imprisoned by Jack, but she remembered the incessant sound of the crashing waves. Max had been there, too, protecting her, although she did not know it at the time. Or rather, she had refused to admit it to herself. She glanced at him again. Sharp horns rose from the top of his skull, and down the back of his neck were spikes, curved like the thorns of a rose. They grew smaller as they descended down his neck, disappearing altogether where it joined his back. From the side of his long snout she could see a hint of his teeth, sharp enough to rip raw flesh from an animal. She had never seen him hunt, but he was a dragon, after all. Which also meant he ate other things, too. Humans, for instance. She pushed the thought away.

"I was also the first person Bronwyn carried," she said.

He turned to look at her. "You were?" he asked, and she could hear the amusement in his voice.

"It was almost as terrifying as when she changed. She raced a waterfall."

Max laughed. "You were the first person I ever carried, too," he said.

"I was?" Anna was surprised. Max was many years older

than Bronwyn.

"Yes. I practiced lifting a log until it was steady before I offered you a ride."

Anna grinned. "Well, you were very good. I would never have guessed."

He grinned. "And then you wanted to have a snowball fight. With a dragon!"

Anna laughed. The snow had just melted against Max's hot hide. But he had gotten his own back when he shoveled the snow over her with his tail, burying her to the waist. "I remember," she said.

She looked back at the palace. Could they see the dragon perched on the hill, she wondered? Max shifted slightly, and she looked down to see that his tail had inched forward and was now stretching in front of her feet. It was armed with fierce-looking spikes, far more dangerous than those on his neck, and even at its narrowest point was too thick for her to wrap her hands around. She nudged him slightly with her foot, and the tip of his tail swished over the ground.

"You're like a dog, with a wagging tail." He dropped his head and rested the tip of his snout against the rock.

"All dogs need petting," he said. He inched forward a little and bumped the side of her leg, his eyes wide. She laughed and stretched out a hand.

"Who can resist such a piteous creature?" she said. She stroked his snout.

"Quite pathetic," he agreed.

She leaned her head back against him as she ran her hand down his neck. "Did you hear the rumors about Rupert?" she asked.

"I did," he said. He drew away from her touch and looked into her eyes. "But I was still right to speak to Alfred. Rupert would have ensured you met his demands before the week was out if I hadn't."

She nodded. "I'm sorry I was so angry."

"So am I." He brought his head closer. "I am usually a

patient man, but no one rouses me to such heights of annoyance as you do, Anna."

She grinned. "I can say the same for you."

He looked away. "Is that why you accepted Garrick's proposal? Because you were annoyed with me?" She pulled away, startled. "I will admit I was rather rude," he said, "but I was taken aback by the strength of his feeling for you." Anna looked away.

"He proposed while I was still at Storbrook," she said.

"And you didn't accept his offer until now?" She didn't reply. "You cannot marry him," he said. She remained silent. "Anna, listen to me. Garrick will not make you happy."

"I don't see what it has to do with you," she said, with sudden irritation. He leaned closer, and when she turned to look at him the yellow of his eyes had been swallowed in a blaze of flames. She drew in a sharp breath as her heart began to pound in her chest.

"Oh, Anna," he said softly, "it has everything to do with me."

"He's a good man," she whispered.

"I know he is," he said. She could smell the flames on his breath. "But he is not the man for you. I told you once that you were made to love wildly and passionately. Garrick loves you, that much is clear, but his calm and steady devotion will quench your spirit." She stared at him until she felt as though she were drowning in an ocean of fire. Her fingers itched to touch him, but she forced herself to look away.

"I should get back," she said. He pulled back, turning away as a blaze of flame spewed from his mouth and spread through the air around him. She rose to her feet and shivered at the loss of heat at her back. He had risen to his full height and towered over her. His tail snaked around her, wrapping around her waist, and she could not resist reaching out her hand and feeling the warm, smooth surface. He stared at her for a moment, then lifting her into the air, gently placed her on his back. She leaned forward and wrapped her hands around his neck as he spread out his wings, opening them like a paper fan, and lifted himself into the air. He rose higher and higher, until the rock she had been sitting on was nothing more than a speck, and then they were surrounded by thick mist. Steam rose from his hide, and she wrapped herself tighter around him.

"Fancy a little ride before I take you back?" he said. He didn't wait for an answer, but angled himself upwards, speeding faster and faster.

"You could crash," she shouted, but he just laughed.

"Into what? The clouds?"

"Another dragon!"

"I won't crash. I promise."

"How do you know?"

"I just know. I can sense when something is approaching, even if I cannot see it. I could walk back to the palace with my eyes closed, and not bump into anything."

"Even as a human?" He turned to look at her.

"I'm always a dragon, Anna. You know that. Taking on the form of a human does not change what I am."

"I know. You are always a monstrous beast."

He grinned. "And you are always a shrew." She kicked her boots against his hide, and he laughed. "Is that supposed to hurt me?"

"No," she said, "I am well aware that it is impossible for me to hurt you."

He turned to face forward in silence. They rose above the clouds, and suddenly the sun was shining brightly on them, making his scales gleam and glimmer. She could see patches of green-blue countryside through the gaps in the cloud, and the twisting, silvery ribbon of the little stream she had forded. He turned to her with a grin.

"I thought I would have to rescue you from the water," he said.

"You saw me?"

"I did."

"And you didn't come to my aid?"

He gave a dry laugh. "I wasn't sure you would welcome my help." Anna didn't reply. The clouds were blocking her view again, but when another patch opened up, she saw they were circling above the wilderness, close to the treetops. He dropped to the ground, landing as lightly as a feather. She slid off his back and walked around to his front.

"Thank you for the ride," she said.

"It's always my pleasure," he said. She stared at him for a moment, her gaze locking with his, then turned and walked in the direction of the palace. Dusk was approaching, and the light was low. Her gown had dried with Max's heat, but the hem was quickly becoming damp once again, and the cold crept through the soles of her feet. She glanced up, once, to see Max circling above her, just beneath the clouds. He puffed out a small flame as she looked up, and she quickly averted her glance.

She was near the courtyard when she saw someone approaching her, and her heart sank when she realized it was Frank, the guard. His arms were crossed over his chest.

"I saw you," he said. "What were you doing with a dragon?"

"I think your eyes are deceiving you," she said, glancing around. "I see no dragon."

He gave a dry laugh. "You think I am fooled so easily? I've wondered before what you are up to, when you go on your rambles. The king will hear of this, and a few coins cannot save you this time. A monster like that always means trouble." She took a step towards him.

"Go and tell the king," she said, "and let's see how much credence he gives to your words."

He nodded. "I will. And if he ignores my warning, well …" The words trailed into silence. He gave another nod, then turning on his heel, strode away.

CHAPTER THIRTY-ONE

The next few days rushed by in a blur of activity. In between accompanying the queen in her duties, the ladies were expected to help with the planning of the ball. They applied to Rupert for the names of his officers so they could be included on the guest list, and the queen insisted that all plans be presented to her for approval.

There was also the added concern about the royal children. Influenza had swept through the nursery, forcing two nurses and all the children to take to their beds. Matilda refused to enter the sickroom, but the concerns for her health did not extend to her ladies, and they were expected to check on the children a few times each day and deliver a report on their progress to the queen. The physician attended the patients daily, offering tonics made of lungwort and laurel, and within a few days the patients were starting to improve. Anna came back one afternoon with a message from Prince John that he wanted to see his mother, but Matilda shuddered slightly and shook her head. "Take a message to the king," she told Anna, "that his children wish to see him."

"Yes, my lady," Anna replied.

A few enquiries gave Anna the intelligence that the king was meeting with his war council in the council rooms, and Anna made her way down the stairs. The door to the chamber was made of solid wood, but as she drew near, she heard the sound of raised voices shouting in anger. She paused, but as she slowly stepped away from the door, it swung open violently. She pulled back against a pillar as Rupert stormed from the room with Lord Hindley on his heels. "Even John could make better decisions than that," he threw over his shoulder, sending an angry glance at the man scurrying behind him. The action brought Anna into his line of sight. "What are *you* doing here?" he demanded. "Are you eavesdropping?"

"What?" she said. "No! I was sent to give the king a message."

"What message? Are you here to tell him that someone tried to give you a kiss?"

Anna flushed angrily. "His son would like him to visit the sickroom," she said.

Rupert laughed dryly. "I would like to watch you deliver that message, but I haven't time for such foolishness." She watched as he marched away, Hindley a step behind, before turning and heading back to the apartments, her message undelivered.

"How goes the training for war?" Anna asked Garrick when she saw him a few days later. As before, he had waited in the courtyard while a message was delivered to Anna in the palace.

"It goes well," he said. "My men can hit a target from a hundred feet." He glanced up at the clouds. "They are eager to put their training into practice, but the king has ordered we wait for the spring storms to be behind us before we start the march."

Anna grimaced. "Men are always so eager to die."

"No," he said. "Just to prove our worth. We can't all be

dragons, after all." A frown crossed his features. "The men at the camp have been talking about a dragon that was seen close to the palace a few days ago."

Anna shrugged. "What of it?"

"The rumor is that there was a woman with the dragon." He glanced down at her. "Was that you?"

"I had gone for a walk," she said. "Max saw me and brought me back."

"You let him carry you? On his back?" His dismay was evident. "Anna, how could you?"

"What do you mean? What's wrong?"

"What's wrong? You let that ... creature ... carry you on his back."

"I have ridden on dragons before, Garrick!"

"That is not just any dragon! That is the dragon you have been hankering after for five years!"

"How dare you?" she said. "I am marrying you, not him!" She turned around, but he caught her by the arm.

"Are you? Are you marrying me?"

Anna turned slowly to meet his gaze.

"Yes," she replied. "I am marrying you. There is nothing between Max and me."

Garrick was silent for a moment, his gaze intent as he stared at her. He nodded slowly and released her arm.

"I'm sorry, Anna. When I heard that you had been with Max, I could hardly contain myself. What am I compared to a creature like that?"

"You are a good man, Garrick. Strong and kind. You don't need to be a dragon to be recognized for your worth."

He smiled and took a step closer. "Thank you," he said. He lifted his fingers and touched her face gently, then dropped his hand. "I've been invited to a ball at the palace."

"I know." She grinned. "I helped with the guest list."

"Ah! I wondered how I came to receive an invitation."

"All the officers were invited, so your name was on the list anyway."

He nodded. "That's what the prince said."

"The prince?"

"Prince Rupert, Commander-in-Chief. All the officers meet with him once a week to discuss training and tactics. He's champing at the bit to start the march to the borders."

Anna felt the color drain from her face. "And ... what do you think of him?"

"Of Prince Rupert?" Garrick shrugged. "He expects his commands to be followed implicitly, and does not tolerate disobedience."

"Have you spoken to him?"

"No. I'm a lowly archer, in command of a unit of eighty men. He takes no notice of me."

"So he doesn't know about our betrothal?"

"No." Garrick looked surprised.

"He must never know. You must not tell anyone."

"Why not?"

"Because he may try and hurt you."

"Hurt me? Anna, what are you talking about?" Anna glanced around, then wrapping her hand around his arm, dragged him away out of the courtyard and towards the river.

"Listen to me, Garrick. Prince Rupert is determined to make me suffer. If he knows that you have feelings for me, he may try to harm you." Garrick was staring down at her in puzzlement.

"Why?" His eyes held hers as his expression changed to one of comprehension. "You're the woman," he said slowly. "The reason the king is unhappy with the prince." She nodded in silence. "Good lord, Anna, how many more rumors am I to hear about you? What happened?"

"Rupert wanted me as his mistress, but Max warned the king to keep him away."

Garrick growled. "Did he force you?"

"No. He would have, if Max had not spoken to the king."

"What did the dragon say? Does the king know what he is?"

"The king knows what Aaron is."

"Ah! I see. So Max went to the king and reminded him of Master Aaron's true nature, and the king told Rupert to stay away." Anna nodded. "So the dragon who left you five years ago is now the one saving your honor." He gave a wry laugh. "I suppose he has his uses, then."

Anna smiled. "From time to time," she said.

"I'm glad he was here to protect you," he said.

"Rupert is determined to have his revenge for the humiliation he suffered, so he must not know that you know me."

"I'm not going to hide from the prince."

"I'm not asking you to hide. Just … don't announce that you know me from the rooftops."

He nodded. "Very well. If it will make you feel more at ease. But if your name comes up, I will not deny you."

"Thank you," she said. She glanced back at the palace. "I need to get going. The queen will be wondering where I have gotten to."

"Very well." He paused. "You know I love you, don't you?"

She nodded. "I know."

CHAPTER THIRTY-TWO

The first buds of spring were starting to swell when the day of the ball arrived. Seamstresses, shoemakers and milliners were continually coming and going from the queen's apartments, arms laden with fabrics, cloaks, shoes and other accessories. The queen had ordered three new gowns made for herself, so that she could choose the one she most fancied on the day of the ball.

The ladies each had new gowns, too. Anna's was of soft blue silk, trimmed in white. A narrow sash of red ribbon had been stitched across the bodice of the gown.

The great hall had been decorated with brightly colored banners displaying the king's standard, with a few of Roderick's colors interspersed. The royal table on the raised dais was decked out in red and white, and on the tables below, red napkins stood stark against the white linen.

As the afternoon light began to fade, Anna could hear the crowds of people starting to congregate on the lawns and within the halls. From the window of their chambers she could see people strolling through the gardens as laughter rang through the air. Strains of music reached her ears, and she hummed to herself as she smoothed down her gown. She had already helped the queen with her garments, and Betsy was helping her get ready for the evening ahead. In the corner of the ladies' chamber the two bright canaries chirped tunelessly, their cheerful sounds making the room seem brighter as Elizabeth and Kathleen added the finishing touches to their outfits.

There was a knock, and a maid peered around the door. "His Highness is here," she said. Betsy carefully tucked the last curl into Anna's braid before she rose to her feet with the other two ladies. They would follow the king and queen when they made their entrance into the hall. In the parlor, Alfred was talking to his son John. This was to be Prince John's first ball, and his father was giving him last-minute instructions.

"You must be sure to dance with lots of ladies," he said. "You cannot be seen to favor one over another." Prince John nodded solemnly. "And look people in the eye when you talk to them. Then they will know you are really attending to them."

Matilda entered the room. "Whenever you are ready, my lord," she said. She was wearing a gown of crimson and gold, the colors of the royal standard, and over her hair she wore a net of red ribbons, studded with tiny pearls. Alfred rose to his feet and gave her a scrutinizing look.

"Very dutiful, my dear." Matilda flashed a smile and dropped a curtsey. Alfred turned to his son. "Lead the way, Your Highness," he said with a smile.

They paused outside the hall a short while later as the chamberlain announced the arrival of the royal entourage. There was a scraping of chairs and benches as the crowds rose to their feet, and the long call of a clarion sounding a single note. The noise died away, and Matilda and Alfred entered the hall with John at their heels. Anna and the other ladies waited a few moments before they, too, entered the large room. Alfred and Matilda were already on the dais, and Anna glanced up to see Rupert smiling at John before nodding with a slight frown at his brother. She looked away and followed Elizabeth and Blanche to their table placed just below the dais, darting a glance around the room as she walked. Garrick was sitting at a table near the back, staring at her intently, and she quickly looked away as she took her seat, Kathleen beside her.

"Master Max Brant is here," Kathleen whispered at the end of the third course. "He's sitting with Mistress Jane." Anna smiled at the footman taking her plate. "He was watching you a moment ago."

Anna looked at her. "I don't know why." She leaned closer. "Perhaps he will dance with you tonight."

Kathleen turned a startled glance on her. "What? No! He wouldn't ... I couldn't ..."

"Nonsense. He will probably dance with every other lady in the room, so there is no reason why he should not dance with you."

"But ... I wouldn't know what to say."

"You don't have to say anything. Just smile, and follow the steps."

The next course arrived, and the ladies were silent as they ate. Once or twice Kathleen glanced up, then hurriedly looked down again. "He's looking this way again," she whispered as the plates were cleared away. "What do you think he's looking at?"

"Who?"

"Master Brant, of course!"

Anna shrugged. "Perhaps he just wants to see who is here."

The music struck up as the last course was removed, and footmen appeared to disassemble the tables and remove them from the room, opening the hall for dancing. Anna moved to the wall, watching as Alfred and Matilda stepped down from the dais. Her hand rested in his, and he led her into the center of the hall. "My lady," he said with a bow. Rupert took her other hand, and soon a large circle was forming as they danced their way around the room. Anna was watching the dancers when a touch on her elbow pulled her attention away. She turned to see Garrick smiling down at her.

"My lady," he said.

She returned the smile, and taking his outstretched hand, allowed him to lead her into the circle of dancers. Someone she didn't recognize held out his hand to the other side of her, and she lightly placed her hand in his as the music of a popular carol was struck up.

"This reminds me of home," Garrick said as they moved around to the simple rhythm. She saw Max join the circle of dancers with Jane at his side.

"Storbrook never had this many people," she replied. She let go of his hand to execute a twirl. "What do you think of Civitas?" she asked as his hand wrapped around hers once more. Across the room she saw Rupert dancing, Blanche on one side, Mary Pritchard on the other. He was watching her, his expression blank.

"Civitas? Too crowded. Too noisy. And too smelly."

Anna laughed. "Is that all?"

Blanche whispered something in the prince's ear. His gaze settled on Garrick for a moment, then moved back to her.

"I prefer the countryside," Garrick said. "But I think you know that." Anna nodded as Rupert dropped out of the circle and left the room through a side door. Anna's glance fell on Max for a moment, and she saw he, too, was watching Rupert, his expression severe. The music ended, and Anna turned to Garrick.

"You must dance with some other ladies, as well." She nodded in Kathleen's direction. "Lady Kathleen is very shy, but she is a good friend. Ask her to dance with you."

"I will be back," he promised, then turned towards Kathleen. The music struck up again, and another man was at Anna's side, begging her to join him. She smiled and nodded, letting him take her by the hand.

The music for the simple carols changed to line dances, where couples danced side by side in line, or facing one another. She danced the first of these with Prince John, accepting his hand with the ceremony befitting a prince of the land. The young prince watched his feet for the entire dance, intent on executing the steps properly, and she smiled at his earnestness. She danced with the officers, smiling at Garrick when he scowled at her partners; and when Garrick pushed his way back to her side, she danced with him again. Kathleen, too, did not lack for dance partners, although Anna noticed that Kathleen tended to look anywhere but at the face of the man holding her hand. She saw Max approach Kathleen during the evening, and she took his proffered hand in flustered confusion, allowing him to lead her into the dance.

"I need some fresh air," Garrick said sometime towards midnight. "I will be back soon." She nodded, and watched as he pushed his way through the crowds. She turned back to the dance floor to see Max making his way towards her.

"It will appear very strange if you are the only lady I don't dance with," he said teasingly, "so will you do me the honor?"

"Maybe I prefer to not be considered one of your adoring admirers," she said with an upraised eyebrow, but she placed her hand in his all the same. She shivered as his fingers curled around hers, and he glanced at her in amusement.

"Perhaps I should be taking you to a secluded corner to warm you up," he said, tightening his fingers when she tried to pull her hand from his grasp. "Don't worry," he whispered, "I have no plans to seduce you." He looked at her with a grin. "At least not tonight when all the other women will watch with raging jealousy."

She laughed. "You are so arrogant," she said.

"I know," he said. "You've told me so before."

The orchestra struck up a new piece, sounding the first few notes of a circle dance, danced in two rings. The men stood in the center facing outwards, while the women formed an outer ring, facing the men. Part way through the dance, each man would step to his right, moving to a new dance partner. Max led her into the formation, and turned to face her as the music swelled. Both her hands were in his as she stepped towards him, while he stepped back in time with the melody. His gaze held hers, and she could see the yellow specks deep in his gray eyes, sparkling when the glow of the candles fell across his countenance. He pulled her a little closer as they moved in silent unison, and her gown swished across his legs. The flame in his eyes flared slightly, and she felt a matching burn growing in the pit of her stomach. Her lips fell open, and he glanced down at them for a moment, before bringing his gaze back to hers. He moved his hands to her hips and she drew in a deep breath. He was lifting her, turning her in a circle, before slowly lowering her back to the floor. Her body slid against his, and the breath caught in her throat as she stared at him. Her toes touched the ground, but he did not move his hands from her hips. Instead, he slid them around her waist and pulled her into the middle of the circle, out of the ring of dancers. She did not notice the other men stepping sideways, closing the space she and Max had created. At that moment, nothing existed besides herself and Max. His long fingers were splayed over her back, and she could feel the trails of heat they made as she gazed at him. His legs were pressed against her skirts and she could feel their muscular strength against her legs. His face was bent down, and just a few inches separated his mouth from hers. She lifted her hands and wrapped her fingers around his arms, and for a moment, she could see the fire blazing in his eyes, right to his very soul. He closed his eyes and breathed in deeply, and her hands slid up to his shoulders.

The sound of her name being called came from far away, and it was only when Max opened his eyes and drew away from her that she heard it.

"It's Garrick," he said. He gave her a rueful smile, and she drew in a shuddering breath as a wave of shame washed over her. She turned and saw Garrick striding angrily across the room towards the circle of dancers, his fists clenched at his sides as he pushed through the crowd. She drew in another deep breath and walked towards him. She felt Max follow her, but ignored him. Max may have behaved indecorously, but that was not surprising – he flirted shamelessly with all the women. It was her own behavior, her response to him, that was inexcusable.

But as she drew closer to Garrick, it wasn't her he was looking at. His attention was focused on the man behind her.

"I need to talk to you," he said angrily. "Outside."

"Garrick," she said. He glanced at her in silence, then looked back at Max.

"Now." Garrick turned and left the room and she watched him leave, her heart sinking. She could feel Max looking at her, but she turned her back to him and walked away.

Garrick did not return to the room, and neither did Max. She was sure Max would do nothing to hurt Garrick, but if it came to a fight, there was no denying who the stronger combatant would be. Matilda took her leave of the remaining company shortly before one o'clock, Elizabeth and Kathleen following her from the room. Kathleen glanced at Anna, but Anna did not follow them. She could not bear to listen to their idle chatter when she was so distraught. Her self-revulsion knew no bounds as she mentally cursed herself. She had behaved no better than a harlot.

She left the hall a little later and walked quickly along the passages towards the wing where the queen's apartments were located. The few lamps that still burned were little more than flickering sparks, and the shadows stretched long fingers along the corridor. She had just reached the foot of the stairs when she heard the sound of footsteps.

"Mistress." She looked up to see Rupert coming towards her, his expression derisive as she took a step backwards. "I could have you right now if I chose," he said.

"You could, but you won't."

His eyebrows rose slightly. "Oh?"

She took in a breath to control the trembling in her voice. "You are too wise to take such a foolish risk. I think you will bide your time until you can bring about complete humiliation."

He snorted dryly. "It is such a pity you forced my hand," he said, "because I would really enjoy tasting that sharp tongue of yours. But you had your chance, and have done us both a disfavor."

She snorted. "Somehow, I don't feel disfavored at all." She nodded her head and started climbing the stairs.

"Oh, Mistress," Rupert said when she was about halfway up. "Who was that man you were dancing with?"

She turned around slowly. "What man?"

"One of my archers. Garrick Flynn, I believe his name is." He regarded her through narrowed eyes. "I know who he is, Anna. I just want to know who he is to *you*."

Anna looked away. "He's just a boy I know from my village."

"So he doesn't mean anything to you, then?"

She shook her head. "No," she whispered. She glanced at him, then turning away, continued up the stairs.

CHAPTER THIRTY-THREE

That night, Anna had vivid dreams. Garrick held her in his arms, his hand stroking her face. "I love you," he whispered. He kissed her, his lips tender and gentle, and when he pulled back to look at her again, his eyes were sad. "Nothing will ever change my love for you," he said, "but I have to let you go."

"No," she whispered, "You can't go. I'm going to marry you," but he stepped back and started walking away, his body growing hazy and insubstantial as he walked. "Stop," she cried, "come back. We have to get married." She started running after him, but he was disappearing in the mist.

"I love you, Anna." His voice was faint, and her name trailed into silence. She looked around wildly, but all around her was inky blackness. There was a rustling sound, a movement, and she turned towards it. Max was walking towards her, his burning eyes the only light in the darkness.

"Garrick's gone," she said, and she could hear the despair in her voice.

"I know."

"I was going to marry him."

"I know." He reached for her hands, but she stepped

away.

"I have to find Garrick," she said.

"Garrick's gone," he said, "but I'm here." He stepped closer, wrapping his fingers around her hands. His eyes were blazing flames that seemed to burn right into her. "I love you," he said. She could feel his breath against her skin.

"Does love last forever, Max?" she asked.

"Forever, my darling," he said. His face was turning to flames as he stared at her, and she was slowly engulfed in a blazing inferno. She gasped, jolting upright in a waking fright as her eyes flew open. Her heart was racing, and when she placed her hand on her chest, she felt it trembling. Across the room a log fell in the fire grate, sending sparks flying into the air, and she jumped, startled. Her hands were slick with sweat, and she had to force herself to lie back down. It was a dream, just a dream. Garrick had not gone, and Max did not love her. But a profound sense of loss settled around her, and it took a long time before her heart stopped racing and her breathing finally settled. She rolled onto her side and stared into the darkness.

She dozed on and off until the morning light, and when she finally rose from the bed, her head was aching. She rubbed her temples with her fingers, but it did little to relieving the incessant pounding. Her eyes were scratchy, as though they had been rubbed in grit, and she closed them as Betsy helped her don her gown. She was hardly aware of what she was doing as she went through the motions of the morning routine, but she managed to hold the tray without spilling. Matilda looked at her sharply.

"What is wrong with you this morning? You look wan and sickly," she said. "Go back to bed; you are no use to me like this."

Anna nodded, not caring what the queen thought of her in that moment, and collapsed gratefully onto her bed with a groan. Her head was too sore to think of anything, and within moments she had fallen asleep. The women came and went through the chamber, but she did not stir until late in the afternoon. She woke to the sound of the canaries chirping brightly as the late afternoon sun streamed through the window, shining on the metal cage. She watched the birds for a moment as she lay on the bed, turning when Betsy came into the room, a pile of linens in her arms.

"You're awake. A letter came for you earlier this afternoon," Betsy said. She lay down the linens she was holding and pulled the missive from her pocket. As Anna took it from her hand, she saw the image of a dragon pressed into the wax. She slid her finger under the seal and opened the letter.

'Dear Anna,' she read. 'We have this morning received word from Aaron that he and Keira are traveling to Drake Manor on a matter of business. They will arrive two days hence, and have requested that I inform you of this decision in the hope that you can arrange a short time of absence from court, and visit with them here. If this plan is amenable to you, and you are able to secure the queen's agreement, Favian will fetch you from court on Thursday morning. The man who brought this message will wait to receive your reply.'

"Is the man who brought this message still here?" Anna asked Betsy.

"I believe so," she replied.

"Good! Do you know where I can find Her Majesty?"

An hour later a reply was in the hand of the messenger, who was already racing through the streets of Civitas, eager to arrive back at Drake Manor before dark. 'I look forward to seeing Favian on Thursday morning,' Anna had written.

When Favian arrived at the palace mid-morning on the appointed day, Anna was ready and waiting. She had written a short note to Garrick explaining her absence, sending one of the many urchins that hung around the palace to the army camp to deliver the missive. She had not seen him since the ball – was he angry with her? She couldn't blame him if he was, she thought, as a wave of self-recrimination washed over her.

She and Favian arrived at Drake House shortly after noon, just a few minutes after Aaron and Keira. Keira rushed out to greet her, throwing her arms around her younger sister.

"Anna! I'm so glad you could come."

Anna pulled back with a laugh. "Of course! Did you think I would miss the chance to see you, even if it meant drawing the queen's wrath? But she was quite happy to give her permission, as long as I am not gone too long."

The hours passed quickly as Anna related all the happenings at court. She told Keira about the queen's ruse to see the city, and how she had coerced Alfred into allowing her to march with the army. She talked about the balls and entertainments, and told Keira about the hospital.

"What about Garrick?" Keira asked. "Do you ever see him?" Anna was sitting on a chair across from the window, and for a moment she stared out at the gardens.

"Yes," she finally said. "I accepted his marriage proposal."

"You did?" Keira leaned back in her chair. "I thought ..." she paused. "Well, I didn't expect this." Anna looked back at her sister.

"It came as a bit of a surprise to me, too," Anna said wryly. "But Garrick loves me, and I think we can be happy together."

Keira nodded slowly. "Aaron says Max is back in the city."

Anna nodded. "He is."

"And yet you still accepted Garrick?"

Anna took in a deep breath. "I didn't mean to, at first. You know how I allow my tongue to run away from me! But when I gave it some thought, I knew that I could be happy with him. He loves me. He is steady, and will work hard to provide for his family. As for Max, well, he has given me no reason to think he cares for me at all. We still annoy each other. And the fact that he stayed away so long shows he no longer has feelings for me." She drew in a ragged breath. "I would rather not talk about Max, if you don't mind."

Keira nodded. "Very well," she said.

As Keira and Anna spent the afternoon talking, dragons were arriving at Drake Manor. Aaron had called a council meeting, and the council members were convening at the manor house before heading into the mountains. The only council member Anna knew was Owain, so she gave the others little attention, but later that day she heard the voice of another dragon drift down the passage from the hall. Max had come to Drake Manor. She darted a quick glance at Keira, then looked away. It mattered not a whit that Max was there. He had come to see his master, and her presence there was just a coincidence. In fact, she could hear Max greeting Aaron, and imagined him thumping a closed fist over his heart, his head bowed before his master. Of all the dragons, only Favian knew Aaron better than Max. Max's connection to his master ran deep, the result of drinking Aaron's blood every day during the conflict with Jack.

Anna rose to her feet. "I think I'll take a walk," she said. Keira nodded, saying nothing. Slipping out the door, Anna turned in the opposite direction from the hall, where the dragons were congregated, and instead headed towards a small side door that led to the kitchen garden. She was almost at the door when she felt a wave of heat wash over her, but she did not glance around. She continued walking, slipping through the door and into the gardens. It was only when she was a short distance from the house that Max called her name, and she turned around to look at him.

"Is Garrick still alive?" she asked.

He looked at her in surprise. "I think so. Why would you ask me that?"

"I haven't seen him since the ball."

"Oh!" Max laughed wryly. "And you think I killed him? Had him for dinner? You should know me better than that!

The last time I saw your betrothed, he was hale and hearty."

Anna nodded. "Good." She turned around and started walking away again, but Max caught her by the arm.

"Anna, we need to talk." She turned back to look into his face.

"There is nothing to say, Max. I should never have danced with you the other night, and I regret the anguish I must have caused Garrick when he saw us. I am marrying Garrick, Max. He loves me, and will always be there for me."

Max looked up at a dragon circling the clouds. "You will never forgive me, will you?"

"Forgive you? For dancing with me?"

"For leaving. After Jack," he added when she was silent.

"Oh." She stared across the garden for a moment, before bringing her gaze back to him. "I don't blame you for leaving," she said softly. "I was a selfish child who was mistrustful and rude, so the apologies should be on my side."

"No," he said. "We were both young and conceited. I should never have stayed away so long." He looked back at her. "I was angry, and told myself my anger was justified. And then, as the years went by, I convinced myself that you had forgotten about me and that you no longer cared. But the truth is, I was too proud to come back." He paused for a moment. "I'm sorry."

She stared up at him. Was he right? Did she resent him for leaving? For not coming back? She had not even admitted it to herself, but as he said the words, she knew what he said was true. Buried deep beneath a load of guilt lay a lake of resentment. He had touched it, and brought it to the surface.

"I'm not going anywhere," he said. "Not this time. I know you are determined to marry Garrick, but I will stay here until there is no hope remaining." She pulled in a deep breath, and turned away.

"It's too late," she whispered, and without a backwards glance, walked away.

CHAPTER THIRTY-FOUR

Favian arranged for a carriage to take Anna back to the palace the next day. The council meetings hadn't finished yet, but Anna had promised the queen that she would remain only a few days. As she approached the apartments, she saw Frank eyeing her narrowly.

"You've been gone," he said as she drew near.

"I was visiting family," she said.

"Your sister is married to Aaron Drake, isn't she?" He didn't wait for confirmation, but stalked towards her until his face was just a few inches from hers. "Does the dragon slayer know that you are friends with a dragon?"

Anna took a step back. "Did you tell the king?" she asked.

Frank glared at her for a moment. "He didn't seem too concerned, so I told the prince."

Anna took a deep breath. "You told Rupert?"

Frank smirked. "That doesn't please you, does it?" He laughed mirthlessly as she pushed the door open to the chambers and went inside.

She had only been back a few hours when one of the maids brought a message from Garrick. He was in the courtyard, and wanted to see her. She nodded and left the room, slipping down the stairs and out the doors. Frank was watching her again, but she ignored him. Garrick stared at her intently as she walked towards him.

She gave him a tentative smile. "Are you angry with me?" she said. He pushed himself upright with a sigh.

"No, I'm not angry with you. With the beast, but not you."

"I didn't see you again after the ball. I didn't know if you had been hurt."

"Why would I have been hurt?" He sounded surprised.

"Because you called a dragon outside!"

Garrick laughed. "The thought that he would injure me never crossed my mind. I'm sorry I caused you concern. Were you waiting for me?"

"I was."

"By the time the dragon and I were done, it was very late. I assumed you had left. If I had known you were waiting, I would have come back."

"Did you receive my note?" she said.

"I did. You went to see your sister and Master Drake at his cousin's house."

"Yes."

"And was the dragon there, too?"

"There were many dragons there, Garrick."

Garrick frowned. "You know who I mean."

"Max went to see Aaron." Garrick's eyes narrowed. "He didn't go because of me," she said.

"The fact that you were there gave him an added incentive to go, however,"

Anna glanced away. "Let's not talk about Max," she said. She brought her gaze back to his. "I told Keira about our betrothal."

Garrick looked at her in surprise. "I thought you wanted to wait."

"I still do, but I didn't want to keep the news from my sister." Garrick nodded in silence. "Aren't you happy?" she asked.

"Of course I am," he said, reaching for her hands. "Very happy." He glanced up at the sky. "The weather has become a lot more settled," he said. "It won't be long now before we march."

"I had better get used to riding," she said.

A look of confusion furrowed his brow. "Why?"

"Don't you know?" Anna was surprised. "The queen plans to follow the troops. She thinks her presence will give the armies across the border a reason to rally to Roderick's cause."

"And you intend to go too?" he said cautiously.

Anna nodded. "Of course."

"No."

"No?"

"You cannot go," he said. "It will be dangerous, not to mention uncomfortable."

"I didn't think it would be anything else."

"Does Master Drake know of this foolish intention?"

"Yes."

"And he is happy with this?" Garrick's eyes bored into her as his features hardened. "He intends to send along a certain dragon to watch over you, doesn't he?"

"I don't know! He said nothing to me." Anna turned away and stared into the distance. "I'm not going to fight a battle," she said. "The queen will stay well back from the battle lines, and I will be attending to her."

"I don't like this."

Anna turned around. "It's not for you to like, Garrick."

"You are my betrothed. Do I not have a say?"

"When we are married, I will submit to your will, although I hope you will give heed to my opinion. But until then, I will do what I feel is right."

Garrick stared at the distant hills. "Very well! It would seem that you have no regard for my feelings in this matter. I can at least be grateful that I will be there to watch over you."

"I'm sorry, Garrick, I know you don't like this, but I cannot stay behind while the queen goes."

Garrick nodded. "I know."

Garrick left a short while later, and Anna returned to the parlor. Kathleen watched her as she walked across the room and took a seat near the window.

"Who is the man who keeps coming to see you?" Kathleen asked.

"His name is Garrick Flynn," Anna said. "We were childhood friends."

Kathleen nodded. "Is he the one who danced so much with you the night of the ball?" Anna nodded. "I wondered if he was something more than a friend." Kathleen looked at the embroidery in her hands as a blush colored her cheeks. Anna looked away.

"Just a good friend," she said.

With the arrival of the warmer, drier weather, preparations for war started to be put into action. The council met every day, and although Rupert wanted to march immediately, the council backed the king when he suggested they wait for Roderick to arrive with the forces he had mustered. Rupert was not pleased, and had left the council chambers tight-lipped and close-fisted.

After much deliberation, Elizabeth announced that she was too old to travel across the countryside on horseback, a decision that Matilda accepted with only a slight flash of annoyance. There would still be three ladies traveling with her, along with numerous maids, footmen, cooks, and the guards, Frank and Tobias. A separate wagon had been arranged for the queen's luggage and that of her entourage, but they would travel at the back of the column on horseback, while the maids and servants traveled with the wagons on foot. Frank and Tobias would ride with the ladies, of course.

Garrick helped Anna choose a fine mare to travel the countryside on, and had commissioned a new saddle from the saddler using funds given to him by Aaron for the supply of his own needs, despite Anna's protestations.

"A good saddle is the key to a comfortable ride," he told her.

Matilda was also having a new saddle made, but she had ordered one of the new-fangled side saddles that were becoming more popular amongst high-born ladies in the foreign courts. It allowed for more fashionable riding attire, but Anna viewed it with scorn. How could you possibly ride comfortably on such a contraption, she wondered?

The packing and preparations continued apace. Matilda ordered her luggage packed, and then, unsure of the gowns she had chosen, ordered everything unpacked again.

"Should I take my red, peasant gown?" she had asked Anna. "Then I could mix with the commoners and encourage their support of Roderick." But Anna had replied that she didn't believe it would be necessary to employ such subterfuge.

Although the ladies would be following the army, they expected to have far more comfortable quarters than a tent and camp cots. Already word had been sent ahead to all the noble houses along the marching route to expect both kings, the queen and her ladies, where the host would have the privilege of feeding and entertaining his guests – at his expense, of course. Once they reached the mountains, however, there were only a few meager villages stretched miles apart, and Matilda and the ladies would have to contend with more primitive accommodations.

Along with an assortment of gowns, boots and riding habits, Anna had also acquired a straw hat for the journey – an item of great amusement amongst the ladies. Blanche had openly sneered at the unfashionable headdress, and even Kathleen had mentioned that it might not seem fitting for a lady in the company of the queen to be seen wearing such an article, but Anna had stoutly refused to part with it.

"You will be wishing I had acquired one for each of you," she told the other ladies, but they just laughed.

As the first day of the march grew closer, Anna saw less and less of Garrick, and when she did see him, she could tell he was distracted.

"My apologies, Anna," he said when she commented on it. "I need to be with my men as we make final preparations." He smiled at her, then hurried away as she watched in bemusement.

Roderick arrived a week after Anna's return from Drake Manor. He brought with him fifteen hundred men, swelling the army to a little over five thousand. More would join along the way, as the army progressed through the kingdom. Added to the soldiers were wagons with supplies, guarded by outriders; a herd of cattle; smiths, with their forges loaded onto carts; and the inevitable camp followers – cooks, washerwomen, wives, children and prostitutes.

Anna had not seen Max at all since her return to the palace. It was not that she hadn't looked for him – she couldn't help herself scanning the crowds for sight of him, but he was never there. So she was surprised when, the day before the army was to start their march, she saw him striding towards her along one of the many palace passages. She watched him as he approached – the one thing she could not do with Max was pretend indifference.

"I'm marching with the army," Max said, "as one of the foot soldiers."

"Why?" Anna asked in surprise.

"Aaron wants me to report back on the king's progress. And I will be able to watch over you." Anna looked away. Why did everyone think she needed watching over?

"Why aren't you flying?" she asked.

"I don't want to be restricted to my natural form, and people will wonder what I am doing there if I haven't marched with the others."

"That sounds very, uh, tedious," Anna said.

Max smiled. "Extremely, but I dare say I will survive. Especially since you will be there to keep things entertaining." Anna stared at the floor. Her feelings for Max were so tangled and confused. He watched her for a moment, then stepped away. "I will see you along the way," he said.

The first soldiers started marching at first light the following morning. It was six hundred miles to the border, a distance that would take a month for such a large army to cover. The people in the rear would only leave the following day – that included the queen, her ladies, her ladies' maids, other servants, the supplies, and Frank and Tobias. That evening Matilda took a fond farewell of her children, staying in the nursery long enough to listen to the nurse tell a story, before bidding each of them a goodnight.

They started their journey early the following morning, shivering as they mounted their horses, before clattering across the courtyard and through the palace gates. Matilda, Blanche, Kathleen and Anna, along with Frank and Tobias bringing up the rear, all rode on horseback. The rest of the entourage walked with the wagons, and it did not take long for the small group of riders to outpace the slower carts. The early morning chill hung in the air as they set out, but as the sun rose higher, Anna could feel little trickles of sweat running down her neck. They soon saw signs of the army's progress from the previous day – trampled grass, broken branches, and as the day progressed, the remains of camp fires. They pushed on through the morning, pausing for a short time at noon, then continued for another few hours until the house of their first host came into sight. They trotted up the road, and were soon welcomed by Lord Southam and his lady. They had had the privilege of entertaining the king the previous night, and they smiled in welcome now as the queen swept through the front door and into the hall. Anna noticed Lady Southam glance anxiously around the hall for a moment before her shoulders relaxed slightly. A roaring fire burned in the grate and the table on the dais had been neatly laid with silverware and porcelain plates, while a flagon of wine and an assortment of glasses lay on a smaller side table at the entrance to the hall.

"Wine, Your Majesty?" Lord Southam offered.

"Thank you, my lord," Matilda replied graciously.

After a long day in the saddle, the hearty meal was fully enjoyed, and when the ladies retired to the chambers prepared for their use later that evening, Anna felt as though every muscle in her body was aching. The bed was soft and inviting, and when she lay down, she was sure she could sleep forever.

"I'm not sure I can ride again tomorrow," Kathleen said with a groan, lying down next to Anna on the wide mattress.

"You'll feel worse in the morning," she assured Kathleen with a grin, and when the girl half-heartedly tossed a pillow in her direction, she laughed. "You can always stay with the Southams," she said. "Your presence here will be a solace to them when the rest of us leave tomorrow," she said.

"Do you really think so?" Kathleen said in surprise, while Blanche snorted from the next bed.

"No, you silly goose," Anna said with a laugh. "I think they will be quite happy to bid us all a pleasant journey and close the door on our backs."

As Anna had predicted, they felt stiff and sore the following morning, and groaned their way into their saddles. The exertion of the ride helped to relieve some of the aching, however, and they soon fell back into the rhythmic motion of the horses. They caught up with the rest of the army shortly after noon. A permanent cloud of dust hung on the horizon, and when they came across the camp fires from the previous night, some were found to still be smoldering. That night, when they arrived at the next house, Alfred and Roderick were there too, bending the ear of their host about the trials of marching. Rupert, Anna discovered, preferred to remain with his troops, for which she was incredibly grateful.

CHAPTER THIRTY-FIVE

As the days progressed, the ladies fell into a pattern of riding for a few hours, resting for a few hours, then riding again. Alfred always ordered an early-morning meal from his hosts, and he and Roderick would leave as soon as they were done eating, but Matilda and her ladies took their time, not leaving until the sun was well above the horizon. Each night they progressed to the next house along the route, partaking of their meals with their hosts before collapsing into their beds. During the day they rode until the late morning sun became unpleasant, then rested for a few hours until it became bearable once more. The wagons and servants did not stop, but continued past the resting group at their slower pace. They would ride for another few hours later in the day, catching up with Alfred and Roderick at the next home they were staying in.

Anna's sense in retaining the ugly straw hat soon became evident – the veils and scarves the other women wore did nothing to keep the sun from their faces, and soon their delicate, pale skin was painted pink by the sun, before the skin peeled away in unsightly patches. The salves and ointments they brought with them did little to protect them, but it was the queen who suffered the most, with her pale complexion and fair hair, until Anna reluctantly offered her the straw hat. It was accepted with alacrity, and Anna handed it over with a sigh. Perhaps she could convince a farm hand to give her another.

Either Frank or Tobias traveled with the women at all times. Whenever Frank was around, his eyes seemed to be trained on Anna, until she felt as though he was boring a hole right through her skin. She ignored him as best she could, and as the weeks went by, he relaxed his vigilance, albeit it ever so slightly. After all, he had seen no more dragons, and apart from her penchant for walking, there was nothing in her behavior to arouse further suspicion. But Anna knew that Frank could not forget the dragon, nor that he had seen her with the creature.

As the days wore on, Anna lost track of the names of their hosts and the places they had stayed. The faces of Lords Bradbury, Cropter, Ludlow and Elliot blurred into one, and she could not remember if Rompton was the town with the huge water mill or the Roman ruins. At each place, they were cheered on by the townspeople, although there were always some in the crowds who scowled and turned away, mumbling to themselves as they dragged their wives and children with them. In one town, a young girl presented the queen with a crown of flowers, and when Matilda asked her name, it was discovered the child was deaf and mute. But the girl smiled sweetly and her father watched her proudly as she presented the gift to the queen, before taking her by the hand and leading her away.

Of Garrick, Anna saw no sign. She hoped he was comfortable at night, sleeping on the cold, hard ground. Sometimes Anna would stand at the window and look out into the dark, watching the stars twinkling in the night sky, wondering whether he was staring up at the stars wondering about her, or whether he was too tired to do anything but sleep. Sometimes, another face would intrude on her thoughts, but she would push it away, angry at herself for her moment of weakness. But she could not help searching the stars, looking for the evidence of twin fires burning in the sky above watching over her. She saw them often, and would turn away, pretending she didn't care.

The first week of traveling was over flat, grassy terrain. Small, spring flowers had once dotted the wide, open fields, but there were few in evidence by the time the queen and her ladies passed by, having been trodden into the ground by thousands of marching feet. In the second week they had to ford a small river, and then the terrain grew more uneven as the mountains in the distance grew ever closer. By the third week they were skirting the mountain range, which lay to the east. Over the towering heights of the mountains lay Storbrook, and Anna wondered whether Aaron was watching their progress. The mountain range ran straight along the trail for a hundred miles, then curved away from them, a distant marker that finally faded into a purple smudge on the horizon. When the path led through dense forests, the army troops would march around them, but the women traveled straight through, enjoying the cool shadows.

It was as they neared the mountains that the homes of noblemen grew further and further apart, and the luxury of a building with separate chambers and comfortable beds became a thing of the past. Instead, the women had to be content with sleeping in tents at night.

"Once we cross the border and reach the towns in the north, there will be people who will gladly open their homes to King Roderick and his sister," Matilda assured her ladies. "These uncomfortable nights, sleeping in tents, will not be of long duration."

Every night, Frank and Tobias oversaw the setup of the camp, and instructed where the tents were to be positioned. Matilda had her own tent, but Blanche, Kathleen and Anna shared another, while the maids slept in a third. Meals were prepared over an open campfire, and as the stars appeared in the sky, the ladies drank their wine from silver goblets and ate from porcelain plates. As often as possible, the guards chose a site that had a source of water, and the queen and her ladies would gratefully wash off the dust and sweat of the day. As the days progressed, Anna could feel her body growing stronger. She was not as tired as she had been at the start of the trip, and when they stopped each afternoon, felt she could travel another few hours at least. Now that they were camping, Anna sometimes caught sight of Garrick marching through the camp. He was often with his men, but when he was alone, he would come over and visit with her briefly. His skin had turned nut brown, and his muscles strained against the shirt and leather jerkin he wore. He only stayed a few minutes at a time, long enough to enquire after her health, before disappearing once more between the many men.

The late spring weather grew hotter and drier as they marched. Dust covered everything, getting into the folds of Anna's gown, into her hair, under her fingernails, and even coating her teeth until her mouth felt gritty. They arrived one hot afternoon to find that Frank had chosen a site near a pond fed by an underground spring. She slid off her horse, and turned to Kathleen. "Come," she said, "let's go swimming." Kathleen looked alarmed.

"I don't know how to swim," she said.

"There's nothing to it," Anna said. "The pond probably isn't very deep."

Reeds and weeds surrounded the small lake, and the two women had to push their way through, scratching their legs, before they reached the water; but once they were in, the water was clear and refreshing. It felt so good to feel the dust wash off her skin, and Anna sighed in pleasure. The roads they traveled in the wake of the army had been trodden to dust, making her eyes water, her scalp itch, and the creases behind her knees turn brown. The water was not very deep, as Anna had supposed, and even at the deepest point she could touch the bottom with her toes. She could feel where the underground spring fed the pond, blasting into the water near the center of the little pool. The pond was shared with a small family of ducks, and Kathleen watched the little ducklings take to the water with delight.

"Have you never seen ducklings before?" Anna asked in amusement.

"Yes, but never this close," Kathleen said, turning to watch the fluffy chicks swim past. She glanced up at Anna. "I don't think I will ever eat duck again, knowing how sweet they are as babies."

"All animals start out small and sweet," Anna said with a laugh. "Even dragons!"

"Yes, but I think even a baby dragon would scare me," Kathleen said with a shudder.

"Don't be too sure of that," Anna said. She lay back in the water and watched the clouds drifting past. She saw a creature circling high overhead and stared at it, but it was a bird which soon disappeared from view. She heard a rustling in the grass, and flipping over onto her stomach, saw Blanche pushing through the weeds. She eyed her warily, glancing around to see if anyone else was with her.

"Don't be so suspicious," Blanche said. "I am quite alone." That did not make Anna feel any easier, but she said nothing. "Doesn't this look like fun," Blanche continued. "But I am surprised, Kathleen, that you would join in such rustic pursuits."

"Oh, shush," Anna said, annoyed. "You can come join us if you wish, otherwise go find your own entertainments."

Blanche raised her eyebrows with a grin, then stripping off her gown, stepped into the water. She sunk down to her knees, and dropped her head back in the water.

"I must admit," Blanche said, "you peasants do have some good ideas at times."

The army reached the border to Roderick's kingdom thirty-five days into the march. A wide river, turned brown by the churning feet of the men seeking its cool relief, separated the kingdoms. It led to the ocean, and Anna could see watercraft plying the tides. Long, flat rafts lay pulled up the banks on the near side, large enough to carry the men and supplies over the water. The army had set up camp near the banks, where Alfred had ordered that the army rest for two days before crossing the border – an order that had Rupert seething with rage, chafing at the delay, if the rumors were to be believed. But if he remonstrated with his brother, it was done beyond the hearing of any of the men.

Garrick found Anna later that day. "How goes the marching?" he asked.

"Exhausting!" Anna averred. "We travel on horseback for at least six hours every day, and have to sleep in a *tent* every night. And then, to make matters worse, our meals are a paltry three courses, and we use the same plate for all the savory dishes!" She grinned at him, and he laughed.

"You have endured terrible hardships, indeed. I did warn you, but you were determined to become a camp-follower." He glanced around, nodding at Kathleen when she looked his way. "I cannot stay," he said. "I just wanted to find out how you are doing. I am glad to see you are still in good health and good spirits."

"Of course," she replied. "Do you think I am a wilting flower?"

"I know you are nothing of the kind," he said. He lifted her hand to his mouth, and quickly brushed his lips over her skin, before turning around and striding away without a backwards glance.

That evening the queen dispatched a message to her husband and her brother, urging them to join her for a meal. A table was set up beneath the shade of a tree, and when Alfred and Roderick arrived, they were ushered to stools at the waiting tables. Tobias had snared a brace of pheasants and a rabbit, and the food simmered over the camp fire as wine from the supply wagon was served in silver goblets.

"Did you follow the army to enjoy picnic meals in the open air?" Alfred asked wryly, but Roderick just laughed.

"What else would you expect of my sister?" he said. He smiled at Matilda. "Only the best for you, eh, Matty?"

"Of course," she said with a smile. "And you must admit that you are quite happy to enjoy a well-cooked and well-served meal, my lords."

"Most definitely," Roderick assured her, but Alfred remained silent.

The rest of the meal passed well. Blanche chatted to Alfred, while Roderick told Matilda about the march. "We lost a dozen horses along the way," he said. "A terrible loss."

"What about men?" Anna asked.

"Men?"

"How many men did you lose on the march?"

Roderick looked at her in confusion, then turned to Alfred.

"Did we lose any men?" he asked.

Alfred glanced up from his conversation with Blanche. "I think Rupert mentioned that there were a few who dropped out. Some of them died, I suppose, after one company got sick with dysentery. I don't know the numbers, however. Fifty. A hundred, perhaps."

"Ah," Roderick said, turning back to Anna. "A few losses are to be expected. But fifty or even a hundred will not affect our chances at victory."

Across the table, Blanche smirked. "Mistress Anna was born in a small village, where they believe each life has value of its own," she said to Roderick. "People like us understand that a few sacrifices must be made to ensure the greater good."

Roderick nodded and looked at Anna. "Clearly you have a kind heart," he said, "but men who have to scrape out a meager existence from the earth or with their hands have little to live for, anyway. At least they died in service to their country."

"And men will fight to death to free themselves from the chains of tyranny," Matilda added.

Anna excused herself as soon as the meal was done, leaving the cheerful party behind her and wandering into the trees. The sun had not yet completely set, and she found her path taking her up a small hillock. She could see the multitude of camp fires as the soldiers prepared their meals – each one a son, a husband, a father or a friend. In the distance, beyond the river, she could see Roderick and Matilda's homeland. It didn't look much different from the countryside they had traversed, and Anna wondered what it was that made men risk hundreds, or even thousands, of lives, so they could lay claim to a corner of the earth. She still did not have an answer when she returned to the tent later that evening and tried to get some rest.

CHAPTER THIRTY-SIX

The broad rafts Anna had seen lying on the river banks were used to carry supplies and the officers, but the rest of the army had to swim across the swiftly flowing current. Anna stood watching from the small hillock overlooking the river as the men swam through the fast-moving water to the other side. She saw one young man, no older than Kathleen, standing on the closer shore, wildly shaking his head. An axe was strapped to his back, and it swayed precariously at his vigorous movements. Another man stood with him, pointing across the river, clearly trying to urge the young man in, but to no avail. Would they leave him behind, Anna wondered, or force him into the water, to be swept away by the current? There had already been a few men washed downstream, their lives sacrificed before they even reached enemy territory, but something about this man drew Anna. Perhaps it was his age. Or the sandy-colored hair which reminded her of a younger Garrick.

As she watched, someone approached the pair. With the sun in her eyes, she could not see at first who it was, but when he turned slightly, she recognized Max. He spoke to the young man, laying his hand on his shoulder, and after a few minutes of earnest conversation, the young man nodded. He followed Max into the water. When it reached his waist, he started to wave his arms wildly, but Max turned and said something to him, and he placed his hands on Max's shoulders. With a kick, Max was in the middle of the river, the man clinging to his back. Max was a strong swimmer, which did not surprise Anna, and it did not take him long to reach the other bank.

As soon as the young man was on the far shore, Max turned and dived back into the current, swimming powerfully and with astonishing speed back to the closer bank where the men stood congregated, attempting their own crossings. He scanned the crowd, then approached someone else. Soon he was swimming once again across the river, with a second man clinging to him. When he came back to the bank the third time, Anna saw Garrick walk towards him. He said something to Max, then turning around, pointed at one of the men congregated on the bank. There was a brief conversation, and then Garrick, too, was in the water, helping a man across. He was not as fast as Max, and when he reached the other side, he paused for a moment, hands on knees, to catch his breath, before diving back into the current. Free of his burden, he moved much quicker, and was soon picking out another man to offer his aid to. As the crowd watched, more men stepped forward, strong and powerful, offering their help to the men who could not swim, until there was a small group of swimmers carting men on their backs through the water, back and forth. Anna smiled to herself when she saw Garrick push some of the larger, heavier men in Max's direction, and when one of the men turned to look at Garrick in surprise, he just shrugged his shoulders as Max laughed. Garrick, of course, was well familiar with Max's strength, but none of the other men knew what Max could do. One by one, twenty or so men were helped across the water, until only Garrick and Max were still swimming back and forth. A small crowd had formed on the far bank to cheer them on, but Anna could see that Garrick was tired, fighting for each stroke through the river. It was after his fourth crossing that he fell to his knees in the shallow water on the far bank, pushing the man he was helping ahead of him. He stayed there for a moment before staggering once more to his feet.

"Stay there," Anna whispered to herself, sucking in her breath when he dived back into the water. She could see immediately that he was in trouble, too weary to lift his arms. She jumped to her feet. "No," she shouted as she ran down the little hill towards the river. "Help him!"

Max was in the water, swimming back to shore, when he heard her voice. He lifted his head in her direction, then swung around to see Garrick floundering in the water. He dived beneath the water's surface, shooting like an arrow through the murky depths. He reached Garrick before Anna could even draw in another breath, grasping him by the waist and towing him back to the far shore. She saw Garrick collapse onto the bank on his knees, Max leaning over him, speaking into his ear. Garrick nodded, and Max pulled away. He turned and looked over his shoulder at her for a brief moment, then rising to his feet, walked out of the shallow water and out of sight. Garrick crawled on his hands and knees onto the muddy grassland where someone grabbed him beneath the arms and hauled him to his feet, dragging him to a high log. A flask was shoved into his hand, and tipping his head back, he threw the contents down his throat before wiping his arm across his mouth.

The soldiers encountered the enemy for the first time that afternoon. A small company of a dozen enemy men put fire to a supply wagon that was left unattended in the chaos of the crossing. Alfred's men had quickly turned on their attackers, but the resulting fight was little more than a skirmish. Three of Alfred's men were taken prisoner, while another two were wounded before the enemy beat a hasty retreat with their prisoners.

"We chased them off!" Alfred said as Rupert finished recounting the events. "Our first battle was victorious."

Rupert snorted. "Their mission was to observe our progress and report back to Terran," he said. "They escaped unharmed, and made off with three of our men, so it seems to me that they are the victors today." He narrowed his eyes. "They had better enjoy it, because it will be the last time."

It took a full day for the entire army to cross the river, and another for the supplies, horses and camp followers. Matilda and her entourage crossed on a raft at the end of the first day, setting up camp along the riverbanks in Matilda's homeland. As she stepped onto the muddy shore, she stretched out her arms and lifted her face to the sun. "At last I have come home," she said. She turned to her brother, waiting nearby, with a smile. "Do you feel it, Roddy?" she said. "The sun shining down on us is a sign that we will be victorious. You will come to your throne, and all will be well."

Roderick smiled. "Aye, my dear," he said, "I feel it. And taste it. Terran will soon be fleeing like a dog with his tail between his legs while the people welcome their true king."

As Anna turned away, she saw Max standing a little further down the bank, looking in her direction. Behind her the sun was setting and as she returned his gaze, she could see his skin shimmering slightly in the low light. "Thank you," she whispered. He smiled, and for a moment she thought she saw the light flare in his eyes, but it might have been the sun shining on him. She turned away, and headed towards the tents.

As the army marched north, they were constantly harried by small groups of enemy men. More men were taken prisoner, and one of the men wounded in the first attack died from his injuries. There were losses on Terran's side, too. One man was taken prisoner, while another was killed by an axe blow to the head. As the days passed, Rupert grew more tight-lipped. The men knew to obey his orders instantly, or face punishment for insurrection. Alfred pleaded for leniency, but his arguments did not sway Rupert. Instead, Rupert snapped out a rude reply that questioned the acumen of his brother before marching away.

Matilda's mood was also affected by news of the skirmishes. "Do they know I am here?" she said one evening, as yet another such report was brought by the guards. "Surely they must know their princess is here, and that their king marches with Alfred."

"I believe they do," Tobias answered cautiously. "The man we captured made, er, mention of your royal name."

"He did?" Matilda leaned forward eagerly. "What did he say?"

Tobias looked at Frank, who shrugged and looked away. Tobias turned back to Matilda in resignation. "He said Your Majesty should return home."

"Home? To the old palace where Roderick and I grew up?"

"No, Your Majesty. Home to Civitas. And to your children."

"Oh."

Tobias nodded his head and quickly walked away.

"It's just the opinion of just one man," Matilda said to Anna. "It doesn't mean anything."

"No, my lady," Anna agreed, keeping her eyes averted as she examined a rip in her gown. "I'm sure the people love you."

Alfred continued to march north, leaving the mountains in the distance as they traversed through wide open plains. They passed by a few isolated homesteads, but when Frank and Tobias approached them to ask for shelter for the queen, they found them locked and barred. They encountered an old woman at one, but she sent them on their way. They did not tell the queen, but Tobias related the incident to Anna in hushed tones.

"The old hag told us the queen is not welcome here, and that Roderick must go back to where he came from," Tobias said, his eyes darting around anxiously as he spoke. "I thought the people here wanted Roderick back on the throne, but that does not seem to be so."

"Perhaps when we reach the towns it will be different," Anna said.

Tobias nodded. "Perhaps. We'll reach the first town tomorrow, and will be on the outskirts of the city within a week. We will soon be engaging the enemy in a proper battle."

"Well, depend upon it, the people in the city will be throwing their support behind Roderick," Anna said. She glanced around the dry and dusty camp. "I'm going to go for a walk," she said.

"You can't!" Tobias was horrified. "It's not safe for a lady."

"I won't go far," Anna said.

"Hey, what's going on there?" Anna had seen Frank watching her and Tobias's whispered conversation. He strode towards them now as Tobias turned to face his fellow guard.

"Mistress Anna wishes to go for a walk."

"A walk? Alone?" Frank's eyes narrowed in suspicion. "Why?"

"Do you think your company is so pleasant I cannot bear to leave it?" Anna said. "I wish for some peace and quiet away from the dust and smoke of the camp." She saw Kathleen come out of the tent. "Besides, I won't be alone. Lady Kathleen is coming with me." She threw a pleading look Kathleen's way.

"Of course," Kathleen said.

"Very well," Frank said. "You can go that way," he pointed to the east, "to avoid the enemy bands seen earlier today. And no further than those trees in the distance." He pointed to a small stand of trees a few hundred yards away.

Anna turned to look where he pointed and nodded. She glanced at Kathleen. "Coming?"

Kathleen nodded. "Yes."

They walked together across the open field. Anna glanced back once to see Frank watching them as they walked, his arms crossed over his chest; but before she looked away again he turned and walked away. The sounds of the army became more distant, until finally they could hear the sounds of bees and other insects darting between the long grasses. Anna swung her arms as she walked, and turned to look at Kathleen.

"Wishing you hadn't come on this march?" she asked.

"Oh, no. It is a wonderful adventure," Kathleen said. "It is a bit tiring at times, and there are so many men who like to stare and make one uncomfortable, but I have never traveled anywhere before except to Civitas and our house in the country."

Anna smiled. "Well, when you look at it that way, this is quite an adventure." They were nearing the copse of trees. There was a slight rustling, and Anna peered into the shadows. The grasses swayed around her feet as strands of hair blew across her face. She turned back to Kathleen. "I saw one of the men greet you earlier today. Do you know him?"

Kathleen blushed. "You mean Lord Giles? No, I don't know him. I mean, not really." She looked down at her feet. They were only a few steps from the woods when Anna heard the rustling sound again. She paused, and so did the sound.

"What is it?" Kathleen said.

"Someone's there," Anna whispered. She grabbed Kathleen's arm and took a step back. "I think we should return." Kathleen nodded, but before they moved another step, Anna saw three men step out from behind the trees. She yanked Kathleen's arm. "Run," she shouted, but it was too late. The first man already had his hands on Kathleen and was dragging her into the shadows. "Stop," Anna shouted. She pounded her fist against the man, but a second man stepped up behind her, and catching her fists he pulled her arms behind her back. She lifted her foot and kicked him in the shin with her boot. The man grunted, but the hold on her arms did not loosen. She heard a voice in her ear.

"A little fighter, eh. Is Roderick recruiting women to do his warring these days?"

"Let me go," she shouted. She rammed her elbow in the man's stomach. His grasp on her arms slackened slightly, and she spun around to look up at the man who had her captive. He was tall, with well-muscled shoulders and arms. His gray eyes were furrowed in a frown, but as he looked down at her his lips stretched into a wide, full smile. He glanced at Kathleen, who stood quiet in the other man's arms, then back at Anna. "Now, what are a pair of women doing wandering around while a war is being waged?"

Anna lifted her eyebrows. "War? The war hasn't even started yet!"

"Really?" The man laughed. "And how many men has Alfred lost so far?" Anna was silent. "So, let me ask my question again. Why are you women wandering around?"

"We are not 'wandering,'" Anna said. "We are taking a walk!"

"A walk? Ah, I see! You decided you must come all the way from your own kingdom and take a walk in ours."

"We are ladies to Queen Matilda," Kathleen squeaked. Anna sighed.

"Queen Matilda, eh? And how is our lovely princess these days?" He didn't wait for a response. "You know, I should return you so you can tell her, from me, to take herself back home again." He raised his eyebrows. "Does that surprise you? We don't want Matilda here, nor her brother, Roderick. We have a king, and are quite satisfied with him."

"But he's a pretender to the throne!"

"Is that what they tell you?" The man laughed again. "No,

Terran has just as much claim as Roderick. But he is a much better man, and a fine king. We do not want Roderick back, thank you very much." Anna was silent. The man looked at the others. "Tie them up. We will take them to Terran. Maybe they will earn us some negotiating power." He looked back at Anna, smiling at her furious scowl. "Don't worry, love," he said. "We will take good care of you. And since we will be together for a while, let me introduce myself." He delivered a courtly bow. "Syngen Gail at your service."

CHAPTER THIRTY-SEVEN

Syngen Gail was charming, handsome and proud – just the kind of man Anna abhorred. She could not believe she had led herself and Kathleen so easily into a trap. She glared at the man, scowling more when his smile grew wider. He was detestable, she thought. She glanced at Kathleen, meeting her gaze briefly. She had yearned for adventure – was this what she had in mind?

The other two men bound the women with ropes as Syngen watched. He checked the knots before nodding his approval. "Let's be off," he said, taking the lead and weaving his way through the trees. One of the men grasped Anna by the arm, but she shook him off.

"I assure you, I am quite capable of walking unassisted," she said. Syngen glanced over his shoulder with a grin.

"Oh, I doubt it's your ability to walk that Danny is questioning," he said. "Unless …" He paused, and turning around, sniffed Anna as she pulled back in horror. "No, you don't smell of drink, so I'm sure you can walk without assistance." He grinned shamelessly then turned back and strode down the path, humming a tuneless song.

The sun dropped behind the horizon, but Syngen did not

slow his pace. A branch caught on Anna's gown, and she winced when she heard it rip along the hem. A twig slapped her in the face, and her eyes smarted. She wondered whether Frank had started searching for them. Or would he just leave them to their fate? But it was no use thinking about such things. She needed to find a way of escaping. As soon as they stopped, she would find a way to speak to Kathleen unobserved.

They cleared the trees and continued walking. The moon was nearly full, and it shone brightly in the night sky, shedding plenty of light to walk by. The ropes around Anna's wrists chafed, and she twisted her hands as they walked. It was another hour before Syngen finally called a halt, and the men allowed Anna and Kathleen to collapse on the ground.

"We'll rest for a few hours, and be on our way again before first light," Syngen said to the men. "And no fire. There will be men out searching for these two."

Anna glanced at Kathleen, but she was staring at the ground a few feet away. She looked at the man standing behind her friend. Syngen had called him Danny. He was short, but built like a bull. He could probably withstand any battering without moving an inch. The other man, however, was much slighter. He was gazing at Anna with sharp, beady eyes, and she looked away. He might not have the same physical prowess as the other men, but not much would escape him. Anna glanced up at the night sky. The stars looked paler than usual against the bright light of the moon. She looked down, but not before a flash caught her eye, making her look up once more. Across the night sky she saw a blaze of light. A falling star, perhaps, or maybe a flash of flame. She glanced back at the men. The big one was sitting on his haunches, staring at the ground, while the beady-eyed one was talking to Syngen. She looked back at the night sky, and there it was again – a flash of flame. She smiled and pushed herself to her feet. Syngen turned to look at her, his eyebrows upraised.

"I, uh, need a few moments of privacy," she said. She twisted her legs together in case her meaning wasn't clear, and Syngen grinned.

"Take her behind the bushes," he said to the man at Kathleen's side. Anna looked at Kathleen.

"Are you coming?" she said. Kathleen glanced up, and meeting her gaze, nodded. Danny looked at Syngen questioningly, but he just shrugged.

"What can a pair of women do?" he said. "Give them a chance to make their plans – it will make them feel better." Anna scowled at Syngen, then turned to follow the small, hulking man. The small clump of bushes was about twenty feet away, and he stopped a few feet shy of them. Anna lifted her bound wrists at him.

"I need my hands free," she said. Danny stared at her for a moment, then nodded.

"Don't try anything funny," he said. "We are a lot faster and stronger than you." It took a while for him to release the bonds, then he turned and undid Kathleen's. "I will wait right here," he said. He turned his back to them and planted his feet solidly on the ground as Anna grabbed Kathleen by both hands and dragged her behind the bushes.

"I want you to forget everything you know about dragons," Anna asked as soon as they were out of sight of the man.

"Dragons? What are you talking about?"

"Shh, keep your voice down."

"Dragons eat people, especially girls," Kathleen whispered. "They are horrible monsters."

"Not all dragons are horrible monsters," Anna said. "And we are about to be rescued by one." She saw Kathleen's eyes open wide. "Shh," she repeated. "I know a dragon, and he is coming to rescue us."

"How do you know a dragon? And how do you know it will rescue us instead of eating us?" Kathleen whispered back.

"Because I saw him." Anna waited a moment. "You have to trust me. Nothing bad will happen, I promise. The dragon will take us back to the camp. We are going to run away from here as fast as we can, do you understand? And when the dragon grabs you, you are not to be afraid."

"When the dragon grabs me?" Kathleen turned as pale as the moon.

"Either we be rescued by the dragon, or we stay with these ... these ... rogues." Kathleen stared at Anna for a moment, then slowly nodded. "Are you ready to run?"

"No!"

Anna grabbed her by the hand. "Run," she shouted in a whisper. "Now!"

They ran into the darkness that lay behind the bushes, stumbling over rocks and shrubs. They had gone a short distance when Anna heard a yell, then the pounding of pursuing feet as Danny started to give chase. "Max," she shouted. She felt a tug as Kathleen tripped to the ground, and she paused to help to her feet. She glanced backwards to see Danny gaining ground, with Syngen a short distance behind, and grabbed Kathleen's hand again. "Come on," she shouted.

"Where's the dragon?" Kathleen huffed. The words had just left her mouth when Anna felt a roll of heat wash over her. She dropped Kathleen's hand, but continued to run. She heard a squeak from Kathleen and knew that Max must have grabbed her.

"Anna!" The dragon roared her name, and she glanced up, slowing when she saw the dragon coming towards her with claws outstretched. "Stop!" But the warning came too late. A log lay in her path, as high as her ankles, and she tripped over it, tumbling head-first into a ravine. She screamed as she tumbled over and over down the steep bank, hitting branches and rocks. She came to a stop against a tree, and lay still.

"Anna!" Anna opened her eyes slowly. Max was hovering

above her, Kathleen dangling in his talons, her face frozen with shock. Anna tried to move, but every part of her body screamed in pain. She was tangled in a bush, her gown and hair caught between twigs and branches.

"Go," she said. "Take Kathleen. Come back for me."

"No, I'm not leaving you."

A shout reached her from above. "Here, she fell down here."

"Go," Anna said. "Quickly. Come back before they find me."

There was a moment of hesitation, then Max nodded. "I will be back very shortly," he said. There was a whoosh of air as Max rose into the air, his huge body fading into blackness.

"Hey, what was that?" Anna could hear the trace of fear in Danny's voice.

"An owl, maybe." Syngen sounded unconcerned. "We need to get the girl out. What happened to the other one?"

"She disappeared. Something dark came out of the night and took her."

"Something dark? A monster?"

"Yes! A monster!" Danny sounded relieved to have an explanation. Syngen cursed softly before replying.

"You should know better than to believe in monsters, Danny." His voice was resigned. "It is too dark to descend the ravine now. The girl cannot go far, and we will retrieve her ..." The voice faded as Anna closed her eyes again. When she opened them again, all was silent. Her eyes drifted closed once more as she wondered how long it would be before Max came back, but when she opened them again, she was lying in the middle of a meadow, the ground beneath her flat and soft. Max was on his knees, leaning over her, his face etched with concern.

"Max," she whispered. He bent closer and gently stroked her cheek.

"My darling, thank God you're awake. You've got quite a few scrapes and bruises. Your wrist is sprained, and you lost a lot of blood from a head wound."

"Nothing too … serious then," she whispered. He smiled slightly.

"You must drink some of my blood."

Anna looked into the darkness. "No," she whispered, "no blood."

"Anna, please," he said. "It will help you heal."

She met his gaze. "If I have your blood, I will be bonded to you, won't I?" He nodded. "I cannot have your blood, Max," she said. He stared down at her for a long time.

"You are the most stubborn woman I have ever met," he said. "Very well. I'll take you back to the camp when it's light. Rest a little more." He lay down on the ground next to her, and gently pulled her against his chest, cradling her head with his arm. She groaned with the movement, but as his heat enveloped her, she closed her eyes with a sigh.

"Is Kathleen all right?" she asked.

"Yes. The poor girl was terrified, but I landed her behind the camp and she managed to walk the rest of the way. I didn't wait to hear her explanation to the others, as I came straight back to get you."

"I didn't see you come."

"You had lost consciousness. I had to untangle you from the trees and bushes, and then I brought you here, away from those men." He paused. "Who were they?"

"Terran's men." Anna started to explain what had happened, but was asleep before she even reached the part where they ran away. When she awoke, the sun had risen. There was a canopy over her, blocking her face from the rays. She stared at it, mesmerized by the way it shimmered in the morning light. Something shifted behind her, and she turned to see Max looking down at her.

"How are you feeling?" he asked.

"Sore," she said. He smiled.

"You need something to eat," he said. "Will you wait here while I find you something?" She nodded. He rose to his feet, and the canopy that had been shading her lifted, stretching out behind him. He flexed the wing and then unfurled the other, and with a quick smile in her direction, shot into the air. He was back within a matter of minutes, his fingers wrapped around the neck of a dead rabbit. He tore the creature apart with his hands, and Anna looked away with a shudder. He glanced down at her with a rueful smile. "I'm afraid I don't have the tools to skin it," he said. "It isn't something I usually need to do."

"It's all right," she said. He ripped off a small piece of flesh, and holding it to his mouth, blew a glowing flame over it, before dropping to his haunches next to her. She lifted her arm to take the piece, and then groaned as a sharp stab of pain shot through her. Immediately Max's arm went around her, holding her carefully against his side as she cradled the arm. He lifted the morsel of meat, his fingers brushing her lips as she opened her mouth. His fingers lingered a moment as she closed her lips over the morsel, and when she glanced up at him, she saw a blaze in his eyes that matched the one in the pit of her stomach. He pulled his eyes away, and shifting his weight slightly, ripped off another piece of meat. Once again he lifted it to her lips, and she took it from his fingers. She did not look at him, and pulled away as soon as it was in her mouth.

He offered her more but she shook her head. He flung the remains of the rabbit aside. Max reached across her legs and slipped an arm beneath her knees, then rose to his feet with Anna in his arms. He held her against his chest, and she nestled into the crook of his arm. She could smell the heat and fire that raged within him, and when he pulled her closer and higher against his chest, she snuggled herself against him, closing her eyes. His wings rustled as he opened them, and they shimmered in the morning light as he stretched them to their fullest extent. He shot into the air and the wind rushed past her, whipping her gown around her ankles. Her sprained arm was cradled between her chest and his, but she reached up with the other arm and slipped it around his neck. She felt him look down at her, and the rushing wind slowed. She opened her eyes, wondering if they had landed, but he was hovering in the air, his wings moving slowly behind him, staring down at her. She closed her eyes again, and after a moment, she felt the soft rush of moving air once again.

She lay in his arms with eyes closed as he drew closer to the camp, but she opened them when she felt the soft thud of his landing. His wings disappeared as he looked down at her. "I'll carry you the rest of the way," he said.

"I can walk," she said, but when her feet touched the ground, her knees buckled beneath her. Max scooped her back into his arms and strode in the direction of the camp. She could hear voices in the distance, and as they grew closer, she heard her name being called. Kathleen had seen them approaching, and came running.

"Anna! Master Brant! What are ...? How is it ...?" She stopped, the confusion clear on her face.

"Anna is badly injured," Max said. "The dragon didn't want to land in the camp, so he gave her into my care."

"You know the dragon?"

Max cast a quick look in Anna's direction. "You could say that. But we need to get Anna somewhere comfortable. Her arm is injured, and she's lost a lot of blood."

Kathleen nodded. "Follow me," she said. She fell in beside Max as they walked. "Master Garrick was here earlier," she whispered to Anna. "He heard that two ladies had been taken."

"What did you tell him?" Anna asked.

"I told him what happened, and that a dragon had returned me to the camp, then gone back for you." Max laughed and Kathleen glanced at him in surprise, before quickly averting her gaze.

"I'm sure he was pleased to hear that," Max said, grinning at Anna when she pinched his neck.

"He was glad that you were being rescued, but he also

seemed sad," Kathleen said.

"Sad?" Anna said in surprise. She glanced at Max again, but he had turned his face away, and she could not see his expression. They were almost at the camp when the others noticed them approaching.

"Mistress. You are back." Frank's voice was cold and suspicious. He glanced at Max's bare chest, and his eyes narrowed.

"Mistress Anna has been badly injured," Max said. "And I would thank you not to make assumptions regarding my lack of attire. I considered her comfort and safety of more importance than stopping to clothe myself more fully."

"Anna? Anna? Is that you? Are you back?" Matilda emerged from her tent and hurried over. "We have been so worried. When Kathleen told us what happened, that you had fallen down a ravine after escaping from your abductors, we feared the worst. But here you are, safe and sound." She stared at Max for a moment, her eyes roving over his bare chest, then looked back at Anna.

"Is there a place I can lay her?" Max asked.

"Of course." Matilda waved towards the other tent.

"Come," Kathleen said, holding open the flap and indicating a low camp cot. "Here is her bed."

Max knelt on the floor and carefully lowered her down. Her arm slipped from his neck. "Thank you," she whispered. Max leaned closer, bringing his mouth close to her ear.

"Rescuing you is always a pleasure," he said, and she could hear the amusement in his tone. He rose to his feet, and turning, walked from the tent.

CHAPTER THIRTY-EIGHT

Anna lay on the bed as Kathleen gently wiped the dirt from her wounds, before coating them with a salve that she had mixed. There was a deep gash on her forehead, and scratches covered her arms and legs. She had twisted her arm in the fall, and Betsy fashioned a sling to keep it secure. She slept after that, drifting in and out of consciousness. Once, when she awoke, she heard Rupert questioning Kathleen outside the tent.

"And you say Mistress Anna was surprised when the men made an appearance?"

"Oh, yes. We both were. We tried to run away, but it was too late."

"I'm sure it was," Rupert replied dryly. What did that mean, Anna wondered? "And did Mistress Anna provide any information about our forces to these abductors?"

Anna could hear the puzzlement in Kathleen's voice. "Information, Your Highness?"

"Yes. About our movements, perhaps?"

"No. Why would she do that? The enemy already knows where we are, do they not?"

There was a moment of silence. "Thank you for your

time, Lady," Anna heard him say, and then the sound of him moving away.

Kathleen came into the tent a few minutes later. "I just had to talk with the prince," she said, her face pale and her hands trembling. "He's so stern!" She sat down on a stool next to Anna. "He asked me a lot of questions about you."

The flap of the tent lifted, and Blanche walked in. "Well, well," she said as she plopped herself down on her cot. "Here is our little Anna, returned safe and sound against the bare, naked chest of Max Brant." She cocked her head. "Tell me, was this a ruse to spend time with your lover, Anna?"

"Her lover?" Kathleen swung around to glare at her. "You are making a horrible mistake, Blanche," she said. "Anna would never do such a thing! We were abducted by Terran's men and taken hostage!"

Blanche laughed. "No need to get so riled up in Anna's defense," Blanche said. "I was only funning!"

Anna took Kathleen's hand in her own. "Blanche is just being spiteful," Anna said. "We both know the truth of what happened, and Blanche knows that defaming my character does not make the words true." Kathleen glared at Blanche a moment longer, then turned and left the tent, leaving Blanche looking at Anna in cynical amusement as Anna turned away and closed her eyes.

Garrick came by later that day, his face etched with concern as he knelt next to the low camp cot with its woven straw pallet.

"Lady Kathleen told me you ran into some of Terran's men." Anna nodded. "Did they hurt you?" He glanced down at the scratches that covered her body.

"No. They held us so we couldn't run, and bound our hands together, but did not mistreat us in any other way. All my injuries are from the tumble I took down the ravine."

"The dragon said he had to untangle you from the trees." His mouth tightened as a frown furrowed his forehead. "It should have been me that rescued you, not that beast."

Anna touched his cheek. "You could not have found us as quickly nor rescued us as easily."

He nodded. "I know."

The army was on the move again the next day, but Matilda offered to keep camp where they were for a few more days so Anna could rest further, although Anna suspected that the queen was tiring of her trek through the countryside and was quite happy to have an excuse to remain behind. The guards, Frank and Tobias, were to stay with them, of course, but when Garrick heard the news, he requested permission to stay as well.

He told Anna later that Rupert had not been happy with the request. "What is your interest in these women?" he asked Garrick.

"I wish to protect my queen and her ladies," Garrick had replied. "She will be an easy target, separated from the main force."

"I see. And is your main interest the queen, or one of the women?"

"Both."

Garrick pulled his eyebrows together in an effort to show Anna what Rupert's countenance had been like, and she laughed.

"You will never be anything like Rupert," she said, "and that is a very good thing!"

Garrick left the tent soon after, but only a few minutes had passed when Anna heard the murmur of hushed voices, the anger evident in the soft tones. She strained her ears to make out the sounds, and Max's low voice reached her through the walls of the tent.

"… not leave her unprotected…"

"I will be here!" Garrick countered, angrily.

"And what good would you be to her when you are dead on the ground, human?"

There was a moment of silence, then Garrick's voice

came again. "Very well. Suit yourself, dragon."

Max's reply was amused. "I will, stable boy."

Anna closed her eyes with a sigh. Garrick hated the sight of Max, that much was certainly clear, but Aaron had ordered him to watch over Anna, and nothing would persuade him to disobey his Master.

Anna's body ached from the bruises and scrapes she had sustained, but as the days went by, she found her strength quickly returning. Each morning and evening Betsy tended to the deeper scrapes with vinegar and yarrow, and brewed her a cup of rosemary tea, which she drank with great distaste. But the concoctions did the trick, and by the next day she was already back on her feet, walking slowly as her aching muscles and bones protested the movement. The wound on her forehead slowly knitted back together, while the skin around the gash turned first purple, then yellow. It was her wrist that gave her the most discomfort. It was twisted and sprained in the fall, and Betsy said it was a mercy she hadn't broken it. It had been swathed in bandages to keep it straight, and she kept the arm in a sling; but at night she would often roll onto the injured hand and wake with a flare of pain. Simple tasks were painful and awkward, and Anna soon found her patience wearing thin. She would walk around the perimeter of the camp in frustration while Frank watched her continuously, warning her to stay close to camp when she wandered too far, his tone indicating that it was not her safety he was concerned about.

She saw Garrick often, but there was little opportunity for conversation. He took his turn with Frank and Tobias, guarding the camp with a bow on his back and a sword in his hand, but he passed her with his quick smile and a brief word whenever he was able.

Only once did Matilda question Anna about the misadventure. "I'm surprised the men who captured you treated you so well," she said.

"There were only three men, my lady, and one of them

was clearly a man of noble birth."

"A man of noble birth? Did he give a name?"

"He did, my lady – Syngen Gail."

Anna glanced at the queen when she remained silent. She looked a little pale.

"Are you all right?" she said. "Do you need to lie down?"

Matilda waved her hand. "No, no, it's just the heat. I was trying to place the name, but I confess it is quite unfamiliar to me. He may have had the appearance of a nobleman, but he is probably a man of low and common birth." She rose to her feet. "Perhaps I will go lie down for a little bit."

As for Max, despite his assertions that he remained behind to protect Anna, it seemed to her that his attention was fixed on the other women in the camp. He flirted with the maids and teased the serving girls, making them blush. He sat with Matilda, laughing and talking, and even managed to get Kathleen to engage in a few shy words. But apart from a few polite greetings, he spoke little to Anna. She was relieved, of course. She could not be comfortable with Max. But she could not help watching him when his back was turned and he was talking to Matilda, or Betsy, or one of the other maids. One time she turned away to see that Garrick had returned to the camp, and was watching her watching Max. He had glanced away, but a wave of shame washed over her. Garrick deserved so much better than she was able to give him. She walked over to him with a smile, and when he looked up at her, his expression was calm.

"How is your arm doing today?" he asked.

"Much better," she said, slowly circling her wrist with only a small wince to show just how much it had improved. He smiled, and nodded.

"I am in desperate need of a wash," he said, "so I will see you later."

"Of course," she said, and turned away. As she walked back towards her tent, she saw that Max was where he had been before, but now it was he who was watching her, his gaze intent. Her eyes met his, and for a moment he held them, but then his expression turned mocking, and he flourished a small bow in her direction. But she had seen a flame in his eyes before it was quickly doused by gray, and could not suppress a slight shiver as Max turned away. There were times when he disappeared from the camp, and she could feel his presence circling above her. She did not look for him then, but she knew he did not go far. How she knew this, she would have been hard pressed to say, but something within her sensed his presence, as tangible as the bench she sat on.

Two days passed before Matilda decided it was time to resume their journey. Plans were made to start the following morning, and Garrick helped Anna mount her horse and take a turn along the dusty path around the camp. It was difficult to control the reins with her injured arm, but her horse was patient, and after a while she had the trick of using just one hand.

They left at dawn, easily following the trail left behind by the army – broken trees and bushes, paths made by thousands of feet, and as they continued north, the occasional cottage burned to the ground. The soldiers were getting impatient with marching and no fighting. Rupert was eager to maintain a good pace, however, and for the most part the villages had been left untouched, but as they neared the first major town, Anna could smell the smoke rising into the air. The town lay behind a small hill, and as they crested the summit she gasped at the destruction. The town walls had been completely destroyed, and within the town only smoldering ruins remained. Anna turned away, horrified at the devastation, wrought by a man who wished to be king. Garrick moved up to stand beside her.

"War is a terrible thing, is it not?" he said quietly.

"I'm glad you weren't a part of this," she said. He remained silent. "What is it for?" she said. She searched his face for an answer, then turned back to the ruins. "All this for the sake of a throne."

"Not just a throne, Anna," he said. "Power, money and supreme rule."

As they drew closer, Anna could see that not everyone had fled the destruction. People picked through the smoldering ashes, using sticks to poke through the hot embers, snatching up anything that still looked useful – pots with broken handles; pans, twisted and bent; melted candlesticks and lanterns. Children wandered around, their arms and faces covered in soot, and dogs nosed their way through the debris. They paused at the outskirts of the town, and Matilda stared with glassy eyes as the people she claimed as her own rummaged through the ashes. One, an old man, looked up and seeing her, spat in her direction.

"See what your people have wrought, Princess," he hissed, shaking his finger as he glared at her. "Take your brother, and your husband, and begone!" Matilda's face was white as she clutched the reins, and without another word, turned her horse aside and traced a path around the town. Anna could see she was shaking, but she held her head high as she rode.

Anna could not sleep that night. Her arm ached after a day of riding, and her heart ached at the destruction wrought by Alfred's army. She wanted to be away from this place, this war between a few power-hungry men. She lay on the cot listening to the heavy breathing coming from the other beds. Outside she heard the low mumble of voices of the guards and servants. She could see the blaze of the camp fire through the thin wall of the tent, the flames casting dancing shadows over the fabric. Cradling her arm against her chest, she rose to her feet and awkwardly slung a robe over her shoulders. Her riding boots sat at the foot of the bed, and she pushed her feet into them, leaving the laces untied as she carefully pushed open the flap to the tent and stepped outside.

Frank was near the fire, and he turned when he heard her

movement. He watched her closely as she stepped up to the flames. "I couldn't sleep," she whispered. He shrugged, and after a moment, walked away.

It was hot next to the fire, and after a few minutes she headed over to a bench that had been placed beneath the trees, and took a seat. She leaned her head back against the trunk and closed her eyes, listening to the crackling flames. She heard a noise and looked up to see Garrick walking towards her. He had been guarding the camp with Tobias, and still wore his sword and dagger. A bow was slung over his shoulder, and an axe hung in his belt. He swung the bow from his back and laid it on the ground.

"Couldn't you sleep?" he asked as he sat down on the bench beside her.

Anna shook her head. "Too many disturbing images in my mind," she said.

Above them the sky was dark as a new moon waxed low above the horizon. Stars sparkled against the black canvas, their glittering pinpricks of light shining brightly. Anna glanced at Garrick as he stared into the flames. The play of light and shadow made him look pensive. "Tell me what you dream about," he said.

"What I dream about?" Anna turned back to the flames. "I don't know. A happy life, with my own home, and children. And you, of course."

A slight smile played over Garrick's lips, but it was quickly gone. "Should I tell you what I dream about?" he said. He took her hand in his as he turned to look at her. "I dream of you, every single night. I dream of you in my arms, your body soft and yielding as I love you the way a man loves a woman." Anna shifted self-consciously as he continued. "I dream of you carrying my seed, nurturing it and bringing forth new life." He glanced down at her hand, lying in his, and gently stroked her fingers. "I dream of us growing old together, your hand in mine as we watch our children growing up and building lives of their own. I dream all of that, Anna, and then it all fades away and I dream of only one thing." He brought his gaze back to hers, his eyes searching as they held hers.

"What, Garrick?" He stared at her for a long moment, then looked away.

"I dream of you happy."

"We will be happy," she said. "We will have a home, and children, and each other." She lifted her hand and placed it on his cheek, and he slowly looked back at her. He covered her hand with his own.

"I love you," he said, "and I dream of a life with you." He closed his eyes for a moment. "But your dreams are your own to follow, Anna. Do not be bound by mine."

He leaned forward and brushed his lips against hers, before rising to his feet and quickly walking away as Anna watched in perplexity.

CHAPTER THIRTY-NINE

Matilda and her party broke camp the following morning, following the trail left behind by the marching soldiers. As they drew nearer to the rear of the army, Anna could see smoke in the distance. Frank and Garrick rode ahead, returning an hour later.

"We engaged the enemy this morning," Frank shouted as they drew near. "One of our companies came upon one of Terran's, and they engaged each other in battle."

"Are we victorious?" Matilda reined her horse next to the two news-bearers. Frank glanced at Garrick.

"No," Garrick said. "By the time our commander reached the skirmish, all was confusion. The officers on both sides were dead, and the men were engaged in hand-to-hand fighting, with some trying to flee the scene. The company was made up of volunteers and new recruits, not trained soldiers. The prince put two of our men to death who were trying to escape, and then recalled the remaining troops and withdrew."

"He withdrew? Leaving the enemy behind?" Matilda said, her tone incredulous. Max had joined them, and was listening to the conversation, his narrowed eyes trained on Garrick.

"Yes, Your Highness," Garrick replied. "There weren't many enemy soldiers remaining – most had retreated behind their lines, leaving the wounded behind. The prince rounded them up as prisoners, and tomorrow he will pitch his forces against the enemy with a definite plan of action."

"I want to see where they were fighting. I want to see the dead bodies of the men who chose to fight against Roderick."

"Uh, my lady," Frank started, but Matilda waved away his protestations.

"I insist," she said. Frank glanced at Garrick, who stared at the queen for a moment, before his eyes flickered over to where Max was standing. After a moment Garrick nodded his head.

"The ladies must stay behind," he said.

"No," Anna said, stepping forward. "I will remain with my lady."

Garrick turned to glare at her, but it was Max who spoke. "No!"

Anna glanced at Max, who was glaring at her with arms folded across his chest.

"Can you give me a good reason why I should not go?" she said. He stared at her, and Anna felt an angry wave of heat roll over her. She narrowed her eyes. "I thought not," she said. She looked at Garrick, who met her gaze with resignation.

Garrick turned back to Matilda. "My lady," he said, "follow me."

Still on horseback, Matilda and Anna followed Garrick as he led them in silence through a small grove of trees. Anna knew Max was following on foot, but she did not look around. Beyond the trees was a large open field, and in the distance she could see large, dark birds circling the sky. She followed Garrick and the queen across the grassland. It had been trampled down by the moving army, walked into dust and chaff.

As they grew closer, Anna could see the remains of soldiers fallen in battle, and the stench of death made her cover her nose. She glanced at Matilda, but the queen was riding with a straight back, her eyes unwavering as she took in the scene before her. Anna followed a few steps behind, pausing when the queen stopped to survey the bloody scene. Max had disappeared through the long grass, heading towards the corpse-strewn field. The bodies of three dozen fallen men lay on the ground, their blood staining the earth beneath them. Flies were already swarming around open wounds, their buzzing making Anna gag. The queen stared for a long moment, then with a nod turned and followed Garrick from the field. Anna turned her horse around, but she stopped when she saw Max standing in the shadow of a tree, his body tense as he took in the sight before him. Anna nudged her horse forward, then changing her mind, drew the horse to a halt. She slipped from her saddle and walked to where he stood.

"Max?"

He turned to look at her, his jaw set, and Anna could see the flames building within his eyes. "Not all the men are dead," he said. "I can hear their heartbeats, stuttering as the agony of death is drawn out." His upper lip curled slightly. "I can smell their blood in the air and taste it on my tongue." He turned back to look at the dead and dying. "You should go," he said, his voice low. "The smell of blood arouses my hunger. I'm not sure I want to test the limits of my control with you."

Anna stared at him, but when he turned to look at her again, his eyes were blazing with flames, the whites completely swallowed in the burning inferno. His mouth was slightly open, his upper lip curled sardonically, and when his tongue traced his lower lip she could see the hint of teeth that no longer appeared flat and human. She took a step back, tripping over a large stick, as fear coiled through her stomach. Turning away, she hurried to her horse and pulled herself inelegantly into the saddle in her sudden haste to be away. Surely Max would never hurt her. But he was a dragon, and if he lost control ... he was the world's most dangerous predator, a fact it would behoove her to remember.

When Anna joined Garrick and the queen, she learned that a messenger from Alfred had sought out Her Majesty with a message from the king.

A loyal Roderick supporter, Cameleus Allen, lived only two miles hence, and had opened his home to Roderick, Alfred and Matilda. At long last, for the first time in weeks, Matilda and her ladies would sleep within four walls, with a roof over their heads.

Anna guessed Cameleus Allen to be in his fifties. He was of middling height, with a rotund belly and whiskers that stuck out from his chin. A friendly, jovial sort of man. He came outside as Matilda and her ladies reached the front door, his round face beaming with a smile of welcome. Anna wondered what he thought of the destruction of the towns and villages to the south.

"Matilda, my dear, how lovely to see you again after all these years," he said, taking her hand and delivering a loud, smacking kiss.

"Thank you for the use of your lodgings, Cameleus," she said. "My ladies and I have not been comfortable in many weeks."

"My home is yours," he said as he led the women into the hall. "The west wing has been closed since my wife passed, but the east wing is open, and chambers are being prepared for you." Roderick and Alfred were already seated in the hall as the women entered behind Cameleus, still chatting to the woman who trailed behind him. "And its proximity to Terranton is certainly an advantage," he added. Roderick glanced up.

"Terranton?" he said.

Lord Cameleus laughed. "That's what the locals have

taken to calling it," he said. "Terran's town, you understand?" He caught Roderick's narrowed look, and cleared his throat. "Not that I call it that, of course. It's just that Terran built a new palace there, and …" His voice trailed off as Roderick continued to glare at him. "Ah, well, yes, enough of that." He turned to Matilda. "A maid will show you and your ladies to your chambers. Dinner will be served in an hour, if that suits you."

"Thank you, Cameleus, that suits me quite well."

Cameleus smiled and glanced at the ladies standing beside Matilda, his gaze pausing on Anna as he took in the healing gash on her forehead. "Have you hurt yourself, my dear?"

"Syngen," Matilda said, flatly, before Anna had a chance to respond. Cameleus's gaze swung back to Matilda in surprise.

"Syngen?"

"He ambushed and abducted two of my ladies."

Cameleus looked back at Anna. "And he did this to you?" he asked.

"No," Anna said. "I fell down a ravine when I tried to escape."

"Ah! I see." He paused a moment. "But how did you escape?"

"We were rescued by, eh —"

"A dragon," Kathleen finished. Cameleus's eyebrows shot up.

"Indeed!"

They supped that night on a sumptuous meal of roasted meats, baked pies and sweetened figs. It was marvelous, and Anna could not help but feel a stab of guilt at the rations Garrick would be enjoying this evening.

"Tomorrow will decide our fate," Roderick said as they ate. "We will face Terran's men in battle and victory will be ours."

"Most certainly it will," Cameleus said.

"I would like to watch," Matilda said. Anna's heart sank

— that was the last thing she wanted to do. She glanced at Kathleen and saw her expression mirrored her own, but Blanche just smiled.

"No!" Alfred's voice was horrified, but it was drowned out by Roderick's louder response.

"Of course, my dear," Roderick said. "We will draw up a carriage to the sidelines so you can observe the proceedings." He turned to Alfred. "She has an interest in seeing Terran defeated, and I, for one, am not concerned that she will be in any danger."

"It's ludicrous," Alfred said, but Anna could hear the resignation in his tone, and when Cameleus offered the use of his carriage, he remained silent.

The next morning dawned overcast and cool, matching Anna's dismal mood. Matilda wasted no time in rising from her bed, urging her ladies to do the same with as much haste as possible. The men had already left at the first light of day, and Matilda did not want to miss a single piece of the action. They left the chambers shortly before nine, to find Cameleus waiting in the hall.

"Ah, there you are." He walked towards Matilda, hands outstretched to take hers. "Did you have a good night's rest, my dear?"

"Thank you, Cameleus, I most certainly did."

"Excellent!" He gestured towards the door. "A carriage has been placed at your disposal and awaits you outside the door. And a basket of food has been placed within."

Matilda smiled. "You are too kind. Will you be joining us today?"

He waved his hand. "No, no, battle scenes are not my thing. I will stay here and await word of Roderick's victory!"

They stepped outside, and in the distance Anna could see trails of smoke rising into the air. The early morning mist had cleared, revealing a clear, blue sky. There was a boom, distant and muffled but still clearly the sound of a cannon, and she saw Kathleen flinch slightly. She took her hand and squeezed gently.

"We'll be perfectly safe," she whispered.

"I know," Kathleen whispered back, "But I don't really want to watch men dying!"

Anna nodded. She was in complete sympathy with Kathleen's sentiments.

As they drew close to the scene of the battle, Anna could see thousands of men ranging the field, arrayed in every direction, swinging swords, axes, maces and spears. Anna wondered where Garrick was, but knew it would be impossible to find him in the melee. The battle seemed to be fiercest on the east side of the battlefield, and towards the back, Anna saw Terran's standard, held aloft on a tall pole. She looked for Roderick's, and saw it at the base of a small hillock, to the west. On the top of the hill were two men on horseback – Roderick and Alfred, Anna supposed.

Matilda pointed out a small mound and the carriage pulled to a stop with one side facing the scene below. Frank and Tobias rode behind the carriage, and they dismounted as the carriage drew to a halt, a sword in each hand. Despite Roderick's confidence that nothing would befall Matilda and her ladies as they observed the unfolding drama, Alfred had ordered the guards to be especially vigilant, wary of a scheming attack against the queen. They stalked around the carriage, swinging their swords through bushes and shrubs, before finally nodding that it was safe for Matilda to alight. The coachman hopped down from his perch, and going to the stowage at the back, pulled out four small stools and a large basket and placed them on the ground. Opening the door of the carriage, he helped Matilda onto a stool as her ladies stepped down beside her. Frank and Tobias stood on either side of the carriage, their bodies at attention as they held their swords at the ready.

A loud boom made Anna turn around in fright, her ears ringing as she saw the smoke rising from the other side of the plain. The thunderous cannon had shaken the ground they stood on, and the carriage rocked slightly. Men dropped to the ground where they stood, injured, or dead, although Anna couldn't tell if they were Alfred's or Terran's. The men carried shields that distinguished the two sides, and brightly painted helmets, but from this distance, it was impossible to tell who was who.

Matilda settled herself on her stool, and patted the one beside her. "Join me, ladies," she said with a smile, as though she were about to watch one of Denton's plays. Blanche took a seat, but Anna stepped back.

"If you'll excuse me, my lady," she said, "I think I would prefer to take a little walk."

There was a loud crack near them, and Matilda turned to seek out the source of the sound. "Do what you will," she said with a wave of her hand. Frank turned to her in protest, but when another cannon boomed across the plain, making the carriage rock once more, he nodded.

"I have to see you at all times," he warned Anna. She gave an exaggerated sigh.

"I'll just be on the other side of the hill," she said.

"I'll come with you," Kathleen said, linking her arm into Anna's as she turned away from the battle and headed down the gentle slope of the little hill. The greenery here had been trampled down by marching feet, the little field flowers crushed and broken. A few small rocks had protected a little spray of blooms, and Anna knelt down to look at them.

"Everything is destroyed," Kathleen said with a moan.

"No, look." Anna beckoned Kathleen to where she knelt. "Not everything." She looked at Kathleen with a smile. "There is always hope!"

There was a rustling behind her, and Anna scrambled to her feet, stumbling slightly, as she felt a wave of heat wash over her. She turned to see Max striding towards them.

"What are you doing here?" he demanded. His eyebrows were gathered in a frown, and fear curled through Anna's stomach as she remembered how he had looked at her the previous evening. Max's nostrils flared slightly, and when he took a step towards her, his voice held a note of seductive challenge. "You aren't scared of me, are you, darling?"

She lifted her chin and met his look. "Most certainly not!"

She shivered when he laughed. "Good girl! But I still want to know what you are doing here."

"Matilda wanted to watch the battle. She hopes to see Terran defeated."

"And she brought her ladies?"

Anna shrugged. "As you can see, Kathleen and I are not watching." Max glanced at Kathleen, who was staring at him uneasily, and his expression softened slightly.

"Apologies for my rude interruption, my lady," he said. He turned back to Anna. "Matilda underestimates Terran's strength," he said. "Roderick will not win today's battle. Already he has lost hundreds of men."

Anna felt the blood drain from her face. "Garrick?" she whispered.

Max quickly covered the remaining distance between them, and his hands wrapped gently around her arms, pulling her close. "He was fine the last time I saw him," he said. "I will watch over him as much as I'm able, but," he dropped his voice low, "I cannot take my natural form with so many men here."

"I know," she whispered. Max's hands were warm on her arms. His eyes held hers for a moment, and then he stepped back.

"I'll be back with news," he said. He nodded at Kathleen, looked once more at Anna, then turned and walked away.

CHAPTER FORTY

The hours wore on, the clanging, booming and shouting becoming a deafening monotone that made Anna's ears ache. Black powder burned through the air, and smoke made the air hazy.

Anna and Kathleen sat on the hill away from the fighting, blocking out the sounds behind them as much as they were able. They checked on Matilda once, but she was so engrossed in the battle below her, she barely noticed their presence. From time to time, Frank walked past, glaring at Anna as he did so, but not pausing to watch their actions.

A few hours after Max had been by, Anna saw another man striding up the hill. She turned to Kathleen. "Is that Lord Giles?" she asked her friend.

Kathleen looked up too, then quickly looked away with a blush, nervously pushing a strand of hair from her face. Lord Giles was of medium height and build, and Anna guessed he was in his early thirties. His face was red from exertion, and a sheen of sweat covered the bald patch that stretched from his forehead across his crown. He walked with a pronounced limp, but it did not appear to slow him down as he marched towards them.

"Lady Kathleen," he said as he drew closer, and Kathleen looked up with a shy smile. "I saw the queen's carriage and wondered whether you were here as well. I'm glad to see you have taken yourself out of direct sight of the battlefield." He glanced at Anna. "Please introduce me to your friend," he said.

"Uh, er –"

"Anna Carver," Anna intervened, nodding at him with a smile. "Have you been injured?"

Lord Giles looked startled for a moment, then glanced down at his leg. "Oh, no, nothing of the sort. A childhood mishap left my leg a little twisted, but I never let it worry me." He patted his thigh. "Lady Kathleen made a balm to soothe it when the weather makes it play up." He smiled at Kathleen, whose blush spread down her neck. "I'd better be off. Have a battle to fight, and all." He stared for a moment at Kathleen, who looked down at the ground; then with a nod at Anna he turned and walked down the hill.

The sun had passed the noon hour when Anna felt Max return. She turned around to see him running towards her, his face etched with concern. She sprang to her feet.

"What is it?" she said. "What's happened?"

"Garrick," he said. He grabbed her by the arm and almost lifting her off her feet, dragged her down the hill. "He's been injured."

She gasped. "What happened?"

"Rupert placed him at the front line in a charge."

"No!" Max pulled her against his side, practically carrying her, as her knees suddenly gave way. "But he's an archer." Archers were always placed at the back of the lines, where they would send their arrows over the field to their enemy targets.

"I know." Max's face was grim. "Rupert knew very well this could cost Garrick his life."

"But why would he do that? Why would he place Garrick in the frontline?"

Max had reached the far side of the plain where the battle was being fought. He skirted around the edges, dragging her around the fallen bodies of dead and dying men. He glanced down at her. "Rupert asked Garrick about his interest in you, but clearly his answer did not satisfy the prince."

"He told him we are betrothed."

"No, he didn't, actually. But Blanche had already told Rupert that Garrick meant more to you than a friend."

Anna closed her eyes in an effort to control the nausea that rose up. "No," she whispered. She gulped in a breath of air, then coughed when sulfur and saltpeter burned the back of her throat. "How badly is he hurt?"

Max came to a stop and slipped his arm from her waist. She turned around to see Garrick lying on the ground, blood covering almost his entire body. The skin around his abdomen hung in ribbons from one side to the other, with black, cloying liquid oozing from the deep gash, and Anna almost gagged at the smell that rose from the wound.

"A flail wound," Max said. "He was hit from the side. He still managed to drag himself away from the fighting, but he has lost too much blood. He does not have long to live."

Anna dropped to her knees beside Garrick, and his eyes fluttered open. "Anna," he breathed. His eyes widened as a spasm gripped him, then fell closed.

"No," Anna whispered, "this cannot be happening." She turned to Max. "You have to give him some of your blood."

"No!"

Anna glanced down at Garrick – his voice had been soft, but no less strident than Max's louder objection. Blood trickled from the corner of his mouth, and another spasm of pain crossed his face. His hand was groping the ground, and Anna wrapped her own around it.

"I will not take the dragon's blood," he finally said. "I have no desire to be bound to a dragon – especially not that one!"

"But you must," she said. "It will save your life." Max was

standing a few feet away, watching in silence, and Anna turned to face him. "You have to give him your blood!" she said. "He's going to die." Her voice was rising. "Are you going to let him die?"

"Anna," Max said, "Even if I wanted to give Garrick some of my blood, I cannot force it on him."

"No," she shouted. "No! You have to! You cannot let him die!"

"Anna." Garrick's voice was barely a whisper. He wrapped his fingers around her hand, and she looked at him. He coughed, and blood splattered from his mouth across his chin. Ripping the hem of her gown, Anna wiped his mouth with the fabric. He smiled faintly. "I'm dying, my love. You have given me such joy and happiness, but I knew that we would not be married."

"What? What are you saying, Garrick? Of course we would have been married."

"Oh, Anna, I know you would have married me." He coughed again, and Anna wiped his face once more. He lay silent for a moment, and when he spoke, Anna had to lean close to his mouth to hear his words. "My dear love, I would not have married you." Anna pulled back, unsure that she had heard correctly.

"You would not have ... not have married me?"

Garrick's nod was barely discernible. "It is Max you love," he whispered. "And Max loves you."

"No, I love you." The tears were spilling down Anna's cheeks. "Please, Garrick, you have to live so we can be married." A ghost of a smile flitted over Garrick's features before quickly turning to a grimace. His skin was pasty, and his hand was cold to Anna's touch, despite the heat of the sun. She leaned forward and kissed his lips. "Please Garrick," she whispered.

"You ... have ..." Garrick drew in a breath, and when he coughed, a stream of blood flew from his mouth, splattering drops over her cheek. He lay, panting for a moment, his eyes closed, his hand clenching hers. He opened his eyes again, but they were unfocused and blood seeped from the corners. His lips moved and Anna placed her ear next to them to catch his last word. "… blessing," he said. His eyes closed, and his hand slipped from hers.

"Garrick," she cried. She lay her ear against his chest and heard the faint fluttering of his heart, as weak as the wings of a butterfly ensnared in a web, and then it fell still. She lay there, her head on his chest, as the tears spilled from her eyes, drenching the shredded remains of the shirt beneath his jerkin. The blood from his wound slowed, then stopped, congealing around the torn edges in a black mass. A fly landed on his open injury, and with a flash of anger she shooed it away.

The battle continued to surge across the plain, with shouts and booms ringing out across the field, but she heard none of them. A man yelled when he tripped over her, then glancing down, muttered an apology, but she neither saw nor heard him. She stared unseeing at the seething mass around her, her mind blank, devoid of thought. If Max had crossed her mind, she would have known he was close by, watching her as she grieved, but she did not think of him, and he made no move to approach her or comfort her. Instead, he sat on the ground and covered her in a cocoon of warmth.

After a time – was it minutes or hours? – she began to take in the scene around her. She was lying on the ground, her arms around Garrick's lifeless body. All that was left was an empty shell – the spirit that had made this body laugh and love and fight was gone. She pushed herself up and glanced around, seeing Max for the first time since Garrick's life had slipped away.

"This is all your fault," she said. Her voice was flat and dull. "You could have saved him."

"He didn't want to be saved," he said.

"You should have saved him for me."

Max rose to his feet and walked over to her, his hand

outstretched. "Come," he said, "let's get you away from here."

She moved away from his reaching hand, and pushed herself to her feet. "Don't touch me," she said. "You killed Garrick." Max's hand fell to his side as she turned around and walked away. She didn't need to look around to know he was following her, but she didn't care. She just had to get away from this battle, this scene of death and despair.

She walked without thinking, stepping over abandoned weapons and pieces of armor, and around the bodies of men whom someone, somewhere, loved. She headed for a small copse of trees, then walked away from them when she heard birds twittering in the branches. Did they not know today was a day of mourning, not joy and celebration? She saw Matilda's carriage perched on its hill, and she turned away from it. The thought of seeing the queen who had been pleased to watch the slaughter was distressing. She longed for Keira, but such thoughts were useless.

She eventually did make her way back to the carriage, when practicality finally overcame sensibility. Already the shadows were growing longer, and soon it would be dusk. The battle was still raging, but Anna could see that both sides were flagging. Bodies littered the ground, and despite Anna's inexperience with war, she could see that neither side would be victorious this day. When she climbed the small hill to the carriage, she saw Matilda watching her curiously, but she made no mention of her absence. Kathleen came running towards her.

"What happened?" she said. "Master Brant took you away and you never returned."

"Garrick is dead."

"Oh, Anna," Kathleen took Anna's hands in her own. "I'm so sorry." Anna felt the tears gathering in her eyes, and looked away.

"I must write ..." the words choked in her throat, and her chest starting heaving. She fell to the ground on her knees as

Kathleen knelt down next to her and wrapped her arms around Anna's shoulders, rocking her gently.

"Shh," she crooned. "It's all right."

"He's dead," Anna whispered. "How can he be dead? We were supposed to be married."

"Married?" Kathleen glanced down at her in surprise, then tightened her arms once more. "It's all right," she said.

She lay in Kathleen's arms until the tears finally stopped and her body went limp. Another set of arms landed next to Kathleen's, and Anna looked up to see Matilda kneeling down beside her.

"Come," she said, "let's get away from this place." Anna nodded and allowed Matilda and Kathleen to help her to her feet. They led her to the carriage, and she collapsed into the corner of the bench. Blanche stepped behind Kathleen and glanced at Anna, and for once, remained silent.

CHAPTER FORTY-ONE

When Cameleus heard that a friend of Anna's had been killed in the battle, he thoughtfully arranged for separate chambers to be prepared, to allow her some privacy in her sorrow. She slept little the first night, the horror and grief of the manner of Garrick's death haunting her dreams, but when the dawn finally lightened the sky, she fell asleep. It wasn't until early evening that she finally opened her eyes to see Kathleen sitting on a stool near the bed.

"I brought you some wine and a little food," she said. She rose to her feet and helped Anna push herself to an upright position, adjusting the cushions behind her back as she winced at the pain that still niggled at her wrist.

"Master Brant came by this morning," Kathleen said as she held out the bowl of beef broth for Anna. "I told him you were sleeping." Anna nodded but said nothing. "Our army made some advances today," Kathleen continued. "But Matilda is weary of watching battles, and chose to remain here, instead." Anna nodded again. She leaned back against the cushions and took the wine from Kathleen's hand.

"Thank you," she said. Kathleen nodded, and taking the bowl, left the room, leaving Anna alone with her thoughts;

but she did not want to think of battles, or Max, or Garrick. She closed her eyes, listening to the sounds of the house around her. She could hear children playing outside the window and the clash of metal pots as they were hauled over the flames of the stove. In the distance, the boom of cannons filled the air. Footsteps sounded outside her room, then died away down the passage. She rose from the bed, carefully wrapping a shawl around her shoulders, and went to stand at the window, staring into the distance.

She fell into an exhausted slumber that night as her aching body and weary mind cried out for rest. When she woke the following morning, there was a maid in the room, carefully pouring fresh water into the ewer.

"Please send someone up to help me get dressed," Anna said. The woman turned, startled, and spilled water on the floor, then hastily dried it with an apron before scurrying from the room. It was Kathleen who entered a short while later.

"I heard you were awake and in need of assistance," she said. She opened Anna's trunk, pulled out a light blue gown and held it out shyly. "I couldn't find Betsy, so I'll help you get dressed," she said. She pulled the gown over Anna's head and tied the laces, and Anna sat down on a stool as Kathleen brushed her hair.

"Cameleus does not have such lovely gardens as we are used to," Kathleen said, "but they have some pretty features. Would you like to explore them a little with me?"

Anna nodded and followed Kathleen through the door. The gardens were in full bloom, but Anna wandered through them listlessly. Each step seemed to take effort as she trailed behind Kathleen. She smiled when Kathleen spoke to her, but it quickly fell away again. How long did it take to heal an aching heart, she wondered?

A few days passed before Max presented himself at the house once more. Even though she hadn't seen him, Anna had sensed his presence during her days of mourning, a warm essence that surrounded her. She had tried to ignore him, but she couldn't deny her awareness of him. He had made no attempt, however, to speak to her since Garrick's death on the battlefield, nor had he shown his physical presence.

She was once again in the gardens, meandering along the paths between the perennials, when Max arrived. She turned when she heard the sound of running footsteps. "Excuse me, Mistress." It was the same maid who had brought water to her room. "There's a gentleman here to see you. He's waiting for you in the parlor."

He was standing at a window when Anna walked into the room, and she saw him straighten his shoulders and breathe in deeply before slowly turning to watch her as she crossed the floor. She drew in a breath when his gaze caught hers, and she looked away.

"What are you doing here, Max?" she said.

"I cannot stay away," he said.

"You stayed away before." She looked back at him as she said the words. He glanced away for a moment.

"You're right, I did. It is a regret I will have for the remainder of my days." He turned to look out the window. "I was so angry with you, at first, but even as I tried to forget you in my waking hours, you haunted me when I slept." He turned to look at her. "In my dreams I would tell you of the things I saw and the places I visited." A smile tugged at his lips. "I held you in my arms in my dreams, and we danced." Anna looked at him in surprise.

"Danced?"

Max walked towards her, and she dropped her eyes. "Yes," he said, his voice low. "Just the two of us, and my hands held you as you danced like a faery." He reached out his hands and brushed them over her hips before dropping them to his sides. She looked up to see his eyes glowing, and she felt herself being drawn like a moth to the light. She tore her gaze away.

"Garrick is dead because of me," she whispered. Max

wrapped his fingers around hers.

"No," he said.

"He would never have joined the king's forces if it hadn't been for me. If I had stayed at Storbrook, he would still be alive."

"You are not responsible for the choices Garrick made. He knew the risks of fighting. He knew that he could die. And even after you agreed to marry him, he did not change that decision."

"He said he would not have married me."

"I know." Max glanced away. "Do you remember when Garrick called me outside at the ball?"

Anna nodded.

"We didn't fight. We talked."

"What did you talk about?"

"Garrick asked me if I would leave you again." Anna drew in a deep breath. "He knew that you would never be able to love him the way he wanted to be loved. He knew," Max paused, "he knew that you loved me, even if you refused to admit it. He had already decided that if he could not have you completely, he would let you go. But he asked me to give him time. To tell you in his own way."

"But ..." Anna shook her head. "I'm confused."

"He loved you so much he wanted you to follow your heart. And he loved you even more because you still chose to marry him, sacrificing your own desires for his."

Tears welled up in Anna's eyes, and turning to a stool, she sat down and buried her face in her hand. "I didn't deserve Garrick's love," she said.

Max knelt down on the floor before her. "Garrick thought you did, and who are you to question a dead man?"

A choked laugh escaped Anna's lips. "I miss him," she said. "I miss knowing that he is out there, living and breathing."

"I know." Max's arms went around her, and she leaned her head on his shoulder, resting in silence for a few moments.

"I forgive you," she finally whispered. His hand moved into her hair, and she felt him smile.

"I love you," he said. She drew in a breath. A flame flickered deep within her, a glowing ember that his words gently fanned. She could feel the warmth spreading through the pit of her stomach, reaching outwards. He lifted her head from his shoulder with his hands and looked into her eyes. "There is something else I need to tell you." She gazed back him, her expression questioning. "When I found you in the ravine," he paused and looked away.

"Yes?" she prompted.

"You were covered in blood. The wound on your head was bleeding profusely, running down your face and into your hair." He stroked his fingers over the red, angry scar on her forehead, then locked his gaze with hers. "I cleaned you," he whispered.

"You mean …?"

He nodded. "I tasted your blood."

She shuddered. "That's —"

"I'm a dragon, remember? It only sounds disgusting to humans. To a dragon …" he smirked, "… it sounds delectable! The blood of the woman you love in your mouth." She felt a sudden ache as the tip of his tongue flicked between his lips. "I have never tasted anything more luscious."

She laughed nervously. "Are you going to eat me now?"

"Certainly not!" He sounded horrified. "Not when I've created a bond with you."

"A bond?"

"Yes, that's what I'm telling you. When I tasted your blood, I formed a bond with you, an unbreakable cord that anchors me to you forever."

She stared at him. "You bound yourself to me? Even though I was going to marry Garrick?"

"Yes." He wrapped his hand around her neck and pulled

her closer. "I love you, Anna. When I was away, I tried to get you from my mind, but you were as stubborn in memory as you are in real life! When I returned, I knew I could never leave you again, and even though you might still have married Garrick, I wanted to know that the creature I am was forever tied to you. I told you I was watching you because Aaron had instructed me to, but that was just an excuse. I just wanted to be near you. I wanted to feel your presence, even if you could not feel mine."

He wrapped his hands around hers and pulled her to her feet. He was standing so close, her gown brushed against his legs. She wanted to press herself closer, but his eyes held her frozen.

"I belong to you forever, Anna," he whispered. "Nothing can ever change that."

"But ... you barely even spoke to me!"

"I wanted to. But my very presence antagonized Garrick. And I knew you felt guilty whenever you spoke to me. So I pretended to ignore you. But just as you could not help watching me when you thought I wouldn't notice, I could not help watching you. I was just waiting for you to realize that you belonged to me, too."

He pushed the hair from her face with light fingers that lingered on her cheek, and glanced down at her lips. He was so close, and she wanted to feel him closer. There was a sound in the hallway and he cocked his head slightly, then stepped away. Even the distance of a few inches was devastating, and she stepped forward. She wanted to feel his arms around her, his body pressed against hers. He took a breath and the light flared in his eyes for the briefest of moments. His hands reached towards her, then dropped to his sides as he took another step backwards.

"Someone is coming," he said softly. "Can I call on you tomorrow?" She nodded. He lifted her hand and brushed her knuckles against his lips. "Until then, my darling," he said.

CHAPTER FORTY-TWO

Anna stood at the window and watched as Max left the house and followed the path around the gardens. He disappeared into the trees, and then a few minutes later she saw a bright flash of light as a dragon rose into the air. He turned towards the heavens, and with a loud roar, blew out a river of flame.

"Goodness, what's that sound?" Matilda said as she entered the room. She walked over to the window and glanced outside, but Max was already too far away to be seen by a casual observer. "I spoke to my brother this morning, and it seems as though this whole affair is going to be far more protracted than they originally thought." She turned to look at Anna. "It is most aggravating. Alfred assured me that Terran's forces were weak and would soon be overrun. If I had known otherwise, I would never have agreed to this scheme of following the army, being dragged over the countryside for weeks on end."

Matilda tapped her fingers against the windowsill. "So I have decided to return home," she said. "My children miss me, and I them, and who knows what a mess our Lord Chamberlain is making of the affairs of state. In fact, it is quite imperative that I return as soon as possible so that I can oversee the running of the kingdom. We will start our return journey at the end of the week."

The end of the week – that left four days.

Anna nodded. "Very well, my lady."

Matilda went over to a seat and sat down. "Pour me a glass of wine, Anna," she said. "I must confess I am quite fatigued." There was a flagon on the table, and Anna poured out a glass and handed it to Matilda before pouring a glass for herself. "Have you gotten over your grief?" Matilda asked.

"No, my lady," she said. "But with each passing day the pain becomes a little duller."

"Then you will be back to your usual spirits by the time we leave?"

Anna looked away. "Yes, my lady," she said.

Max met Anna in the gardens the next day. She knew he was there before he even came around the corner, and smiled when he strode towards her. "You were spying on me," she said. "Wanted to make sure I was alone before you presented yourself."

He laughed. "Most definitely. I always want you to myself. But how did you know?"

She wrapped her hand around his arm as they walked along the path. "I can feel when you are near."

He turned to look at her in surprise. "What do you mean?"

Anna shrugged. "Just that. I don't know how else to explain it except to say that even when I don't see you, I can feel your presence." Max was silent, and when she glanced at him, she saw his forehead was furrowed in thought. "What is it?" she said.

"Well, it's just that it's impossible. What you are explaining is a blood bond, but you haven't had my blood."

"Are you sure you didn't slip me some when I was unconscious?" she said teasingly.

He smiled. "I will admit the thought crossed my mind, but no, I didn't." They continued walking as he reached into his pocket. "I have something for you." In his hand lay a simple, silver band.

"What is this?" She took the ring, holding it closer to the see the love knot etched into the metal.

"It belonged to Garrick. He had it made for you when you first agreed to marry him."

She glanced up at him. "How do you know?"

"He showed it to me the night of the ball. He had already decided it could not be a wedding band, but he still wanted you to have it. He just hadn't decided how to give it to you." Max paused. "He had it on him when he died."

Anna closed her hand over the ring and looked away, blinking back the tears that suddenly filled her eyes. "I cannot take it," she whispered. "My heart was not faithful and true to him."

Max stopped walking, and stepping back, pulled his arm from hers. "Anna," he said sternly, "did you not hear what I said? Garrick knew that you could not love him, but he loved you anyway. This is not a gift based on what *you* think or feel, but a gift based on what *he* felt for you! It is not a reward. It is a gift of friendship. You will take it, and will wear it. And it will be a reminder that before he even asked for your hand in marriage, he was your friend." His eyes narrowed as she turned and continued walking down the path, away from him, but she could not shut out the sound of his voice. "You keep telling yourself that you failed Garrick, but he did not see it that way. You were not unfaithful to him. You did not choose me over him. Instead, you remained true even when your heart cried for you to make a different choice."

No, her mind shouted, it was her fault he was dead. She hadn't loved him enough. She heard Max following her, but his next words stopped her in her tracks. "He told you to follow your own dream, and not be bound by his," Max said softly. "It was his last wish." She turned around slowly, but he was hazy through the tears.

"You heard," she whispered. "You heard him talking to me." He nodded. "I wanted to love him," she said. "I wanted to make him happy. Why could I not love him?" In a few quick strides, Max was wrapping his arms around her, pulling her head against his shoulder.

"There is no guilt," he said. "Garrick loved you. Let that be enough. It was enough for him." A sob rose in her throat, and she turned her face into Max's shoulder as the tears ran down her cheeks, pouring out from the crack in her soul that was ripping wider apart. She didn't notice when he slipped his arm beneath her knees and carried her to a quiet bench in the corner, settling her in his lap as he continued to rock her. His hand was in her hair, soothing her like an infant. Finally the tears slowed, and then ceased altogether, and she lay spent against his chest. She felt extremely weary, and for a moment, closed her eyes.

"I shouldn't have blamed you for Garrick's death," she finally said.

"I understood," he said.

"Thank you," she whispered. She lay against his chest for a few more minutes, until the sound of other voices in the distance penetrated her mind. She disentangled herself from Max's arms and slid off his lap onto the bench beside him. He kept his arm around her, and she leaned against his shoulder.

"Did you hear that Matilda has decided to return home?"

She felt Max smile. "I think all the king's forces have heard that piece of news. I'm not sure who is more relieved – Alfred or Roderick!"

Anna gave a half-hearted smile. "Maybe Rupert?"

Max's grin fled and he looked away. "Rupert doesn't care one way or the other. He just wants to win this war, whatever the cost."

"But why? It's not his war."

"Pride. Or maybe it's because he wants to prove his worth

as the second son. But he will not back down."

"And Alfred?"

"I think Alfred is starting to recognize the toll this will take on his kingdom, both in terms of money and lives lost. He entered this war confident of an easy victory, but he underestimated Terran's support and strength. If he's wise, he would cut his losses and return home with his wife."

"Is he wise?"

"I don't know." Anna thought about this for a moment.

"Have you heard from Aaron lately?" she said.

"I'm going to see him tomorrow. I'll leave early in the morning and return the following afternoon." He paused to look at her. "Will you be all right if I'm gone for a few days?"

"You will be back before we start our return journey?"

"I will. I won't tarry at Storbrook, and will return as soon as my business with Aaron is done."

"I'm sure I can survive without you for a few days!" she said wryly.

He laughed. "I'm sure you can! I'm more concerned about your personal safety. Stay here at the house, and you should be fine."

CHAPTER FORTY-THREE

Alfred and Roderick also had chambers at Cameleus's house, and every day, as the residents gathered for meals, they discussed the progress of the war. Roderick wanted to keep fighting, but Anna could tell that Alfred's heart was not in it. His and Terran's forces were similar in both size and strength, with neither side coming out as the clear victor. One day, Alfred's losses were significant – dozens of men dead or captured – but the next day, fortunes were reversed. As frustrating as this was, what troubled Alfred even more was that the support of the locals which Roderick had assured him would be forthcoming had not materialized. The citizens of Terranton – as everybody was now calling it – had not streamed out of the city to back Roderick, as he had assured Alfred would happen. In fact, the farmers in the surrounding countryside had gone so far as to kill their livestock and burn what was left of the previous harvest, to prevent the invaders from laying their hands on their supplies, before fleeing into the safety of the city. Rupert had been furious when he heard the report, and laid waste to the surrounding countryside, setting fire to empty cottages and new crops.

Rupert had refused Cameleus's welcome, preferring to remain close to the action, but rumors were rife in the camp of his increasingly tyrannical manner and merciless vengeance against any who crossed him. It had not gone unnoticed amongst the soldiers that he felt nothing about risking the lives of his men, sending them into situations that were essentially suicide missions, then dismissing the numbers lost with barely a nod. Discontent was rife within the camp, and fights between the men were not uncommon. The stocks and posts were filled each day with men being punished for some infraction or other, and the smiths were kept busy making locks and chains to keep pace with the punishments.

For Anna, just the mention of Rupert's name made her tremble with rage. He had sent Garrick into a battle for which he was not trained, knowing that his chances of survival were slim. And all for what? To revenge himself on Anna? She had not seen him since before that day, but she smiled grimly at the thought of someone burying a dagger in his chest.

But he was the army commander, and brother to the king, and the day Max left for Storbrook, Rupert arrived at the house, demanding to see Alfred at once. Anna did not see him arrive, but everyone in the house could hear the ruckus he made as he marched into the hall, and the book Anna held in her hand trembled as her grip around it tightened.

"I don't care what he is doing," Rupert shouted at the footman who had answered the call. "Find him and bring him to me. Now!"

Anna felt a roaring in her ears, and rising to her feet, she walked to the window, placing her forehead against the cool glass. She saw Matilda cast a disinterested glance her way as she threw down the sheet of paper in her hand. Their departure was set for just two days hence, and the page contained a list of items still to be attended to before they started their journey.

"I will be very glad to leave this place," Matilda said,

leaning her head back against her chair. "Although, I would be more content knowing that Roderick was firmly back on his throne."

"I don't think the people here want him back," Blanche said.

Matilda's head shot up. "Nonsense," she said sharply. "Of course they do. They have been led astray by Terran's smooth talk and empty promises, but mark my words, there will be rejoicing when Roderick is king once more."

Anna glanced away. She was quite in agreement with Blanche, but there was no point voicing that opinion to the queen. Out of the corner of her eye she saw a maid shake out a gown. Their clothes had been washed and ironed in preparation for their long journey home, and all that remained was to stow them in the trunks. Without the army to slow them down, they would cover the distance back home in twice the speed, but it would still be many weeks before they were back in their own chambers. Anna wondered how her canaries were faring. She had left them in the care of one of the maids, and she missed their bright chirping.

"Someone needs to remind the stables to clean and oil my saddle before we leave," Matilda said. She rose to her feet and glanced out the door. "Where are those guards when you need them?" She pulled back into the room and looked around, her eyes roving over Kathleen, who quickly looked down at the work in her lap, before stopping on Anna. "Go and tell them in the stables that my saddle must be well oiled," she said.

Anna nodded. She was quite certain the stables knew what to do with a saddle, but she was glad of a task to engage herself in. "Yes, my lady," she said.

She left the room and strode along the passage. The corridors were dark, the stone worn to a smooth surface by the passing of many feet. It was a large house, three storeys tall. At the main entrance to the house was a wide staircase which split the house into two wings. To the right an arched doorway opened into the hall. Behind the hall ran a narrow passageway which led to the study and a parlor. On the left side of the house was another arched doorway, but a screen barred entry, and the rooms beyond were bare. Like many large houses, it had been built atop a small hill, with the main front entrance at a higher level than the back of the house, where a small staircase led to the lower level where the kitchens and storage rooms were located. These led out to the courtyard behind the house.

On the second floor, as with the main floor, the rooms to the left were closed off and left unused. When Anna asked a maid about it, she explained that Cameleus's children were all grown and married; when his wife died, leaving him alone, he had ordered the second wing closed, feeling that the house was too large for the use of just one man. The rooms were empty, the maid explained, except for a few pieces of broken furniture.

Anna walked along the upstairs corridor, down the stairs and into the narrow passage behind the hall. It ran past the parlor, and as she drew close, she saw that the door had been left ajar. The king and his brother were within, and their voices, raised in anger, spilled through the open door. She paused, considering her options. She had no desire to eavesdrop on the conversation, but if she walked past, they would see her and might think she had been listening.

"You are a fool," she heard Rupert saying as she drew herself against the wall, and slowly slid one foot behind the other.

"Terran wants to negotiate terms, and you would continue fighting," Alfred shot back. "How many men have we lost already, Rupert? And for what? To gain a throne for Roderick?" Anna held her breath, sliding backwards an inch at a time.

"You thought it was a good enough cause a few months ago," Rupert sneered.

"Aye, that I did, because you assured me that Terran was weak, and did not have the backing of his people. It turns out you were wrong on both counts."

"So you would turn tail and run now because of a few losses. A strong leader would stay the course, Alfred." Anna froze when she heard Rupert's voice grow louder. He stopped near the door, but a moment later was pacing away again.

"What do you know about being a strong leader? You take what you want without regard for anyone but yourself."

"You are nothing but a weakling," Rupert said. "You do not deserve to wear the crown."

"Think what you will, Rupert, but I am your king, and you will do as I say." There was the sound of someone dropping heavily into a chair. "I have considered Terran's request to parley, and have decided to meet him on the morrow. I will invite him to meet us here, and you will join us." There was a long moment of silence.

"If you are intent on doing this," Rupert said, his voice speculative, "then we should meet him at his court. Ask him to send some men to escort us." Anna paused at the words. She had already moved a few feet from the door. Just a little further and she could turn and walk away without fear of discovery.

"Why?" Alfred's voice was filled with suspicion.

"It will demonstrate your faith and goodwill." There was another moment of silence.

"What are you up to?"

"Is it not good leadership to flatter your enemy, while forcing your own demands? Tell Terran that as king and leader of this land, he should not have to travel into the countryside to confer with us." There was another moment of silence, and Anna could imagine Alfred slowly nodding his head.

"I will think about it. Now go." Anna quickly scurried backwards, but Rupert marched out of the room before she could get beyond sight of the door. She turned and ran down the corridor, but no sooner had Rupert slammed the heavy wooden door shut than he was behind her, his hand grabbing her arm and swinging her around against the wall. She cried out when her arm hit the stones.

"What are you doing here?" he hissed. "You are eavesdropping so you can report back to Terran and his spies."

"What? No! I was going to the stables with a message from the queen."

Rupert laughed dryly. "Stables? For the queen? Is that the best you can come up with?" He leaned closer. "You are a spy and a traitor. One of the guards saw you with a dragon. And I did admire the way you made it seem as though you had been abducted by Syngen Gail, when all along you had planned to meet with him and pass along our plans."

Anna glared at him, twisting and turning in an effort to free herself from his grasp. "Is that the best *you* can come up with?" she said. "What plans could I possibly discover that would make such a deception of value to him?"

"Your lover was passing information along to you," he replied. "I heard he died. Took a blow to the stomach."

"Let me go," she growled. There were footsteps in the distance, growing closer, and she glanced in the direction of the sound. But her heart sank when she saw Frank striding towards them, his eyebrows drawn together in a frown.

"Your Highness," he said to Rupert, "is everything all right?" Rupert glanced down at Anna, then pulling her away from the wall, thrust her towards Frank.

"This woman is a traitor," he said. "Take her to the west wing and lock her in one of the empty rooms. I will deal with her later."

Frank nodded. "Yes, Your Highness," he said.

"Oh, and make sure she is bound and gagged," Rupert added. "We don't want people thinking we have bagged ourselves a witch."

Frank grinned. "Yes, Your Highness. It will be my pleasure." He wrapped his hand around Anna's arm. "I always knew you were a traitor," he said to her. She scowled at him, but kept silent as he dragged her down the hall, along the empty corridors and into the west wing.

It was clear that that part of the house had been closed up for years. The passages were coated in a thick layer of dust, and the room at the far end of the passage that Frank pushed her into was dark and damp. The shutters hung askew from the open window, and the broken bed had become a nest for breeding mice. Frank glanced around the room with a look of disgust, then looked back at Anna. "Not what you are used to, but it will have to do." There was a pile of linen in the corner, moldy and chewed, but Frank lifted one of the sheets, and finding a piece that still looked fairly intact, ripped it into long strips. She winced when he pulled her wrists behind her back, and he gave her a look of sympathy.

"Can't have you trying to escape, now can we?" he said as bound her hands with a strip of linen. He glanced at her mouth, then down at the strips in his hands. "If I leave you ungagged, will you promise not to scream out the window?"

"I cannot promise anything," Anna said, "but I'm sure I won't have to resort to screaming out the window. The queen will soon hear what has happened, and it won't be long before she sees me released."

Frank nodded. "If I hear a squeak, I will be back with enough gags to choke you." He checked the knots around her wrists one more time and left the room. The key creaked as it turned in the lock, sliding the bolt into place, and Frank's footsteps grew fainter as he walked away.

CHAPTER FORTY-FOUR

Anna looked around the room she had been locked into. It was once a bedchamber, but all that remained of the furnishings were the mice-ridden bed and a broken stool. One look at the bed was enough to convince her that she did not want to be anywhere near it. She sank down to the floor, turning her face into her shoulder as the dust rose from the floor and settled over her. Had Matilda noticed her absence yet? Had Rupert informed the king of her arrest? Alfred would not believe the ludicrous charges against her, she was sure of that. She leaned her head against the wall and watched as a spider scurried across an exposed rafter then swung to the corner of the room, leaving a fine, glistening thread trailing behind it.

She pulled her knees up to her chest, and waited.

It was a long time before she heard the sound of returning footsteps. The door was pulled open, and Frank stepped inside, a steaming plate of roasted meat and vegetables in his hand. He placed it on the floor, and crouching before her, loosened the bonds holding her wrists together. Anna's arms were numb, and it took a moment before she could move them again, but slowly the feeling began to return. She took the plate held out to her, and looked up at Frank.

"I'm not guilty of treason," she said.

Frank shrugged. "Your actions would suggest otherwise."

Anna sighed. "What did the queen say?"

Frank glanced away. "She hasn't been told."

Anna looked up at him in surprise. "Why not? What does she think has happened to me?"

Frank rose to his feet. "I am not privy to the prince's thoughts," he said. "As for your disappearance, I overheard Lady Blanche say you had run away with your lover."

"What?" The fork slipped from Anna's grasp and clattered to the plate. "What lover? Master Garrick is dead!"

"Not Garrick. Max Brant."

"Ah!" The memory of Blanche sneering words about Max carrying her back to camp came flooding back. "She would say that," Anna said, lifting the fork and taking a mouthful of food. It was hot, for which she was grateful.

"Yes, well, I didn't suspect you of *that*," Frank said dryly.

"Has the queen sent anyone to look for me?" she asked.

"No."

Anna nodded. The food was sticking in her throat, and suddenly she was unable to eat. She handed the plate back to Frank. He took it without meeting her gaze and left the room in silence. He returned a short while later with a quilt in his hand, which he threw at her without a word, before leaving once more. He had left her hands untied – by accident or design, she wasn't sure.

The shadows in the room grew longer as the sun dropped towards the horizon. Soon it would be dark, and she would be alone with the mice. But she did not expect to remain that long. As soon as Alfred heard of her imprisonment she would be released. He knew that Aaron would not look kindly on his sister-in-law being imprisoned on trumped-up charges.

She sat with her head against the wall, waiting. The stone was hard and cold, and after a while she rose to her feet and started pacing the room. Why was it taking so long for Alfred to set her free? The minutes ticked by, and she sat once again, drawing the quilt around her shoulders. It was growing darker in the room, and she wished someone would come to release her from this prison. She could not believe Alfred had left her for so long. She rose to her feet and walked over to the window. The room she was in overlooked the courtyard, three storeys below. What if Rupert had not told his brother what he had done? What if Rupert did not intend to tell him at all? Frank was the only other person who knew where she was, and he already believed her guilty of the crimes of which she had been accused. Would he think it strange if Rupert instructed him to remain silent about what happened? Would she be able to convince Frank to involve the king?

The hours passed, and the moon rose in the night sky, sending a pale shaft of light into the room. Anna could see the mice scurrying on the floor. She tried to count them, but they would pause for only a moment before running off, scurrying through a crack in the wall, or squeezing through the gap beneath the door. She guessed there must be at least two dozen. At some time during the night she drifted off to sleep.

She awoke with the sound of birds chirping in the trees, their cheerful chatter filling the air. They reminded her of Garrick, and she felt a pang as she thought of him. She rose painfully to her feet and walked over to the window and watched as the sky lightened.

The morning wore on without any sign of Frank. She paced the small room, counting the cracks in the floor. The courtyard was alive with sound, and she stood at the window, watching people coming and going. Children were running around, playing, and from time to time a woman would come out of the kitchen, wooden spatula in hand, and yell at them. The noon hour passed, and the sun was nearing the western horizon by the time the door finally creaked open. Frank stepped into the room, a hunk of bread and cup of wine in his hands.

"Thank you for remembering me!" she said. He stared down at her for a long moment, then dropped down to his haunches before her.

"The king is dead," he said. Anna stared at him. She didn't understand.

"What did you say?"

"The king is dead. He was killed on his way to Terran's court."

"But … how?"

Frank slumped onto the ground and covered his face with his hands. "He was killed by his brother," he said, his voice low.

"What?" Anna stared at Frank, trying to make sense of his words. Frank lifted his head.

"A contingent arrived from Terran this morning to escort the king and the prince to his palace."

"Yes...?"

"Matilda wanted me to give the king a message, but he had already left. She told me to chase after him to deliver her missive. I didn't think it was important, but I must obey the queen, so I went." He glanced at the floor. "The king was riding at the back of the group, between the prince and one of Terran's men. It struck me as strange. Why would the king be at the back, unprotected? I rode faster, determined to deliver my message and be gone, but as I drew closer, I saw the prince pull a dagger from his waist. With the noise of the other horses, he hadn't heard me.

"He held the dagger down by his side and fell back half a pace, pretending to fiddle with the stirrup. I saw the king glance back at him, then turn to say something to Terran's man. As soon as the king turned away, the prince plunged the knife into his brother's back, leaning over to sink it in the side furthest from him. I wasn't sure at first what had happened, for the king sat straight in his saddle for a moment. But then he fell forward onto the neck of his horse, and I knew."

Frank's face was pale, his eyes wide and staring. He pushed himself to his feet and went to stand at the window. "I spurred my horse forward, but then Rupert was yelling, shouting that Terran's man had stabbed the king. The king's men started attacking Terran's, and I knew that the guards would believe Rupert over me, so I pulled away, and fled into the forest." He looked up to meet Anna's horrified gaze. "I ran like a coward."

Anna stared at Frank in a daze, then slowly shook her head. The king was dead! Killed by the hand of his own brother! He was not coming to help her. She looked up at Frank. His fist was pressed against the wall, his face anguished. She rose to her feet and walked over to where he stood. "You are the only witness to what happened," she said. "Rupert would have killed you if you had stayed." She turned and paced the room. "Did you tell anyone what you saw?"

Frank looked out the window. "No."

"This will continue the war. I overheard ..." She stopped and looked at Frank.

"Go on," he said wearily. "At this stage I have no idea who I believe any more."

"I was on my way to the stables when I walked past the parlor. I heard the king say he wanted to negotiate with Terran. He realized that Terran had the backing of his people, and he did not want to drag the war out any longer. Rupert accused him of being a coward."

"Rupert wants his victory, and killed his brother to achieve it," Frank said.

"Yes!" Anna resumed her pacing. "Terran needs to know what happened. He needs to know that Rupert is determined to drag out this war at any cost, and that it is up to him to stop it. But how to tell him? If only ..." She paused. She had been so caught up in Frank's story, she had not noticed the return of a heated, musky presence. She turned excitedly to

Frank.

"Max! You have to find Max! He can help us reach Terran safely."

"Max Brant? What makes you think he would help us? Can he even be trusted?"

"Yes! Yes! You must find him, and bring him back here." She paused, considering. "Tell him to come when it's dark. He will want to come straight away, but you mustn't let him."

"There must be a better plan."

"No! Max is the best help we could have!" She walked over to Frank, her eyes locking with his. "Do you believe I have been falsely accused?"

He stared at her, then turned to gaze out the window. He shrugged his shoulders. "Perhaps."

"Even if you are not completely certain, you agree that I *may* be innocent?" Frank was silent. "Does the queen know where I am? Did the king?"

Frank sighed. "No."

"Why wouldn't Rupert tell them if I was guilty? Why would he keep it a secret?" Frank turned to look at her. "Please, go and speak to Max. He is the only one who can help us."

Frank said nothing for a moment. "Nothing makes sense anymore," he said. He dropped his eyes to the ground. "I'll do it," he said slowly, "but only because I have no idea what else to do." He paused as Anna watched him intently. "But why would he come with me? He has no reason to trust me any more than I do him."

"Tell him I sent you. No. Wait." Anna smiled. "Tell him that the shrew needs a dragon."

"The shrew needs a dragon? What does that mean?"

"It doesn't matter! Tell him that and he will know I sent you. Quickly now. Go find him. And remember what I said – do not let him come straight away. He must wait until dark. Bring me word when you have delivered the message. We will reach Terran tonight."

Frank nodded, his expression resigned. "I will give him your message, but if you are wrong about him, then we could all be dead by morning." He turned and left the room, locking the door behind him.

Anna paced the room anxiously. She had no doubt that Max would help her. She only hoped he would see the sense in her plan, and not come charging in to rescue her straight away. He needed to fly her to Terran's court, and he needed the cloak of night to pass by unnoticed.

For a second time, Anna watched the shadows lengthen in the room as she waited for the lock to turn and the door to open. This time her patience was rewarded when Frank returned two hours later. He closed the door behind him and nodded at her.

"I found him and gave him your message. He said he will be here as soon as night falls."

"Is that all he said?"

"No. He said a few choice words which I will not repeat. Then he demanded I bring him here straight away, but I told him what you said. He was not happy, but agreed he would wait."

Anna smiled. He must love her.

CHAPTER FORTY-FIVE

Anna could feel Max's presence growing closer as he strode down the corridor. It was dark, and once again a narrow moonbeam was the only light illuminating the room. Max pushed the door open and strode over to Anna, wrapping his arms around her.

"My darling," he whispered, "you are very cruel to make me wait."

"A little lesson in patience would not go amiss," she said.

"Patience?" He raised his eyebrows as he pulled away from her. "Have I not been patient enough? I have waited years to hold you in my arms!"

Behind them Frank cleared his throat, and Anna pulled away. "Did Frank tell you what he witnessed?"

Max nodded. "I cannot say I'm surprised. I never trusted Rupert."

"We need to warn Terran."

"Why?"

"So that this war can be stopped!"

Max glanced at Frank, then motioned with his head toward the door. Frank glanced between them, then with a resigned expression left the room.

"This is not my war, Anna," Max said as Frank disappeared around the corner. "Humans have been fighting each other over one petty thing after another for centuries."

Anna crossed her arms over her chest and glared at him. "That may be true, but it is *my* war, and I want it to stop! Garrick has already died, and if it continues, many more men will lose their lives. How many humans must die, Max, before dragons decide that they should help?"

Max stared at her for a moment, then turned away with a growl. "Aaron instructed me not to get involved," he said.

"Aaron does not know that Alfred is dead," Anna said. "He was fond of the king, was he not?"

"Yes, but Alfred was just a human."

Anna stared at Max's back in disbelief. "*I* am human, Max, or have you forgotten? And so is your Master's wife! Do you think he would be so unconcerned if the human involved was Keira?" Max's fists clenched at his sides, and flames glowed between his fingers. Anna stepped up to him, and laid her hand on his back. She could feel the ridges along his spine, and she traced her fingers along the raised edge.

"Please, Max," she whispered. "You say you love me, but then you must accept who I am. I am human, and always will be. And being human means caring about the fate of others." She dropped her hand, and slowly wrapped it around his glowing fist. At her touch his hand relaxed, and with a sigh he turned to face her, weaving his fingers between hers. He stared down at her with blazing eyes, and she could feel the heat pouring off him.

"I know you are human," he said. He smiled wryly. "I remember it every time I come to your aid. But you also have such a strong character, that sometimes I forget, too." He shut his eyes, and when he opened them, they were no longer glowing but were a cold, flinty gray. "I will take you to Terran, but it is for your sake I do this, not his, nor Alfred's." He glanced at the door and raised his voice. "Frank!" Frank's face appeared at the door a moment later as he stepped into the room.

"Mistress Anna and I will go talk to Terran," Max said, "but you must remain here."

"But —"

"The queen is in need of your protection, now more than ever," Max interrupted. "Rupert may decide he wants a throne, which places her and her children in danger. You must see her away as soon as possible, and get them back to Civitas. When you arrive there, speak to the Lord Chamberlain at once. Also Lord Eastwich. He's a bit of a fool, but he will know the truth of what you say and will seek to protect Matilda and the new king."

"But what about the prince? He needs to pay for what he has done!"

"Terran will make him pay. And," he continued when Frank opened his mouth to protest, "your first duty is to your queen. And there is no time to lose. You must tell Matilda that you leave at first light, and do not tarry along the way."

Frank stared at Max for a moment, then finally nodded. "Yes, milord," he said.

"Good! Quickly now. Rupert is with his men tonight, so you can prepare to leave the palace without his notice."

Frank looked at Anna. "You will tell Terran all I have told you?"

Anna nodded. "I will. Thank you, Frank."

He glanced at Max, then turning on his heel, left the room. Anna looked back at Max. He was already stripping off his tunic. "Will you hold this?" he asked. She took the heated garment from his hand. Max glanced out the window. "We will need to find a room where our exit will go unnoticed," he said. "Come." He took her by the hand and led her across the passage to the opposite room, where the window overlooked the empty gardens. "This will have to do," Max said. He pulled his boots off his feet and handed them to Anna, standing before her wearing only his breeches. "Turn around," he said.

She blushed when Max kicked his breeches over to her, but remained still until a bright light filled the air then dispersed into the night sky. Scooping up the breeches, she turned to see Max hovering outside the window. She flung her legs over the window ledge and waited as he curled his tail around her, lifting her onto his back. His clothes were between her chest and his neck, but she wrapped her arms around him and held on tight as he lifted himself above the building and into the dark night sky.

Terran's palace lay only a few miles north of Cameleus's estate, and in a few minutes Max was dropping down towards a field just beyond the city of Terranton. A flash of light shot through the air as he transformed once more, but when Anna turned around to look at him, his chest was still bare, his tunic in his hand. She looked at him questioningly as he grinned at her.

"Easier this way," he said. He grabbed her around the waist and shot back into the air, his wings opening behind him as she gasped in fright. She had barely had time to draw in breath when they were falling back to the ground, his wings folded against his back as they fell freely through the air, landing in a dark corner a few hundred feet from the palace. Max had to hold Anna upright as her knees threatened to give way beneath her and her chest heaved from fright. She leaned her forehead against his chest, breathing deeply as her heart slowed to its regular pace. When she was finally able to pull away, she glared at him, but he grinned shamelessly in return before taking her by the arm.

"This way," he said.

The palace Max led her into was not as big as Alfred's, but it was very grand. A staircase of white marble welcomed them into a large, domed room, from which passages exited on either side. Max paused a moment, glancing between the two directions, before settling on the one to the right. He pulled Anna a little closer as he headed towards the arched doorway, then paused again. Someone was coming towards them. Anna recognized him right away, but it was Max who greeted the man who had taken her hostage a few weeks before.

"Syngen Gail."

Syngen stopped in his tracks for the briefest of moments, then continued walking towards them with a grin. "Well, well! Max Brant! And my pretty little hostage. I wondered if you were somehow involved when she and the other girl disappeared. Are you returning her to me, Max?"

"I heard you cursing me," Max said. "And no, I'm certainly not returning her to you."

Anna glanced between the two men before settling her gaze on Max. "You know him?" she hissed.

Max looked down at her. "Unfortunately, I do. Syngen is part of Aaron's clan."

Anna looked at the other man in surprise. "You're a —"

"No!" Max quickly intervened, looking pointedly at a footman who had entered the palace and was hurrying across the floor in their direction. Max waited until he was out of earshot before turning back to Anna. "Syngen was adopted by his aunt and uncle when he was …" He looked up at Syngen. "How old were you?"

"Three." Syngen looked at Anna. "My mother died when I was an infant, and her sister took me in. She was married to a, er, Aaron's distant cousin, and I grew up with them." He looked at Max. "I take it the girl belongs to you?"

Anna frowned and took a step towards Syngen. "Certainly not!" she said. She turned to glare at Max when he grinned down at her. "What?" she said. Max reached out and took her hand in his, squeezing it gently, before turning back to Syngen.

"Actually," Max said, "she's under Aaron's protection."

Syngen looked surprised. "Aaron's?"

"My sister is Aaron's wife," Anna said.

"Ah! Well, if I had known that," he said, raising his

eyebrows with a sly look, "I would not have allowed you out of my sight."

Next to her Max snorted, but when she turned to glare at him, he quickly cleared his throat. "We need to see Terran," he said to Syngen.

"Yes, that reminds me. Were you not marching with Alfred? Since when do your kind concern yourself with human affairs?"

"Since Aaron's sister-in-law serves the queen," Max said.

Syngen nodded. "Of course. That makes sense. You were her protection."

"Enough chitchat," Anna interrupted. "You can enjoy your reunion later, but right now, we need to speak with your king."

"Why?"

"We have news that he will wish to hear regarding Alfred's death," Max said.

"Hmm. He's not in a very good mood, I must warn you."

"Just take us to him," Anna said.

Syngen nodded, and inclined his head. "Follow me," he said. Max kept hold of Anna's hand as they walked, and Syngen glanced down in amusement. "I thought she didn't belong to you," he said to Max.

"Not yet," Max replied.

Syngen led Anna and Max into a large, square, windowless room, leaving them alone while he went to advise Terran of his visitors. Tapestries covered every wall, and in each corner stood a small table, with a large, wooden-cased clock on each. The face of each clock differed from the others, but they ticked in unison, each second reverberating through the room from corner to corner. In the center of the room was a wooden chair with a velvet-covered seat. The chair was plain, but unique in the fact that it was the only other furniture in the room apart from the corner pieces.

Anna moved to the wall to get a closer look at the tapestries, recognizing scenes from the tale of Beowulf. She studied the tapestry depicting Beowulf's battle with the dragon. The dragon in the picture was huge, with bronze wings that stretched from one side of the canvas to the other, while flames poured out from his mouth and over the armor-clad warrior. As she studied the form, it seemed to her that the dragon looked suspiciously like Max, and she turned to look at him. He smiled wryly, and his eyes flicked over to the next scene. The dragon lay defeated on the ground, a sword buried in his chest, the blaze in his eyes dulled as he breathed his last. Anna walked up to the picture, and gently traced her fingers over the face of the dragon. She felt as though a band was tightening around her heart at the thought of the magnificent creature dying, and she drew in a ragged breath. "Don't die," she whispered. She felt Max's footsteps behind her, and the brush of his fingers against her neck, and she turned to look at him. She pulled in a breath when she saw the look in his eyes, and then his mouth was on hers, his lips hard and demanding. He pulled back a second later, and turning around, strode away from her. She was still staring at him, trying to collect her scattered thoughts, when the door to the chamber opened and a man she did not recognize strode into the room, closely followed by Syngen.

"This is Master Brant, Your Highness," Syngen said. "And ..?" He turned to look at Anna. Anna pulled her attention away from Max.

"Er, Anna Carver, lady-in-waiting to the queen Matilda," Anna said, with a curtsey in Terran's direction. He was a tall man, with dark hair and a neatly trimmed short beard. His dark eyes were brooding, and he studied her with open scrutiny. He frowned when Anna mentioned Matilda's name and turned to Syngen.

"What is this? What are these people doing here?"

"We have some news that will interest you, Your Majesty," Max said. "Mistress Anna was recently imprisoned by Rupert after she overheard a conversation he had with the king. He accused her of spying for you, Your Majesty." Max

313

paused as the words sank in, then he looked at Anna. "Tell him what you know."

Anna nodded, and slowly started to tell her story. She was hesitant at first, but was soon caught up in relating the events of the past few days. Terran muttered a curse when she repeated Rupert's words about flattering the king, but when she started relating Frank's part of the story, his face grew livid with rage.

"Where is the man who saw these events?" he demanded.

"He's guarding the queen," Anna said.

Terran turned to Syngen. "Does the girl speak the truth, you think?"

Syngen looked at Max, locking his eyes with the dragon. "I believe she does," he said.

Anna watched as Terran paced the room, his hands behind his back. "Roderick was always a fool," Terran said. "The people never wanted him as king. Alfred should have known better than to listen to his urgings. But Rupert! If what you say is true, then he is less than despicable."

"He definitely is that," Max said, "and I'm sure you will find a way to punish him for what he has done. But you will understand when I say that our involvement in this matter ends tonight." Terran looked at Max with eyes narrowed in speculation as Max stared back; then dropping his gaze, he nodded.

"Very well. I would have welcomed your support in this battle, but clearly you have other ideas. You have relieved me of the burden of thinking my people murdered a king while he rode under an agreement of truce. Our council will meet to discuss our next move." He turned to Syngen. "I will take the night to consider the matter more thoughtfully, and will meet with the council in the morning. Ensure that they know." Syngen nodded as Terran left the room.

"What are your plans now?" Syngen asked Max.

"Anna needs to sleep before we travel to Storbrook. If you can arrange chambers we will leave at first light."

"Storbrook?" Anna said. "But I need to return to the queen."

"Anna," Max said gently, "you cannot return to Matilda. Blanche has been spreading rumors that you ran away with your lover."

"I know what Blanche has been saying," Anna said, "and to whom she is referring." She gave Max a pointed stare. "But the queen will not believe such a slander against my name."

"It does not matter whether she believes it or not," Max said. "Your name has already been tarnished."

"Tarnished? And would my name have been tarnished if I had given into Rupert's demands?"

"Being mistress to the prince is quite different from running away with your lover," Max said. Anna glared at him angrily.

"I didn't run away with my lover," she ground out. "I was imprisoned by the prince!"

"And Matilda might even believe that! But Blanche's tale has already been spread too far and wide to be ignored." Max paused. "Besides, yours is not the only name being disparaged in this affair."

"Oh? Are you referring to the tarnishing of your name, Max? Because I think you will be applauded by the men at court, while I will be considered a trollop!" She turned on her heel and stormed out of the room, but she heard Syngen laugh.

"She's not even yours yet, and you are fighting like a pair of cats!" he said.

"Oh, well," Max replied with a sigh, "it keeps me humble."

Anna was halfway down the passage when she realized she had no idea where to go. She paused, struggling with her pride at the thought of returning to the room, when a woman appeared further along the corridor. Anna hurried over to her.

"Master Gail was to send a message that a room be prepared for me, but I'm afraid I've lost sight of him. Can you help me?"

Word of her arrival must have already spread through the palace, as the woman did not appear surprised. "Of course, my lady," she said. "Follow me." She led Anna up a stairway and into a small chamber, already freshly prepared. She was back a short while later with warm water and fresh linens. "Would you like me to take your gown?" she asked. "I can clean it and have it back by morning." Anna glanced down at the gown she had been imprisoned in. She had not given consideration to her appearance since her capture, but the question made her realize how unkempt she must appear.

"Yes, please," she said with relief, stripping off the offending article. "And if you can find a clean chemise somewhere, I would be most appreciative!"

The maid gave a small curtsey. "I will see what I can do, my lady," she said, before leaving the room with the gown and closing the door firmly behind her.

CHAPTER FORTY-SIX

As soon as Anna lay down on the bed, exhaustion washed over her. She closed her eyes, and was asleep before she had time to consider the past few days.

She awoke late the following morning. Her gown had been washed, dried and pressed, and was hung over the back of a chair, but Anna could not see it for the man who occupied the seat. He smiled at her when she opened her eyes, and moving to the bed, sat down next to her.

"Good morning, my darling," he said. "You must have been exhausted. You have been sleeping these last twelve hours."

Anna smiled at him sleepily. "How long have you been sitting there?" she asked.

"All night. It reminded me of the times I used to watch over you. And in the morning I would brush your hair. Should I do that again?"

"I don't have a brush with me," Anna said.

"I can at least untangle the knots," he said. "Sit up."

Anna sat up and placed her back to him, shivering slightly when she felt his fingers against her scalp. "Why did you always brush my hair?" she asked.

Max laughed softly. "It was the only time you would relax in my presence. The first time you were feeling unwell, remember? And I offered to brush your hair since you seemed incapable of doing it yourself. But when I did, I could see how it soothed you. So I kept offering to do it."

Anna smiled. "I'm sorry I snapped at you last night," she said.

"That's all right. I'm quite used to it," he said, and she could hear the amusement in his tone.

They left the chamber a short while later, and Max easily led Anna through the passages and down the stairs to the wide open hall where they had met Syngen the previous evening. The white, marble steps beyond the doorway glittered in the morning sun, but it was the commotion at the bottom of the steps, where two armed men were wrestling a man down the stairs, that drew Anna's attention. Another three guards blocked the view, and all Anna could see was legs kicking and flailing. "Let me go," the man shouted.

Anna glanced at Max. "Is that –?"

"Frank," he finished. He strode forward, pushing his way through the growing crowd. "Let him go," he ordered the men.

The guards looked at Max in surprise, keeping a firm grip on Frank. "This man was storming the palace," one of them said.

Max laughed wryly. "One man! Quite a threat against …" – he glanced around – "… five armed men!"

"He's wearing Alfred's colors! And is covered in blood!"

"I will vouch for him."

The men glanced at one another. "We only follow orders from the king," one of them finally said, but before Max could answer, someone approached from behind. The guards shifted their attention to the newcomer, and Anna glanced back to see Syngen Gail.

"Bring the man here," he said. The guards hauled Frank up the stairs and threw him on the ground at Syngen's feet.

Syngen looked at Max. "You know him?"

"He's the man we told you about," he answered softly.

Syngen stared at Frank for a long moment, then looked back to the guards.

"Leave the matter with me," he said. He turned on his heel, and flicked his hand. "Come, let's find a more private place to talk." Anna glanced at Max, who shrugged, then pulling Frank up by the shoulders, pushed him after Syngen. A sheen of sweat covered Frank's forehead, and dark patches of blood stained the front of his tunic, splattered from top to bottom. Mud and blood were smeared over his face, and a bloodied dagger hung from the belt of leather tied around his waist.

"You better have a very good reason for being here," Max said.

"Rupert's dead," Frank replied. Max looked at him sharply, but remained silent. He gestured for Anna to go ahead of him, and they followed Syngen into a small, windowless room. Syngen turned around to look at Frank.

"What is the meaning of this?" he said. Frank glanced at Max, who, after a speculative glance at Syngen, nodded.

"I killed Rupert," Frank said. He ran his hand over his head, and Anna could see dried blood beneath his fingernails.

"What happened?" Anna asked softly. Frank turned to her.

"He attacked me, so I killed him."

"And then you came here? Why?" Max said.

"Rupert's men were after me."

"And what of Matilda?"

"She's safe, as far as I know."

"I see," Max said. He glanced at Syngen, then with a slight sigh, looked back to Frank. "Perhaps you should start at the beginning. Tell us exactly what happened."

"Well … it happened this morning. We were just about to leave. The queen was finally ready, and she and her ladies were mounting their horses when Rupert rode up."

Max held up his hand. "And who was riding with her?"

"The king's men. And Lord Giles."

"Lord Giles?" Anna said in surprise.

"Yes. Do you know him? He walks with a limp." Anna nodded. "He heard that the queen was leaving this morning, and insisted on accompanying us."

"How did he hear that?" Max asked.

"His cousin is one of the king's guard."

"His cousin needs to have his tongue checked," Max said wryly. "Do they know Rupert killed Alfred?"

Frank shook his head. "No. I told Tobias, but we decided that the queen's safety was our first priority, and didn't want the men seeking revenge. We told the king's guards that since the king was dead, the queen needed to get back to Civitas and to her son as soon as possible. They agreed to ride with us to ensure her safety through hostile enemy lands." Frank glanced at Syngen as he spoke.

"Good thinking," he said with a grin.

Max nodded. "Very well. So you and Tobias were outside in the courtyard with the king's men when Rupert arrived. What happened next?"

"Rupert wanted to know where we were going. We told him that the queen was returning home."

"And he was happy with that?"

"No. He ordered the queen to return to the house and await his instruction." A ghost of a smile crossed his face as he looked at Anna. "You know the queen. She will not be ordered around. She told the prince that he had no authority to order her about, and then started riding. We all turned to follow her, but I was at the back, and Rupert stopped me."

"But she got away?" Max said. Frank turned his gaze back to him.

"I think so. He ordered his guards to give chase, but there were only three of them."

"Very well. And then what?"

"Rupert wanted to know what had happened to Mistress

Anna."

"What did you tell him?"

"I told him that she was safely locked away. He wanted to see you for himself," Frank said, glancing at Anna.

"What happened?"

"I took him to the room, but when he saw you weren't there, he rounded on me with his fists. He thought I had been lax in my duties. I didn't resist too much at first, but when he pulled out his dagger, I knew he was beyond reason. He managed to get the first swipe and drew blood on my arm." Frank pushed up the sleeve of his tunic and showed them where the dagger had sliced through his skin above the elbow. "That's when I drew my own knife. I knew then that I had to kill him. It was not an easy fight, but I told him I had seen him kill his brother. That's when he made a careless mistake which left his belly exposed."

"An advantage you made use of," Max said.

"I did. I stabbed him in the stomach, and as the dagger ripped open his belly, I knocked him to the ground. The dagger was buried to the hilt, so I twisted it and wrenched it down to his groin. I watched him die a slow and agonizing death." Anna felt her stomach heave, and she turned away, steadying herself against the wall. "But I was still there when his guards came looking for him," Frank continued. "I jumped out the window to escape them."

Anna turned around. "You jumped out the window?" she exclaimed. "You could have been hurt. Or killed!"

"I didn't stop to think. I knew I was a dead man if the guards found me, so I jumped and ran. My horse was still in the courtyard, so I threw myself over him and spurred him to motion. And I figured this was the only place I could come where the guards could not follow me."

Syngen snorted. "They could have tried, but they would not have gotten very far." He gave Frank a scrutinizing look. "So you have brought our war to an end."

Frank's eyes narrowed as he returned the look. "Who are

you, exactly?"

"Syngen Gail, advisor to King Terran."

"And the man who kidnapped me," Anna added. She frowned when Syngen grinned.

Frank glanced at Anna, then looked back at Syngen. He crossed his arms over his chest. "You will allow the queen to return home without hindrance."

"Why should I do that?"

"Because I have twice been the instrument of you receiving news that helps you in your cause."

"And this is your price?"

"Yes."

Syngen laughed. "You do know it is a little late to start negotiating?"

"I do. But I believe your king is an honorable man who will do what is right."

Syngen nodded thoughtfully. "Very well. I will see what I can do to persuade the king. But I can give no assurances for Alfred's men."

Frank looked down at the floor. "I know," he said. "Just give them a few hours before you begin the chase."

"I will relay your request to the king," Syngen said. "And now, you will come with me to bring news of Rupert to the king yourself."

"You will guarantee my safety?"

"I will. And I will also ensure your freedom to remain here, should you so choose." Syngen turned to Max. "What about you? Do you leave?"

"We will leave immediately," Max said. "This is no longer our affair." He glanced at Anna as he spoke.

"But …" Anna began, before falling silent. In fact, she was quite happy to leave all this behind her. She nodded. "Yes," she said.

CHAPTER FORTY-SEVEN

Anna and Max left shortly afterwards, with Max spreading his wings and turning his long neck and huge body towards the mountains, and Storbrook.

"What did Syngen mean when he said he could give no assurances about Alfred's men?" Anna asked as she lay against Max's neck. Max glanced back at her for a moment.

"They will be rounded up and brought back to Terranton as prisoners of war," he said. "Those from wealthy families will be ransomed, while the rest ..." Max lifted a claw. "They will be put to work."

"But they are needed back home!"

"Those are the fortunes of war, Anna," Max said. "Men join an army in the hopes of winning women and plunder. But there can only be one victor."

"But some of the men were forced to join the army by their lords and landowners."

"True."

"But that's not fair!"

Max snorted. "War is never fair. And Terran was invaded by Alfred without provocation. He needs labor to rebuild."

Anna was silent for a moment. "So what was it all for?"

she finally said.

"Alfred preferred the idea of Roderick on the throne rather than Terran, and was willing to gamble with the lives of his subjects to try and gain it. Such is the nature of war."

"And Roderick?"

"Roderick is probably already aboard a ship, fleeing with the few men still loyal to him."

"Do you think he will return?"

"He may be foolish enough to try again, but I trust that Alfred's son and his advisors will show a little more wisdom than Alfred did when he agreed to support Roderick."

Anna was silent until the turrets of Storbrook came into view, like sentinels against the dusky sky. Max flew around the castle once, before landing in one of the huge chambers on the top floor.

"How do you know which room to land in?" Anna said.

"This is always my chamber when I stay at Storbrook," Max replied. "And Aaron told me to come straight here."

"He did? When?"

Max looked at her in amusement. "Two minutes ago."

Anna did not have time to reply. The door flew open, and Keira hurried into the room, Aaron striding in behind her. "Anna!"

Anna turned to Keira with a smile. "Home at last!" Keira said. Anna was engulfed in her sister's warm embrace as Aaron stood behind his wife, smiling at them.

"Welcome home, Anna," he said. "I didn't expect to see you here so soon."

"Alfred is dead," Max said, "and so is Rupert." Aaron looked at Max in surprise.

"What happened?"

"It is a long story."

"Does Terran know?"

Max glanced at Anna. "Your sister-in-law insisted we tell him about Alfred. We were there last night. We learned about Rupert before we left."

"Anything else?"

"Syngen sends his regards."

Aaron grunted. "Syngen? You spoke to him then?"

"Yes. Briefly."

"Come," Keira said, pulling Anna from the room, "let's leave these men to their discussions of war. The children are longing to see you. And your chambers are exactly as you left them." She led Anna down the stairs.

"Is Peggy still here?" Anna asked.

"She is, but Corbin, the tutor, spends most of the day with them. You will meet him tomorrow – he likes to come and go."

Keira pushed open the door, and Anna stepped into the nursery. The children were seated at the table, a plate of sliced fruit before them, while Peggy hovered nearby. For a moment, it seemed to Anna that she had stepped back in time, but as she looked at the twins she could see that they had grown, their faces a little leaner than they were a year before. Lydia looked up from her plate, her eyes growing wide as she took in the visage of her aunt.

"Antana!" She pushed herself to her feet, then paused; but when Anna dropped to her knees and held out her arms, the little girl rushed into them. Zach looked up, then he too was scrambling over to his aunt, knocking her to the ground as she wrapped her arms around them both.

It had been dusk when Max and Anna arrived at Storbrook, and the children were soon sent to bed as the adults made their way to the parlor. The evening passed comfortably as they talked of things at Storbrook. Max had already given Aaron a brief outline of what had happened, but for now, they pushed concerns of kings and kingdoms from their minds. Anna sat with Keira, listening to her talk about her children, before asking about their parents.

"Father is fine, but Mother lingers on. She will be very happy to see you."

Anna nodded. "I will visit her soon," she promised.

Anna's chambers were exactly as she left them, as Keira had said, and when she stepped into the room later that night, she breathed out a long sigh. Except for the few nights at Cameleus's, she had not had a chamber to herself for more than a year. She buried her toes in the fur rug in front of the fire, before heading over to the bed and sitting down. Someone had been in and opened the shutters, allowing the air to flow in from three different directions. She leaned against the wall and stared out the window, remembering how many times she had gazed at this same view. Somewhere, out there, was a pair of dragons, one of whom had bound himself to her forevermore. She shrugged her gown off her shoulders and lay down on the bed, leaving the shutters open to let in the night air. There was the screech of an owl in the distance, but she had already fallen asleep.

She was still in her bed the next morning when the sound of her name being called broke through her dreams. She rose to her feet and went to the window, staring at the huge dragon hovering just a few feet away, his huge wings barely moving as he held himself aloft. The morning light glimmered against the smooth surface, making it sparkle, while the sun caught his horns and made them shine, as deadly as a pair of swords. The dragon smiled. "Good morning, my darling."

She smiled, and reaching out a hand, stroked his snout. "Good morning," she said. He rubbed himself against the palm of her hand, then drew back.

"Come for a ride with me," he said. She nodded, quickly dragging on a gown before lifting her feet over the edge of the window. Max wrapped his tail around her and lifted her onto his back. He was silent as he flew through the air, the peaks of mountains still covered with snow drifting past below them. A large clearing opened up below them, and Max headed towards it, landing on a patch of a grass. A fallen log lay over the ground, and Max's tail draped over it, the sharp spikes rising upwards as they marched along the tail's length. Max made a motion with his head, and Anna turned around as the light filled the air. When she turned back, he reached out a hand and pulled her closer. He wrapped his hands around her face and stared into her eyes.

"I have to return to Civitas," he said. "I wanted to say goodbye."

"Goodbye?" Anna pulled free from his clasp and stepped away.

"Just for a short time." He reached for her hands. "We are bound together, you and I, my darling, even though you haven't yet tasted my blood. I could never leave if I didn't know I would be returning."

"Then why are you leaving?"

Max pushed his hands through her hair, allowing the strands to run over his fingers. "Aaron needs me to take care of a few things in the city, and I need to tie up my own loose ends."

"But you will be back?"

"I will not be able to stay away," he whispered. "I will be back before the first snowfall."

Three months. His mouth was just above hers, and she could feel his breath against her lips. She leaned forward as his arms slid down her back, coming to rest on her hips. He lowered his head, his gaze holding hers as he searched her eyes, and then he was kissing her. His lips were soft and gentle, and she felt the flick of his tongue, teasing her. She slipped her arms around his waist and pulled him closer. He had donned a pair of breeches when he changed his form, but his back was bare and she felt the ridges along the length of his spine, pulsing with heat. His breath filled her mouth, and she moaned as something clenched deep within her. She opened her mouth to him, tasting him and wanting more. He growled, a deep sound that reverberated in his chest, and his kiss became more demanding. His wings spread open, straining against his back as he wrapped his arms around her. She felt as through every nerve ending pulsed with life as his heat covered her, wrapping around her. She wanted to drown in him, and feel him drowning in her, too.

He pulled away, and stared into her eyes. His were blazing, open flames, and as she stared back, she felt as though she were being burned alive.

"Snowfall is too long. Look for me when the leaves start turning," he said. His mouth descended to hers once more, and she smiled. He pulled away a moment later. "Let's walk through the woods," he said, "before I take you right here and now."

"I don't mind," she said with an impish smile, and for a moment the blaze burned even brighter, before he tempered the flames.

"But I do," he said softly. "I will not take you like a common wench when we are not even bound together. I love you, and I wish to honor you in every possible way." She glanced away, suddenly embarrassed, but he dragged her face back to his with his fingers. "And I love the fact that you want me too. I told you once before that you were made to love wildly and passionately, and Anna, just the anticipation of that will fill my dreams every night."

She smiled. "I love you," she whispered. "Hurry back to me."

CHAPTER FORTY-EIGHT

Max left that afternoon. He and Anna had spent the morning walking through the woods, her hand clasped in his; although, if truth be told, they stopped more than they walked. She felt the loss of his presence as soon as he left Storbrook, and watched from her chambers as he circled through the air above the castle before disappearing further from view. There was a gap in the mountains which he headed towards, but in the moments before he reached it, he turned to look at her, and she heard his roar echo between the rocky cliffs and resound within her heart. His fiery breath lit the sky, and then he was gone. She stared out the window for a long time after, hoping to see one more glimpse of him, before turning away. The rest of summer stretched out before her, but after all she had already been through, she could wait a few more months.

"Do Father and Mother know where I have been?" Anna asked Keira the following morning.

Keira shook her head. "News about the war is scant in the village, and since it never came up, we never told them that you had gone with the queen to the battle lines. It just seemed best not to worry them."

"And did they know about Garrick?"

"No." Keira looked at Anna keenly. "Should I have told them?"

Anna looked away and stared out the window for a long moment. "No," she finally said.

As Keira nodded, Aaron walked into the room. "I heard you discussing your parents. I will take you into the village if you wish to visit them."

Anna looked at him in surprise. "I thought you only flew Keira."

"True. But I will make an exception this time. I'm sure you are anxious to see them, and Thomas is busy with other duties today and cannot accompany you into the village."

Anna smiled. "Excellent. I will be ready in half an hour."

An hour later Aaron landed in a field beyond the village and Anna slid off his back. "Are you coming as well?" she asked.

"Not today," he said. "I have other matters I need to attend to, but will return for you in a few hours. Is that enough time?"

"Yes," she said. "Thank you."

Richard and Jenny lived on the outskirts of the village, and it was not long before Anna reached their small house. Richard was inspecting the vegetables in the garden as she drew near, and he looked up with a wide smile.

"Anna! Daughter! You're back!" He wrapped his arm around her shoulder and drew her close, before quickly stepping away again and looking her up and down. His gaze touched the scar on her forehead, now faded to dark pink, and his eyebrows drew together in concern. "You've been injured."

"I fell down a ravine."

Richard's expression turned puzzled. "What were you doing near a ravine? Weren't you in the city?"

"I was." She paused. "I have much to tell you. Why don't

we go inside and sit down. How is Mother?" she asked as they walked into the house.

"Asleep," he replied. "Dame Lamb has been giving her sleeping draughts to help alleviate the pain in her belly."

They entered the house, and Anna took a seat in the small parlor opposite her father, and started relating the events of the past year.

"The prince imprisoned you for treason?" Richard said incredulously as Anna finished her tale. She had sketched the bare bones of the story, from her time with the queen and the march to Terranton, omitting any mention of Garrick, and only touching on the fact that she had been helped — twice – by a dragon.

"Yes."

"And Aaron knew that you were traveling with the queen?"

"He did." Anna paused a moment. "It was he who sent the dragon to ensure my safety."

"Ah!"

The sound of a bed creaking came from one of the adjacent chambers, and Anna glanced in its direction.

"Should I go and check on Mother?"

"She will be very happy to see you," Richard replied with a sad smile.

When Anna walked into Jenny's room, she wrinkled her nose at the stale air. Jenny turned to look at her, and for a moment, her eyes shone with excitement. "Anna," she whispered, "My daughter. You're finally here. I've been waiting for you."

Anna sat down beside her mother and took her hand. "Hello, Mother."

"Are you well, Anna? The house is so empty without you here. Are you coming home soon?"

Anna sighed. It had been more than six years since she had lived at home. "Not yet, Mother," she said. Jenny's hand was soft and frail, and Anna thought of the old woman she had seen in the hospital.

"You've been gone so long," Jenny said. "It's time to come home."

"I've been visiting the queen, Mother," Anna said.

"The queen?"

"That's right. She lives in a beautiful palace. Should I tell you about it?"

Jenny nodded. "Have you really been to the royal palace?" she said.

"I have." The next hour passed quickly as Anna described life at the royal court. Jenny listened eagerly, asking questions about Matilda's clothes, the king and the little prince. By the end of the hour, however, Anna could see that her mother had grown weary, and she leaned down and kissed her forehead. "Sleep now," she said softly. "I will be back to visit again very soon."

Anna wandered into the village after leaving the house. It was market day, and the village market was teeming with people who had come from around the country to buy and sell their wares. She passed the stall that held Richard's wooden tableware. It was manned by a young girl she didn't recognize, but she paused to stroke her fingers over the smooth surfaces. She thought of the many times she and Keira had sat in this same spot, selling the items for their father. Jenny had been there too, her mind active and her body strong. Anna heard a voice calling her name, and she turned around, her heart sinking when she saw Sarah Draper walking towards her.

"Anna," she said, "I haven't seen you in months. Where have you been?"

Anna glanced away. What to say? The city for a coronation? Drake Manor to watch a girl change into a dragon? The court to serve the queen? The next kingdom to watch a war?

"I've been away," Anna replied.

"Oh." Sarah glanced around, then dropped her voice to a

whisper. "Did Garrick Flynn come into the village with you?"

Anna dropped her gaze. "No," she said. She started to move away, but Sarah grabbed her by the arm.

"Wait," she said, "where is he? When will he be in again?" Anna stopped, then turned to face Sarah.

"Garrick is not coming back," she said. "He's dead. He died fighting for the king." Sarah dropped her arm.

"Dead?" She stepped back. "That is ..." But Anna did not hear what Sarah thought. She turned around and walked away without a backward glance.

A few days later, Corbin invited Anna to accompany him and the children on an excursion through the woods. "We will be studying the fauna and flora of the area surrounding Storbrook," Corbin explained to Anna when he invited her to join them. "There is life within every nook and cranny."

"Are you enjoying being at Storbrook?" Anna asked as she fell in step with him.

"Oh yes," he answered, pausing to inspect a small clump of flowers at the base of a tree. He called the children over. "Can either of you tell me the name of these?" he asked, crouching down and pointing. Zach and Lydia stared at the flowers for a long moment. "Lydia?" Corbin prompted.

"Blue, er, fox flowers?" she answered. Corbin smiled.

"Almost. Bluebells." He picked a flower between his fingers and pointed out the shape to the children as they listened solemnly. "Now go find five other specimens of forest flora and bring them back to me," he said. He rose to his feet as the children scampered away. "What were we talking about?" he said.

"How much you are enjoying Storbrook."

"Ah, yes! I enjoy being here very much. I'm not one for city life. I can come and go as I please here, and I find Zach and Lydia easy to teach. Of course, although I've never lived at Storbrook before, like most of our kind I have been here many times before, so when Aaron asked me if I was interested in tutoring his whelps, I accepted with alacrity."

"Are you related to Aaron?"

Corbin nodded solemnly. "All dragons are related somehow. Aaron's great-grandfather and my grandfather were bothers. And Max's father, James, is my cousin." A spider's web stretched between the trees, distracting Corbin once more, and then the children were back, carefully cradling a variety of flowers and leaves in their hands. Their enthusiasm reminded Anna of Garrick, and she smiled sadly. She had loved Garrick, in her way. And although the guilt she felt over his death had lessened, it had not completely lost its grip. But for the first time, perhaps in her life, she also felt a sense of peace and belonging. She belonged to Max, and he belonged to her, too. She glanced down at the ring she wore on her finger as a reminder of Garrick. Friendship had been all she could accept from him, but his friendship had helped her when she needed it most.

"Antana!" Lydia's voice broke through Anna's thoughts, and she looked up to see the girl running towards her. "Look," she shouted. "A ladybird!" Her hands were clasped together as she ran, and Anna dropped down to her knees with a laugh, bringing her head close to Lydia's to examine the precious find.

CHAPTER FORTY-NINE

'Dear Kathleen,' Anna wrote one afternoon, 'I've been wanting to write to you to explain the events leading up to my disappearance from Lord Cameleus's home, and to deny the spurious allegations against my name that have been set abroad by Lady Blanche. I did not leave the queen's side in the company of a lover, but was imprisoned in a room within the west wing by Prince Rupert on suspicion of treason, another spurious allegation. For the truth of this matter, please apply to Tobias who can confirm the events of the night. I was rescued by Master Brant and he returned me to Storbrook. Please write back to me and relieve me of the fear that you have believed the falsehoods spoken against me. I remain forever your friend, ...'

There was a noise at the door, and Anna turned to see Lydia standing at the entrance to her chambers. "Antana," she said, "what you doing?"

"I'm writing a letter," Anna explained. "What are you doing? Shouldn't you be with Master Corbin?"

"Master Corbin took Zach to see a eagle nest, but I didn't want to go. Can I go for a walk with you?"

Anna smiled and nodded. "Yes, but first you need to let

me finish my letter and deliver it to Thomas. Can you do that?"

Lydia nodded eagerly. "Yes!" Anna signed her name to the bottom of her letter, then folding the sheet, sealed it with a wax wafer.

"Come," she said, holding a hand out to Lydia, "let's go give this to Master Thomas."

As it turned out, Thomas had gone into the village for Aaron that morning, and had not yet returned, but she left the letter on his desk, knowing he would see it there. She and Lydia walked out into the hot summer sunshine, and headed across the courtyard into the gardens. Lydia let go of Anna's hand and started twirling on her toes around her.

"Look at me, Antana," Lydia sang out. "I'm dancing," Anna caught her by the hands and danced around in a circle with her. They reached the shade of the spreading oak, and Anna dropped to the green lawn with a gasp, dragging Lydia down with her. Lydia lay giggling for a few moments, then was back on her feet, scrambling into the tree. "Look at me, Antana," she shouted. She was standing on a long thick branch that spread out a few feet above the ground. She held out her arms to her sides. "I can fly!" she yelled. She launched herself from the branch, and landed easily on her feet as Anna let out a sigh.

"You cannot fly yet, baby girl," Anna said. "You have to grow some wings first."

Lydia nodded. "Like Papa." She cocked her head as she looked at Anna. "When will you grow wings, Antana?"

"I will never grow wings," Anna said. "I'm not a dragon."

"You're not? What are you?"

"I'm human."

"But I'm human, too."

"No, you're not human. You just look like a human, but you are all dragon."

"Like Papa," Lydia said. Anna nodded. "And Master Corbin? And Uncle Max?"

"That's right."

"Oh." Lydia stared down at the ground for a long time.

"What is it, Lydia?" Anna asked, seeing the girl's forehead furrow.

Lydia lifted her gaze to look at Anna. "Will I be a boy when I grow up?" she said.

Anna stared at her in confusion for a moment. "A boy? No, why would you ...?" Her voice trailed away as Lydia looked back at the ground. "Girls are dragons, too," Anna said softly.

"But you're not a dragon. And Mama isn't either."

"Your Mama and I were born human, but you were born a dragon. Should I tell you about another girl who was born a dragon? You have even met her. Do you remember Bronwyn?"

Lydia wrinkled her nose. "Bronny?"

"Yes. I saw her when she grew her wings."

"You did?"

"Mmm-hmm. She turned into a dragon right in front of me."

Lydia looked at her in surprise. "Were you scared?"

"We were both a little scared. She wasn't sure, at first, what was happening, and I didn't know what to do. But her father was close by, and he came to help her."

"What did she look like?"

"She was beautiful. A beautiful girl and a beautiful dragon." She wrapped her arm around Lydia's shoulders. "Just like you." Lydia smiled and jumped back to her feet, tugging on Anna's hand. She pulled her along the path, and Anna recognized the spot where Garrick had rescued the injured bird.

"Antana?"

"Yes."

"Why is Nursey scared of Papa?"

"A lot of people are scared of dragons. Sometimes dragons hurt people and then people think all dragons are like that. And humans don't have long tails or huge wings to help them. And they can't breathe fire."

Lydia nodded. "It doesn't smell so good when Peggy gets scared."

Anna looked at Lydia in surprise. "It doesn't?"

Lydia shook her head. "You know, she smells all … smelly."

"No, I don't know," Anna replied. "I cannot smell what people are feeling."

This time is was Lydia's turn to look surprised. "You can't? Why not?"

Anna laughed. "Because I'm human."

Lydia's forehead furrowed a little as she thought about it. "Humans can't smell?"

"Humans can smell some things, like the scent of a flower or a tasty dish, but we cannot smell if someone is happy, or sad."

"Oh!" Lydia took a moment to absorb this, then turned to Anna with a shy smile. "You smell happier when Uncle Max is here."

Anna gave Lydia a startled glance as a blush rose in her cheeks. "I do?"

"Yes."

"And Uncle Max? Does he smell happier?"

"Oh yes! And he shines more too!"

"He shines?" Anna said weakly.

"He goes all glowey and shiny," Lydia said with a giggle. She grabbed Anna by the hand. "Come, let's run," she said.

Returning to the castle with Lydia sometime later, Anna was passing Aaron's study when he called her name. She turned to enter his study. "Thomas has been in the village and brought back a letter for you." Anna took the missive from him, clasping it in her hand. "He also brought back news that Matilda has made it safely back to the city and has been reunited with her children."

"And how many of the men returned?"

Aaron shrugged. "It's difficult to say, but we heard that Terran has about fifteen hundred prisoners. Some of them have been ransomed and returned to their families." Anna nodded as Aaron continued. "John has been crowned king, and Matilda has been named one of his advisors."

"She has? I wonder how she managed that?"

Aaron grinned. "You should know Matilda's skill in getting her own way! The Lord Chamberlain has also been named to the king's council, as well as his great-uncle Eastwich."

Anna left the room, pressing the letter against her chest. She had known immediately who it was from, and she smiled at the thought of reading his words. She left the castle and quickly walked to the bench in the corner of the gardens, where she took a seat. She slipped her finger beneath the wax seal and spread the page open wide.

'My darling Anna,' she read. 'I have just arrived at my home in the city, and every thought I had as I traveled here was of you. By the time you receive this, a few weeks will have passed since I saw you last, but you have been in my thoughts every day and in my dreams every night. I long to see you again, and hold you in my arms. I almost turned around when I saw you standing at your window when I left, but knew that if I did that, I would be unable to make the attempt again!

'You will be interested to know that young John has been crowned king. His coronation was not as grand as Alfred's, but it was very solemn, given that he is just a boy of eight and still mourning the death of his father. Of course, the kingdom will be ruled by his advisors until he comes of age. I saw Matilda, who looks well, but did not exchange any words with her. Your friend, Kathleen, was not in attendance.

'I count the days until I can once more be at your side. I dreamed of you dancing last night. Will you dance for me, my darling, when I see you again?

'I remain, for now until eternity, yours.

'Signed, Max Brant'

CHAPTER FIFTY

Anna and Keira visited Jenny every week, watching as she slowly declined in health, until she was no longer able to leave her bed. She smiled whenever she saw her daughters, and reached out her hand to her grandchildren as Keira pushed them closer. Zach would escape the sickroom as soon as he was able, creeping into Richard's workshop to watch him carve his wooden pieces, but Lydia would sit with her grandmother, a silent sentinel to her passing. Richard had started teaching Zach how to carve, and after a while he gave Zach his own piece of wood and a small knife, and they sat carving together in silence at the long bench where Richard worked.

Anna waited for a letter to arrive from Kathleen, but week after week passed with no letter. "Did you see the letter I left on your desk?" Anna asked Thomas one morning. "It was a few weeks ago."

"The letter addressed to Lady Kathleen?" he said. "I sent it with the other city communications."

But the weeks passed, and there was no reply.

One late summer afternoon, Anna and Keira were seated in the parlor, laughing over something Aaron was saying. He had just joined the ladies, bringing Corbin with him, as they sat together in the afternoon sun, while on the floor the children were trying to figure out a puzzle that Corbin had made for them. As they sat together, Peggy came into the room, searching for her charges so she could give them their supper.

"There they are!" she said with a relieved sigh, and Anna and Corbin swapped an amused glance. Peggy seemed to spend her whole life searching for the children. She stood in the doorway for a moment, staring into the room as if unsure whether she should enter, but Aaron waved her in with a smile.

"Join us for a glass of wine, Mistress," he said.

Peggy looked startled, and for a moment she hesitated, but when Corbin gave her a smile and a small nod of encouragement, Anna could see her uncertainty melting.

Like all dragons, Corbin made a handsome man. He had light hair, which had been braided in a single braid down his back, and his eyes shone with a color that was neither gray nor blue. He did not appear older than thirty-five or so years of age, although Anna knew he topped Aaron's one hundred and ten years. He caught Anna's glance and pulled a wry smile, shrugging slightly.

A clatter in the passage outside the parlor had Anna pulling her attention away from Peggy and towards Thomas as he stepped into the room. His boots were dusty from riding, and he held a small pouch in his hand. He passed the pouch over to Aaron, who took it with a nod.

"Any news?" he asked.

"A few soldiers took up at The Bell Inn a few days ago, causing a ruckus amongst some of the villagers who wanted them gone. They feared for their daughters' safety, and I cannot blame them! Richard sent a message to Warren, and he sent some men to deal with them, and they have since moved on." Richard Carver, Anna's father, was the reeve of the village in the service of Lord Warren, earl of the county.

Aaron gestured towards the flagon of wine on the table. "Anything else?"

"No, milord," Thomas said, pouring himself a glass and taking a seat on the bench beside Corbin. Aaron nodded and opened the package that Thomas had given him, pulling out a small handful of letters. He flipped through them quickly, separating them into piles. He handed Anna two of the letters and passed the rest back to Thomas. Anna took hers eagerly and glanced at the writing on each. One was from Max, and the other from Kathleen.

"At long last! I was beginning to wonder what had happened!"

"Is that the letter you have been waiting for?" Thomas said, placing his pile beside him, and she nodded. She slipped the letter from Max into her pocket, to be read later in private, but then turned the letter from Kathleen over in her hands, slipping her finger beneath the seal. She glanced at Keira.

"Do you mind?" she asked. Keira shook her head with a smile. Anna opened the missive and spread it over her lap, her eyes skimming the page as she read in silence.

'Dearest Anna,' it read, 'I was very relieved to receive your letter and learn that you had not run away with Master Brant as we had been led to believe, although I am shocked that the prince could have treated you so. Since I last saw you, I have married Lord Giles, whom you may remember from the march, and have retired from court life. I believe my father was very relieved to see me so happily united. I thank you for the kindness you showed me at court, and am sorry that we can no longer pursue our friendship, but you will understand that as a wife and future mother I cannot be too careful about my reputation, and by extension, the reputation of my friends. I trust you are well, and wish you a long and happy life. Yours fondly, Lady Kathleen Giles'

The chatter in the room had resumed as Anna started reading the letter to herself, but Keira was watching her sister, and she touched her arm as she finished reading. "Is everything all right?" she asked quietly. Anna pressed her lips together and passed the letter over to Keira, who read it with a frown. "I'm so sorry, Anna," she said. Anna nodded.

"I thought Kathleen was my friend." She took the letter back, and folded it into a tight wad before stuffing it into her pocket. She turned to Keira and forced her lips into a smile. "I have all of you," she said, indicating with her hand around the room. "What more do I need?"

"And Max," Keira added softly. Anna smiled. Yes, she had Max too, and that was the most important thing. But until he came back, she would not claim him as her own. But soon, she hoped, he would be back, and then he would be hers forever.

CHAPTER FIFTY-ONE

Anna was in her chambers when she first became aware of Max's presence, like a soft hint of musky fragrance in the air. It was early afternoon, and she had been sorting out some ribbons for Lydia. She closed her eyes with a smile, and waited as the knowledge of his presence grew stronger, before finally rising to her feet and heading to the window. He was still just a smudge against the horizon, but as she stepped into the opening, she felt a flare of heat, a burning awareness that surged towards her, and she knew he had seen her, too. She watched him grow closer, his huge body cleaving through the sky, held aloft by his glorious, massive wings. She lifted her feet over the window ledge and sat down. She could see the blazing fire in his eyes as he raced towards her. Flames poured from his mouth, rolling over his body before dissipating in the air. He drew closer, but instead of pausing at her window, he circled around and snatched her with his tail, lifting her onto his back.

She grabbed his neck as he plunged through the air, immediately heading away from Storbrook. She leaned forward and stroked his scales, resting her cheek against his neck, and when he turned to look at her, the breath caught in her throat. They gazed at each other in silence, before he turned his head back and leaned into the wind. He dropped lower, below the tall mountain peaks, and Anna saw a splash of green in the distance. He headed towards it, landing with a soft thump on the mossy grass. She slipped off his back, and before she even had a chance to completely turn around, he transformed. Placing his hands on her shoulders, he turned her around to face him, and then his mouth was on hers. His kiss was hungry and savage, and he pulled her closer as he groaned into her mouth. She wrapped her arms around him and pressed her hands into the small of his back. His hands were all over her, as if he was reacquainting himself with the shape of her body, and she could feel his heat caressing her skin. She was panting when she finally pulled away, gasping for air, and he laid his forehead against hers.

"I love you," he whispered. "I've missed you so much. Marry me."

"Yes," she said.

He pulled back to look in her eyes. "Now?"

"We need to find a priest."

"Only for a human marriage. For a dragon mating, we just need to share our blood."

"What about witnesses?"

"We can repeat the vows with God as our witness. Any dragon seeing us together will know we've mated. Humans may not see the bond, but dragons can sense it, as tangible as an iron chain that locks my heart to yours. Once formed, it cannot be unbroken."

"I thought you wanted a ceremony?"

"I only want to take you as my mate, which means creating a blood bond. I didn't want you to bond with me before I left, knowing that it would make the absence harder for you to bear."

"You could have taken me with you to the city instead of leaving me at Storbrook."

"I could have. But you needed some time to grieve for

Garrick."

She stared at him, then slowly nodded. "Thank you," she whispered.

"But now I am impatient to make you my own."

"And we can do it now? Here?"

"Yes. And we will have a nuptial mass on the morrow to make it humanly official, too. In the meantime, we will be handfast."

Anna nodded. "Yes. Is there a special dragon vow?"

"Just these words: I choose you to be my lifelong mate. As your blood runs through my veins, we are bound together until parted by death." Anna repeated the words under her breath as Max drew out a short knife. He flipped it in his hand and offered her the handle. "I don't have a chalice, so you will have to drink the blood from my veins."

Anna looked up at him, startled. "From your veins." She shuddered slightly.

"We can wait, if you prefer," he said.

"No. Where do I cut you?"

"Anywhere you want." Anna lifted his hand, but he drew it away. "No," he said, "too impersonal." He pointed to his chest. "Cut me here."

"On your chest?" A feeling of horror swept over her. "I can't do that!" Max lifted her hand which held the knife, and wrapping his over hers, pressed the blade against his skin. She stared at the point for a moment – the area around it was draining of color – before looking up into his eyes.

"Are you sure?" she said.

"Yes! I'm eager to know that you have tasted me. Are you ready?" She nodded, and he pressed the blade into his flesh. There was a moment of resistance, but then it slid in, silently, immediately drawing blood. Anna tried to draw her hand back, but Max held it fast on the handle of the knife and pushed the blade in deeper. He grunted slightly as the blood gushed from the wound, and allowed his hand to fall from hers.

"Taste it," he whispered.

She looked at the blood that was staining his chest, and slowly brought her finger up to it, dipping the tip in the red liquid. She raised it to her lips, and cautiously licked her finger. The blood was hot, and as soon as it touched her tongue, she could feel it spreading through her. It tasted like a thick brandied sauce, sweet and delicious. Her eyes flew up to his, then returned to his chest. She leaned forward and licked his skin, running her tongue over the blood that was trailing a path to his stomach.

He shuddered, and gripped her shoulders as she continued to chase the bloody trail. His wings were still stretched out behind him, and they strained against his back, reaching to the furthest reaches of the air around them. She placed her hands against his chest, the knife still loosely gripped in her fist, as she continued to lap the liquid. It was no longer flowing, but she did not want to leave a single trace. She could feel it weaving through her, reaching into every distant corner of her body, while at the same time she felt invisible threads leaving her and reaching him, tying them together with invisible cords. She could never be apart from him again without feeling those cords stretch and tighten.

She wanted more of him, wanted to know that he pulsed through her veins, and her grip around the knife tightened again.

He felt her movement and groaned. "Yes," he whispered. "Taste me some more."

She dragged the knife against his skin and moaned when the blood welled up once more, this time not hesitating as she placed her mouth over the gushing flow. She sucked and swallowed, tasting him as he became one with her. When the flow stopped, she leaned her cheek against his chest. His arms wrapped around her and held her tight.

"I can feel it," he whispered. "I can feel your bond with me." He pushed the hair away from her face and gently stroked her cheek. "Repeat the vow," he whispered.

"Maximilian Brant," she said, "I love you and take you as my mate." She slid her hands behind his neck. "As your blood runs through my veins, we are bound together forever," she finished.

Max smiled as he ran a finger down her neck. "I want to taste you too," he said.

"Yes," she whispered. She pulled away slightly to look into his eyes. He glanced down at her shoulder, pushing the gown away to reveal her bare skin.

"Here," he said. She nodded. She held the knife out to him, but he shook his head. "No," he whispered. "I'm a dragon." He lowered his mouth to her shoulder. She felt a flash of fear and he pulled away. "I won't hurt you," he said, "But if you prefer the knife —"

"No," she said. "You're a dragon." He smiled, and lowered his head again. She could feel his teeth against her skin. They were no longer flat, but sharp, and she felt them prick against her shoulder before sinking into her skin. She felt a slight stab of pain, but then it was gone. The wounds he made would quickly heal, with his blood in her veins. He drew deeply and she felt her blood gush into him. The invisible cords tightened. He pulled again, and she felt him swallow as his hands tightened against her back and his wings lifted behind him, straining even more than they had before. His mouth left her shoulder and trailed up her neck, and she heard him whisper in her ear.

"I love you Anna, and take you as my mate." His lips reached hers, and he whispered against them. "As your blood runs through my veins, we are bound together forever," he said, and then he was kissing her. He slid the gown off her shoulders and onto the ground. His hands wandered over her bare flesh, then dropping lower, clasped her around the thighs. He lowered her onto the mossy grass and when he pressed against her, she lifted her hips to meet him. He shuddered, and she gasped as her own pleasure burst open, flooding every part of her. He rolled over onto his back, pulling her with him, and she lay against his chest, listening to the pounding of his heart, like a wave crashing against the shore.

"You asked me once about the purpose of my life," he said softly. "You, Anna, have given my life purpose. Without you, I am nothing, but with you, I can do anything."

She lifted her head to gaze at him. "I love you," she whispered.

They lay in the mossy grass of the meadow as the sun passed above them, watching the clouds paint patterns in the sky. Max told her about his time in the city, while she talked about the happenings at Storbrook and in the village. They watched as the sun moved across the sky, and when a slight breeze rustled through the trees above them, Max drew her closer, wrapping his heat around her. The sun was starting to sink behind the mountains, casting long shadows on the ground, when Anna let out a long sigh. "We should get back," she said.

Max was lying on the ground, his hand stroking her back as she sat against his side. "Why?" he said.

"Because Keira and Aaron will wonder where I am."

Max laughed. "Aaron already knows," he said.

Anna pulled away to look at him in consternation. "How does he know that?" she asked suspiciously.

"Because he's Dragon Master." Anna raised her eyebrows, and Max lifted himself onto his elbow. "You forget I have a bond with him. He knows that I have taken a mate." Anna's eyebrows rose even higher.

"No!"

Max nodded, grinning shamelessly. "He also knows, through my connection with him, that it is you I have claimed."

Anna dropped her head into her hands. "That's –"

Max laughed, and pulled her hands from her face. "He doesn't know your intimate feelings, Anna, although he may hazard a guess, I suppose. All he knows is that we are now bonded."

"So if he knows, then Keira knows too?"

"I would imagine so!" Max sat up and pulled her into his lap. "So there's no need for us to return to Storbrook."

"Actually, I don't think I ever want to return," she said.

He grinned. "You will have to face them sometime, my darling. But there's no rush. We will remain here for the night."

Anna darted a look into the trees. "But there might be wolves. Or wild cats."

Max laughed, and rising, lifted her to her feet. "You are with a dragon," he said. "Nothing will venture anywhere near you when you're being protected by the world's most dangerous creature. Except maybe faeries."

"Faeries?"

"Hmm. Faeries like to come out and dance on moonlit nights, and this looks like a perfect place for dancing." He leaned closer, and his breath brushed her cheek. "Will you dance for me, Anna?"

She pulled in a shuddering breath. "There isn't any music."

He placed his hands on her hips and swayed to an unheard rhythm. "The music is within you," he said. "Dance like a faery for me." She caught the pace of his movements and started to glide with him, her skin brushing against his. He took a small step backwards. "Don't stop," he said when she paused.

She resumed the motion, swaying gently, then lifting her hands, moved them through the air above her shoulders. Max dropped his hands and took another step backwards as she glided on her feet, sashaying from side to side. She twisted slightly, her arms curving to follow her movement, then throwing back her head, spun around in a circle. Her hair flew out around her face, whipping through the air. She closed her eyes and danced as heat wrapped around her, the swish of her feet moving on the ground the only sound.

She felt Max stepping up behind her, and she shivered slightly when his hands stroked her upraised arms. He clasped them in one of his, and slowly pulled them backwards behind his neck as she leaned her head against his shoulder. The movement thrust her chest forward, and his hands slid down her arms and gently stroked her skin, cupping her breasts. Her movements slowed as he swayed behind her, and when his lips dropped to her shoulder, she was barely moving. He caressed her skin with his tongue, stoking a burning flame within her that slowly consumed her.

There was a movement of air as he unfurled his wings, slowly and languorously, and the ground disappeared from beneath her feet. She lay against him as he hovered in midair, caressing her with his hands, and when his mouth moved along her neck she groaned with pleasure. His wings were stretched outwards, and he leaned back against them, pulling her against his chest, before slowly turning her in his arms.

She stared down at him as he lay beneath her, floating through the sky, supported by his outstretched wings. His arms wrapped tightly around her, one beneath her thighs, the other around her head, and his feet tangled around hers. He pressed his lips against hers, and slowly rolled himself over in the air until she was beneath him, only his arms wrapped around her preventing her from falling. Her head rested heavy in his hand, and he pulled her closer as he slipped into her, catching her gasp with his mouth. She wrapped her legs around his waist, and when his lips slid to her neck, she cried out, before biting down on his shoulder when it seemed she would be ripped apart. She tasted his blood, and swallowed it as he grunted, grasping her so tightly she felt as though they had melded together into one.

Her hands slipped from the clasp around his neck, and her arms fell back, hanging limply in the air. He rolled over again, and she collapsed against his chest. His fingers trailed over her back as they drifted through the air, his wings outstretched beneath him. She stretched out her hand and stroked his wing, taut behind his back, her fingers weaving patterns as she watched the moonlight glitter against the smooth surface. He sighed into her hair, her name a whisper that filled his lungs and turned into a flaming blaze.

CHAPTER FIFTY-TWO

They slept in the alpine meadow, Max curled around Anna as he held her against his chest. And when she awoke, she watched the sun rise over the peaks of the mountains as his arm cradled her head.

They were flying back to Storbrook when Anna asked him the question that had been teasing the edges of her mind. "Max?" she said as they flew through the air. He turned to look at her.

"Hmm?"

"That time at the battlefield, you told me to stay away from you. Was that because of the blood?"

Max turned back to look at the mountains. "The blood heightened my desire for you. If you had come closer, or touched me, I might not have had the control to stay away from you."

"You would have killed me?" Anna's voice was a whisper. Max turned to look at her again.

"Killed you? Is that why you were afraid of me the next day?" His fiery breath filled the air around them. "I wanted you, Anna – wanted to taste your blood, and have you taste mine. I wanted to feel you in my arms, and might have taken you right there and then, whether you were ready or not."

Anna blushed. "Oh," she said, looking away from him. Max stared at her for a long moment.

"Know this, Anna," he said. "There will never, ever, be a time when you need fear that I will harm you in any way. Your life will never be in danger because of me." Anna nodded, but kept her eyes averted. "Look at me," he said. She dragged her gaze back to his. "I love you more than anything else this life has to offer me, either as a man or a dragon," he said.

"I love you, too," she whispered.

He landed them back in Anna's chambers, and no sooner had Anna slipped off his back than the door was flung open and Aaron strode into the room.

"Max," he said, "good of you to seek out your Master on your return."

Max grinned. "I was just about to do that, Aaron, but I had some other matters to attend to first."

Aaron nodded sardonically, but he turned to Anna with a smile. "You were already my sister, Anna, but now you are doubly part of my family. I'm glad this lad has finally come to his senses and taken you as his mate." Next to her, Anna heard a soft snort. She lifted her chin.

"Thank you, Aaron," she said. Aaron grinned.

"Keira is in the parlor, making plans for your human ceremony," he said. "If you want any say in the matter, you had better go find her."

Anna nodded. "I will." She turned to the doorway, but Max grabbed her hand, and pulling her into his arms, kissed her, before releasing her with a look that made her wish they were alone again.

Anna found Keira in the parlor, scratching her quill over a sheet of paper. She looked up as Anna walked into the room, then quickly replacing the quill in a pot of ink, rose to her feet and wrapped Anna in an embrace. "Finally," she whispered. Anna pulled back.

"Finally?" she said. Keira smiled.

"When Max returned to court, I told Aaron it would just be a matter of time," she said.

"But I was engaged to Garrick."

Keira frowned. "I know, and I'm so sorry Garrick had to die before you discovered it was Max you loved."

Anna turned away. "Garrick told me he wouldn't have married me," she said softly. "He gave me his blessing as he lay dying."

Keira was silent. Anna turned around and tapped the sheet that Keira had been writing on. "What is this?"

Keira glanced down. "I was making a list for your human ceremony."

"Perhaps we aren't going to have one," Anna said teasingly as Max and Aaron walked into the room.

"We're not?" Max said, taking her hand. "I don't mind."

"You can't do that," Keira said with a look of consternation. "What will you tell Mother?"

Anna laughed. "I wasn't being serious," she said. "Of course I want a human ceremony – I am human after all! I want all the world to know that Max and I belong to each other. And Mother *has* been longing to hear news of my nuptials." She glanced at Max, who was watching her with a peculiar look.

"If Mother was well enough we could have the ceremony here," Keira said, "but she is quite unable to travel the distance, so we will ask the village priest to marry you, and then have a dance in the village square, as we did for our wedding."

"I'll speak to Father Brown," Aaron said. "I'm sure he will be willing to do the honors later this week."

"But we must first tell Mother and Father the good news," Keira said, glancing at Aaron.

"Of course," he agreed.

"And you need a dress," Keira said. "I have some fabric in my chambers."

"You have fabric?" Anna said.

"Yes." Keira's tone was defensive. "I wanted to be prepared for any eventuality."

Anna shot a quick grin at Max. "Just tell us when and where, and we will be there."

Keira sighed. "Don't be silly, Anna," she said. "We will go find that fabric now, and then this afternoon we will go into the village to make the arrangements and inform Mother and Father." She turned to Aaron. "Meet us in our chambers at noon. And you, too," she added, wagging a finger in Max's direction.

"Yes, Mistress," he said meekly.

Richard came out of his workshop as the two couples walked up the path to the house. "Aaron," he said with a smile. He turned to look at Max. "I remember you," he said. "You were at Storbrook a number of years ago. Max, is it?"

Max nodded. "It is good to see you again, Master Carver." He glanced at Aaron, then at Anna. He reached out his hand and wrapped it around hers, pulling her closer. "We have come to bring you some news," he said.

Richard looked at Anna, his eyebrows raised. She had not mentioned Max in any of her visits. She smiled sheepishly, and he looked back at Max. "You are not after my permission, I take it?"

"No. It is too late to ask your permission. But we would like your blessing."

Richard's eyes narrowed, and his gaze flew back to Anna, but it was Aaron who spoke. "Richard," he said, "I think you are well aware of what Max is. He is a member of my clan, and has claimed Anna as his mate. They have already shared a blood bond, but they wish to have a human ceremony as well."

"I see," Richard said. "Is the ceremony for Jenny's benefit?"

"Partly," Max said as Richard looked back at him. "Even

though Anna is already my mate, she is human, and I want to honor her by having a human ceremony, too." Anna glanced at him as he squeezed her hand. She smiled and turned back to Richard, who was watching them intently.

"When is this ceremony to take place?"

"If Jenny is well enough, we will speak to the priest and settle on a day as soon as possible."

"I see," Richard said. He stared at the ground for a long moment, then raised his head with a nod. "I will provide fare for a village dance." He held up his hand when Aaron started protesting. "I insist," he said. "There has been precious little I've been able to do for Anna these last few years, and I will not forfeit this right too." He turned to look at Anna. "I wish you many years of blessing and happiness, my daughter," he said. Anna felt the tears welling in her eyes as his gaze moved to Max. "Welcome to the family," he said. "If Aaron believes you worthy of my daughter, then so do I."

"Thank you," Max said.

Richard nodded, then turned towards the house. "Let's go give Jenny the good news," he said.

Jenny was lying in bed when they stepped into the room, her eyes closed. Her face was pale against the pillow, and the outline of her body was barely noticeable beneath the blankets. She opened her eyes as Anna drew closer. "Anna," she said softly. Her glance flickered between Aaron and Max, then came to rest on Keira. "Where are my grandchildren?" she asked. Keira stepped forward.

"Anna has come to give you some news," Keira said. Jenny's gaze traveled slowly to where Anna stood.

"What is it? Are you finally getting married?"

"Yes, Mother, I'm going to be married," Anna said. She reached out a hand to Max and drew him closer. "You remember Max, don't you?"

"Max?" She frowned for a moment, then smiled. "Yes, I remember him. Charming and honest. I thought you didn't like him." Max shot Anna an amused grin, before stepping forward and leaning down next to the bed.

"Mistress Carver," he said, "I love your daughter. I have loved her for many years, and would like your permission to take her as my wife."

Jenny reached out a thin, wavering hand and took Max's in hers. "Yes," she said. "Take the girl and marry her. I must warn you, though, she is rebellious and disobedient. She gave her sister many hours of grief. But if you want her, she's all yours."

Max glanced at Anna, his eyes shining with laughter as Anna glared back at him. "Thank you, Mistress Carver," he said. "I will be sure to keep her under control." He lifted the frail hand and gently kissed it before returning it to the coverlet.

Jenny beckoned Anna forward. "Better make it quick before he changes his mind," she said. Anna drew back and bit her lip.

"I will, Mother," she said. "Right away."

The wedding was two days later. The morning dawned rainy and gray, and cloud covered the tops of the mountains, swathing Storbrook in mist. But as the morning wore on, the cloud lifted and a few weak rays of sun broke through the thick covering. Anna wore a gown of dark blue linen, the color of a clear night sky when the moon is full. It had been finished the night before, and as she slipped it over her shoulders, Anna smiled in satisfaction. It fitted her form perfectly. One of the maids had brushed and braided Anna's hair, twisting it in complicated braids that wound around her head and joined at the back, secured by a pair of combs made from the antlers of an elk, a wedding gift from Max, given to her the night before. They had been carved with the image of a flaming dragon, each comb carrying half the design which became complete when they were combined.

Max was already at the church when Anna arrived with Aaron. He was standing at the bottom of the stairs, Lydia's hand in his, but as Anna crossed the square towards him, his eyes were intent upon her. The cords between them flexed and tightened as her heart gave a little lurch. She dragged her gaze away and glanced around the square. A few of the villagers had gathered to watch, including Sarah Draper, who was staring at Max, her mouth hanging open. Corbin stood a little to the side, along with Zach; and Thomas and Peggy stood together at the edge of the square. They had traveled from Storbrook on horseback, starting their journey at dawn. Near the church sat Jenny on a wooden chair, a blanket wrapped around her legs. Richard was standing behind her, his hand resting protectively on her shoulder.

Anna looked back at Max, then smiled down at Lydia. The little girl had a small posy clutched in her hand. As Anna drew nearer, she dropped Max's hand and ran up to Anna, holding up the posy.

"For you," she said.

Anna bent down and took the flowers. "Thank you," she whispered.

Max stepped up to her as she straightened, and taking her hand in his, pulled it through his arm, squeezing her fingers gently as he did so. He led her up the stairs and to the doors of the church where Father Brown waited with an open book.

Father Brown nodded and cleared his throat, then glancing down, recited the marriage vows, pausing as Max repeated the words after him. He turned towards Anna, and she too repeated the vows, before the priest led them into the church for the nuptial mass. As they entered the shadowy recesses of the building, Max leaned down and brushed his lips against her ear.

"You belong to me in every way now," he whispered against her skin, and she smiled. She might belong to him, but he belonged to her, too. They knelt down to receive the mass, then followed the priest from the church as the people gathered in the square let out a cheer. Tears streamed down

Jenny's cheeks, and Keira beamed at her sister. Lydia, who had joined Keira when the vows were recited, broke free from her mother and ran over to Anna, wrapping her arms around Anna's legs. Max lifted the girl and settled her in his arms as Lydia reached out her hand and stroked his face.

"You are *very* glowey now," she said. "Will you also live at Storbrook?"

Max laughed. "Your aunt makes me burn very much, little dragon." His face sobered slightly. "When people are married, they live together, so I will live wherever Aunty Anna lives. But I'm not sure that it will be at Storbrook." He glanced at Anna. With how quickly things had happened, there hadn't been a chance to discuss where they would live. She gave a slight nod in agreement.

"Uncle Max and I will have our own home, somewhere other than Storbrook, but you can visit us, and we will visit you," she said. Lydia opened her mouth to protest, but then she was being pulled into her father's arms, her protests unnoticed, as Aaron thumped Max on the back and embraced Anna, and others swarmed around to share their own good wishes.

Richard and Aaron had arranged musicians for dancing and food from the innkeeper whose inn backed the square. Max later told Anna that with the hard work of the two men, there had been nothing for him to do. The musicians struck up a lively carol, and soon a dance was twisting its way around the square as more and more people joined in. There were no fancy court dances, but country carols that weaved around the square as dancers laughed gaily. Sarah Draper tried to position herself next to the groom as much as possible, but he only had eyes for his mate.

"My wife, in every possible way," he whispered in her ear. "I love you."

CHAPTER FIFTY-THREE

"I want to return to the city," Anna told Max a few days later. They had returned to Storbrook after the wedding, moving between Anna's chambers and Max's.

"Why the city?"

"I need to finish business with the queen."

"What do you mean? You cannot return to her service."

"I know that. But I would like a chance to explain why I left. Kathleen believed Blanche's story that we had run away together, and I want to convince Matilda that that was not the case and try to salvage what I can of my reputation."

"Kathleen is naïve and gullible, and she should have trusted her friend," Max said, "but Matilda knows better than to give credence to what Blanche says. But that being said, Blanche's tale has already spread through the court."

"You heard it when you were back?"

Max nodded. "I denied it, of course, but it is far too salacious to be forgotten."

"I know." Anna glanced away. "But I must try."

"Very well. We will go to Civitas, and you can help me decide whether I should keep my house there. When shall we leave?"

"Tomorrow," Anna said, with a smile.

Max wrapped his arms around her. "Always eager, aren't you?"

"Just eager to be alone with you," Anna whispered.

They left the following morning. The first snows had already fallen in the mountains, and the fresh snow gleamed in the early morning light. They flew until dusk, when Max saw a small lake in the distance. He headed towards it, and Anna gasped when he struck the water, plunging his lower body beneath the frigid surface as he sped through the spray. He ducked his long neck into the depths, then lifted it with a fish clamped between his teeth. He threw it into the air, and catching it in his mouth, swallowed it whole.

"Urgh," Anna said. "Raw fish."

"It wasn't raw by the time it reached my stomach," Max said. He ducked his head down again and came up with another catch. Instead of swallowing, he skimmed across the water and dropped it on the beach. "That's your supper," he said. Anna looked at it in distaste as Max changed his form. He scavenged along the shore for a moment before returning with a handful of sticks. Two of them were forked, and he pushed them into the sand, forked ends up, before spearing the fish with a thinner branch, which he laid across the two forks. He placed a few larger logs on the sand, and with a snap of his fingers shot a flare of flame onto the wood.

"How can you do that?" Anna asked.

"What?"

"Make flames come from your hand."

"That's Aaron's trick, not mine," Max said, drawing her down onto the sand next to him. "Only dragons far older and stronger than myself can control the burn that way, and Aaron is the most powerful dragon I know. He can turn himself completely into flame, and since I've had his blood, a tiny amount of his ability also resides in me."

"I thought all dragons had tasted Aaron's blood."

"Hmm, the dragons of Aaron's clan have, but I drank more than most." He turned to look at her. "When we were facing Jack," he said.

"Yes, I heard!" Anna looked away. "I'm sorry I didn't listen to you, back then. If I had, things would have been so different! You risked your life for me, and I acted like a child," she said.

He smiled and gently lifted the hair that was blowing around her face. "You *were* a child, my darling. And we were both a little proud. Perhaps both of us needed to grow up a bit," he said.

She smiled. "Yes, maybe we did." She stared into the flames as they flickered and danced, searing the fish above them. "Keira said one time that Aaron talked of a dragon savior."

"That's just a legend."

"You don't believe it is true?"

Max shrugged. "If it is, it will come from a very powerful line. Aaron's the most powerful dragon I know."

"So perhaps Zach or Lydia is the savior."

Max laughed. "I think we would already have some indication if they were. Maybe it will be one of Zach's offspring."

"Not Lydia's?"

"Female dragons cannot bear children."

"Oh, yes. I knew that." Anna turned back to the flames. Lydia would never be able to have children. Would she be able to find a man who would love her and cherish her, or would he run away when he discovered her true nature? Perhaps she would mate with another dragon, but most male dragons would want to mate with a human so they could continue their line. The challenges facing Lydia seemed too much for a young girl to bear, but of course, every other female dragon shared the same fate. At least she was not alone.

Max and Anna left again the next morning, flying over open fields and countryside. "I need to hunt," Max said as he rose into the air. "I'm consuming more energy than usual." He turned to look at her with a leer, and she grinned back.

"Then you'd better make sure you find an especially large creature to feast on, because you will be consuming a whole lot more," she said. He groaned, and his eyes flared into blazing flames. He turned ahead to watch where he was flying.

"If you keep talking like that, we will never get anywhere," he said, his tone low. She leaned forward and wrapped her arms around his neck.

"I know," she whispered.

Max started losing height as they approached a small forest. "I can see a ledge above the forest floor," he said. "I will drop you there to wait for me."

"Why can't I stay with you?"

"I don't want you to get hurt," he said. A sheer rock face, rising about ten feet from the forest floor, provided a rocky outcropping, and it was here that he landed. She slid off his back as he lifted his head and sniffed the air. "There's something just beyond the trees," he whispered. "Wait here."

He turned and rose silently into the air again, changing direction as he reached above the height of the forest canopy. Anna watched as he glided above the green branches. She lost sight of him for a moment, but then he was back in view. She saw his eyes brighten as he turned downward towards the earth, then silently he gathered speed and plunged towards the ground. Anna gasped when she saw how fast he was going, and a roar broke through the air, shattering the silence. She could feel it in her bones and she shuddered. If she had not known it was Max she would have turned and fled in terror.

She shifted herself on the rock and tried to see him between the trees. There was furious rustling, and she sidled over some more, then stopped when he came in sight. The dragon's jaws were clamped on a large animal on the ground, the blood seeping between his teeth. He stayed like that for a moment, and she could see his throat working as he swallowed the warm liquid. He pulled back slightly and shook his head from side to side, tearing the body apart, then used his claws to rip the animal open. He buried his snout in the bloody flesh, tearing off chunks of blackened meat with his teeth. She watched, a combination of awe and horror twisting through her. How could she love such a vicious creature? She could see the sharp horns on his head glimmering in the sunlight as he buried his head in the steaming carcass of his prey. He ripped off another piece of flesh and lifted his head, growling as his powerful jaws chewed and swallowed. He looked in her direction and his blazing eyes caught hers, holding them until he dropped his head and ripped off more flesh. She felt a clenching in her stomach as she watched, but it was no longer born of fear.

He lifted his head again as he ripped off another chunk of flesh, then stiffened as a breeze swept lightly through the air. He turned slowly to look at her, and his gaze met hers through the trees. His tail swished on the ground, raising swirling leaves and dust into the air as it flicked from side to side. He stared at her for a moment, then lifted his face to the sky and like an arrow, hurled himself up into the clouds. His wings were spread out wide as he flew higher and higher. Flames spewed from his mouth and rolled over his huge form, and as she watched, a roar ripped through the air. He turned, doubling back on himself, and she gasped when she saw he was heading straight towards her, his tail streaming behind him as he sped closer. He raced through the sky, his huge body flashing like a streak of lightning, his talons outstretched before him.

She scrambled to her feet as he drew closer, fear making her fumble. He had said he would never hurt her, but was this ferocious monster hurtling towards her really the husband she loved?

His talons clamped around her arms and she flew through the air, landing on the ground beneath him, his talons penning her in on the sides. His claws had ripped the top of her bodice and scratched her skin, bringing a few drops of blood to the surface. He glanced down at the exposed skin, then bending his head, slowly licked her. His forked tongue was long and hot, and it dragged over her skin as she shivered. He pulled back to look at her, his eyes flaming as he stared into her eyes. His tail swished against the ground, curling around her legs as it moved from side to side, and slowly, she pushed the ripped gown off her shoulders. He glanced down at her, then bent his head close to her ear.

"You're playing with fire," he whispered, his voice tight. She reached up her hands, and grabbing his horns, pulled him closer. They were long and smooth, and as she ran her fingers over the tips, she could feel how sharp they were.

"Then make me burn, dragon," she whispered back. A shudder passed through him, and he growled as his tail swished harder. His snout was in her hair, and as he breathed in deeply, a rumble reverberated through his enormous chest. There was a flash of light as he shifted into his human form, and then his lips were on hers, his tongue devouring her. She gasped when he claimed her, and she claimed him, too. They flew higher than they had ever been before, beyond the clouds and past the stars until they reached the edge of heaven, and even then there was no limit to the pleasure they took in each other. Max raised himself up from her, pushing his arms straight and throwing back his head, and roared out a stream of flame that rolled down his neck and over his back. The roar shuddered through her and left her trembling to her toes. She wrapped her arms around him as he collapsed back onto her, and they lay together until the night fell.

CHAPTER FIFTY-FOUR

Anna and Max arrived at Drake Manor the next day. As they approached, a dragon flew towards them, and Max glanced back at Anna. "Bronwyn is coming to meet you," he said.

"Anna!" Bronwyn shouted, speeding towards the pair with eyes bright with excitement. "When I heard you were back at Storbrook, I thought I wouldn't see you again for ages. But here you are. And mated to Uncle Max!"

Anna laughed. "No getting rid of me now," she said.

Bronwyn grinned. "Brilliant!" she said. She glanced at Max. "You know we have visitors?"

Max lifted his head and sniffed the air, suddenly slowing down to a hover.

"What is *he* doing here?" he said. His voice was hard, and when Anna glanced at him, she saw that his eyes were a dull, flat yellow.

Bronwyn shrugged. "He heard you were coming. I think he wants to see you, Uncle Max."

"Who is it?" Anna asked.

"James," Max said.

"James? Your father?"

Max growled. "No! Just the beast who left his seed with

my mother."

"What about his wife? Is she here too?" she asked. James was married to Beatrix, who was also a dragon. They had mated long after Max was born, but she was furious when she learned that James had fathered two children before they were married, abandoning both mothers before they even delivered their babies and not bothering to find a way to tell his children about their true natures.

"Yes," Max said. He was circling the manor house, and Anna saw a small party forming at the entrance to the building. She could easily pick out Owain and Favian, with their red coloring, which meant that the other man must be James. She nudged Max with her knees.

"Are you going to hover all day?" she asked.

"I suppose not," he said with a grimace.

He circled around one more time, then landed on the ground before the party. Bronwyn landed next to him as he nodded at the two red-heads.

"Owain. Favian. It is good to see you again."

Owain nodded, then glanced at Anna as she slid off Max's back. Favian gave her a grin.

"It is good to see you, Anna. I'm glad to see you have finally brought this beast to heel." Favian glanced at his father, Owain, and with a quick gesture towards Bronwyn, they turned and walked back inside. Bronwyn rose into the air, too, leaving Max and Anna alone with James.

"Max," James said. He was a little shorter than Max, with a slighter build. His hair was straight brown, but bronze highlights were evident when he cocked his head. His dark brown eyes regarded Max steadily.

Max nodded. "James."

"I was sorry to hear about your mother," James said.

"Well, at least you spared a thought for her in death, since you never did while she lived," Max replied.

James sighed. "I heard you had mated, and it is clear that this is the woman. Are you going to introduce us?"

Max stared at James for a long time, then bent his head down to Anna.

"Anna, this is James." He glanced at the other man. "James, Anna."

James took a step towards Anna. "I'm Max's father," he said.

"I'm pleased to meet you," Anna said. Next to her Max snorted.

"Well, at least that makes one of you," James said. He turned to Max. "Beatrix is inside and eager to see you again." He turned and walked into the house.

"Why are you so angry with him?" Anna asked as James disappeared into the shadows. Max lifted Anna with his talons and flew onto the roof of the manor.

"James is *not* my father," Max said, taking the satchel from Anna's neck after transforming. He pulled on a pair of breeches. "He may have planted the seed that resulted in my mother breeding, but that is where his involvement in my life ended. He didn't even stay around long enough to find out he had a son." Max tugged a pair of boots onto his feet. "I had no idea what was happening to me when I first changed, and now he claims me as his own. But where was he when I needed him?" He pulled on his tunic and turned to face Anna. "James means nothing to me."

"Well, clearly you mean something to him," Anna said.

Max gave her a look of disbelief. "Are you defending him?"

"Of course not! I think what he did was terrible. But sometimes people need a second chance. Imagine what would have happened if you hadn't given *me* a second chance."

"That is quite different," Max growled, turning away and opening a door that led to a staircase.

"What happened to your mother?" Anna asked as she followed him down the stairs.

"She died before I returned to Civitas," he replied.

"I'm sorry," Anna said.

Max paused, turning to look at her. "I left my childhood home when I was fifteen, determined to find the man who fathered me so I could learn why I was changing. I saw little of her over the years, but before she died I returned to my childhood home to see her. I had given someone my word that I would show my mother what I was. I spent a few months with her before she died." He glanced away. "It wasn't long enough, but long enough to tell her about you."

Anna smiled, and reaching out her hand, traced the line of his jaw. "I'm always on your side," she whispered. He smiled, and taking her by the hand, led her down the stairs.

Beatrix was a large, matronly kind of woman, and she immediately enveloped Anna in a warm embrace. In addition to being Max's stepmother, she was also Aaron's aunt. She had tawny, gold eyes, like Aaron's, but her hair was darker. She pulled back and looked at Anna. "The poor child looks exhausted, Max! You really need to keep in mind that she is only human, and needs to stop and rest when you travel." Max stepped next to Anna, and rested his hand on her back as he looked down at her in amusement.

"If the truth be told, Beatrix, Anna is the one who doesn't give me a moment's peace." Anna slowly ground the heel of her boot into Max's foot, smiling when she heard him shuffle slightly. His arm wrapped around her, and he pinched her side as she squirmed. "She really drives me too hard, but I cannot deny my mate," he said.

Behind her, Anna heard Cathryn laugh, and she turned around with relief. "Cathryn, how lovely to see you!"

Cathryn grinned, then shook her head at Max with an expression of disapproval. She leaned closer to Anna. "You and I have much to discuss, like how to tighten a dragon's leash." She glanced around as Margaret came into the room.

"Anna! Congratulations, my dear!" said Margaret, stepping towards them. "I'm glad you both finally came to your senses."

Max grinned, and leaned forward to kiss Margaret on the cheek. "Eventually," he agreed.

It was a tight squeeze in the parlor, and with so many dragons in the room the temperatures soared. Anna took a seat next to Max, who wrapped his arm around her, drawing her close. His fingers trailed over her shoulder, and Anna pressed herself to his side. James took a seat across from them.

"How's Jane?" he asked Max. Anna looked at James in surprise then turned to Max. How did James know Jane? She was about to ask him, when Beatrix took a seat beside her.

"How is Aaron doing?" she asked. "I haven't seen him since his mating, which is quite inexcusable, really. But his uncle over there," she nodded in Owain's direction, "sees him every few months, and he assures me that Aaron is doing very well. You know, Aaron is a lot like his uncle, which is a good thing. Not that I have anything against his father, of course – he was my brother, after all, but he lacked the steadiness of character that both Owain and Aaron possess." Beatrix patted Anna's hand. "And how is that lovely sister of yours? I can see the resemblance between the two of you. And the children? They must be growing up. How old are they? Two? Three?"

"They turned five last spring."

"Five! I remember when Aaron was that age. He and Favian were such little scamps." Beatrix leaned back with a smile as she reminisced about the past while Anna nodded politely. She grew more interested when Beatrix talked about Max, but there was not much she could tell Anna. "He only remained with us a few months, and then he was off to the city to make a name for himself." Her forehead furrowed, but when she saw Anna watching her, she quickly smiled.

Later that evening, James glanced around the room. "I need to go hunting," he said. "Does anyone care to join me?"

"Not me," Owain said. "I was out yesterday."

"So was I," Favian said with a glance in his children's

direction. "And Bron and Will were with me."

Max looked around at the group. "*I* have no need to go hunting. Besides, you cannot expect me to leave my new mate."

Across from them, Anna could see James watching Max intently. "Actually, Beatrix is right," she said, "I'm not getting enough sleep. I think you should go."

Max looked down at her with eyebrows raised, then bent close to her ear. "We can sleep, if you want." Anna glanced at Cathryn, who was suddenly deep in conversation with Margaret, while Favian and Owain leaned together, talking quietly. Only James and Beatrix were watching them. She pulled back to look at Max, then brought her lips to his ear.

"That's just the problem. I cannot sleep with you around. If you don't go out, I'll have to find somewhere else to rest for the night."

Max pulled away with a scowl, and dropping his arm from her shoulder, moved away. "Very well," he said softly, "if that is how you feel." He leaned close to her once more, his eyes holding hers. "But I will make you pay, you little shrew!" She drew in her breath, biting her lower lip, and his gaze dropped to her mouth. She saw the flick of his tongue as a flare of heat clenched her stomach. "Sure you want me to go, darling?" he whispered. She stared at him for a moment, then dragged her eyes away with a nod.

"Yes," she breathed. He grinned and turned to face James, the smile vanishing a moment later.

"Clearly I'm being set up, with even my wife chasing me away, so I will join you. But hunting is all I intend to do. This is not a chance to catch up with hours of conversation."

James nodded. "Very well. Let's go." He rose to his feet and strode out the door, Max a few steps behind. Anna released a slow breath as the door closed behind the two men. The conversations in the room had stopped, and she looked down, embarrassed. Had they all heard the exchange between her and Max?

Cathryn cleared her throat. "Will and Bron have been practicing a duet. Will, why don't you get your fiddle?"

Will sighed, but a moment later was reaching into a corner to bring out a four-stringed instrument. He plucked the strings for a moment, then picking up a bow, scraped the hairs across the strings as Bronwyn rose to her feet to sing her tune. Their voices harmonized well together, and soon the others were joining in, tapping their toes or clapping their hands. Cathryn grabbed Anna and pulled her to her feet, linking their arms as they hopped in a circle in time to the music.

It was a cheerful evening as the small party laughed, sang and danced, and when Anna pleaded exhaustion a few hours later, she stumbled her way up the stairs and fell onto the bed she was to share with Max. She fell asleep instantly, but awoke a few hours later shivering with cold. The fire had died down to a few low embers, and she turned to glare at them balefully, but something else caught her eye. Max was seated in the chair near the fire, his long legs stretched out as he leaned against the back. His eyes were closed, but Anna could see the light of flames shining beneath his lashes, making his cheeks glow. She watched him for a moment, her eyes sweeping over his handsome form as she shivered. She saw the light grow slightly and knew he was not asleep, and she smiled.

"Come to bed," she coaxed.

"No," he replied, his eyes still closed. "I'll not lie with a shrew."

"Your mate is cold," she whispered. His eyes opened slowly and his gaze caught hers as he looked at her in silence. "Is a dragon really scared of a shrew?"

He rose to his feet and walking to the bed, leaned over her. "Even a dragon feels the bite of such a nasty little creature."

She reached up a hand and ran her fingers over his face. "Then let me kiss it better," she whispered. He groaned, then collapsing onto the bed next to her, pulled her into his arms.

"A very persuasive and manipulative little shrew," he whispered, bringing his lips to hers.

She pulled away. "In that case," she said, her voice breathless, "I can just leave you in peace," but he wrapped his arms around her and no more was said for a long, long time.

CHAPTER FIFTY-FIVE

They left Drake Manor the next afternoon, after a leisurely morning and a hearty dinner. James and Beatrix left before them, but Anna noticed that even though Max tensed at the sight of James, he did not seem quite as angry as he had the night before.

"How was your hunting last night?" she asked as they flew towards Civitas.

Max looked at her with a grin. "I don't think I should tell you," he said. Anna gave him a small kick and he laughed. "James wanted to apologize for leaving when my mother was with child."

"And did you accept his apology?"

Max was silent for a moment as he turned his head forward. "What he did was inexcusable. He was thoughtless and arrogant. He abandoned his children – children who desperately needed to know their father. But I suppose we all make mistakes, and if you can extend forgiveness to me for leaving you for so many years, then I can try and extend it to him. Not," he added quickly, "that I am willing to make James a part of my life. But maybe I can let go of the anger a little."

Anna leaned forward and ran her hand over his neck. "Good," she said. "Because if it hadn't been for James, I would never have had you!" She rested her cheek against the shiny bronze scales, and when her arms wrapped around his neck, he leaned down and bumped her hands with his snout, his warm breath washing over her skin.

They landed behind the small hillock that hid the city from view, and followed the path that led them over the bridge and through the gates. It was a gray, wintry kind of day, and the mud was thick on the ground. Max led Anna along the sludgy streets before turning onto a wider, cobbled boulevard that led towards the nicer part of town. Anna recognized the road where Favian and Cathryn had a house, but Max walked past it, turning in the opposite direction onto a street that was little more than an alley. He stopped outside a narrow building, the walls abutting similar houses on either side. The house had two storeys; the lower was built of dark, age-stained wooden planks, while the walls of the upper floor were whitewashed mud and wattle. Windows made up of many small squares of leaded glass overlooked the street from both floors.

Max lifted the latch and pushed the door open, then swept Anna into his arms. "Welcome home, my darling," he said with a smile as he stepped over the threshold. His arms were warm around her, and as he slid her to her feet she took a deep breath before glancing around the room they had entered. A long, narrow passage stretched out in front of her, with a staircase at the end. To the left was a small room, with a table, and a few chairs and benches. Behind it was a kitchen, with a long bench and a brick stove built into the wall. The walls were stained black, but the room was clean and ordered. Max took her by the hand.

"Come," he said. "I'll show you upstairs." He led her from the room and up the rickety staircase. Another long passage stretched down the length of the house, directly above the other. There were two rooms upstairs – one furnished as a study and the other a bed-chamber. "It's not much," Max said, "but it is mine."

Anna glanced into the bedroom, then back at the study. The rooms were small, and the house was only as wide as one room plus the passage. The staircase was unsafe, the passages were dark and the windows did not let in much light. She turned to Max with a smile. "It's perfect," she said.

Max wrapped his arms around her and pulled her against his chest. "It will do for now, but when the baby dragons come, we will need something larger."

Anna shivered. "Baby dragons?" she whispered.

"Hmm," Max breathed into her hair as his hands explored her back. "We will start with a dozen and take it from there."

Anna pulled away with a laugh. "Why don't we start with one, and take it from there!" She walked over to the window and looked down at the street. A woman was walking along the road, her head covered with a gray cloak. She stepped off the street at Max's house, pausing a moment before walking up to the door. She lifted her face and pushed off the hood, glancing up as she did so. Anna stepped back into the shadows, but not before she had a chance to see the smiling countenance of Mistress Jane. She heard the door downstairs being pushed open and a voice calling out Max's name. Anna swung around, but Max was already striding out of the room, taking the stairs two at a time in his eagerness to greet the visitor. Anna hurried after him, her face set in anger, reaching the top of the stairs as Max arrived at the bottom.

"Jane!" he said, and Anna could hear the pleasure in his voice. Jane smiled at him, and gently touched his face.

"I came as soon as I knew you were back," she said. She glanced up as Anna started descending the stairs, and stepping around Max, hurried towards her. "Mistress Anna," she said, "I would have come to see you at Drake Manor, but Max told me to wait here."

Anna stared at the woman for a long moment, her

forehead creased with a frown as she glanced at Max in confusion. She knew that Max had created an unbreakable bond with her, but then why was Jane here? He stepped towards her with a gentle smile.

"Anna, this is my sister, Jane." Anna looked back at the woman in confusion.

"Your sister? But ... why ...?"

Jane took another step towards her, her hand outstretched. "I wanted to tell you, but Max asked me not to. But now that you know who I am, I want to say how glad I am that you are finally my sister. It is all very well having a brother like Max, but I have always wanted a sister."

Anna was still standing next to the stairs, and she sat down with a thump. "Jane is your sister?" she said to Max. "Why didn't you want me to know?"

"I wasn't meaning to keep it a secret, at first," he said. "The first time you saw us together, Kathleen was there too, and it just seemed easier to keep silent. But then the rumors started swirling, and you made your own assumptions, so I didn't contradict you. It gave me an excuse to always be at court, while giving you time to untangle your own feelings."

Anna looked at Jane again. Her resemblance to Max was so clear, she wondered that she hadn't seen it before. "I'm sorry I made the wrong assumptions about you," she said. Jane smiled.

"I hold Max completely responsible," she said.

"So are you also a ..." Anna paused.

"A dragon? Yes. Max and I share the same father." She turned to Max. "I can smell James' scent. Was he at the manor?"

Max sighed. "Yes. I went hunting with him."

"You did?" Jane was clearly surprised. "Why?"

Max smiled wryly. "My mate would not allow me in her bed."

Jane turned to Anna with a laugh. "Well, you have accomplished more in a few weeks than the rest of us have in years."

Anna blushed. "Perhaps we can all be a little more forgiving," she said.

Jane stayed with Anna and Max until long after the sun had disappeared and the sky turned dark. She was six years younger than Max, she told Anna, and had lived with her grandmother until James and Beatrix finally found her and invited her to live with them. She had only been nine years old, but her grandmother was relieved to be free of the burden and expense of caring for a young child. It was while she lived with Beatrix and James that she learned of her true nature, and when she first changed, it was Beatrix who had helped her through the transition.

"I know that Max is unable to love James," Jane said, "but I am grateful that he found me when he did." Max had scowled at that, but Anna ignored him.

"How long did you live with them?" she asked.

"I came to Civitas five years ago, after Max left, and lived here while he was away."

"You lived here? Where are you living now?"

"I'm staying with a friend," she said.

"But you must stay here!"

Jane laughed. "Actually, I think I will find more peace where I am for now, but thank you for the offer."

Max grinned, and wrapped his arm around Anna's shoulder, drawing her close. "Absolutely right," he said. "It would be very noisy here. Best to stay away." Anna turned to glare at him, but he grinned back shamelessly. "What?" he said. "Am I wrong?"

It was late when Jane rose to leave. She clasped Anna by the hands as they stood at the door. "I could not be happier about Max's choice of mate," she said. "I already know how well suited you are. He has been as cross as a bear these last few years, but it is clear that each of you completes the other. I wish you many, many years of happiness!"

"Thank you," Anna said, clasping her hands tightly

around Jane's. "I have already been blessed in Max, and now I am doubly blessed, knowing I have such a wonderful new sister."

CHAPTER FIFTY-SIX

Anna and Max went to the palace a few days later, crossing the courtyard to reach the doorway on the opposite side. It was bustling with people as they went about their duties, shouting at the children and animals that were underfoot. Anna looked at the low wall where she had been wont to meet Garrick, then glanced away as Max squeezed her hand.

They asked the whereabouts of Matilda, and were directed to the throne room, where she was listening to petitions with the new king. As they made their way through the passages, a familiar face stepped out of a doorway.

"Tobias!"

Tobias looked up at the sound of his name, an expression of surprise crossing his face before quickly being replaced with a smile. He hurried towards them.

"Mistress. What brings you here?" He looked at Max, and his eyebrows drew together in a slight frown. "Master Max. You, too."

"We are here to see the queen," Anna said.

Tobias looked away. "You may not find her as welcoming as before," he said.

"I know," Anna said with a sigh. "Do you believe the

rumors, Tobias?"

Tobias glanced at Max again, but when he looked back at Anna, he smiled. "Frank told me what happened, so no, I don't believe the rumors."

"Is Frank here?" Anna asked.

"No." He frowned again. "The last time I saw Frank was when we left Master Cameleus. I thought he was behind us, but he never showed up."

"He was detained by Rupert," Max said.

Tobias's eyes opened wider as he looked at Max. "We heard that Rupert was found dead. Do you mean to say ...?"

Max nodded, and Tobias looked away, his expression troubled. "He escaped and went to Terranton," Max said.

"He's alive?"

"I believe so."

Tobias smiled. "Good." He looked back at Anna. "It is good to see you again, Mistress," he said. "Good luck with the queen."

"Thank you, Tobias," Anna said. She and Max continued along the passage, heading to the small, windowless antechamber off the throne room where petitioners waited to see the monarch. Long benches ran down one side of the room for the commoners, while on the opposite side were wooden chairs with velvet seats for the more nobly born. Max led Anna to one of the chairs to wait.

Only a few minutes had passed when the door to the hall opened, and the Lord Chamberlain stepped into the room, his gaze searching the people gathered there. His eyes fell on Anna, then moved on to Max, narrowing as he stared at him searchingly. Max returned the gaze, until finally the Chamberlain turned to look at the people seated on the other side of the room. He waved to a young man carrying a roll of parchment under his arm. "The king will see you now," he said. He glanced once more at Max with a slightly perplexed expression, then disappeared through the door.

As he left, Anna looked at Max questioningly, but he

shrugged his shoulders. "He's not sure what to make of me." They waited in silence for a few more minutes, until the door swung open and the young man stepped out, his expression resigned and disappointed. The Lord Chamberlain nodded in Anna's direction and she rose to her feet, Max a step behind her. They entered the hall, and Anna paused to take in the scene. Young King John was seated on the throne that had so recently been occupied by his father, while his mother sat beside him. His back was straight as he stared at the two entrants, and he gave a slight nod, beckoning them forward. There was no one else in the room except Lord Eastwich, and he glanced at Anna and Max without interest. As they entered Matilda had been whispering something to her son, who nodded at her words; but as she turned to look at the new entrants, her expression froze.

"Anna!" She paused and took in a breath. "Mistress Anna, you are very brave, returning to court with" – her eyes flickered over to Max – "with him." She turned to King John. "This is Mistress Anna, my lord," she said, "my late lady-in-waiting, and Max Brant." Anna shivered at the choice of words. She wasn't dead, after all.

"I remember," the king said. "I danced with you at the spring ball."

"Yes, Your Majesty," Anna said, sinking into a curtsey. "Please allow me to offer my condolences for your loss."

"Thank you."

Matilda rose to her feet. "You have nerve, returning to my court with the lover you ran away with!" She stepped off the dais and walked over to her. "Do you expect me to forgive you, Mistress?"

Anna bit her tongue as a wave of heat rolled over her. "My lady, let me introduce my husband."

"Your Majesty," Max said. Matilda glanced at him, then returned to Anna.

"You married the man who dishonored you? Well, I suppose there was nothing else you could do."

"You are mistaken, my lady," Anna said, her rising dander making her tone flat. "Max did not dishonor me. The day I disappeared I had been taken prisoner by the king's brother, Prince Rupert."

Anna saw King John start at her words. Matilda stared at her for a long moment, before glancing out the window. "Pray tell, Mistress, why would my late husband's brother do such a thing?"

"I overheard him talking to His Majesty, and he accused me of spying."

"And were you?"

"No, my lady."

Matilda turned and paced the room. "Why should I believe you?"

Anna took a step forward. "Please, my lady," she said, "did I ever displease Your Majesty while I served in your chambers?"

Matilda stared at her for a moment before replying. "You did not."

"Did I act dishonorably or give you cause to doubt my word?"

The queen turned away and started pacing the room again. "No."

"I did not do what I was accused of, my lady," Anna said softly.

Matilda stopped her pacing and turned to look at Max. "What about you?" she said. "You vanished about the same time as Mistress Anna."

"I freed her from her prison and returned her to her family," Max said.

"So you also claim wrongful accusation?" she said.

"Of course," he replied.

Matilda resumed her pacing and for a moment all that could be heard were her footsteps against the stone floor. King John was watching his mother intently, and Eastwich stared out a window. Matilda halted and turned once more to Anna. "Be this as it may, I cannot receive you back at court," Matilda said. "I was sorry to hear that you had run away, and I would be glad to think you are innocent of the charges, but even if that proves to be the case, you cannot return."

"No, my lady," Anna said. "I did not come here today to seek reinstatement. But I did want to give you an explanation, as well as offer my fealty to you and our new monarch."

Matilda nodded, then turned to look at Max. "No-one will believe you have allowed yourself to be snared into marriage," she said.

Max's hand rested on Anna's back. "I am not concerned what others may believe, my lady," he said, "just as long as Anna knows that she alone holds my heart."

"Even though she may not come back to court, you will always be welcome. You do know that, Max?" she said.

Max looked down at Anna, and she felt the heat spread through her back where his fingers splayed over her skin. "Thank you, Your Majesty, but if my wife is not welcome here, then neither am I. I have no desire to be anywhere except at Anna's side."

Matilda laughed dryly. "As you wish," she said. She turned and walked back to her throne, throwing aside her train as she took her seat and looked again at Anna. "You know that Kathleen is no longer in my service?"

"Yes, my lady. I understand she is married."

Matilda nodded. "Yes. But before she left she packed up your belongings." She waved over a footman and whispered something to him before looking back at Anna. "Wait in the antechamber and someone will bring them to you."

"Thank you, my lady," Anna said. She turned to the young king. "Your Majesty, I wish you a long and prosperous rule." King John glanced at his mother before nodding.

"Thank you, Mistress," he said.

Anna and Max waited in the antechamber in silence. Half an hour had passed when Betsy hurried into the room, holding the cage of canaries in one hand while she clutched a wooden chest against her hip with the other. She greeted Anna with a small curtsey. "I'm so relieved to see you well!" She glanced at the floor. "I never believed the rumors set about by Lady Blanche."

"Thank you, Betsy," Anna said. "I didn't run away with Master Max, but I did end up marrying him!"

Betsy looked up with a smile. "I wish you all the happiness in the world, my lady." She nodded at the canaries. "I took over the care of these when I returned from the march. I am very glad to deliver them safely into your hands." Max relieved Betsy of the cage, and Betsy pressed the chest she was holding into Anna's hands. "I'm afraid Mistress Blanche raided your gowns," she continued, "but I managed to keep a few things safe for you, in case you ever returned." She leaned closer. "Your pearls are in there, as well as your personal correspondence," she said in a low voice.

"Thank you," Anna said. Betsy bobbed her head, and without another word left the room. The box she had given Anna was made of wood, with a small latch on one side. Anna pulled the pin free and glanced inside. Her string of pearls lay on top of a pile of letters, and tucked into the corner she saw a piece of paper, folded into a tiny square. She placed the box on the bench and pulled out the note, unfolding it slowly. 'A mere arrow is useless against a beast,' she read. She turned to look at Max, who glanced down at the note.

"I knew then that you still cared for me," he said.

"Why didn't you say anything?" she said.

"Because you needed to know it too, my darling."

She smiled. "I know it," she said. She linked her arm into his as they walked out of the room, the box tucked under her other arm. "I believe I'm done here," she said. "What about you?"

Max smiled down at her. "I think I can safely say I never want to return to this place again."

Anna drew back in mock consternation. "But what about all the women who will be left utterly distraught at your absence?"

Max grinned and drew her closer. "I thank you for your consideration," he said, wrapping his arm around her shoulder. He buried his nose into her hair, drawing in deeply. "But you," he said, and she could hear the laughter in his tone, "are as much shrew as one dragon can handle."

GLOSSARY OF TERMS

The setting for this story is the Medieval period or the High Middle Ages, which covers roughly the time period from AD 1000 to 1300. In the course of the story I have used terms that not everyone is familiar with. Below is an explanation of these terms.

Bower – a private study or sitting room for the lady of the house.

Cabinet – a study or library.

Carol – a dance (not a song) where everyone holds hands and dances in a circle.

Doublet – a tight-fitting jacket that buttons up the front.

Great Hall – a multi-purpose room for receiving guests, conducting business, eating meals, and when necessary, sleeping.

Kirtle – a gown worn over a chemise and laced across the front, side or back.

Reeve – an overseer of a town, reporting to the local lord. (In this story, Aaron Drake is referred to as 'milord', a title used for someone of superior social standing. However, he is not the lord of the district, and the reeve does not report to him.) The word 'sheriff' comes from the word reeve. The reeve carries a white stick as a symbol of his authority.

Solar – a private sitting room used by family and close friends. The word solar does not refer to the sun, but rather to the fact that the room has sole or private use.

Tunic – a garment pulled over the head that reaches around mid-thigh. It is worn over a shirt and cinched at the waist with a belt.

A note about meals. During the Early and High Middle Ages, the entire household typically ate meals together. There were only two meals a day, although the working classes would usually eat something small, such as a piece of bread, when they first arose and before they started working. The first meal, called dinner, was served at around 11 a.m. and was the larger meal, with numerous courses. A second meal was served in the late afternoon.

If you are interested in learning more about the Medieval period, head over to the author's website, www.lindakhopkins.com.

ACKNOWLEDGMENTS

Once again, thank you to Belinda, Tara and Vickie for your valuable feedback!

And to my family, my greatest supporters!

ABOUT THE AUTHOR

Linda K. Hopkins is originally from South Africa, but now lives in Calgary, Canada with her husband and two daughters. Head over to her website, www.lindakhopkins.com, to learn more about the author. Sign up for updates, and be among the first to hear when the next story from The Dragon Archives will be released.

BOOKS BY LINDA K. HOPKINS

The Dragon Archives
Bound by a Dragon
Pursued by a Dragon
Loved by a Dragon
Facing a Dragon: A novella *(free ebook for subscribers)*
Dance with a Dragon
Forever a Dragon (2016)